A Harvest of Stories

A HARVEST OF STORIES

From a Half Century of Writing by

DOROTHY CANFIELD

HARCOURT, BRACE AND COMPANY, NEW YORK

Acknowledgment is made to Henry Holt and Company, Inc. for stories from
Hillsboro People and *Home Fires from France,* and to the following magazines for stories first published in their pages: *Yale Review, Woman's Day,
Woman's Home Companion, Delineator, Ladies' Home Journal, Good Housekeeping, The American Heritage.* Stories have also been selected from *Raw
Material, Basque People, Fables for Parents,* and *Four-Square,* all published
by Harcourt, Brace and Company, Inc.

LIBRARY OF CONGRESS CATALOG CARD NUMBER: 56-11298

PRINTED IN THE UNITED STATES OF AMERICA

PUBLISHERS' NOTE

The stories in this volume are laid in very different backgrounds: in eighteenth-, nineteenth- and twentieth-century Vermont; in France; in the Basque country of the Pyrenees; and in the United States at large, or, in the phrase which might perhaps, to the amusement of most Americans, be used by the Green Mountain people, "in the United States outside of Vermont." Yet all the stories are told from the point of view of one observer who has shared the life portrayed. To the reader who might ask how any one person could have this intimate feeling of having been a part of four such diverse ways of life, the explanation is simple.

As to Vermont from 1764 to our time, the explanation is contained in the phrase often used by the author's father, when asked how long the Canfields had lived in Arlington. "Let me see—," he would say reflectively. And then, "It will be, come next May, a hundred and seventy-two years." Now, in 1956, it is nearly two centuries. In a close-knit, stable, old community, such as a mountain town anywhere, people live in the past, as well as in the present, through the folk practice of telling family and town old stories. From many repetitions, generation after generation, such a true fable as "Nothing Ever Happens" (what was done by one's great-grandmother), and such a satiric comment on social pretentions as "Uncle Giles" become a factor in the growing understanding of life by children in the third grade of school today, although both tales are of the Civil War times. Dorothy Canfield Fisher has been a member of this fable-narrating community for seventy-seven years.

But Vermont, like all other states, is a part of American life, and Americans live all over the map. So has the clan Canfield. Mrs. Fisher's grandfather was for many years the rector of a New York City parish; her father was a professor and president in several state universities; her mother was an artist who spent much time in Paris

vii

studios (her little and young-girl daughter with her). Mrs. Fisher herself went with her children to France when her husband became a
member of the volunteer American Field Service in the First World
War, staying on after the United States joined forces with the Allies.

During this wartime sojourn in France, which lasted so long that
the Fisher children forgot their English, Mrs. Fisher was a volunteer
worker in what was being done for the war-blinded soldiers, for the
families of men on the fighting line, and for the countless children
who were, in one way or another, as truly war victims as those
wounded in battle. It was in the effort to help restore to normal life
and health children from those northern *départements* of France
which were occupied by German invaders that she shifted her own
home and children from Paris to the foot of the Pyrenees. There, with
the aid of Basque country neighbors, she helped establish a convalescent home for undernourished and ailing children. The stories in this
book of France in war, like those of Basque life, came out of the intensive effort-in-common with French and Basque helpers of these
years. These people became lasting and much-cherished friends, never
lost from view, often revisited in later years.

These transatlantic years, lived at the other end of the gamut from
Vermont, were for Dorothy Canfield Fisher, like her grandfather's
lengthy life in New York City and her father's experiences as a university educator in the American Middle West, only part of a life-
time deeply rooted in Vermont. For those three generations of Canfields, Arlington was home, as it had been for the generations before
them. The big-city life, the state university years, the close sharing of
everyday living in France, have widened the family awareness of
other horizons, have brought to these Vermont mountain-town people
the most inescapable conviction that human life, everywhere it is
lived, is like cloth of identical texture—of different colors.

TABLE OF CONTENTS

x   *Table of Contents*

ஃ *War*

What My Mother Taught Me

*When I was asked by my publishers to collect a bookful of stories from among the many I have written, I did not at once realize that even to begin this task—to justify selecting one, discarding another—would call for a long look into the years back of me. But it soon became clear that an author of fiction cannot reread page after printed page, written during half a century or more, without being forced into serious reflection on the past. By no means only a narrow, individual past. Even more on the timeless elements which always have been, are now, and always will be the reasons why anybody tells stories.

The earliest in date of the tales in this volume, "The Bedquilt," for instance, or "The Heyday of the Blood," were published more than fifty years ago. The latest, "The Washed Window," was written only last October. What has made an adult citizen, who was free to do any of a great many other things, keep up so long the baffling struggle with her own limitations in the effort to get stories told? For that, I meditated, there must have been some deeply rooted driving impulse, and not only a root-impulse, but food to nourish it in the places, persons, happenings of the outer world.

What was—what is—this impulse? It is to try with all one's might to understand that part of human life which does not lie visibly on the surface. And then to try to depict the people involved, and their actions, so that they may be recognizable men, women—and children.

To attempt this means to have one's primary interest concentrated on, and absorbed by, human beings and their doings. But why that one special concentration? Why not science, or music, or mathematics, philosophy, or any one of the myriad other aspects of existence in our cosmos?

Pondering this question as it affected my own case, "Better disregard internal motivation," I thought. "Nobody really knows anything about that. It can't be proved, one way or another. As for external influences, no doubt many of them were combined. Usually that's what happens. But I wonder if I cannot put my finger on one of them stronger than the others. . . ."

Of course I could. The moment I had formulated that question I knew the answer. I knew whose influence it was. My mother's! Let me tell you something about her.

She was a Vermonter of undiluted blood stream, was Flavia Camp Canfield; yet all her long life she set herself in word and deed against most of what was implicit in her inheritance. A few rebels and plenty of deviationists, of course, are to be expected in any society—especially in one like ours in Vermont, where fierce individualism rejects enforcement of a rigid party line for tribal customs. Still here, as elsewhere, there are preponderant tendencies—nine-times-out-of-ten accepted rules of thought and action.

These were anathema to my mother!

For example, though Vermonters may backslide, most of us never doubt the value of regularity and stability as essential cogwheels in the clockwork of daily life. Many a time my mother has told me how every Sunday, her grandfather, Deacon Barney of the Rutland Congregational Church, drove with his family from his farm, put his team in the church shed, sat in his pew through the service—and never missed once in half a century. If you only knew what weather an occasional Vermont Sunday can produce in January or February—! But you can guess again if you think she told that story with pride in her grandfather's remarkable resolution, stamina, and loyal adherence to a cherished faith. On the contrary, all she saw in it was a hidebound devotion to routine for the sake of routine. She herself preferred to miss trains rather than to put herself out to be punctual to the hour or the minute, or, indeed, to the day. For she detested the frozen rigidity (as it seemed to her) of set plans.

Our valley lies on a reasonably straight line between Montreal and New York. This fortunate situation brought it for many years a single-track railroad and two trains a day, one south, one north—both called "Flyers" with the poker-faced irony of our regional talk. As the distance is about equal in both directions, the schedule often called for them to meet and pass at Arlington. One morning, many years ago, my mother decided that she would go to New York to buy some artist's materials she needed (she was a painter), which could not be found in Vermont. I'll say they could not! They can now. So she asked a neighbor who was going to drive to the village to take her as far as the railway station. That day the train for New York was late, and the north-bound express was the first to come along. The next afternoon we had a postcard from her in Montreal, delighted to be doing her shopping 500 miles away from where she had planned to go when she left us.

Living all her life—well, for as much of her life as she could not avoid them—with people who made plans and carried them out, my mother developed an almost miraculous skill, eel-like and sinuous, for avoiding limiting certainties. At the start of a journey she was never willing to say when she would come back. She invoked reasonableness to explain this unwillingness—how could she tell beforehand? When she went away, as she constantly did (my father's half-rueful, half-amused phrase was that she had never found a place on the globe that seemed to her fit to live in for more than a fortnight), she always called back to us the same farewell phrase. Leaning out of the train window, or waving from the deck of a departing ship, "Expect me when you see me!" shouted my smiling mother, elated to be leaving her family tiresomely rooted in a tradition of stability.

It did not dim her elation that this uncertainty was sand in the house-machinery of those left behind. The door must always be left unbolted so that she could get in if she happened to take a notion to come home on a midnight train; a bedroom must be kept empty and ready to receive her; someone must always stay within sound of the telephone bell in case she should call up and ask to be met at Pittsfield, Massachusetts, where some oddity of her fancy and her disdain of railway timetables had landed her. Such precautions for the care of an absent member are minimum requirements in any traditional family code. Her family, like most others, cherished that code. But she did not. She would have died of ennui if she had been the one to stay at home and make such provisions for someone else. Or, rather, more accurately, it would have been inconceivable to her that she should be expected to make sacrifices to keep regular machinery running, when she disapproved of machinery as a part of pulsingly irregular human life.

No, do not jump to conclusions. These first strokes of a portrait-sketch of my mother's way of life do not mean what, probably, you take them for—a one-sided negative. She did not say a frowning "No" to aspects of human existence she did not wish to admit as valid. Rather she ignored them, did not see that they were there. She turned a glowing, ardent welcome to what she was willing to recognize.

She was a dedicated lover of art. As unswervingly as her deacon grandfather, she cherished a faith. The core of hers was an absolute certainty in the infallible, unique perfection of the Greeks in their great period. This was a theoretic creed. Born in 1844, before modern archaeology had more than scratched the surface of Hellenic civilization, and never crossing the Atlantic until after she was grown up and married, her devotion rested on decidedly unstable foundations. No matter! Dogmas need no material proof. This was her dogma. But her worship of the Greeks in no way blinded her to the achievements of their successors. Any art of the first rank was sacred to her. The best in fiction, in music, above all, in the art she herself tried to practice—painting—those were to her the true realities of life.

She never confused the pursuit of art with sipping absinthe in a bohemian café, or with the impermanent love affairs of the Left Bank. (At the remote date of which I write, Montmartre hadn't been discovered.) It was a new art-experience which gave her the gloriously pulsing emotion which for most people is associated with falling in love.

Falling in love was one of the things my mother had not much use for. Since that experience has nothing to do with the enjoyment of the first-rate best in art, it had no special interest for her. When there was talk of it (there often is talk of it, you may have noticed), my mother's delicately modeled face took on a rather grim, aloof look. People who did not know her intimately thought her expression was "the Puritan look." This idea caused considerable mirth among those who did know her. Nobody could have been further away from Puritanism. Her excitements—she had plenty of them—came in other ways.

Here is a report on one such typical excitement of hers. As it turned out, it was one of mine too. Many of hers did so turn out. We were in Paris that winter. My mother, as usual, was studying and painting in one of the well-known studios, Carlorossi's, it was, I remember. I was regularly enrolled as a student, attending lectures at the Sorbonne, and the Ecole des Hautes Etudes. I had naïvely thought we were settled for some months. I was, you see, barely twenty, and still uninstructed by experience.

All at once the name of Velasquez roared through the Paris ateliers like a hurricane on the Florida coast. Of course he had been known and admired by an inner circle ever since he had been "discovered" by the Romantic School, in the early nineteenth century. But at this time his fame became a craze. Such crazes have always been frequent in that world. You must have seen many come and go just as this one did.

The word went around, excitedly (part of the creed of that world was that to be really alive, to be excited was essential)—"The greatest master of all time!" "Oh, yes, yes—of course, there *are* samples in the Louvre. The little Infanta in the Salle Carrée." "But you can't begin to guess his power until you see his work in Spain."

So my mother and I went to Madrid.

Everyone with a grain of common sense tried to head us off. They pointed out loudly that Spain and Russia alone in Europe were so backward that they still insisted on passports for foreign visitors. In those long-ago, politically tranquil days, none of us had ever seen a passport. My mother said easily, "Oh well, we'll get passports."

"But the language! Nobody speaks anything but Spanish."

"Dolly will soon learn Spanish. She always picks up new languages," said my mother. She herself was detached from the stupid, wasteful Tower-of-Babel multiplicity of languages, never bothered to learn a word of anything but her native Vermontese.

The French members of our circle who had friends or relatives forced by business to go to Spain, cried out that the sanitary arrangements south of the Pyrenees were of a filthiness beyond imagination. Everybody who went there, they said, fell desperately ill with prodigious intestinal troubles (yes, then, half a century ago, just as now, only more so!). To this warning, my mother did not respond, because she was already throwing her artist's materials into a suitcase—we called them valises or satchels in those days.

You wouldn't believe me if I told you all the details of that endless, rumbling, jolting trip from Paris to Madrid—the old-fashioned railway compartments (we always traveled third class not to waste money on non-essentials) had no toilet arrangements of any kind. Such needs were to be taken care of in the stinking, foul outhouses at the railway stations. No food, save what could be snatched from unwashed hands and counters during stops of the train. No water save what was sold by old women carrying bloated goatskins, walking up and down the platforms, screaming, "Quien quiere agua-a-a?" in a shrill refrain which rang in my ears for—well, it still does at times. No heat. On the dirty wooden floor of our compartment lay flat tin containers filled with water. Cold water. Looking back now after later experiences with Spain, I imagine that if we and our fellow-passengers had bribed the conductors, the water might have been—at intervals—hot. But those suffering travelers were too poor and too unsophisticated to think of that. And the season of the year of our hastily-decided trip was still so early that the cold was penetrating. I can close my eyes and see the bleak, snow-covered Pyrenees as we saw them by starlight from the windows of the stone-cold train.

By the time we had inched our endless way to Madrid, my mother was ill. Very. The people at the hotel looked at her, groaning, racked with pain, ashy-faced, bowed together weakly as she hung on my arm. Evidently they thought she was likely to die, and felt a superstitious fear against letting her into the house. But we pushed our way in and upstairs, behind a reluctant chambermaid, to a tile-floored room, as cold as the train we had left.

There was a fireplace in it. It was a black, empty, yawning, dust-filled cavity. But a fireplace. I hurried my mother into bed with a hot brick or two beside her. My considerable acquaintance with unheated European hotels had made me hope there would be soapstones or bricks on the back of the cookstove in the big kitchen, and I ran down and snatched them.

Then I began to argue with the hotel people about firewood. Nobody at the hotel spoke a work of French or English, it being a meager little inn, all that we could afford. But, as my mother predicted, I did learn Spanish, with as scared a speed as a chased cat climbs a tree. One of the first sentences I understood was that there was no firewood. I pointed out to the proprietors that if a fireplace had been built there must have been something to burn in it. No, the season had gone by for heat in bedrooms. Winter was over—or would be soon. No firewood in the fuel-merchants' shops. But how about sick people, new babies, very old people, I insisted, in what rags and scraps of Spanish I had, raising my voice belligerently to match their attempt to drown me out by vociferations. Finally to get rid of me, they admitted that sometimes one could buy a sack of dug-up dried tree roots, said to be combustible. Leaving my poor mother huddled in bed, looking and feeling deathly sick, I raced away to find a merchant who would sell tree roots.

One of the dangers which kind French friends had tried to impress upon my mother was that Spain was still medieval in its ideas about women. Any personable young female taken there, they explained, *must* be carefully protected, *must not* go out alone on the streets, "because, Mrs. Canfield, it is simply not *safe* for a respectable girl to leave the house by herself."

Having for years scurried along Paris streets without a companion, I had already discovered that pleasure-seeking men are repelled (as a dog by a pail of cold water) by a swift ejaculation of obviously sincere exasperation, the equivalent of "Oh! For goodness' sakes! I've got something else on my mind! Go along and find someone else."

Hastily learning enough Spanish phrases for an approximation of these sentiments, I rushed here and there, up and down all kinds of Madrid streets and alleyways, by day and night; to the pharmacist's; to the doctor's; to the fuel merchant's; to the markets, trying to find something that could be made fit for an invalid to eat; to the householdware shops hunting for utensils in which I could cook that food over an open fire. It turned out, as I expected, that my mother had been accurate in her estimate of the perils of the late nineteenth-century equivalent of wolf-calls. I had some disagreeable but no alarming experiences, in my headlong, hurried errands.

With what doctoring could be found for her, with what nursing could be improvised, with a fire in her bedroom, with a diet she could digest, my mother slowly got better. As a matter of record, she lived for thirty-five years after this, to the venerable age of eighty-five. The instant she could stand on her feet, she had me take her to the Prado.

All this happened when I was just past twenty. I have now passed my seventy-seventh birthday. It must have been fifty-six years ago, and that was long before sight-seers had begun to swarm into Spain. It was also so early in the year that Baedeker warned tourists away, and sensible Spaniards were staying at home or hugging sunny street corners. If there were any other sight-seers, they were lost in the interstellar spaces of the Prado. My memory of that vast museum, on our first visit, and on all the other days we spent there, is of empty, long, and cold, cold, cold galleries. Each room had a *brasero* of burning charcoal as its sole means of heat. Over each *brasero* hovered an elderly uniformed guardian, fanning the red coals feebly with a turkey wing. His frozen old body was evil-smelling because nobody in his senses would take a bath in that weather, and because his unwashed person was wrapped, many layers deep, in equally unwashed woolens.

I don't suppose my mother with her unrivaled ability to ignore whatever seemed unessential to her saw or smelled any of that.

She saw Velasquez.

White-faced, her legs trembling under her with weakness and cold, her Victorian false front pinned crookedly on her head (before we had come out I had tried to straighten it in the hotel bedroom but she had waved me aside), she tottered into the Prado, hanging all her weight on my arm—the arm that was not carrying the campstool for her. When she could stagger no further, she sank down on the stool and gazed up. That first halt happened to be before the great canvas called "Las Meniñas."

How long did she gaze, ecstatic as a saint in prayer, enraptured as Adam and Eve when "Lo, Creation widened on man's view"? Hanging by her hands to the guardrail to keep from falling from her seat, she forgot for a while to breathe—then drew a deep lungful of air on a quivering a-a-ah, and forgot to breathe again. All her life was in her eyes, feasting on the luminous atmosphere which filled that seventeenth-century room, peopled by those exquisitely painted court figures.

When she came to the surface enough to move, it was to the antithesis of the Spanish court that she went, to the magnificent, Rembrandt-like "Aesop." Perhaps in the end this was her favorite canvas. There she sat, gazing into those rich browns, making little swimming motions with her arms as though drowning in pleasure. In front of the particularly luscious flesh, miraculously painted, of a young woman's back and shoulders—in "The Weavers," I think it was—she wiped tears of joy from her eyes. In front of the cheerful, vulgar, life-enjoying materialism of "Los Borrachos," she laughed out loud in sympathy. To the "Christ on the Cross" she gave but one fleeting glance. A too-zealously pious clergyman stepfather had set her, as a girl, against religious people, and to his memory she dedicated a lifelong anticlericalism. (Could this have been one reason for her feeling about Greek art?)

But she almost cried out, did fling up one arm as if to ward off the overpowering impression of artistic power, when she lifted her eyes to the two mighty equestrian portraits of Oliveres and Philip IV.

As you can see, I too remember those masterpieces, because by that time I had been following my mother's flickering course from one picture gallery to another for so many years that I had absorbed something of her burning conviction that masterpieces of great art are important beyond anything else in the world—beyond taking reasonable care of one's health in order not to be a burden; beyond, far, far beyond comfort—one's own or one's family's; beyond regret at seeing the disagreeable consequences of one's own actions weighing on other people. My mother's eyes were shocked wide open at that moment of her first contact with masterpieces new to her. Mine were, too. I too gazed, my heart shaken. Now after half a century I can still see, so deep was the impression made on me, the golden reflection of that splendor of art which I encountered in the course of living with my mother.

Of course my mother had to stay on in Madrid—no matter what the reasons were for going back to Paris. Among these reasons was my

winter's work at the Sorbonne. She could not leave until she had
made copies of some of the pictures she especially adored. For her
excellent way of penetrating herself to the last fiber by a picture she
loved was to make a careful, detailed copy of it, just as painters of the
great centuries often did. A fine Velasquez copy of a Titian was one
of the canvases in the Prado.

Did you ever, I wonder, carry through from beginning to end the
complex undertaking of getting permission from a European Museum
of Art for a foreigner to make copies? If not—and why should you
have been forced to struggle through those labyrinths?—there's no
use trying to tell you where the trail led which I followed in Madrid,
pantingly learning more Spanish with every step, from one bureau-
crat's office to another, in and out of the Prado. In fact I couldn't tell
you if I wanted to, because all the times, all the cities, all the museums
connected with that often-repeated process have rather run together
into a blur in my memory. From the Prado struggle with entrenched
red tape, the only detail I recall was that at one point I found myself
improvising the birthday dates of my mother's parents. The museum
and government authorities would not put their seal on the permission for her to copy, unless every line of every questionnaire was
completely filled in. She herself had no idea of her parents' birthdays.
"Oh, gracious, child, tell them anything that comes into your head,"
she said carelessly.

So we stayed on in Madrid for a long time. My mother fell ill occasionally. She was often ill all through her life, as why wouldn't she
be? But after nursing and special food, she recovered from each attack
and returned to her copyist's easel. Every day I was needed to carry
back to the hotel that part of the paraphernalia of painting which
copyists were not allowed to leave at the museum. And naturally the
duration of each day's work was unpredictable, depending as it did
on the ups and downs of my mother's health. A good deal of waiting
around was part of my daily routine.

Some of those waiting hours I conscientiously spent in book study—
Spanish, philology, the history of French and Italian literature, subjects on which I was supposed to be working at the Sorbonne. More
of those marking-time weeks were wasted, as was natural to my age,
dawdling, fidgeting or yawning vacantly. But since those pictures hung
there before my eyes, I did look at them as no casual visitor to a gallery ever has time to look. One day I found myself noting broad lines
of composition; on another my attention chanced to be fixed on detail;
sometimes I could not see beyond the marvel of color. Once in a
while, just because the clock seemed to stand still, and there was no

reason for moving on, I stood before a picture until I sank deep into that rare, trancelike, timeless gaze, which penetrates by divination to the inner meaning which, perhaps, in spite of the theories of the professional technicians, is the core of every great artist's intention.

It was with this mesmerized gaze that I looked long at one of the Velasquez court dwarfs. There are several of these strange figures in the Prado. From one of them, a lack-witted, simpering moron, I turned away with a shudder. But another—was he called Sebastian de Morra?—that name sticks in my mind when I remember him—was not young. Above his dwarfed body, there looked out a full-grown man's face, terrible in its quiet sadness. I could not pass along that wall without stopping to meet his darkly shadowed eyes. It was as if he had a wordless message for me, a compelling one. In the end even the hard, adolescent crust over my shallow, undeveloped young heart was pierced with an involuntary, persistent compassion for human ills, which has been for me, as for everybody who admits that skeleton into his inner closet, a disquieting cause for heavy-heartedness.

Of course the superbly painted, horrible detail in Brueghel's "Triumph of Death" caught, shocked, and held my young eyes as sensational, materialistic horrors always do fix the attention of inexperience and ignorance. Many years went by before I saw the much more there is in Brueghel, but even then to look from corpses and hell-fires and gloating devils, up into the patient, steadfast understanding in the shadowed wise eyes of the ugly old Aesop—that gave the inexperienced girl a hint of what serene maturity might bring.

Weeks slipped by. I came and went in the Prado. I passed the time of day with the bored, elderly, underpaid guardians, rubbing their chilblained feet in their patched shoes. I explored the basement. It was tomblike, colder even than the upper floors. My mother never went down those stairs because only etchings, engravings, drawings—all black-and-whites—were in the glass showcases. She burned all her incense before color. I loitered long over the Goya drawings. It was there, I remember, that I saw for the first time the skeleton, his winding-sheet trailing from his frantic bones, struggling out of his tomb, propping up with one fleshless arm the lid of the coffin so that he could scrawl on it "Nada"—"Nothing."

But that black negation faded to less than a shadow in the life-giving warmth which streamed from the "Surrender of Breda" upstairs in the long gallery. Upstairs in the long gallery? In my memory forever, there, in front of a forest of slim lances, the conquering general with a sublimely gentle gesture of respect for human dignity accepts the sword from his defeated opponent.

After a while we moved back to Paris.

One more brush-stroke on this portrait of my Vermont-anti-Vermont mother, whose attitude towards life really—although at the time this was not obvious—was all the while pointing out for me a road I could follow with wholehearted acceptance, leading me on into the country where my nature could most deeply live.

Many years had passed since the trip to Madrid. During them the direction of my life—apparently through no volition of mine—had totally changed. I had turned away to the writer's world from the scholar's world where I had been contentedly working. This abrupt transfer had taken place so wholeheartedly that I had not tried to understand why it caused neither hesitation nor regret. The subjects, the plots of the many novels and stories I had written, seemed to be chosen by accident. I had not bothered my head to consider whether there might be some general underlying principle which made one kind of plot seem valueless to me, while I grudged no amount of hard, long-continued labor to the development of another.

Also by this time I had married, had children, and with my husband set up a home wherever we went. My mother, now nearly eighty, greatly disliked the routine drudgery of managing domestic arrangements. She equally disliked hotel life. Since my father's death she had divided her time, as the whim took her, between my brother's home and mine. Thus I was not at all surprised when I found myself in mid-December boarding a north-bound train for Rotterdam to meet the ship on which she had come from New York to spend the rest of the winter with us in Paris.

It goes without saying that my brother and his wife in New York had tried their conscientious best to persuade her not to take that trip at all. After a good many arguments, they had recognized the meaning of her mouth's set lines, and shifted their ground: "Not in midwinter, anyway," they pleaded. "Why not wait until good weather in spring?" Her face did not soften.

"Well, at least not alone. Plenty of women, young or old, would jump at the chance of earning a free passage to Europe in return for acting as companion—little personal services, you know, reading aloud, finding mislaid shawls, eyeglasses . . ." their baffled voices trailed off before her silence. My mother had recognized perfectly the real intention her children always had, she thought—not as we claimed, to make her life more comfortable and safe, but to make her less of a bother to others. She appeared to be turning their suggestion over in her mind. Finally she said, using the patient intonation of a mature, reasonable adult, trying to make ignorant children aware of the nature of things, "But that's out of the question. You see—I hate her already! How could I live with her?"

So she came alone. So I traveled from Paris to her port of debarkation, making the trip as quick a one as possible not to interrupt Christmas doings for my home and family. Someone was needed to get her through the customs and on the right train. There are, you may remember, a good many noble masterpieces in the Dutch art museums!—hence Dutch is one of the languages with which I have some enforced acquaintance.

As I waited for the fine, Holland-American liner to dock, I looked around at the clean, warmed, well-ordered customs office and thought of another time when I had helped my mother to get safely on land from a ship. That was in Naples, the wild, old pre-Mussolini days, when trains did not run on time and Naples was Naples. What ferocious screams from the dirty pirate-porters, profiting by the venality of the customs officials to snatch, overcharge, frighten. How helplessly and shamefully—to resist their bullying—I had let myself be dragged down to their level. How I had lost my self-respect, had screamed, shaken my fist, snatched back valises from their clutches, spat out threats. I felt sick at the memory of the foul, unswept paving stones from which all those trampling feet sent up a cloud of pulverized horse manure and ever-renewed rotten refuse. The insane bedlam of noise! The lice crawling visibly on those thick necks caked with sweat and dirt! The garbage smell of everything!

Now the Holland-American liner was there, warped quietly into its place. The gangplank was pushed out, making contact between dock and ship in one accurate gesture. A stream of clean, silent stewards filed down, carrying valises and suitcases. The passengers appeared.

There was my mother, stooped, tiny, looking so infirm in her old-lady blacks that a strong steward had been told off for her to lean on. Suiting his step with gentle kindness to her slow, uncertain progress, the big Hollander brought her to me, transferred her familiar weight to my arm (but I had the folding campstool ready for her to sit on) and took his departure. I noticed that my mother did not tip or thank him, but looked the other way. I recognized the signs. Something had evidently gone wrong on that crossing.

But when I asked her, "Yes, yes," she told me absently, the trip had been all right. It had been long enough for her to reread, yet once more, every word of *Portrait of a Lady*. She enjoyed, in books, what she loved in pictures—the best. Never, in all her life, did she read five minutes' worth of poor-quality writing. That was a golden part of what I inherited from her example.

But her old face, which the years had worn almost to translucence like a winter leaf, had a severe look.

I inquired farther, "Was the trip stormy?"

"Yes, rather," she replied casually. "To be expected on a midwinter crossing." But she was never bothered by storms, she reminded me. Enjoying intensity as she did, she liked their ferocity. Another joy— an epic one—which was part of what I learned from her.

What could be, I wondered, the reason for her cold look of disapproval. It continued during all the process of my seeing to the examination of her steamer trunk. She sat on her campstool gazing back at the ship and its personnel still treading up and down the gangplank, carrying baggage in unhurried, well-disciplined order.

I knew the reason as soon as we were outside in the comfortable cab, on our way to the station. As its door closed smoothly behind us, she broke out heatedly, "Of all the dreary, cold, inexpressive, cheerless people—! I hope I never have to see one of the race again as long as I live! They are like men walking in their sleep. Rembrandt *couldn't* have been a Dutchman! I don't believe it!"

The scene at Naples had so freshly hung before my memory that— it was, you see, some time since I had stepped into my mother's aura— I remarked, "Why, I was just thinking how deliciously peaceable and decent this debarkation has been, compared to the time at Naples."

My mother turned to me in amazement. "How *can* you compare that—that wonderful flood of light, that wild, free animation, that life, life, life—with these glum, congealed, *worthy* people! I'd a thousand times rather have my purse stolen by a smiling, dirty, charming pickpocket than have money put into it by a priggishly honest closemouthed Hollander—or Swiss—or Vermonter!"

I said no more. The time had long passed—of course I mean it had never been—for discussion with my mother along lines on which our minds could really meet.

We looked out of the windows at the well-swept streets of Rotterdam, and very soon the smooth motion of the solidly constructed Dutch cab sent her off into the light, dozing sleep of old age.

The trip from the Rotterdam dock to the railway station is not long but in it I had time for considerable reflection about the bases of human life.

No, don't think that a cab in motion is an odd place for a grave, deep, inner effort to understand. The technique for thus using quiet intervals of any kind no matter how short is one of the skills acquired, out of necessity, by any woman trying to turn a house into a home. The sands of the sea are not more multifarious than the hurricane of details which constantly hurtles around her. A drive in a cab with a sleeping companion is, for her, essential silence.

Looking out unseeingly at stepped gable roofs and well-scrubbed white doorsteps, I drove my mental probe down, down, to inner depths where I hoped to find an honest answer to the honest question which for so many years had been at the back of my mind: "What are they all trying to say—the people who talk like that?"

For, long ago, I had realized that my mother did not by any means speak for herself alone. She was an extremist, to be sure, but she had plenty of company, much of it very brilliant. In my youth I had listened during innumerable studio bull-sessions to people talking just as she did. All my life I had read similar ideas, mordantly expressed in magazines representing one generation after another of the always recurrent rebel-youth movement. Briefly unhampered now, by material worries, since I could trust a Dutch cab driver to land us at the station in time for our train, and not to overcharge us, I tried to reach the bedrock of that abstract question.

I did not get far—although my speculations ranged very far and very wide. Yet like Peer Gynt with his onion, I came to no definite "yes," or "no." Every time I peeled off a layer marked, "On the one hand," I found below it another, distinctly labeled "On the other hand."

Before I could command my mind to honestly non-partisan reflection, I found myself (as often cheaply happens even to those who are trying to be fair) substituting a wisecrack for thought. "When they bring up, once again, their old threadbare notion that they would prefer having their pockets picked by a filthy thief who is laughing and charming, rather than . . . what they mean is that they can count on some tiresomely decent stupidly honest person feeling it his priggish duty to replace the stolen money."

But I knew at once that this was no more than petulant. "No," I thought. "They can't count on help—except occasionally from those who love them. Far more often they are rebuffed, like Le Fontaine's grasshopper." When I first read that fable, a little nine-year-old in a French classroom, did I admire the prudent responsible ant? Not at all. I was revolted by his self-righteous cruelty. I still am.

I tried to penetrate to deeper motives. "What they think is, isn't it, that the only two alternatives open to us are, either to repudiate the whole idea of human responsibility, or else year by year to shut out any glimpses of the spaciousness of beauty, of poetry, of the deeper intuitions, "Brush your teeth, balance your checkbook, wash behind your ears, catch trains, watch the clock. . . . That's the way to make sure you have three square meals a day." On such terms I would be the first to agree that life's not worth living, no matter how conventionally virtuous. But, of course, the fallacy was obvious—those two extremes are not the only ways of life open to us. Bach, Wordsworth, Darwin, Einstein—I snatched up the great names at random, as representing their peers—they had all known that great wild pulse of intuition which Beethoven called his "raptus"; but they had also accepted their share of responsibility for others. After all Rembrandt *had* been a Dutchman, had lived his life in Holland, not in an artist's Utopia.

Unfortunately I was not battling by hook or by crook to beat down an opponent in a law suit. I was trying to search out the rights of the question, and I recognized at once that the example of those illustrious men had two sides. True, they had lived orderly lives. But did their *primary* interest lie in the quality of human relations? Certainly it did not. They and all others in their richly gifted group have unutterably longed to reach not a human but a non-human goal . . . the creative constructive ordering of elements such as colors and lines, musical sounds, mathematical conceptions, the mysteries of astronomy, theology, biology.

A little cast down now, I admitted, "Yes, nobody can feel responsible for the whole universe. We have to make a choice, shut our minds to many things, concentrate on the few which to us seem vital."

Something far away from thoughts fumblingly trying to take shape . . . something up there on the surface of things—it was the dimly perceived railway station just coming into view down the long street— warned me that I was near the end of the short truce with personal responsibility which gave me time to think . . . to try to understand the metes and bounds of such responsibility. It also supplied an example as I hastened to go on.

"I never bother my head, do I, about the train in which I am a passenger. I don't feel any duty toward the cylinders, pistons, connecting rods, under the steel flanks of the locomotive. Isn't this just the spirit in which my mother and those who speak her language brush off the intricate mechanisms which keep human relations going? They admit no obligation to understand human nature, to moderate it, to learn how to help it survive its self-secreted poisons. Why not, if they have other things to do?"

We were now, I saw dimly, not far from the station. Dull, banal thoughts began to trickle into my mind like water under a closed door. Had I the right change in Dutch coin, I wondered, to pay the driver?

Only a moment was left. Trying hard to concentrate, I continued my thoughts. "When I hear an engine laboring painfully on an up-grade, I know in a vague way that it cannot function without oil. But do I feel that I must share in the responsibility for providing the oil? Not in the least. How am I different from those who refuse to take seriously such qualities as self-discipline, fair play, thoughtfulness for others, promise-keeping? To them, humanity's pathetic aspiration to virtue is no more than useful . . . as a social lubricant."

The cab slowed down, swerved gently towards the curb. A last thought called out from the depths. "There is more to it than that. The more comes in because they themselves, like all of us, are human beings and live with men and women, not with locomotives, or colors, or musical notes."

The shift of the cab's wheels was enough to unbalance my mother's ancient, frail, sleeping body. It swayed, slowly tipped against me. Her head rested on my shoulder. The human touch moved my heart, and lifted my thoughts to a wider viewpoint. "Why, all this is meta-physics . . . or something. Not for me. Sort of self-righteous too. How did I get so deep in it?" I put my arm protectingly around her. "After all, what she's always done," I reflected, "is to reach for the only stars she sees. What better can any of us do than to reach for our own stars . . . and know which they are?"

The cab, with dreamlike smoothness, came to a halt. The motor stopped purring. My mother did not wake. We were poised in stillness.

In that silence occurred the miracle when thought and emotion crystallize. As by a flash of lightning, a vivid memory thrust me through and through. For the instant which is long enough for memory to unroll a piece of the past, I was not grown up, married, a mother, in a cab in Holland. I was again young—crassly young—and in Madrid, in the Prado, standing beside my artist-mother. She was lifted out of herself by the ethereal radiance of light-suffused air, presented on nobly painted canvases. I was looking at the same pic-tures. I too was exalted by them. But although she was the force which had brought me there, what I saw, even in my raw youth, was not what my mother saw.

The sad-faced dwarf, bearing with patience the ignominy of his misshapen body, was a victim of man's inability in the 17th century to cure glandular lacks which now our modern medical skill easily sets straight. The tragedy of the dwarf man, the dignity of that help-lessly suffering face . . . they had opened my heart to share the sor-row of the victims of modern man's ignorant inability to mend flaws in the social structure and standards, which cause just as much misery as glandular lacks ever did centuries ago.

The subject of one of the first stories I wrote, "The Bedquilt," was as helplessly starved as the Spanish dwarf of what all human beings need for growth . . . was as humbled before her fellow-men through no fault of hers . . . as defenselessly given over to the care-less mockery of those luckier than she. This by no glandular lack . . . by the social code of her time which decreed that plain women with-out money, who did not have husbands, who had never been admired by men, were only outcasts from the normal group . . . grotesque deformities, so that to look at them was to laugh at them!

I had never known, had never before thought, what had been the impulse which in my youth had inexplicably detached me from the study of phonetic changes in Old French, to which I had been set as a part of the training to earn my living; the impulse which had lifted me away from my textbooks to gaze, deeply sorrowing with her, into the patient remembered eyes of an insignificant old maid whom I had known in my careless childhood; the impulse which had forced me into facing the enormous difficulties of story telling, often enough too great for my powers to cope with.

Well, now I had a clue to that impulse. A message received from the marvelously painted, dark, tragic eyes of Sebastian de Morra had forced me to look deep into the faded blue eyes of Aunt Mehetabel. With that look the walls which keep a scholar's room windless and still, had fallen, leaving me in the heartsick turmoil of a compulsion to imagine and desperately to try to portray a human being not as what she seemed, but what she was . . . to convince people who in life hardly even noticed her existence that she shared in the human dig-nity of the instinct to create.

They were not all somber—far from it—those memories from the Prado . . . those early premonitions of the interests which were to govern my outlook on life. What had I seen in "Los Borrachos," The Topers, for example? The simple, close-to-earth satisfaction of work-ingmen, neither quarrelsome nor rapacious, eating and drinking on a holiday . . . a gusto in merely being alive. Perhaps some great-great-grandchild of that perception led to my writing "The Heyday of the Blood."

"How could they ever—the studio-people of my youth," I wondered, "have endured me at all, incorrigibly transposing their technical glories into mere human terms? The pure linear beauty of those slim lances clustered back of the two generals—he who had conquered—he who had been defeated . . . that noble triumph of color and composition had been transparent to my eyes. I had looked through it to the magnanimity of Spinola's courteous deference toward his beaten enemy—whom he could have ground brutally down in humiliation—whom he did not humiliate, but with radiant gladness respected. That, and not the beauty of the painting, had been a bulwark in my heart against those dark hours which come to the stoutest spirit when overpowering disgust for the despicable aspects of our human race batters at the inner door.

The driver climbed down from his seat. The flash-of-lightning memory dimmed. In my last glimpse of it, I saw that what had lifted me out of myself in the Prado was an idea which, expressed in the language of my mother's inner world, was irrelevant . . . even heretical: that art with its magical intuitions brings, and should bring, to the observer an enrichment of human life . . . of humanity's ceaseless Pilgrim's Progress through the years.

The driver opened the door of the cab. All that turmoil and searching sank down to the inner depths. I was at the Prado no longer. I was in front of the big modern railway station.

My mother woke up, refreshed by her nap, smiling cheerfully at the prospect of the long rail trip which would carry her away from the prison bars of bleak Dutch integrity. We got out of the cab. I paid the courteously silent driver the legal fare and the specified tip. A porter emerged from the railway station, ready to carry our bags. That would be another tip, I thought calculatingly.

It was at the moment when I looked down into my purse for the right Dutch coins, that I first became consciously aware that, for good or ill, for success or failure, my fate had been settled long ago. I was marching in the right regiment—the right one for me.

Because, whatever may be true for other branches of the arts, no novel—and no novel condensed into its bare essentials and written as a short story—is worth the reading unless it grapples with some problem of living. Beauty of description, a stirring plot, the right word in the right place . . . all these are excellent. But without that fundamental drive, they are only words—words—words. My task, I saw it clearly, was to go on as inner bent and outer circumstances had started me . . . to focus what powers I had on the effort to understand and to invite readers to join me in trying to understand what happens to and within our poor, fumbling, struggling human race.

Nobody can hope to understand the whole human race. But everyone can make a beginning. The essential first step for any reader, and for any writer of fiction, humble or great, is to bend the utmost effort of mind and sympathy on the lives nearest at hand. More often than not those lives appear in no way remarkable, seem barren of all external drama.

What if they do?

Only those of our fellows whom we have really known and lived with can we, if we are fortunate, after long meditation see with the intuition of imagination. And only from achieving such intuition about lives we have shared comes the broader vision which lifts our eyes to those other men, women—and children, outside our personal circle . . . brings them so close that—if our own hearts are big enough—we can share their joys and sorrows—understand the meaning of their lives.

Once, in a Boston street, my father used to tell us, he chanced to ask a doleful, grizzled Irish immigrant, "What part of the Old Country do you come from?"

"I was born in Mayo—God help me!" said the old man.

As the porter picked up the bags and we turned into the station, I thought wryly:

"I was born to be a teller of stories . . . God help me!"

Wryly, but gladly too. For in the obscure labyrinth of the inner world, it is comforting to be sure of anything.

Vermont Memories

Nothing
Ever Happens

~§ W̲e live—as my father used to say laughingly, we have lived for the last hundred and eighty years—in a pleasant, long valley in Vermont. The ancient, weather-worn mountain ranges almost meet each other's gently-flowing downward lines, so that, at the bottom, there is room only for a few fields and houses, a small factory or two, the meandering river, the highway, and—for the last century—the railway. Its steely tracks are like clean penstrokes, their straightness setting off the curves of the rest of what we see from our homes. Many of the farmhouses, fields, barns, stone walls, pastures, lie along the narrow side roads which branch off from the valley highway and for a mile or so climb the lower slopes of the Taconic Range. One elevation up there is just right for orchards. The good pasture land is a little higher. Above this broad band of human habitation, up to the high-lying long line of the mountaintops on each side, stand the forests, thick and dark. Summer and winter, this tranquil scene is bathed in the mild, north-country light, which grays a little all it falls upon, and blends into one peaceful whole the subtly varied colors and forms of a well-watered, time-honored landscape.

This is the way it looks to us. Evidently it does not look like that to the people who come in from the high-speed, modern world outside. You will see, as well as we do, what their impression is, if I quote a question many of them ask after they have been here a day

3

or so, fidgeting and restless. They look up and down and all around, and inquire with a razor-edged intonation, "For heaven's sakes, does anything ever happen here?"

We know what they mean. And we know that what they mean would stand in the way of their understanding our words, if we tried to answer their question. So we just change the subject.

If they could understand, we would be glad to tell them some of the things which have happened around us and our forefathers; for a few of them we are very proud of. We don't mention these often, even to each other, but we think of them, and are nourished by them. We do talk to each other endlessly about some others of the happenings, for they are cram-full of comedy, and make us laugh whenever they are mentioned. Their humor is like good cheese, mellowed and ripened by age. And some—our valley looks peaceful but is inhabited by fully human men and women—we are so ashamed of that we hang our heads to remember them, although they may have happened a hundred years ago.

I'll tell you one of our small, plain old tales, so that you can see for yourself why we don't bring them out to people who know beforehand that our life is stagnant. We too know something beforehand: that our events are modeled in such low relief as to make them invisible to folks who get their idea of something happening from newspaper scareheads, from the radio, and from the sex-and-crime in the movies.

Many years ago when my great-grandmother was a brisk, withered old woman, she heard that on one of the mountain farms 'way up on a steep side road, the farmer's wife never came down to the village to buy things or go to church because she was afraid people would laugh at her. Her mother had been an Indian, and her skin was very dark. They were plain folks with little money, and she didn't think her clothes were good enough to go to church. She'd stayed away from people so long that she was shy—the way a deer is shy—and felt "queer," and went into the house quickly and hid, if a stranger happened to stop at the farm.

My great-grandmother no sooner heard that, than she got into the small battered old family phaeton and had a boy drive her to the other end of the valley and up the long, narrow road to the Hunter farm. Mrs. Hunter was hanging out her clothes on the line when Great-grandmother drove into the yard. Before she could dodge away and hide, Great-grandmother hopped out of the low, little carriage and said, "Here, let me help you!" In a minute, with her mouth full of clothespins, she was standing by Mrs. Hunter, pinning up sheets and towels, and men's shirts. "My, how clean you get them!" she said mumblingly around the clothespins. "They're as white as new milk! How do you make your soap? Do you put any salt in it?"

By the time they had the big basket of wet clothes hung up, the dark-skinned, black-haired mountain wife couldn't feel shy of the quick-stepping little old woman from the valley. They had a pleasant time talking in the kitchen as they washed the breakfast dishes, and sat down together to the basket of mending. The question of going to church came up, along with all sorts of other subjects. Great-grand-mother asked to see the coat and hat Mrs. Hunter had, and said they were just as good as hers, every bit. Before the old visitor had gone, Mrs. Hunter said she would go to church the next Sunday, if she could go with Great-grandmother and sit in the same pew with her.

"Yes, indeed," said Great-grandmother. "I'll be waiting for you in front of our house with my daughter and my little granddaughter. We'll all walk across to church together." For Great-grandmother lived just across the street from the church.

Sure enough, the next Sunday, Great-grandmother, her young-lady daughter and her little-girl granddaughter stood on their front porch. They were all in their best Sunday dresses, wore bonnets, had their prayer books in their hands. They smiled at Mrs. Hunter as Mr. Hunter drove her up in the lumbering farm-wagon.

Mrs. Hunter had a bonnet on over her sleek black hair. Her dark face was creased with nice smile-wrinkles as she climbed out on the old marble mounting block and started up the front walk to the house. It was a cool day, she had put on a warm cloak, her shoes were brightly black with polish. And (she was a real country-woman whose idea of dressing up was a freshly ironed clean apron) she had put on a big blue checked-gingham apron, nicely starched, over her coat, and tied the strings in the back.

My aunt, who was Great-grandmother's granddaughter, and who was the little girl on the front porch that day, used to tell me, when I was a little girl, about what happened next. She said she and her young-lady aunt were so astonished to see a woman starting to church with a big apron on, *over her coat,* that their eyes opened wide, and they were just ready to put their hands up to their mouths to hide a smile. But Great-grandmother swung the little girl sharply around and shoved her back into the house, calling over her shoulder to Mrs. Hunter, "Well, would you believe it, the girls and I have forgotten to put our aprons on. We won't keep you waiting a minute." She took hold firmly of her young-lady daughter's wrist and pulled her in, shutting the front door behind them.

Once inside, she hustled them into gingham aprons, which they tied on over their coats. She herself put on the biggest one she had, tied the strings in a dashing bowknot behind, and they sailed across to the church with Mrs. Hunter, aproned from chin to hem, all four of them.

People already in their pews looked astonished, but Great-grandmother put on a hard expression she sometimes used, and faced them down, so that they got the idea and made their children stop giggling.

At the end of the service, everybody came to shake hands with Mrs. Hunter. They knew Great-grandmother would have a thing or two to say to them, if they didn't. They told her and the rector of the church told her they were glad to see her out at church and they hoped she'd come often. After that Mrs. Hunter came every Sunday, the rest of her life—without an apron; for sometime during the next week, Great-grandmother let fall negligently that it wasn't really necessary to wear them on Sundays.

Well, that is one of the stories we laugh over. My great-aunt to her dying day sputtered over her mother's tyranny. But we're silently very proud of it. We were prouder yet when long, long years after Great-grandmother and Mrs. Hunter were both in the old Burying Ground with tombstones over their graves something else "happened" that would make you think, almost, that one action makes a natural channel along which other actions like it can flow more easily. Or perhaps it is rather that both actions grow from the way of feeling about life most familiar to the people who live in that region.

We would never try to put this idea into our talk, of course. It is rather a mystic notion anyhow, and our tradition is that such conceptions, made of half-glimpsed spiritual starlight, are bruised and deformed if anybody tries to cram them into the muddy vesture of words. More than this, we fear that such an idea would make the story sound sentimental, and we value the little, twofold, communally-remembered incident too much to risk that.

It was this way. One of the families in our town was very poor. The father had died, the mother was sick, the five children scratched along as best they could, with what help the neighbors could give them. But they had to go without things that you'd think were necessary.

Not only did they never have good "dress-up" clothes, but they never even had new work clothes. They wore things that other people had given up because they were too ragged. Their mother, sitting up in bed, patched them as best she could, and the children wore them. When the oldest boy—he was a thin little fellow about fourteen years old—got a chance to go to work for a farmer over the mountain from our valley, he had nothing at all to wear but a very old shirt, some faded, much-patched blue denim overalls, and his work-shoes.

The farmer and his wife had never seen anybody in such poor working-clothes. It did not occur to them that the new hired boy had no others at all. Saturday when the farmer's wife went to the village to sell some eggs, she bought young David a pair of blue jeans, so stiff they could almost stand alone—you know how brand-new overalls look.

The next day at breakfast they said they were going to church, and would David like to go along? Yes, indeed he would! So they went off to their rooms to get into their Sunday clothes. The farmer was dressed first, and sat down by the radio to get the time signals to set his watch. David walked in. His hair was combed slick with lots of water, his work-shoes were blacked, his face was as clean as a china plate. And he had on those stiff, new blue jeans, looking as though they were made out of blue stovepipe.

The farmer opened his mouth to say, "We're almost ready to start. You'll be late if you don't get dressed for church," when he saw David's face. It was shining. He looked down at the blue jeans with a smile, he ran his hand lovingly over their stiff newness, and said ardently to the farmer, "Land! I'm so *much* obliged to you folks for getting me these new clothes in time to go to church in them."

When the farmer told about this, he said he had to blow his nose real hard before he could say, "Wait a minute." He went to take off his own black suit and put on a pair of blue jeans. Then he and David walked into church together, sat in the same pew, and sang out of the same hymnbook.

So when visitors from the city say, "Goodness, how ever do you *stand* it here, with nothing to do, and nothing ever happening?" we think, "Well, that depends on what you mean by 'happen.'"

Flint
and Fire

&ℳy husband's cousin had come up from the city, slightly more fagged and sardonic than usual. As he stretched himself out in the big porch-chair he lost no time in taking up his familiar indictment of what he enjoys calling Vermonters' emotional sterility.

"Oh, I admit their honesty. They don't forge checks. And they're steady. Sure. They never burn their neighbors' barns. You can count on them to plug ahead through thrifty, gritty, cautious lives. But no more! No inner heat. Not a spark ever struck out. They're inhibition-bound! Generations of niggling nay-sayers have dried out all feeling from them except . . ."

I pushed the lemonade pitcher nearer him, clinking the ice invitingly. With a wave of my hand I indicated our iris bed, a more cheerful object for contemplation than the flat monotony of rural life. The flowers burned on their stalks like yellow tongues of flame. The strong green leaves, vibrating with vigorous life, thrust themselves up into the spring air.

In the field beyond them, as vigorous as they, strode Adoniram Purdon behind his team, the reins tied together behind his muscular neck, his hands gripping the plow handles. The hot sweet spring sunshine shone down on 'Niram's head with its thick crest of brown hair. The ineffable odor of newly turned earth steamed up around him like

8

incense. The mountain stream at the fence-corner leaped and shouted. His powerful body answered every call made on it with the precision of a splendid machine. But there was no elation in the set face as 'Niram wrenched the plow around a fixed rock, or as, in a more favorable furrow, the gleaming share sped along before the plowman, turning over a long, unbroken brown ribbon of earth.

My cousin-in-law followed my gesture. His eyes rested on the sturdy, silent figure, as it stepped doggedly behind the straining team, the head bent forward, the eyes fixed on the horses' heels.

"There!" he said. "There is an example of what I mean. Is there another race on earth which could produce a man in such a situation who would not on such a day sing or whistle, or at least hold up his head and look at all the earthly glories about him?"

I made no answer, but not for lack of material for speech. 'Niram's reasons for austere self-control were not such as I cared to discuss with my cousin. As we sat looking at him the noon whistle from the village blew. The wise old horses stopped in the middle of a furrow. 'Niram unharnessed them, led them to the shade of a tree, and put on their nose-bags. Then he turned and came toward the house.

"Don't I seem to remember," murmured my cousin under his breath, "that, even though he is a New Englander, he has been known to make up errands to your kitchen to see your pretty Ev'leen Ann?"

I looked at him hard; but he was only gazing down, rather cross-eyed, on his grizzled mustache. Evidently his had been but a chance shot. 'Niram stepped up on the grass at the edge of the porch. He was so tall that he overtopped the railing easily, and, reaching a long arm over to where I sat, he handed me a small package done up in yellowish tissue-paper. Without a nod or a good morning, or any other of the greetings usual in a more effusive culture, he explained briefly:

"My stepmother wanted I should give you this. She said to thank you for the grape juice." As he spoke he looked at me gravely out of deep-set blue eyes, and when he had delivered his message he held his peace.

I expressed myself with the babbling volubility of another kind of culture. "Oh, 'Niram!" I protested as I opened the package and took out a finely embroidered old-fashioned collar. "Oh, 'Niram! How *could* your stepmother give such a thing away? Why, it must be one of her precious family relics. I don't *want* her to give me something every time I do her just a neighborly favor. Can't a neighbor send her in a few bottles of grape juice without her thinking she must pay it back somehow? It's not kind of her. She has never yet let me do the least thing for her without repaying me with something that is worth ever so much more than the little I've done."

When I had finished my prattling, 'Niram repeated, with an accent of finality, "She wanted I should give it to you."

The older man stirred in his chair. Without looking at him I knew that his gaze on the young rustic was quizzical and that he was recording on the tablets of his merciless memory the ungraceful abruptness of the other's action and manner.

"How is your stepmother feeling today, 'Niram?" I asked.

"Worse."

'Niram came to a full stop with the word. My cousin covered his satirical mouth with his hand.

"Can't the doctor do anything to relieve her?"

'Niram moved at last from his Indian-like immobility. He looked up under the brim of his felt hat at the skyline of the mountain, shimmering iridescent above us. "He says maybe 'lectricity would help her some. I'm goin' to git her the batteries and things soon's I git the rubber bandages paid for."

There was a long silence. My cousin stood up, yawning, and sauntered away toward the door. "Shall I send Ev'leen Ann out to get the pitcher and glasses?" he asked in an accent which he evidently thought very humorously significant.

The strong face under the felt hat turned white, the jaw muscles set, but for all this show of strength there was an instant when the man's eyes looked out with the sick, helpless revelation of pain they might have had when 'Niram was a little boy of ten, a third of his present age, and less than half his present stature. That chance shot rang the bell.

"No, no! Never mind!" I said hastily. "I'll take the tray in when I go."

Without salutation or farewell 'Niram Purdon turned and went back to his work.

The porch was an enchanted place, walled around with starlit darkness, visited by wisps of breezes shaking down from their wings the breath of lilac and syringa, flowering wild grapes, and plowed fields. Down at the foot of our sloping lawn the little river, still swollen by the melted snow from the mountains, plunged between its stony banks and shouted to the stars.

We three—Paul, his cousin, and I—had disposed our uncomely, useful, middle-aged bodies in the big wicker chairs and left them there while our young souls wandered abroad in the sweet, dark glory of the night. At least Paul and I were doing this, as we sat, hand in hand, thinking of a May night twenty years before. One never knows what Horace is thinking of, but apparently he was not in his usual captious vein, for after a long pause he remarked, "It is a night almost indecorously inviting to the making of love."

My answer seemed grotesquely out of key with this, but its sequence was clear in my mind. I got up, saying: "Oh, that reminds me—I must go and see Ev'leen Ann. I'd forgotten to plan tomorrow's dinner."

"Oh, everlastingly Ev'leen Ann!" mocked Horace from his corner. "Can't you think of anything but Ev'leen Ann and her affairs?"

I felt my way through the darkness of the house, toward the kitchen, both doors of which were tightly closed. When I stepped into the hot, close room, smelling of food and fire, I saw Ev'leen Ann sitting on the straight kitchen chair, the yellow light of the bracket-lamp beating down on her heavy braids and bringing out the exquisitely subtle modeling of her smooth young face. Her hands were folded in her lap. She was staring at the blank wall, and the expression of her eyes so startled and shocked me that I stopped short and would have retreated if it had not been too late. She had seen me, roused herself, and said quietly, as though continuing a conversation interrupted the moment before:

"I had been thinking that there was enough left of the roast to make hash-balls for dinner"—Ev'leen Ann would never have used a fancy name like croquettes—"and maybe you'd like a rhubarb pie."

I knew well enough she had been thinking of no such thing, but I could as easily have slapped a reigning sovereign on the back as broken in on the regal reserve of Ev'leen Ann in her clean gingham.

"Well, yes, Ev'leen Ann," I answered in her own tone of reasonable consideration of the matter, "that would be nice, and your piecrust is so flaky that even Mr. Horace will have to be pleased."

"Mr. Horace" is our title for the sardonic cousin whose carping ways are half a joke, and half a menace, in our household.

Ev'leen Ann could not manage a smile. She looked down soberly at the white-pine top of the kitchen table and said, "I guess there is enough sparrow-grass up in the garden for a mess, too, if you'd like that."

"That would taste very good," I agreed, my heart aching for her.

"And creamed potatoes," she finished steadily, thrusting my unspoken pity from her.

"You know I like creamed potatoes better than any other kind," I concurred.

There was a silence. It seemed inhuman to go and leave the stricken

young thing to fight her trouble alone in the ugly prison, her work-
place, though I thought I could guess why Ev'leen Ann had shut the
doors so tightly. I hung near her, searching my head for something
to say, but she helped me by no casual remark. 'Niram is not the only
one of our people who possesses to the full the supreme gift of silence.
Finally I mentioned the report of a case of measles in the village, and
Ev'leen Ann responded in kind with the news that her Aunt Emma
had bought a potato-planter. Ev'leen Ann is an orphan, brought up
by a well-to-do spinster aunt, who is strong-minded and runs her own
farm. After a time we glided by way of similar transitions to the mention of his name.

"'Niram Purdon tells me his stepmother is no better," I said. "Isn't
it too bad?" I thought it well for Ev'leen Ann to be dragged out of her
black cave of silence once in a while, even if it could be done only by
force. As she made no answer, I went on. "Everybody who knows
'Niram thinks it splendid of him to do so much for his stepmother."

Ev'leen Ann responded with a detached air, as though speaking of
a matter in China: "Well, it ain't any more than what he should. She
was awful good to him when he was little and his father got so sick.
I guess 'Niram wouldn't ha' had much to eat if she hadn't ha' gone
out sewing to earn it for him and Mr. Purdon." She added firmly,
after a moment's pause, "No, ma'am, I don't guess it's any more than
what 'Niram had ought to do."

"But it's very hard on a young man to feel that he's not able to
marry," I continued. Once in a great while we came so near the matter
as this. Ev'leen Ann made no answer. Her face took on a pinched look
of sickness. She set her lips as though she would never speak again. But
I knew that a criticism of 'Niram would always rouse her, and said:
"And really, I think 'Niram makes a great mistake to act as he does.
A wife would be a help to him. She could take care of Mrs. Purdon
and keep the house."

Ev'leen Ann rose to the bait, speaking quickly with some heat: "I
guess 'Niram knows what's right for him to do! He can't afford to
marry when he can't even keep up with the doctor's bills and all. He
keeps the house himself, nights and mornings, and Mrs. Purdon is
awful handy about taking care of herself, for all she's bedridden.
That's her way, you know. She can't bear to have folks do for her.
She'd die before she'd let anybody do anything for her that she could
anyways do for herself!"

I sighed acquiescingly. Mrs. Purdon's fierce independence was a
rock on which every attempt at sympathy or help shattered itself to
atoms. There seemed to be no other emotion left in her poor old

work-worn shell of a body. As I looked at Ev'leen Ann it seemed rather a hateful characteristic, and I remarked, "It seems to me it's asking a good deal of 'Niram to spoil his life in order that his stepmother can go on pretending she's independent."

Ev'leen Ann explained hastily: "Oh, 'Niram doesn't tell her anything about—she doesn't know he would like to—he don't want she should be worried—and, anyhow, as 'tis, he can't earn enough to keep ahead of all the doctors cost."

"But the right kind of a wife—a good, competent girl—could help out by earning something, too."

Ev'leen Ann looked at me forlornly, with no surprise. The idea was evidently not new to her. "Yes, ma'am, she could. But 'Niram says he ain't the kind of man to let his wife go out working." Even while she drooped under the killing verdict of his pride she was loyal to his standards and uttered no complaint. She went on, " 'Niram wants Aunt Em'line to have things the way she wants 'em, as near as he can give 'em to her—and it's right she should."

"Aunt Emeline?" I repeated, surprised at her absence of mind. "You mean Mrs. Purdon, don't you?"

Ev'leen Ann looked vexed at her slip, but she scorned to attempt any concealment. She explained dryly, with the shy, stiff embarrassment our country people have in speaking of private affairs: "Well, she *is* my Aunt Em'line, Mrs. Purdon is, though I don't hardly ever call her that. You see, Aunt Emma brought me up, and she and Aunt Em'line don't have anything to do with each other. They were twins, and when they were girls they got edgeways over 'Niram's father, when 'Niram was a baby and his father was a young widower and come courting. Then Aunt Em'line married him, and Aunt Emma never spoke to her afterward."

Occasionally, in walking unsuspectingly along one of our leafy lanes, some such fiery geyser of ancient heat uprears itself in a boiling column. I never get used to it, and started back now.

"Why, I never heard of that before, and I've known your Aunt Emma and Mrs. Purdon for years!"

"Well, they're pretty old now," said Ev'leen Ann listlessly, with the natural indifference of self-centered youth to the bygone tragedies of the preceding generation. "It happened quite some time ago. And both of them were so touchy if anybody seemed to speak about it, that folks got in the way of letting it alone. First Aunt Emma wouldn't speak to her sister because she'd married the man she'd wanted, and then when Aunt Emma made out so well farmin' and got so well off, why, then Mrs. Purdon wouldn't try to make it up because she was so poor.

That was after Mr. Purdon had had his stroke of paralysis and they'd lost their farm and she'd taken to goin' out sewin'—not but what she was always perfectly satisfied with her bargain. She always acted as though she'd rather have her husband's old shirt stuffed with straw than any other man's whole body. He was a real nice man, I guess, Mr. Purdon was."

There I had it—the curt, unexpanded chronicle of two passionate lives. And there I had also the key to Mrs. Purdon's fury of independence. It was the only way in which she could defend her husband against the charge, so damning in her world, of not having provided for his wife. It was the only monument she could rear to her husband's memory. And her husband had been all there was in life for her!

I stood looking at her young kinswoman's face, noting the granite under the velvet softness of its youth, and divining the flame under the granite. I longed to break through her wall, to put my arms about her. On the impulse of the moment I cast aside the pretense of casualness.

"Oh, my dear!" I said. "Are you and 'Niram always to go on like this? Can't anybody help you?"

Ev'leen Ann looked at me, her face suddenly old and gray. "No, ma'am; we ain't going to go on this way. We've decided, 'Niram and I have, that it ain't no use. We've decided that we'd better not go places together any more or see each other. It's too—if 'Niram thinks we can't"—she flamed so that I knew she was burning from head to foot—"it's better for us not—" She ended in a muffled voice, hiding her face in the crook of her arm.

Ah, yes; now I knew why Ev'leen Ann had shut out the passionate breath of the spring night!

I stood near her, a lump in my throat, but I divined the anguish of her shame at her involuntary self-revelation, and respected it. I dared do no more than to touch her shoulder gently.

The door behind us rattled. Ev'leen Ann sprang up and turned her face toward the wall. Paul's cousin came in, shuffling a little, blinking his eyes in the light of the unshaded lamp, and looking very old and tired. He glanced at us as he went over to the sink. "Nobody offered me anything good to drink," he complained, "so I came in to get some water from the faucet for my nightcap."

When he had drunk with ostentation from the tin dipper, he went to the outside door and flung it open. "Don't you people know how hot and smelly it is in here?" he said roughly.

The night wind burst in, eddying, and puffed out the lamp. In an

instant the room was filled with coolness and perfumes and the rushing sound of the river. Out of the darkness came Ev'leen Ann's young
voice. "It seems to me," she said, as though speaking to herself, "that
I never heard the Mill Brook sound so loud as it has this spring."

I woke up that night with the start one has at a sudden call. But
there had been no call. A profound silence spread itself through the
sleeping house. Outdoors the wind had died down. Only the loud
brawl of the river broke the stillness under the stars. But all through
this silence and this vibrant song there rang a soundless menace which
brought me out of bed and to my feet before I was awake. I heard
Paul say, "What's the matter?" in a sleepy voice, and "Nothing," I
answered, reaching for my dressing-gown and slippers. I listened for
a moment, my head ringing with frightening neighborhood tales I
had been brought up on—that despairing Hilton boy who, when his
sweetheart—the Raven Rocks loomed up, with their hundred-foot
straight drop to death—and the deserted wife—. There was still no
sound. I stepped rapidly along the hall and up the stairs to Ev'leen
Ann's room, and opened the door. Without knocking. The room
was empty.

Then how I ran! Calling loudly for Paul to join me, I ran down
the two flights of stairs, out of the open door, and along the hedged
path that leads down to the little river. The starlight was clear. I
could see everything as plainly as though in early dawn. I saw the
river, and I saw—Ev'leen Ann!

There was a dreadful moment of horror, which I shall never remember very clearly, and then Ev'leen Ann and I—both very wet—
stood on the bank, shuddering in each other's arms.

Into our hysteria there dropped, like a pungent caustic, the arid
voice of Horace, remarking, "Well, are you two people crazy, or are
you walking in your sleep?"

I could feel Ev'leen Ann stiffen in my arms, and I fairly stepped
back from her in astonished admiration as I heard her snatch at the
straw thus offered, and still shuddering horribly from head to foot,
force herself to say quite connectedly: "Why—yes—of course—I've always heard about my grandfather Parkman's walking in his sleep.
Folks *said* 'twould come out in the family some time."

Paul was close behind Horace—I wondered a little at his not being
first—and with many astonished and inane ejaculations, such as people
always make on startling occasions, we took our way back into the
house to hot blankets and toddies. But I slept no more that night.

Some time after dawn, however, I did fall into a troubled unconsciousness full of bad dreams, and only woke when the sun was quite high. I opened my eyes to see Ev'leen Ann about to close the door.

"Oh, did I wake you up?" she said. "I didn't mean to. That little Harris boy is here with a letter for you."

She spoke with a slightly defiant tone of self-possession. I tried to play up to her interpretation of her role.

"The little Harris boy?" I said, sitting up in bed. "What in the world is he bringing me a letter for?"

Ev'leen Ann, with her usual clear perception of the superfluous in conversation, turned away silently, went downstairs and brought back the note. It was of four lines, and—surprisingly enough—from old Mrs. Purdon, who asked me abruptly if I would have my husband take me to see her. She specified, and underlined the specification, that I was to come "right off, and in the automobile." Wondering extremely at this mysterious bidding, I sought out Paul, who obediently cranked up our small car and carried me off. There was no sign of Horace about the house, but some distance on the other side of the village we saw his tall, stooping figure swinging along the road. He carried a cane and was characteristically occupied in violently switching off the heads from the wayside weeds as he walked. He refused our offer to take him in, alleging that he was out for exercise and to reduce his flesh—an ancient jibe at his bony frame which made him for an instant show a leathery smile.

There was, of course, no one at Mrs. Purdon's to let us into the tiny, three-roomed house, since the bedridden invalid spent her days there alone while 'Niram worked his team on other people's fields. Not knowing what we might find, Paul stayed outside in the car, while I stepped inside in answer to Mrs. Purdon's "Come *in,* why don't you!" which sounded quite as dry as usual. But when I saw her I knew that things were not as usual.

She lay flat on her back, the little emaciated wisp of humanity, hardly raising the piecework quilt enough to make the bed seem occupied, and to account for the thin, worn old face on the pillow. But as I entered the room her eyes seized on mine, and I was aware of nothing but them and some fury of determination behind them. With a fierce heat of impatience at my first natural but quickly repressed exclamation of surprise she explained briefly that she wanted Paul to lift her into the automobile and take her into the next township to the Andrews farm. "I'm so shrunk away to nothin', I know I can lay on the back seat if I crook myself up," she said, with a cool accent but a rather shaky voice.

I suppose that my face showed the wildness of my astonishment

for she added, as if in explanation, but still with a ferocious determination to keep up the matter-of-fact tone: "Emma Andrews is my twin
sister. I guess it ain't so queer, my wanting to see her."

I thought, of course, we were to be used as the medium for some
strange, sudden family reconciliation, and went out to ask Paul if he
thought he could carry the old invalid to the car. He replied that,
so far as that went, he could carry so thin an old body ten times around
the town, but that he refused absolutely to take such a risk without
authorization from her doctor. I remembered the burning eyes of resolution I had left inside, and sent him to present his objections to
Mrs. Purdon herself.

In a few moments I saw him emerge from the house with the old
woman in his arms. He had evidently taken her up just as she lay.
The piecework quilt hung down in long folds, flashing its brilliant
reds and greens in the sunshine, which shone so strangely upon the
pallid old countenance, facing the open sky for the first time in years.

We drove in silence through the green and gold lyric of the spring
day, an elderly company sadly out of key with the triumphant note
of eternal youth which rang through all the visible world. Mrs. Purdon
looked at nothing, said nothing, seemed to be aware of nothing but
the purpose in her heart, whatever that might be. Paul and I, taking
a leaf from our neighbors' book, held, with a courage like theirs, to
their excellent habit of saying nothing when there is nothing to say.
We arrived at the fine old Andrews place without the exchange of a
single word.

"Now carry me in," said Mrs. Purdon briefly, evidently hoarding
her strength.

"Wouldn't I better go and see if Miss Andrews is at home?" I
asked.

Mrs. Purdon shook her head impatiently and turned her compelling
eyes on my husband. I went up the path before them to knock at the
door, wondering what the people in the house *could* possibly be thinking of us. There was no answer to my knock. "Open the door and
go in," commanded Mrs. Purdon from out her quilt.

There was no one in the spacious, white-paneled hall, and no sound
in all the big, many-roomed house.

"Emma's out feeding the hens," conjectured Mrs. Purdon, not, I
fancied, without a faint hint of relief in her voice. "Now carry me upstairs to the first room on the right."

Half hidden by his burden, Paul rolled wildly inquiring eyes at me;
but he obediently staggered up the broad old staircase, and, waiting

till I had opened the first door to the right, stepped into the big bedroom.

"Put me down on the bed, and open them shutters," Mrs. Purdon commanded.

She still marshaled her forces with no lack of decision, but with a fainting voice which made me run over to her quickly as Paul laid her down on the four-poster. Her eyes were still indomitable, but her mouth hung open slackly and her color was startling. "Oh, Paul, quick! quick! Haven't you your flask with you?"

Mrs. Purdon informed me in a barely audible whisper, "In the corner cupboard at the head of the stairs," and I flew down the hallway. I returned with a bottle, evidently of great age. There was only a little brandy in the bottom, but it whipped up a faint color into the sick woman's lips.

As I was bending over her and Paul was thrusting open the shutters, letting in a flood of sunshine and flecky leaf-shadows, a firm, rapid step came down the hall, and a vigorous woman, with a tanned face and a clean, faded gingham dress, stopped short in the doorway with an expression of stupefaction.

Mrs. Purdon put me on one side, and although she was physically incapable of moving her body by a hair's breadth, she gave the effect of having risen to meet the newcomer. "Well, Emma, here I am," she said in a queer voice, with involuntary quavers in it. As she went on she had it more under control, although in the course of her extraordinarily succinct speech it broke and failed her occasionally. When it did, she drew in her breath with an audible, painful effort, struggling forward steadily in what she had to say. "You see, Emma, it's this way: My 'Niram and your Ev'leen Ann have been keeping company—ever since they went to school together—you know that's well as I do, for all we let on we didn't, only I didn't know till just now how hard they took it. They can't get married because 'Niram can't keep even, let alone get ahead any, because I cost so much bein' sick, and the doctor says I may live for years this way, same's Aunt Hettie did. An' 'Niram is thirty-one, an' Ev'leen Ann is twenty-eight, an' they've had 'bout's much waitin' as is good for folks that set such store by each other. I've thought of every way out of it—and there ain't any. The Lord knows I don't enjoy livin' any. I'd thought of cutting my throat like Uncle Lish, but that'd make 'Niram and Ev'leen Ann feel so—to think why I'd done it; they'd never take the comfort they'd ought in bein' married. So that won't do. There's only one thing to do. I guess you'll have to take care of me till the Lord calls me. Maybe I won't last so long as the doctor thinks."

When she finished, I felt my ears ringing in the silence. She had walked to the sacrificial altar with so steady a step, and laid upon it her precious all with so gallant a front of quiet resolution, that for an instant I failed to take in the sublimity of her self-immolation. Mrs. Purdon asking for charity! And asking the one woman who had most reason to refuse it to her.

Paul looked at me miserably, the craven desire to escape a scene written all over him. "Wouldn't we better be going, Mrs. Purdon?" I said uneasily. I had not ventured to look at the woman in the doorway.

Mrs. Purdon motioned me to remain, with an imperious gesture whose fierceness showed the tumult underlying her brave front. "No; I want you should stay. I want you should hear what I say, so's you can tell folks, if you have to. Now, look here, Emma," she went on to the other, still obstinately silent, "you must look at it the way 'tis. We're neither of us any good to anybody, the way we are—and I'm dreadfully in the way of the only two folks we care a pin about—either of us. You've got plenty to do with, and nothing to spend it on. I can't get myself out of their way by dying without going against what's Scripture and proper, but—" Her steely calm broke. She burst out in a scream. "You've just *got* to, Emma Andrews! You've just *got* to! If you don't, I won't never go back to 'Niram's house! I'll lie in the ditch by the roadside till the poor-master comes to git me—and I'll tell everybody that it's because my twin sister, with a house and a farm and money in the bank, turned me out to starve—" A spasm cut her short. She lay twisted, the whites of her eyes showing between the lids.

"Good God, she's gone!" cried Paul, running to the bed.

Instantly the woman in the doorway was between Paul and me as we rubbed the thin, icy hands and forced brandy between the flaccid lips. We all three thought her dead or dying, and labored over her with the frightened thankfulness for one another's living presence which always marks that dreadful moment. But even as we fanned and rubbed, and cried out to one another to open the windows and to bring water, the blue lips moved to a ghostly whisper: "Em, listen—" The old woman went back to the nickname of their common youth. "Em—your Ev'leen Ann—tried to drown herself—in the Mill Brook last night . . . That's what decided me—to—" And then we were plunged into another desperate struggle with Death for the possession of the battered old habitation of the dauntless soul.

"Isn't there any hot water in the house?" cried Paul, and "Yes, yes;

teakettle on the stove!" answered the woman who labored with us. Paul, divining that she meant the kitchen, fled downstairs. I stole a look at Emma Andrews' face as she bent over the sister she had not seen in thirty years, and I knew that Mrs. Purdon's battle was won. It even seemed that she had won another skirmish in her never-ending war with death, for a little warmth began to come back into her hands.

When Paul returned with the teakettle, and a hot-water bottle had been filled, the owner of the house straightened herself, assumed her rightful position as mistress of the situation, and began to issue commands. "You git right in the automobile, and go git the doctor," she told Paul. "That'll be the quickest. She's better now, and your wife and I can keep her goin' till the doctor gits here."

As Paul left the room she snatched something white from a bureau drawer, stripped the worn, patched old cotton nightgown from the skeleton-like body, and, handling the invalid with a strong, sure touch, slipped on a soft, woolly outing-flannel wrapper with a curious trimming of zigzag braid down the front. Mrs. Purdon opened her eyes very slightly, but shut them again at her sister's quick command, "You lay still, Em'line, and drink some of this brandy." She obeyed without comment, but after a pause she opened her eyes again and looked down at the new garment which clad her. She had that moment turned back from the door of death, but her first breath was used to set the scene for a return to a decorum.

"You're still a great hand for rickrack work, Em, I see," she murmured in a faint whisper. "Do you remember how surprised Aunt Su was when you made up a pattern?"

"Well, I hadn't thought of it for quite some time," returned Miss Andrews, in exactly the same tone of everyday remark. As she spoke she slipped her arm under the other's head and poked the pillow up to a more comfortable shape. "Now you lay perfectly still," she commanded in the hectoring tone of the born nurse; "I'm goin' to run down and make you a good hot cup of sassafras tea."

I followed her down into the kitchen and was met by the same refusal to be melodramatic which I had encountered in Ev'leen Ann. I was most anxious to know what version of my extraordinary morning I was to give out to the world, but hung silent, abashed by the cool casualness of the other woman as she mixed her brew. Finally, "Shall I tell 'Niram— What shall I say to Ev'leen Ann? If anybody asks me—" I brought out with clumsy hesitation.

At the realization that her reserve and family pride were wholly at the mercy of any report I might choose to give, even my iron hostess faltered. She stopped short in the middle of the floor, looked at me silently, piteously.

I hastened to assure her that I would attempt no hateful picturesqueness. "Suppose I just say that you were rather lonely here, now that Ev'leen Ann has left you, and that you thought it would be nice to have your sister come to stay with you, so that 'Niram and Ev'leen Ann can be married?"

Emma Andrews breathed again. She walked toward the stairs with the steaming cup in her hand. Over her shoulder she remarked, "Well, yes; that would be as good a way to put it as any, I guess."

'Niram and Ev'leen Ann were standing up to be married. They looked very stiff and self-conscious, and Ev'leen Ann was very pale. 'Niram's big hands, crooked as though they still held an axhelve or steered a plow, hung down by his new black trousers. Ev'leen Ann's strong fingers stood out stiffly from one another. They looked hard at the minister and repeated after him in low and meaningless tones the solemn and touching words of the marriage service. Back of them stood the wedding company, in freshly washed and ironed white dresses, new straw hats, and black suits smelling of camphor. In the background, among the other elders, stood Paul and Horace and I—my husband and I hand in hand, Horace twiddling the black ribbon which holds his watch and looking bored. Through the open windows into the stuffiness of the best room came an echo of the deep organ note of midsummer.

"Whom God hath joined together—" said the minister, and the epitome of humanity which filled the room held its breath—the old with a wonder upon their life-scarred faces, the young half frightened to feel the stir of the great wings soaring so near them.

Then it was all over. 'Niram and Ev'leen Ann were married, and the rest of us were bustling about to serve the hot biscuit and coffee and chicken salad, and to dish up the ice cream. Afterward there were no citified refinements of cramming rice down the necks of the departing pair or tying placards to the carriage in which they went away. Some of the men went out to the barn and hitched up for 'Niram, and we all gathered at the gate to see them drive off. They might have been going for one of their Sunday afternoon "buggy-rides" except for the wet eyes of the foolish women and girls who stood waving their hands in answer to the flutter of Ev'leen Ann's handkerchief as the carriage went down the hill.

We had nothing to say to one another after they left, and began soberly to disperse to our respective vehicles. But as I was getting into our car a new thought suddenly struck me.

"Why," I cried, "I never thought of it before! However in the world did old Mrs. Purdon know about Ev'leen Ann—that night?"

Horace was pulling at the door. Its hinges were sprung and it shut hard. He closed it with a vicious slam. "I told her," he said crossly.

Old
Man Warner

~~**W**~~hen I was a little girl—and that is a long long
time ago—everybody worried about Old Man Warner—what would become of him—what to do with him. It was not that old Mr. Warner
was a dangerous character, or anything but strictly honest and law-
abiding. But he had his own way of bothering his fellow citizens.

In his young days he had inherited a farm from his father, back
up in Arnold Hollow, where at that time there was a cozy little
settlement of five or six farms with big families. He settled there,
cultivated the farm, married, and brought up a family of three sons.
When the Civil War came, he volunteered together with his oldest
boy, and went off to fight in the second year of the war. He
came back alone in 1865, the son having fallen in the Battle of the
Wilderness.

Naturally he went back to live in Arnold Hollow. So did a few
of the older returning veterans. But the younger ones, after one look
at those steep rocky fields, set off for the West, the two remaining
Warner boys now old enough to go along with them.

Gradually the Hollow settlement shrunk. Old folks died, others
moved down close to the new railroad track in the valley. Mr. Warner
stayed on. He hardly ever left the farm, even to go to the village.
His wife said he told her once that it seemed as if he never could get
caught up for what he'd missed in all that time he was slogging

through Virginia mud. "He always thought the world of his own home," she added.

Finally all the neighbors were gone. Then in 1898, the wife died, leaving her husband alone at seventy-one. Meanwhile after the usual ups and downs of pioneer farmers, the sons had done pretty well out in Iowa. Now in their late forties they had comfortable homes. They wrote, inviting their father to pass his old age with them.

Everybody in our town began to lay plans about what they would buy at the auction, when Old Man Warner would sell off his things, as the other Arnold Hollow families had. The Selectmen planned to cut out the road up into Arnold Hollow, and put the tidy little sum saved from its upkeep into improvements on the main valley thoroughfare. But old Mr. Warner wrote his sons and told the Selectmen that he saw no reason for leaving his home to go and live in a strange place and be a burden to his children, with whom, having seen them at the rarest intervals during the last thirty years, he did not feel very well acquainted. And he always had liked his own home. Why should he leave it? It was pretty late in the day for him to get used to western ways. He'd just be a bother to his boys. He didn't want to be a bother to anybody, and he didn't propose to be!

There were a good many protests all round, but of course the Selectmen had not the faintest authority over him, and since, quite probably, his sons were at heart relieved, nothing was done. The town very grudgingly voted the money to keep some sort of road open to Arnold Hollow, but consoled itself by saying freely that the old cuss never had been so very bright and was worse now, evidently had no idea what he was trying to do, and would soon get tired of living alone and "doing for himself."

Twenty-two years passed. Selectmen who were then middle-aged grew old and decrepit, died, and were buried. Boys who were learning their letters then, grew up, married, had children, and became Selectmen in their turn. Old Man Warner's sons also grew old and died, and the names of most of his grandchildren, scattered all over the West, were unknown to us. And still the old man lived alone in his home and "did for himself."

Every spring, when road work began, the Selectmen groaned over having to keep up the Arnold Hollow road, and every autumn they tried their best to persuade the old man to come down to a settlement where he could be taken care of. Our town is very poor, and taxes are a heavy item in our calculations. It is just all we can do to keep our schools and roads going, and we grudge every penny we are forced to spend on tramps, paupers, or the indigent sick. Selectmen in whose regime town expenses were high, are not only never re-elected to town office, but their name is a byword and a reproach for years afterwards. We elect them, among other things, to see to it that town expenses are not high, and to lay their plans accordingly.

One Board of Selectmen after another, heavy with this responsibility, tried to lay their plans accordingly in regard to Old Man Warner, and ran their heads into a stone wall. They knew what would happen; the old dumb-head would get a stroke of paralysis, or palsy, or softening of the brain, or something, and the town treasury would bleed at every pore for expensive medical service, maybe an operation at a hospital, and after that, somebody paid to take care of him. If they could only ship him off to his family!—One of the granddaughters, now a middle-aged woman, kept up a tenuous connection with the old man, and answered, after long intervals, anxious communications from the Selectmen.—Or if not that, if only they could get him down out of there in the winter, so they would not be saddled with the perpetual worry about what might be happening to him, with the perpetual need to break out the snow in the road and go up there to see that he was all right.

But Old Man Warner was still not bright enough to see any reason why he should lie down on his own folks, or why he should not live in his own home. When gentle expostulations were tried, he always answered mildly that he guessed he'd rather go on living the way he was for a while longer; and when blustering was tried, he straightened up, looked the blusterer in the eye, and said he guessed there wasn't no law in Vermont to turn a man off his own farm, s'long's he paid his taxes and didn't owe any debts that he knew of.

That was the fact, too. He paid spot cash for what he bought in his semi-yearly trips to the village to "do trading," as our phrase goes. He bought very little, a couple of pairs of overalls a year, a bag apiece of sugar and coffee and rice and salt and flour, some raisins, and pepper. And once or twice during the long period of his hermit life, a fleece-lined work-jacket and a new pair of trousers. From time to time he drew a few dollars from the tiny savings account started years ago when he sold his timber-lot. But not often. For mostly what he brought down from the farm was just enough to pay for such purchases, for he continued to cultivate his land, less and less of it, of course, each year, but still enough to feed his horse and cow and pig and hens, and to provide him with corn and potatoes and onions. He salted down and smoked a hog every fall and ate his hens when they got too old to lay.

Of course, as long as he was economically independent, the town, groaning with apprehension over the danger to its treasury though it was, could not lay a finger on the cranky old codger. Yet, of course, his economic independence couldn't last! From one day to the next, something was bound to happen to him, something that would cost the town money.

Each year the Selectmen, planning the town expenditures with the concentrated prudence born of necessity, cast an uneasy mental glance up Arnold Hollow way, and scringed at the thought that perhaps this was the year when money would have to be taken away from the road or the school fund to pay for Old Man Warner's doctoring and nursing; and finally for his burial, because as the years went by, even the tenuous western granddaughter vanished: died, or moved, or something. Old Man Warner was now entirely alone in the world.

All during my childhood and youth he was a legendary figure of "sot" obstinacy and queerness. We children used to be sent up once in a while, in summer, to take our turn in seeing that the old man was all right. It was an expedition like no other. You turned from the main highway and went up the steep, stony, winding mountain road, dense with the shade of sugar maples and oaks. At the top, when your blown horse stopped to rest, you saw before you the grassy lane leading across the little upland plateau where the Arnold Hollow settlement had been. The older people said they could almost hear faint echoes of whetting scythes, and barking dogs, and cheerful homely noises, as there had been in the old days. But for us children there was nothing but a breathlessly hushed, sunny glade of lush meadows, oppressively silent and spooky, with a few eyeless wrecks of abandoned farm houses, drooping and gray. You went past the creepy place as fast as your horse could gallop, and clattered into a thicket of shivering white birches which grew close to the road like a screen; and then —there was no sensation in my childhood quite like the coming out into the ordered, inhabited, humanized little clearing, in front of Old Man Warner's home. There were portly hens crooning around on the close-cropped grass, and a pig grunting sociably from his pen at you, and shining milk-pans lying in the sun tilted against the white birch sticks of the wood-pile, and Old Man Warner, himself, infinitely aged and stooped, in his faded, clean overalls, emerging from the barndoor to peer at you out of his bright old eyes and to give you a hearty, "Well, you're quite a long ways from home, don't you know it? Git off your horse, can't ye? I've got a new calf in here." Or perhaps if it were a Sunday, he would be sitting in the sun on the front porch, with a clean shirt on, reading the weekly edition of the *New York*

Try-bune. He drove two miles every Saturday afternoon, down to his R.F.D. mailbox on the main road, to get this.

You heard so much talk about him down in the valley, so much fussing and stewing about his being so "sot," and so queer, that it always surprised you when you saw him, to find he was just like anybody else. You saw his calf, and had a drink of milk in his clean, well-scrubbed kitchen, and played with the latest kitten, and then you said goodby for that time, and got on your horse and went back through the birch thicket into the ghostly decay of the abandoned farms, back down the long, stony road to the valley where everybody was so cross with the unreasonable old man for causing them so much worry.

"How *could* he expect to go along like that, when other old folks, so much younger than he, gave up and acted like sensible people, and settled down where you could take care of them! The house might burn down over his head, and he with it; or he might fall and break his hip and be there for days, yelling and fainting away till somebody happened to go by; or a cow might get ugly and hook him, and nobody to send for help." All these frightening possibilities and many others had been repeatedly presented to the old man himself with the elaborations and detail which came from heartfelt alarm about him. But he continued to say mildly that he guessed he'd go on living the way he was for a while yet.

"A *while!*" He was ninety years old.

And then he was ninety-one, and then ninety-two; and we were surer and surer he would "come on the town," before each fiscal year was over. At the beginning of last winter our Selectmen went up in a body to try to bully or coax the shrunken, wizened old man, now only half his former size, to go down to the valley. He remarked that he "guessed there wasn't no law in Vermont" and so forth, just as he had to their fathers. He was so old that he could no longer straighten up as he said it, for his back was helplessly bent with rheumatism, and for lack of teeth he whistled and clucked and lisped a good deal as he pronounced his formula. But his meaning was as clear as it had been thirty years ago. They came sulkily away without him, knowing that they would be laughed at and blamed, in the valley, because the cussed old crab had got the best of them, again.

Last February, a couple of men, crossing over to a lumber job on Hemlock Mountain, by way of the Arnold Hollow road, saw no smoke coming out of his chimney, knocked at the door, and, getting no answer, opened it and stepped in. There lay Old Man Warner, dead on his kitchen floor in front of his well-blacked cookstove. The tiny, crooked old body was fully dressed, even to a fur cap and mittens, and in one hand was his sharp, well-ground ax. One stove-lid was off, and a charred stick of wood lay half in and half out of the firebox. Evidently the old man had stepped to the fire to put in a stick of wood before he went out to split some more, and had been stricken instantly, before he could move a step. His cold, white old face was composed and quiet, just as it had always been in life.

The two lumbermen fed the half-starved pig and hens and turned back to the valley with the news, driving the old man's cow and horse in front of them; and in a couple of hours we all knew that Old Man Warner had died, all alone, in his own kitchen.

Well, what do you think! We were as stirred up about it—! We turned out and gave him one of the best funerals the town ever saw. And we put up a good marble tombstone that told all about how he had lived. We found we were proud of him, as proud as could be, the darned old bulldog, who had stuck it out all alone, in spite of us. We brag now about his single-handed victory over old age and loneliness, and we keep talking about him to the children, just as we brag about our grandfathers' victories in the Civil War and talk to the children about the doings of the Green Mountain Boys. Old Man Warner has become history. We take as much satisfaction in the old fellow's spunk as though he had been our own grandfather, and we spare our listeners no detail in his story: ". . . And there he stuck year after year, with the whole town plaguing at him to quit. And he earned his own living, and chopped his own wood, and kept himself and the house just as decent, and never got queer and frowzy and half-cracked, but stayed just like anybody, as nice an old man as ever you saw—all alone, all stark alone—beholden to nobody—asking no odds of anybody—yes, sir, and died with his boots on, at ninety-three, on a kitchen floor you could have et off of, 'twas so clean."

Uncle Giles

Few personalities of bygone years survive the blurring erasure of time. For the most part, family talk preserves of past generations no more than a date, an anecdote. But the personality of my Great-Uncle Giles has suffered no such partial obliteration. It has come down to us, entire, with outlines sharply etched into the family consciousness by the acid of exact recollection. To us all, down to the one latest born, he has been an example. What kind of an example, the story of his life well known to us will tell you.

By people outside the family, Uncle Giles was thought to be a man of charm and distinction. This was his own opinion, too. He felt that he was the only member of the entire tribe with any fitness for a higher sphere of activities than the grubby middle-class world of his kinsmen. Yes, that is what Uncle Giles thought, probably adding to himself that he was a "gentleman among canaille." To this day the family bristles at the mention of anyone who openly professes to be a gentleman and claims the privileges traditionally belonging to that class.

A gentleman should not be forced to the menial task of earning a living. Uncle Giles was never forced to the menial task of earning his living. None of the coarsely materialistic forces in human life ever succeeded in forcing him to it, not even the violent efforts of a good many able-bodied and energetic kinspeople. The tales of how Uncle Giles blandly outwitted their stub-fingered attacks on his liberty and succeeded to the end of a very long life in living without work are part of our inheritance. For three generations now they have wrought the members of our family to wrath and laughter. He was incredible. You can't imagine anything like him. Unless you have had him in your family too.

For many years of his youth Uncle Giles was "preparing for the ministry." These were the candid years of hope when his older generation did not know him so well as later, and still believed that with a little more help Giles would be able to get on his feet. He was a great favorite in the Theological Seminary where he was a student for so long, a handsome well-set-up blond young man, with beautiful large blue eyes. I know just how he looked, for we have an expensive miniature of him that was painted at the time. He paid for that miniature with the money my great-grandfather pried out of a Vermont farm. It had been sent to pay for his board. A conscientious family can't abandon a son just on the point of becoming a clergyman. Great-grandfather himself had no more money to send at that time, but his other sons, hard-working, energetic, successful men, clubbed together and made up the amount necessary to settle that board bill. Uncle Giles thanked them and forwarded with his letter, to show them, in his own phrase, "that their bounty was not ill-advised," a beautifully bound, high-priced little red morocco notebook in which he had written down the flattering things said of him by his professors and others—especially others. He underlined certain passages, thus: ". . . a very worthy young man, *most pleasing in society.*" "A model to all *in the decorum and grace of his manners.*"

His board bill had to be paid a good many times before Uncle Giles finally gave up preparing himself for the ministry. The summer vacations of this period he spent in visiting first one and then another member of the family, a first-rate ornament on the front porch and at the table, admired by the ladies of the neighborhood, a prime favorite on picnics and on the croquet ground. He always seemed to have dropped from a higher world into the rough, sweaty and hard-working existence of his kin; but his courtesy was so exquisite that he refrained from commenting on this in any way. Still you could see that he felt it. If you were one of the well-to-do neighbors on whom the distinguished young theological student paid evening calls, you admired his quiet tact and his steady loyalty to his commonplace family.

The effect which his quiet tact and steady loyalty had on his commonplace family was so great that it has persisted undiminished to this day. Any one of us, to the remotest cousin, can spot an Uncle Giles as far as we can see him. We know all about him, and it is not on our front porches that he comes to display his tact and loyalty, and the decorum and grace of his manners. As for allowing the faintest trace of Uncle-Gilesism to color our own lives, there has never been one of us who would not rush out to be hired man on a farm, or to clerk in a ten-cent store, rather than accept even the most genuinely voluntary loan. We are, as Uncle Giles felt, a very commonplace family, of ordinary Anglo-Saxon stock, with no vein of fanciful, imaginative Irish or Scotch or Welsh blood. I think it very likely that if we had not experienced Uncle Giles, we would have been the stodgiest of the stodgy as far as social injustice is concerned. But our imaginations seem to have been torn open by Uncle Giles as by a charge of dynamite; and, having once had it pounded into our heads what he stood for, we hold on to the idea with all our dull Anglo-Saxon tenacity.

We have a deep, unfailing sympathy with anyone who is trying to secure a better and fairer adjustment of burdens in human life, because we see in our plain prosaic way that what he is trying to do is to eliminate the Uncle Gileses from human society and force them to work. And we are always uneasily trying to make sure that we are not, in the bigger scheme of things, without realizing it, Uncle Gilesing it ourselves.

After a while Uncle Giles stopped preparing for the ministry and became an invalid. He bore this affliction with the unaffected manly courage which was always one of his marked characteristics. He never complained: he "bore up" in all circumstances; even on busy washdays when there was no time to prepare one of the dainty little dishes which the delicacy of his taste enabled him so greatly to appreciate. Uncle Giles always said of the vigorous, hearty, undiscriminating men of the family, that they could "eat anything." His accent was the wistful one of resigned envy of their health.

It has been a point of honor with us all, ever since, to be able to "eat anything." Anyone, even a legitimate invalid, who is inclined to be fastidious and make it difficult for the others, feels, even when he is alone at the table, a family glare concentrating on him, which makes him, in a panic, reach out eagerly for the boiled pork and cabbage.

Uncle Giles's was a singular case, "one of those mysterious maladies which baffle even the wisest physicians," as he himself used to say. A good many ladies in those days had mysterious maladies which baffled even the wisest physicians, and they greatly enjoyed Uncle Giles. No other man had such an understanding of their symptoms and such sympathy for their sufferings. The easy chair beside Uncle Giles's invalid couch was seldom vacant. Ladies going away after having left a vaseful of flowers for him, and a plate of cake, and two or three jars of jelly, and some cold breasts of chicken, would say with shining, exalted countenances, "In spite of his terrible trials, what an inspiration our friend can be! An hour with that good man is like an hour on Pisgah."

They would, as like as not, make such a remark to the brave invalid's brother or cousin (or, in later years, nephew) who was earning the money to keep the household going. I am afraid we are no longer as a family very sure what or where Pisgah is, although we know it is in the Bible somewhere, but there is a fierce family tradition against fussing over your health which is as vivid this minute as on the day when the brother or cousin or nephew of Uncle Giles turned away with discourteous haste from the shining-faced lady and stamped into another room. Doctors enter our homes for a broken leg or for a confinement, but seldom for anything else.

When the Civil War came on, Uncle Giles was the only man in the family left at home. He rose splendidly to the occasion and devoted himself to the instruction of his kinswomen, ignorant of the technique of warfare. From his invalid couch he explained to them the strategy of the great battles in which their brothers and husbands and fathers were fighting. As a rule the women of his family were too frantically busy with their Martha-like concentration on the mere material problems of wartime life to give these lucid and intellectual discussions of strategy the attention and consideration they deserved. When the letters from hospitals came with news of the wounded, who but Uncle Giles was competent to understand and expand the tragically bare surgical reports.

The war, however, though it seemed endless, lasted after all but four years. And when it was over, Uncle Giles was free to go back to discussions more congenial to his literary and esthetic tastes.

By this time he was past middle age, "a butterfly broken on the wheel of life," as he said; it was of course out of the question to expect him now to think of working for his living. He had become a family tradition, embedded in the solidly set cement of family habits. The older generation always had taken care of him, the younger saw no way out, and with an unsurprised resignation bent their shoulders to carry on. So, before any other plans could be made, Uncle Giles had to be thought of. Vacations were taken seriatim not to leave Uncle Giles alone. In buying or building a house, care had to be taken to have a room suitable for Uncle Giles when it was your turn to have the invalid under your roof. If the children had measles, one of the first things to do was to get Uncle Giles into some other family home so that he would not be quarantined. Everyone bowed to that unwritten law of family life which ordains that, in the long run, everyone submerges his personal preference in the effort to conform to that of the member of the circle who complains most loudly and is most difficult to satisfy. The dishes Uncle Giles liked were the only ones served (since other men could "eat anything"); the songs Uncle Giles liked were the only ones sung; the very partitions of the houses were adjusted to him; the color of the rugs and the pictures on the walls were selected to suit Uncle Giles's fine and exacting taste.

Looking back, through the perspective of a generation-and-a-half, I can see the exact point of safely acknowledged middle age when Uncle Giles's health began cautiously to improve; but it must have been imperceptible to those around him, so gradual was the change. His kin grew used to each successive stage of his recovery before they realized it was there, and nobody seems to have been surprised to have Uncle Giles pass into a remarkably hale and vigorous old age.

"Invalids often are strong in their later years," he said of himself. "It is God's compensation for their earlier sufferings."

He reaped the full rewards of the most rewarded old age. It was a period of apotheosis for him, and a very lengthy one at that, for he lived to be well past eighty. In any gathering Uncle Giles was conspicuous and much admired, erect and handsome, specklessly attired, his smooth old face neatly shaved, with a quaint, gentle, old-world courtesy. The protecting chivalry in his manner to ladies was a model for imitation, so elderly visiting ladies thought.

He became one of the sights of the town. Strangers and newcomers were brought to see him, and to hear him tell in his vivid, animated way of old times in the country. His great specialty was the Civil War. At any gathering where veterans of the War were to be honored, Uncle Giles held everyone breathless with his descriptions of Gettysburg and Chancellorsville; and when he spoke of Mobile Bay and Sherman's march, how his voice pealed, how his fine eyes lighted up! Strangers used to say to themselves that it was easy to see what an eloquent preacher he must have been when he was in the active ministry. The glum old men in worn blue coats used to gather in a knot in the farthest corner, and in low tones, not to interrupt his discourse, would chat to each other of crops, fishing, and politics.

Somewhere we have a scrapbook in which an ironic cousin of mine carefully pasted up all the local newspaper articles that were written about Uncle Giles in his old age, and the many handsome obituary notices which appeared when he finally died. I can remember my father's getting it out occasionally, and reading the clippings to himself with a very grim expression on his face; but it always moved my light-hearted, fun-loving mother to peals of laughter. After all, she was related to Uncle Giles only by marriage and felt no responsibility for him.

The other day, in looking over some old legal papers, I came across a yellowed letter. It had been folded and (as was the habit before envelopes were common) sealed with three handsome pale-blue seals on its back. Although now broken one could see that the sealing-wax had been stamped with the crested cameo ring which Uncle Giles always wore, bearing what he insisted against constant sour contradiction, was the "coat of arms" of our family. The handwriting of the letter was beautiful, formed with an amorous pride in every letter. It was from Uncle Giles to one of his uncles, my great-grandfather's brother. It had lain there lost for half a century or more, and of course I had never seen it before. Yet every word of it was familiar to me as I glanced it over.

It began in a manner characteristic of Uncle Giles's polished courtesy, with inquiries after every member of his uncle's family, and a pleasant word for each. He then detailed the state of his health, which, alas, left much to be desired, and seemed, so the doctors told him, to require urgently a summer in the mountains. Leaving this subject, he jumped to the local news of the town where he was then living, and told one or two amusing stories. In one of them I remember was this phrase, "I told her I might be poor, but that a gentleman of good birth does not recognize poverty as a member of the family." Through a neat transition after this he led up again to the subject of his health and to the desirability of his passing some months in the mountains, "in the pure air of God's great hills." Then he entered upon a discreet, pleasant, whimsical reference to the fact that only a contribution from his uncle's purse could make this possible. There never was anybody who could beat Uncle Giles on ease and grace, and pleasant, pungent humor when it came to asking for money. The only person embarrassed in that situation was the one from whom Uncle Giles was expecting a loan.

I read no more. With no conscious volition of mine, my hand had scrunched the letter into a ball, and my arm, without my bidding, had hurled the ball into the heart of the fire.

But as I reflected on the subject afterwards, it occurred to me that I was wrong. I thought of the wonderful back-stiffening influence which Uncle Giles has always had on our family. His memory has—how many times!—made us stand up to life, come to grips with reality, unrelentingly harsh though reality often is. No, I told myself, Uncle Giles ought not to be forgotten. I should have saved that letter to show to my children.

Ann Story

Ann Story is, literally, one of our Vermont great-grandmothers. Perhaps she is one of yours too, for she had five children, every one of whom she brought up to strong, useful maturity. They all married, had children, moved with their families here and there in our country as is the American way. Since she was born about 1739, and all her children before 1774, there has been plenty of time for one or the other of her descendants to have become one or another of your ancestors.

Whether they factually did or not, she is, spiritually, an ancestress for every American. Yet I doubt if you ever heard of her, perhaps because her story has in it neither mating, nor murdering. Nor yet money-making. Mostly, if you'll notice, those are the elements considered essential to a "dramatic" script or news report. We who were brought up on old Vermont stories think hers quite dramatic enough.

We know most of the homely-heroic details of her life, for the people who settled Vermont, from 1764 to the 1790's, were younger sons and daughters of decently educated Connecticut, Massachusetts, and Rhode Island people, hence quite literate. They left behind many kinds of written records of those first years—letters, diaries, account books, memoirs, amateur local histories.

In addition, Vermont oral tradition is vivid and unbroken. The grandparents of my youth had heard from their grandparents all about the life of the early settlers. It is from talk as well as from yellowed letters, deeds, and daily journals that we know accurately how the primeval Vermont forests were turned into the mellow home-farms now all around us.

Usually the first of the family to come into Vermont over the Indian trails was the father, always a young father. He brought a helper; a son if he had one old enough, or a brother, or a friend who also planned to settle in Vermont. If the waterways ran in the right directions, these men came by canoe. But mostly on foot or with a pack horse, carrying the minimum of tools and supplies—axes, wedges, a gun, powder, lead, salt, flints, seed for the first crop of grain, a kettle or two (very precious), a frying pan (called a spider because it had legs), blankets, and a very small iron ration of food, generally Indian corn, to fall back on in the infrequent days when neither fish nor game could be had.

Thus in September, 1774, did Ann Story's husband, Amos, arrive at the spot in the dense forest which was to become the town of Salisbury, Vermont. With him was his son, Solomon, then thirteen years old. Look attentively at the next boy of thirteen you see (perhaps there is one in your family circle) so that you will know how old was the boy who swung an ax beside his father, then perhaps thirty-five years old. Together, through that long, cold, dark Vermont winter, they felled trees, built a strong log house, and constructed a chimney. As spring came on, the man and boy (he was fourteen then) called the new home done, and turned to clearing a field in the forest, to make a planting for the family bread the next winter.

And as they toiled together, forward-looking, creative-minded, peaceable young father and sturdy son, disaster struck. A huge sugar maple (we know exactly what kind of a tree it was, for this is one of the details of the story, told and written down over and over) did not fall as Amos Story had thought it would. As it plunged downward, its great branches roaring in the air, it turned and, crashing to the earth, pinned Amos Story's body beneath it.

He died instantly. But his son could not believe it. Snatching up his ax the boy began frantically chopping at the giant cylinder of the granite-hard tree so that he could roll it away from the crushed body. Hardly more than a little boy, he swung his ax desperately, with the skill learned in the long winter's chopping. But when, dripping with sweat, his heart pounding, he had driven his ax blade clear through the great tree-trunk, he still could not stir it. He knelt down by his father again, and saw that he was dead. He was quite alone in the wilderness. Getting up to his feet, he laid his young hand again to the ax, chopping slowly now but delivering steadily those powerful well-aimed blows, till once more he had gone through the thickness of the primeval giant. Then he could roll away the section which lay across his father's dead body, and straighten it for burial.

The nearest human being was in a clearing where the town of Middlebury now stands—miles away from the solitary fatherless boy. The young woodsman knew where the trail ran, followed it, and brought back one Benjamin Smauley (we know the names of the people in this story) and his two sons. They carried the body to lie beside the grave of one of Smauley's daughters who, at twenty years of age, had lost her way in the forest and starved to death before she could be found—this as a reminder to the fourteen-year-old boy of what the wilderness meant.

And after that funeral, what? The fourteen-year-old boy was a good deal more than a hundred and fifty miles from where his mother waited with the little brothers and sisters. There was no way of reaching her except by walking—over a trail through the deep woods most of the way. In those days, the long distances, the lack of roads or bridges or places of shelter along the way, the absence of any system of mail communication, quite often resulted simply in the breaking apart of families. How could it be otherwise? Sturdy young people were assets in any frontiersman's house. Boys and girls separated by chance from their parents were welcomed as helpers to the nearest log cabin. What else could they do?

Ann Story's son could do something else. As steadily as he had driven his ax through the great tree which had killed his father, he set off on foot to go back to tell his mother.

The many accounts of this homespun epic which have come down to us are Vermontishly factual. We know fully the details of what was done. But not what was felt. Nobody has ever told us about the day when young Ann Story (for she was thirty-three when her husband died) back in the Connecticut town, weary with waiting for news, watching the road anxiously, saw her eldest son, foot-sore, dusty, ragged, his head hanging, trudging in on the highway from the north. When Vermonters, telling this story, come to the meeting of mother and son, they stop, swallow hard, and are silent for a moment.

But that is the last pathos in this tale. From that point on the story of this woman and mother rings with vitality, like ax-strokes on oak. This seemed natural to those around her. To us too, who live a good deal by old rather than modern ideas. Not till the Victorian and Romantic-School tradition of females as frail, timorous sofa-creatures, were women admired for being cowards and weaklings. In the pioneering boat they were generally expected to pull their full weight. So they could—and did.

Ann Story had planned with her husband the creation of the new home in the north woods where their boys and girls could grow up children of free and independent landowners. For I must tell you that there was much more in the migration to Vermont, after the ending of the French-and-Indian War, than just the random itching foot common to returned soldiers, more than the stories then going the rounds in New England homes, of good land, and plentiful game in the Green Mountain forests, now newly opened to settlers.

The ferment, political, economic, social, which boiled over into our Revolution, was bubbling hotly among the younger people in the settlements to which the colonial soldiers returned after they were mustered out from the British army at Quebec, in 1763. That date was, note well, only ten years before the Boston Tea Party, twelve years before the shooting at Lexington and Concord, and the rhetorical demand of Ethan Allen for the surrender of Ticonderoga. Men who had been in the colonial troops were still young when they set out to make homes in the Vermont woods.

They were looking for new land and good hunting, just as debunking modern historians tell us, yes, of course. But we who know them very well from the records they left, have plenty of proof that they were also simple-hearted enough to be on fire with the love for liberty, which they spelled, pronounced, and lived for with a capital L. When, before long, they drew up a constitution for the new state, those buckskin-clad farmer-hunters laid down their rifles and their axes to write into it (the first state which did this on the North American continent as far as we can find out) a clause forbidding human slavery in any form. The rising wind of the passion for human freedom, for the recognition of individual human dignity sang loudly in the ears of these young family men, then British Colonials, soon to become Americans, who pushed into Vermont along Indian trails.

And of their wives and sisters, too, as you will see from what Ann Story did.

Her sorrow over her husband's death seemed to her a mighty reason for carrying out what they had planned together, to make free landowners and citizens of their children. Without him, she took up alone the effort they had thought to share. She made the usual preparations of people who went into the wilderness of the North to found new homesteads. She bought a pack horse with the money from the sale of most of her household gear; she gathered her brood around her and set out—a young widow with three sons and two daughters. Wouldn't you like to know their names? Stout Yankee Bible names—

Hannah and Susanna, Samuel, Ephraim, and Solomon. Their ages ran from fourteen down.

Ann carried a rifle over her shoulder as her husband would have done, and so did her first-born. After plunging into the Vermont forests, they knew they would depend largely for food on what game they could shoot. They slept out at night, around a campfire, over which, turn by turn, one of them kept watch. Steadily, slowly, held back by the short steps of the younger children, drawn forward by Ann's vision of earned independence, they pushed on, day after day, week after week, through the great dark trees.

It was about a year after her husband had reached the spot in the forest which was to be their home-farm—in the latter part of 1775—that Ann Story led her children into the ragged, bramble-overgrown clearing, into the log cabin built by her children's father.

At this point, every one of us should shake from his imagination the thick layer of dust deposited on it by too many movies, and too much romantic fiction. You will not get the flavor of this true story unless you try to realize that this woman and her children were real, actually did live and do all this. This is no historical novel printed in a book or flickering on a movie screen. Ann Story was only thirty-three years old, a sore-hearted, lonely widow, who left the safety of a settled, century-old town to carry out single-handed the hopes which she and her husband had shared of freehold citizenship for their children. Those were flesh-and-blood little boys and girls, journeying on, day after day, through the primeval forest. If you ever took five lively children, running from fourteen years down, out for a single day's walk in the country, you know that you were lucky if you brought all five back without minor mishaps—bumped heads, stubbed toes, skinned knees, thorns in fingers, quarrels, queasy stomachs, hurt feelings—up to scalp wounds, a sprained ankle or maybe even a broken arm. Ann Story's five were exactly like yours—don't look at them with the glassed eye we all turn on Hollywood children pretending to be something different from what they are. Everything happened to them that is likely to happen to any children. Yet their young mother brought them through weeks and weeks of solitary journeying. Along that Indian trail was no doctor. Not a grocery store to sell food. There was no man with them to cut wood for the campfire; to pitch the bit of sloping canvas under which they slept; to shoot the game to keep them alive; to keep off the wolves and catamounts which screamed around their fire at night; to deal with casual Indians encountered on the trail. Little and bigger, boy and girl, every one of the five who started out with their young mother stood around her, safe, when she lighted the first fire on the hearth of the new home.

She set to work at once to provide for her children, inside the cabin and out of it. They soon came to be as much at home in the woods as the squirrel and partridge. The boys helped as they could to clear the land of the "monstrous great trees," to plan the crops for the food there was no other way to get, to chop and split the mountains of firewood needed in the long Vermont winter. The little girls helped too, cooking, mending, picking and drying wild fruits, manufacturing soap out of grease and lye made from the wood ashes. They used this soap to keep the family clothes and home spotlessly clean. They smoked the haunches of the deer their mother and the boys shot. They rendered into birch-bark pails the great slabs of fat from the occasional bear brought down by their mother. She, like any other pioneer, kept her rifle as close to her hand as her ax.

One of the smaller details of the old-time stories told us by the oldest of our Vermont old folks, was the lament of *their* old folks about the lack nowadays of the wonderful provision of bear-fat every family then had. Sweet and tasty it was for cooking, they said. Every meat dish made with it was strengthening and appetizing. Wonderful for greasing your thick leather winter boots, a fine preparation for keeping your hair in good condition, excellent for the wooden axles of the first clumsy carts. And such a lot of it. All you wanted. No measly little paper-wrapped pounds you had to pay the grocer good money for.

We who had never tasted bear-fat and didn't like the sound of it any too well, used to think these nostalgic yearnings rather comic. They took on another aspect after what we learned in the two great world wars of the intense sufferings of people deprived of fats and oils.

On this diet of venison, fish, bear-fat, wild fruit, Indian corn mush, and maple syrup, Ann Story's children grew strong, hardy, muscular, alert, and as boldly courageous as their mother, who was said by those who knew her not to be afraid of anything. As her grief for her husband's death was buried deeper under the activity and responsibility of every day, she herself grew, too, not taller, like the children, but stronger in mind and body and spirit. An old settler, reminiscing about her in his last years, said, "She was a busting great woman who could cut off a two-foot log as quick as any man in the settlement." She had always been a good-looking woman, and as she grew in power, she took on a stately handsomeness which became legendary. With her tanned, bright-eyed, lithe, disciplined, and skilled boys and girls about her (she taught them to read the Bible she had brought up in the packsaddle, from the old home) she was a model mother and homemaker, the admiration of all who passed that way.

But she was more than a homebody. She was a citizen. And a patriot. Like the stout, plain chairs of our great-grandfathers, which we still keep in our Vermont living rooms, not for show as antiques but to rest ourselves in after a day's work, we still keep such words as "patriot" in our everyday vocabulary. This mother had set her bold, fiery heart on independence for her children. She wanted the same thing for other people's children—her country. In a time when political opinions meant something, showed the stuff men and women were made of, she was passionately on the side of self-government by the people.

At the dedication in Salisbury of the monument in Ann Story's honor, a justice of the Supreme Court of the District of Columbia said of her, "She gave herself, heart and soul, to the great cause of the people against their tyrants. She was a revolutionary. The American Revolution was not at bottom a struggle between the colonies and Great Britain. It was a line of cleavage which divided the English-speaking people wherever they happened to be—on one side those who believed in self-government, in the people, on the other those who believed in the doctrine that 'one part of the race is born booted and spurred, ready to ride, and the other part is born ready saddled and bridled to be ridden.' Ann Story had the vigor of mind to do her own thinking, to take in the whole scope of the question at issue. She was brave and strong, and what her mind approved her arm did not tremble to execute."

As Ann Story saw it, what she wanted for her children as Vermonters was the right to own their land as free men and not to be forced into semi-feudal subservience to rich folks, like the tenant farmers in New York, dependent on patroons. As Americans, what was at stake was their right to free themselves from traditional obedience to an overseas political authority over which they had no control. She was ready to stand by both those causes with as forthright a civic conscience and courage as, in her personal life, she showed in taking care of her children.

After the beginning of the Revolutionary War the British hired the Indians to fight for them against the colonial rebels. As soon as they heard this dire news, those few Vermont families who had begun building up their homes in the region north of Rutland knew that they would not be safe. They were scattered sparsely around in the forests, dangerously close to the Canadian border. They gave up their dearly earned log homes, they abandoned their laboriously cleared fields, they moved to the southern part of the state, where the settlements were more numerous.

But not Ann Story.

It was her home-place. It had been founded by the father of her children, she herself was building it up. It was all she had for her sons and daughters. But for her it had a far more than personal value. It was an outpost of the fighting front. If she stayed in it she could be of use in the battle for freedom. She was already a valued aid and adviser to the loosely organized guerrilla fighters called the Green Mountain Boys. A few of those men, either single, or whose families had been moved back of the lines at Rutland, came and went and camped out, over this now deserted region, ostensibly as casual hunters. They were to keep track of enemy movements, coming from the north, from Canada. To them, as she boldly announced her determination to stay on, she now said—the exact words of her phrase are carefully preserved, and passed on to us, in all the Vermont stories, written and oral—"Give me a place among you, and see if I am the first to desert my post."

It was not long before the British-led Indians came, torch and tomahawk in hand.

The Story children had been trained to act as sentinels, and there were enough of them so that in every direction around the house, some sharp young Story ear was cocked for suspicious sounds. One spring day, in 1776, a little boy came running—but silently—to tell his mother in a whisper that an Indian war-party, about half a mile away, was pillaging and setting fire to the cabin of a neighbor, one of those who had gone south for safety, leaving his home empty.

The river was high with melted snow, had overflowed its banks and flooded low-lying parts of the forest. Working at top speed, Ann and her children loaded their big canoe with the most vital household belongings—blankets, the precious "iron kittle" and spider, the bags of seed soon to be planted, the wooden tub of maple sugar, and the birch-bark pails of bear grease. Stepping in themselves, they paddled off swiftly on the flood-waters in amongst the dense trees, which hid them, but through which they could see everything done by the Indians, who soon came whooping into the clearing. The Story family watched them ravage the carefully kept home, set it on fire in a dozen places. When the cabin was quite burned down, they shouldered their booty and were off.

Ann and her children waited cautiously till it was safe to return to the desolation which had been their home. We do not need to try to imagine what they felt as they stood by the smoldering logs, for

Ann's words have come down to us, accurately repeated by people who heard her tell the story with terse Vermont understatement. She evidently did not even once think of giving up and beating a retreat to safety. Nor did she waste an instant's time in laments. She resolutely presented this as an incident, not a catastrophe. Her account of her reason for staying on is dry and matter-of-fact. "If the smoking ruins of our home disheartened us," she explained, years afterwards, "the hope arose that the Indians had made so little in this excursion, they might not visit the region any more. So we began cutting and laying up small trees, such as the children and I could handle, and it was not long before we had quite a comfortable cabin, made of poles instead of logs, on the spot where the former one had stood."

Watching from a distance we of the twentieth century have seen the savage forces of war pillage and burn down our old home of isolated nationalism, very dear to us. We too stand beside ruins, and face the need of building up a new home, somehow, out of the materials available to us, whether or not they are as good as we would like.

The most visibly picturesque part of this homespun Ann Story epic begins here, the part in which the imaginations of Vermont children have reveled ever since—for did a child ever live who did not love the idea of a cave hide-out? In the daytime, the Story children and their mother could risk growing food, preparing it, keeping house (and incidentally gathering valuable information for the guerrilla forces on their side), because they could stand guard, and at the first sound of danger could take to their canoe and paddle noiselessly out of sight. But at night?

It was as patriot that she stayed on, at the front. It was as patriot as well as homemaker that she kept her house of poles clean, snug and smelling pleasantly of good food. It continued to be what it had been from the first, like the switchboard of a modern telephone system. To it came singly, or in small sauntering groups, men who looked like trappers or hunters, dropping in for a chat with the widow Story over a dish of her excellent venison stew. But they left an important message to be passed on orally to other buckskin-clad, musket-carrying men who were to drop in, some days or weeks later. Or, while the children scattered into the woods in a wide circle, all around the clearing, to keep watch, a canoe would come up the creek, loaded with kegs of gunpowder, which would be hastily rolled out and hidden, till a party of the Green Rangers later arrived with the right password. Often these roving scouts stopped to get what information Ann

and her active children had picked up about British or Indian movements, for the children were everywhere, and Ann acquired an F.B.I.
ability to piece together isolated odd items to make a clear whole.
Or, perhaps the visitors came just to get Ann Story's slant about what
to think of some new move, political or military. For, of course, as
always happens to people who are in the thick of things and not
sheltered, her understanding fed on experience and grew stronger.

As to what the family did at night, for a long time nobody knew.
Ann kept her own counsel and the children were as mum as young
partridges hiding in the dry leaves at the mother bird's command.
But we now know the device.

The banks of the Otter Creek where their home stood were high
above the water. Selecting a place where tall old trees stood thickly,
their roots intertwining into a strong, wiry network, the Storys began
to dig an underground passageway into the bank. Prisoners digging
escape tunnels have trouble hiding the fresh dirt. The Story diggers
slid this into the swift-flowing stream. The mouth of the passage, at
the water level, they made just large enough to let the canoe float in,
all its passengers lying flat. And they kept that entrance thickly
planted with overhanging bushes, so it would not be seen by any of
the men in canoes, pro-British, Indian, or pro-American, who used
the Otter as a road into and out of the northern wilderness. A place
to sleep was dug out at one side, well above the level of the water.
Here the roots of the trees acted as a natural arch to hold up the
roof, over what was a sizable underground room.

Till her husband's death, Mrs. Story had been an indoor house-
mother in an orderly, safe old Connecticut town. But she had now
learned well the lessons of wood lore, and so placed the cave that,
entered as it was from the ever-flowing water, no sign of trodden leaf
or broken stick could betray it to the sharpest Indian trackers. A well-
worn path led down, naturally enough, to where, during the day, the
canoe lay moored, back of the cabin.

Every night, after dark, they filed silently down to the river, stepped
into the canoe, pushed it out without a sound, and glided between
the high wooded banks, around a bend in the Otter. With one deft
paddle stroke, the bow of the light craft was swung sidewise, and the
canoe slid in under the overhanging bushes. The Storys were gone,
all six of them, as if they had evaporated.

I have said that this great-grandmother of yours and mine was not
only a good woman but a good citizen. As Justice Stafford said of her,
"She was one of Plutarch's women." The other way around, also. She

was no less a woman, mother, and protector to human beings in distress because she was on fire with passion for the ideals which we Americans are brought up to revere.

She did not hesitate, the day one of her children returned from a far-ranging wood expedition, reporting that he had heard somebody crying. Going cautiously to see, noiseless on his moccasined feet, he had peeped through the leaves from a distance and had seen a woman, a white woman, sunk in a heap on the forest floor, sobbing.

Ann Story reflected. It might be an Indian trick. But it might not be. Everybody in those times knew that when Indians, under British instructions, burned the homes of the American revolutionaries, part of the recompense for the red-skinned allies was to carry off as many white captives as they could. This was not to scalp and torture them. It was a business operation. If the captives could be taken along, alive and well as far as Canada, they could be sold as servants to white Canadians. This too was a commercial matter. The Canadians who bought those captives often made a big cash profit on the venture, through the ransom exacted for them from their New England families.

Yes, this weeping young woman alone in the forest might well be such a captive left to starve. Or she might be a decoy, carrying out some plot against the guerrilla "resistance" fighters called the Green Mountain Boys.

Rifle on shoulder, guided by the little boy, both of them as silent as cloud-shadows, Ann Story made her way to a place where she could see and not be seen. The child had told the truth. The mother waited a long time, with Indian patience, standing invisible in the forest, till she was sure it was no trick. Then she stepped forward.

We rather like to imagine the moment when that girl, abandoned by her Indian captors, saw before her the "busting great" tall, stately, homespun-clad Ann.

The girl came from a settlement far inside the American lines, which had been raided by a war-party of Indians in the service of the British. The prisoners were hurried along the trail to Canada. And this girl (here is one name that has not come down to us, in story-lore, so I can only call her the girl) was far advanced in pregnancy. Quite as much afraid of the wilderness as of their tomahawks, she had tried desperately to keep up with the swift dog-trot of the Indians. But she had fallen so far behind as to be out of their sight. They had gone on. It was less trouble to leave her there to starve than to turn back and split her skull.

Ann Story had borne five children. She knew that the young
woman's time was near. Vermont-fashion, she said in her later safe
and comfortable years very little about what she had thought or felt
during those years of danger. All we know is what she did. What she
did now was, instantly, to add another to the incredible sum of her
responsibilities. The young mother was taken in, the baby was born—
Ann Story midwife—and like all babies, he was anything but self-
controlled and disciplined. One of the stock sayings of her contempo-
raries about Ann Story was that "she feared neither Tory, Indian, nor
wild beast," because she felt herself to be stronger than they. But
even she could not keep a baby from crying when he felt like crying.
The soundless caution of the canoe-approach to the underground
shelter, the whispers of their talk in the cave, were ruthlessly broken
by the baby's lusty yells when something displeased him. If you have
ever been acquainted with a baby, I need say no more. You can
imagine what the Storys' situation now became.

Ann had not shrunk back from what she thought a patriot's duty,
because it was dangerous. Nor did she now from a woman's obligation.
Babies and their mothers must be cared for at no matter what peril.
For the present, till the mother could walk, there was no way of
moving them on to another place of safety. So the baby stayed, continuing to cry when the spirit moved him.

And he was the hinge on which a small—but not unimportant—
piece of American history swung into place—the right place.

As the Honorable Justice from Washington, D. C., pointed out in
his address delivered at Ann Story's monument, the American Revolution was not at bottom a struggle between the colonists and Great
Britain. It was between those, everywhere, who steadfastly believed
that people should be free to govern themselves and those who did
not. In the colonies there were many men and women who took no
stock in the republican ideas which, with Cromwell, had shaken the
English state to its foundation, which were in a few years to flame
all over France. Always, everywhere, there are plenty of backward-
looking lovers of the past, and of old ways hallowed by old traditions.
Even in Vermont, so new that the bark was still on it, there were
people deeply attached to the much-loved old Church, and to the institution of the Crown, which seemed to them the only basis for a decent orderly society. They were, also, alarmed about their property
and social position, for lovers of the past usually have more money
and put on more style than those who press forward into the future.
Naturally such people hated and feared the rawly new, violently

egalitarian principles announced in the 1776 Declaration of Independence—principles sacred to Ann Story—and to us, her descendants.

Nowhere were these Vermont royalists—"Tories" they were called—strong enough to stand against the overwhelming popular majority. Their only hope was to bring in help from the British. To this end, a number of them arranged to slip quietly away from their separate communities, join together once they had passed beyond the last blockhouses of the Revolutionary forces, and march north to Canada. The actual fighting strength they could give the enemy was negligible. Their threat lay rather in the exact detailed information as to the location and defenses of the Vermont settlements, and about the movements, organization and resources of the guerrilla forces which they could turn over to His Majesty's troops and His Majesty's savage Indian allies. With such information the weaker settlements could have been overwhelmed one after another. In fact all Vermont frontier settlements might have been wiped out if their carefully devised plan had succeeded. And succeed it almost did.

Traveling separately to avoid suspicion, they were on the last lap of their journey, crossing the no-man's strip of the extreme picket line, where Ann Story lived and kept her eyes open. They went by night. During the hours of darkness the keen Story eyes were underground, asleep. All these northbound plotters might have reached their rendezvous unobserved, if just before dawn one morning that baby had not taken it into his head to cry. At the sound coming from the ground under his feet, one Ezekiel Jenny, following the trail north along the riverbank, stopped and stood still. He was of that region, had long suspected the part Ann Story was playing in the resistance movement. So this, he thought in exultation, was the key to the secret of the Storys' vanishing by night.

He tiptoed to the edge of the water, hid himself in the bushes, looking keenly up and down the river as the dawn slowly broke. Before long, sure enough, just under where he stood, the tip of a canoe was silently pushed through the bushes. It hung there a moment, probably to make sure no one was passing. Then with one swift paddle-thrust, it reached mid-stream, loaded with women and children, and shot toward the bend of the river and the landing place back of the Story cabin.

Now, thought Ezekiel Jenny, putting his musket on the cock, and darting across the neck of land to lie in wait for the unsuspecting party, now is the time to make that pestiferous woman rebel talk. Crouched in the bushes beside the landing place, he waited till Ann had stepped out of the canoe and then springing up, he presented the muzzle of his gun at her very breast, and proceeded to terrorize her into betraying her allies.

Ann Story was not one to be terrorized. Let her talk for herself here. Her own inimitably dry words have come down to us. Beside them, anything I could write would be as boneless as boiled macaroni. "I gave evasive and dissatisfactory replies to his questions. This exasperated Jenny and he threatened to shoot me on the spot; but to all his threats I bid defiance, and told him I had no fears of being shot by so consummate a coward as he, and finally he passed along down the creek."

Ann Story thought him a coward. Perhaps he was, perhaps not. For my part I never could see that great courage is required to kill a defenseless woman. It seems more likely that the reason why he held his fire was that a shot might be heard—that a dead woman's body if found would call for much searching and beating the bushes. He could not risk the chance that some party of hunters might be within earshot. His associates needed at least another day of concealment to carry out their getaway.

But coward or not, he was a blunderer. Instead of making a crafty detour he stamped straight off toward his destination, not dreaming that, back of him in the remote clearing, the motherly woman encumbered with young children, and a new baby, had wit enough to note which way he went and inside information enough to guess what his purpose was, or had any means of calling help.

What she did was to snatch a flyleaf from her Bible, the only paper she had, write a hasty note on it, and send one of her sons flying to the camp of the nearest Green Mountain Rangers. Part of their advance-scout system was always to keep her informed of the whereabouts of the buckskin-shirted guerrillas who patrolled that section of the Vermont wilderness. The long-legged, sure-footed Story boy knew the dimly marked forest trail as our children know the way to the nearest movie theater, knew when he could make a short-cut across its windings, wade a stream, dodge a swamp, climb a hill, and come racing down to the camp of the Vermonters.

It was not long before Daniel Foot, Samuel Bentley (don't you like their names?) and other Americans had snatched up their rifles and set off in pursuit, following the broken twigs and scuffed-up dry leaves of Ezekiel's well-marked trail. From my little girlhood, I have always hoped that the men let that Story boy who took them the message go along with them. I was sure he would not have felt he needed to get his mother's permission.

That evening the Tory fugitives were so far north of the last cabins that they felt it safe to come together, make camp, and lie down to sleep around their fire. Suddenly, from every side, came piercing yells and a volley of shots. Waking, they found themselves surrounded. Escape or resistance, both were impossible.

Those Green Mountain Rangers, leaping into the firelight with savage whoops and leveled rifles were, all of them, hunters to whom shooting was as natural as breathing. They were members of a rough-and-ready organization, loosely held together with practically no military discipline. With them in that hour of red-hot excitement there was present no curbing "higher" authority to hold them back from acting like a lynching rabble, or scalping Indians on the warpath—nothing except their self-respect.

True, the men now huddled together with hands raised in surrender had intended the betrayal of American families to fire and tomahawks. But their capture had prevented that. What need to kill them? Those ancestors of ours were bred in a civilized tradition. They were fathers and husbands and citizens as well as guerrilla fighters. They carried their higher authority in their own hearts.

The prisoners were not harmed. Prosaically the Vermont captors marched their prisoners across country to Fort Ticonderoga, then in American hands, and in the words of their own report, "gave them up to the proper constituted authorities."

To us, in the mid-twentieth century, that report sounds anything but "prosaic." We are grateful to the Vermonter who recognized and wrote thus clearly into that late-eighteenth-century record the principle for living, deep-lying, still honored by us today—self-control.

You'll hear it said that our self-control robs us of the most glorious thrills of human existence. We don't believe a word of it. We know that from its very start, our history has been full of hotly pulsing enthusiasms. The code handed down to us by our forefathers bids us, when something needs to be done, to throw our whole strength into doing it, even if it calls for violence—for war. But once the crisis is passed, the need met—no more hot blood, no more excitement for the sake of excitement. Like the men of that Green Mountain Commando, we turn our backs, without regret, on whooping and shouting, and go back to our trust in law and order, in "constituted authority."

Ann Story's monument stands on the spot where her husband built their first log cabin home. On it are these plain unrhetorical words:

ANN STORY
In Grateful Memory of Her
Service in The Struggle of The
Green Mountain Boys for Independence

You might think that those who designed the monument would have added that well-known saying of hers to the defenders of Vermont when she was urged to be wholly mother, not also citizen and patriot—"Give me a place among you, and see if I am the first to desert my post."

But that doesn't need to be carved in stone, or cast in bronze. We remember it, all right.

The Bedquilt

Of all the Elwell family Aunt Mehetabel was certainly the most unimportant member. It was in the old-time New England days, when an unmarried woman was an old maid at twenty, at forty was everyone's servant, and at sixty had gone through so much discipline that she could need no more in the next world. Aunt Mehetabel was sixty-eight.

She had never for a moment known the pleasure of being important to anyone. Not that she was useless in her brother's family; she was expected, as a matter of course, to take upon herself the most tedious and uninteresting part of the household labors. On Mondays she accepted as her share the washing of the men's shirts, heavy with sweat and stiff with dirt from the fields and from their own hard-working bodies. Tuesdays she never dreamed of being allowed to iron anything pretty or even interesting, like the baby's white dresses or the fancy aprons of her young lady nieces. She stood all day pressing out a monotonous succession of dish-cloths and towels and sheets.

In preserving-time she was allowed to have none of the pleasant responsibility of deciding when the fruit had cooked long enough, nor did she share in the little excitement of pouring the sweet-smelling stuff into the stone jars. She sat in a corner with the children and stoned cherries incessantly, or hulled strawberries until her fingers were dyed red.

The Elwells were not consciously unkind to their aunt, they were even in a vague way fond of her; but she was so insignificant a figure in their lives that she was almost invisible to them. Aunt Mehetabel did not resent this treatment; she took it quite as unconsciously as they gave it. It was to be expected when one was an old-maid dependent in a busy family. She gathered what crumbs of comfort she could from their occasional careless kindnesses and tried to hide the hurt which even yet pierced her at her brother's rough joking. In the winter when they all sat before the big hearth, roasted apples, drank mulled cider, and teased the girls about their beaux and the boys about their sweethearts, she shrank into a dusky corner with her knitting, happy if the evening passed without her brother saying, with a crude sarcasm, "Ask your Aunt Mehetabel about the beaux that used to come a-sparkin' her!" or, "Mehetabel, how was't when you was in love with Abel Cummings?" As a matter of fact, she had been the same at twenty as at sixty, a mouselike little creature, too shy for anyone to notice, or to raise her eyes for a moment and wish for a life of her own.

Her sister-in-law, a big hearty housewife, who ruled indoors with as autocratic a sway as did her husband on the farm, was rather kind in an absent, offhand way to the shrunken little old woman, and it was through her that Mehetabel was able to enjoy the one pleasure of her life. Even as a girl she had been clever with her needle in the way of patching bedquilts. More than that she could never learn to do. The garments which she made for herself were lamentable affairs, and she was humbly grateful for any help in the bewildering business of putting them together. But in patchwork she enjoyed a tepid importance. She could really do that as well as anyone else. During years of devotion to this one art she had accumulated a considerable store of quilting patterns. Sometimes the neighbors would send over and ask "Miss Mehetabel" for the loan of her sheaf-of-wheat design, or the double-star pattern. It was with an agreeable flutter at being able to help someone that she went to the dresser, in her bare little room under the eaves, and drew out from her crowded portfolio the pattern desired.

She never knew how her great idea came to her. Sometimes she thought she must have dreamed it, sometimes she even wondered reverently, in the phraseology of the weekly prayer-meeting, if it had not been "sent" to her. She never admitted to herself that she could have thought of it without other help. It was too great, too ambitious, too lofty a project for her humble mind to have conceived. Even when she finished drawing the design with her own fingers, she gazed at it incredulously, not daring to believe that it could indeed be her handiwork. At first it seemed to her only like a lovely but unreal dream. For a long time she did not once think of putting an actual quilt together following that pattern, even though she herself had invented it. It was not that she feared the prodigious effort that would be needed to get those tiny, oddly shaped pieces of bright-colored material sewed together with the perfection of fine workmanship needed. No, she thought zestfully and eagerly of such endless effort, her heart uplifted by her vision of the mosaic-beauty of the whole creation as she saw it, when she shut her eyes to dream of it—that complicated, splendidly difficult pattern—good enough for the angels in heaven to quilt.

But as she dreamed, her nimble old fingers reached out longingly to turn her dream into reality. She began to think adventurously of trying it out—it would perhaps not be too selfish to make one square—just one unit of her design to see how it would look. She dared do nothing in the household where she was a dependent, without asking permission. With a heart full of hope and fear thumping furiously against her old ribs, she approached the mistress of the house on churning-day, knowing with the innocent guile of a child that the country woman was apt to be in a good temper while working over the fragrant butter in the cool cellar.

Sophia listened absently to her sister-in-law's halting petition. "Why, yes, Mehetabel," she said, leaning far down into the huge churn for the last golden morsels—"why, yes, start another quilt if you want to. I've got a lot of pieces from the spring sewing that will work in real good." Mehetabel tried honestly to make her see that this would be no common quilt, but her limited vocabulary and her emotion stood between her and expression. At last Sophia said, with a kindly impatience: "Oh, there! Don't bother me. I never could keep track of your quiltin' patterns, anyhow. I don't care what pattern you go by."

Mehetabel rushed back up the steep attic stairs to her room, and in a joyful agitation began preparations for the work of her life. Her very first stitches showed her that it was even better than she hoped. By some heaven-sent inspiration she had invented a pattern beyond which no patchwork quilt could go.

She had but little time during the daylight hours filled with the incessant household drudgery. After dark she did not dare to sit up late at night lest she burn too much candle. It was weeks before the little square began to show the pattern. Then Mehetabel was in a fever to finish it. She was too conscientious to shirk even the smallest part of her share of the housework, but she rushed through it now so fast that she was panting as she climbed the stairs to her little room.

Every time she opened the door, no matter what weather hung outside the one small window, she always saw the little room flooded with sunshine. She smiled to herself as she bent over the innumerable scraps of cotton cloth on her work table. Already—to her—they were ranged in orderly, complex, mosaic-beauty.

Finally she could wait no longer, and one evening ventured to bring her work down beside the fire where the family sat, hoping that good fortune would give her a place near the tallow candles on the mantelpiece. She had reached the last corner of that first square and her needle flew in and out, in and out, with nervous speed. To her relief no one noticed her. By bedtime she had only a few more stitches to add.

As she stood up with the others, the square fell from her trembling old hands and fluttered to the table. Sophia glanced at it carelessly. "Is that the new quilt you said you wanted to start?" she asked, yawning. "Looks like a real pretty pattern. Let's see it."

Up to that moment Mehetabel had labored in the purest spirit of selfless adoration of an ideal. The emotional shock given her by Sophia's cry of admiration as she held the work towards the candle to examine it, was as much astonishment as joy to Mehetabel.

"Land's sakes!" cried her sister-in-law. "Why, Mehetabel Elwell, where did you git that pattern?"

"I made it up," said Mehetabel. She spoke quietly but she was trembling.

"No!" exclaimed Sophia. "Did you! Why, I never see such a pattern in my life. Girls, come here and see what your Aunt Mehetabel is doing."

The three tall daughters turned back reluctantly from the stairs. "I never could seem to take much interest in patchwork quilts," said one. Already the old-time skill born of early pioneer privation and the craving for beauty, had gone out of style.

"No, nor I neither!" answered Sophia. "But a stone image would take an interest in this pattern. Honest, Mehetabel, did you really think of it yourself?" She held it up closer to her eyes and went on, "And how under the sun and stars did you ever git your courage up to start in a-making it? Land! Look at all those tiny squinchy little seams! Why, the wrong side ain't a thing *but* seams! Yet the good side's just like a picture, so smooth you'd think 'twas woven that way. Only nobody could."

The girls looked at it right side, wrong side, and echoed their mother's exclamations. Mr. Elwell himself came over to see what they were discussing. "Well, I declare!" he said, looking at his sister with eyes more approving than she could ever remember. "I don't know a thing about patchwork quilts, but to my eye that beats old Mis' Andrew's quilt that got the blue ribbon so many times at the County Fair."

As she lay that night in her narrow hard bed, too proud, too excited to sleep, Mehetabel's heart swelled and tears of joy ran down from her old eyes.

The next day her sister-in-law astonished her by taking the huge pan of potatoes out of her lap and setting one of the younger children to peeling them. "Don't you want to go on with that quiltin' pattern?" she said. "I'd kind o' like to see how you're goin' to make the grapevine design come out on the corner."

For the first time in her life the dependent old maid contradicted her powerful sister-in-law. Quickly and jealously she said, "It's not a grapevine. It's a sort of curlicue I made up."

"Well, it's nice-looking anyhow," said Sophia pacifyingly. "I never could have made it up."

By the end of the summer the family interest had risen so high that Mehetabel was given for herself a little round table in the sitting room, for *her,* where she could keep her pieces and use odd minutes for her work. She almost wept over such kindness and resolved firmly not to take advantage of it. She went on faithfully with her monotonous housework, not neglecting a corner. But the atmosphere of her world was changed. Now things had a meaning. Through the longest task of washing milk-pans, there rose a rainbow of promise. She took her place by the little table and put the thimble on her knotted, hard finger with the solemnity of a priestess performing a rite.

She was even able to bear with some degree of dignity the honor of having the minister and the minister's wife comment admiringly on her great project. The family felt quite proud of Aunt Mehetabel as Minister Bowman had said it was work as fine as any he had ever seen, "and he didn't know but finer!" The remark was repeated verbatim to the neighbors in the following weeks when they dropped in and examined in a perverse Vermontish silence some astonishingly difficult tour de force which Mehetabel had just finished.

The Elwells especially plumed themselves on the slow progress of the quilt. "Mehetabel has been to work on that corner for six weeks, come Tuesday, and she ain't half done yet," they explained to visitors.

They fell out of the way of always expecting her to be the one to run on errands, even for the children. "Don't bother your Aunt Mehetabel," Sophia would call. "Can't you see she's got to a ticklish place on the quilt?" The old woman sat straighter in her chair, held up her head. She was a part of the world at last. She joined in the conversation and her remarks were listened to. The children were even told to mind her when she asked them to do some service for her, although this she ventured to do but seldom.

One day some people from the next town, total strangers, drove up to the Elwell house and asked if they could inspect the wonderful quilt which they had heard about even down in their end of the valley. After that, Mehetabel's quilt came little by little to be one of the local sights. No visitor to town, whether he knew the Elwells or not, went away without having been to look at it. To make her presentable to strangers, the Elwells saw to it that their aunt was better dressed than she had ever been before. One of the girls made her a pretty little cap to wear on her thin white hair.

A year went by and a quarter of the quilt was finished. A second year passed and half was done. The third year Mehetabel had pneumonia and lay ill for weeks and weeks, horrified by the idea that she might die before her work was completed. A fourth year and one could really see the grandeur of the whole design. In September of the fifth year, the entire family gathered around her to watch eagerly, as Mehetabel quilted the last stitches. The girls held it up by the four corners and they all looked at it in hushed silence.

Then Mr. Elwell cried as one speaking with authority, "By ginger! That's goin' to the County Fair!"

Mehetabel blushed a deep red. She had thought of this herself, but never would have spoken aloud of it.

"Yes indeed!" cried the family. One of the boys was dispatched to the house of a neighbor who was Chairman of the Fair Committee for their village. He came back beaming, "Of course he'll take it. Like's not it may git a prize, he says. But he's got to have it right off because all the things from our town are going tomorrow morning."

Even in her pride Mehetabel felt a pang as the bulky package was carried out of the house. As the days went on she felt lost. For years it had been her one thought. The little round stand had been heaped with a litter of bright-colored scraps. Now it was desolately bare. One of the neighbors who took the long journey to the Fair reported when he came back that the quilt was hung in a good place in a glass case in "Agricultural Hall." But that meant little to Mehetabel's ignorance of everything outside her brother's home. She drooped. The family noticed it. One day Sophia said kindly, "You feel sort o' lost without the quilt, don't you, Mehetabel?"

"They took it away so quick!" she said wistfully. "I hadn't hardly had one good look at it myself."

The Fair was to last a fortnight. At the beginning of the second week Mr. Elwell asked his sister how early she could get up in the morning.

"I dunno. Why?" she asked.

"Well, Thomas Ralston has got to drive to West Oldton to see a lawyer. That's four miles beyond the Fair. He says if you can git up so's to leave here at four in the morning he'll drive you to the Fair, leave you there for the day, and bring you back again at night." Mehetabel's face turned very white. Her eyes filled with tears. It was as though someone had offered her a ride in a golden chariot up to the gates of heaven. "Why, you can't *mean* it!" she cried wildly. Her brother laughed. He could not meet her eyes. Even to his easy-going unimaginative indifference to his sister this was a revelation of the narrowness of her life in his home. "Oh, 'tain't so much—just to go to the Fair," he told her in some confusion, and then "Yes, sure I mean it. Go git your things ready, for it's tomorrow morning he wants to start."

A trembling, excited old woman stared all that night at the rafters. She who had never been more than six miles from home—it was to her like going into another world. She who had never seen anything more exciting than a church supper was to see the County Fair. She had never dreamed of doing it. She could not at all imagine what it would be like.

The next morning all the family rose early to see her off. Perhaps her brother had not been the only one to be shocked by her happiness. As she tried to eat her breakfast they called out conflicting advice to her about what to see. Her brother said not to miss inspecting the stock, her nieces said the fancywork was the only thing worth looking at, Sophia told her to be sure to look at the display of preserves. Her nephews asked her to bring home an account of the trotting races.

The buggy drove up to the door, and she was helped in. The family ran to and fro with blankets, woolen tippet, a hot soapstone from the kitchen range. Her wraps were tucked about her. They all stood together and waved goodby as she drove out of the yard.

She waved back, but she scarcely saw them. On her return home that evening she was ashy pale, and so stiff that her brother had to lift her out bodily. But her lips were set in a blissful smile. They crowded around her with questions until Sophia pushed them all aside. She told them Aunt Mehetabel was too tired to speak until she had had her supper. The young people held their tongues while she drank her tea, and absent-mindedly ate a scrap of toast with an egg. Then the old woman was helped into an easy chair before the fire. They gathered about her, eager for news of the great world, and Sophia said, "Now, come, Mehetabel, tell us all about it!"

Mehetabel drew a long breath. "It was just perfect!" she said. "Finer even than I thought. They've got it hanging up in the very middle of a sort o' closet made of glass, and one of the lower corners is ripped and turned back so's to show the seams on the wrong side."

"What?" asked Sophia, a little blankly.

"Why, the quilt!" said Mehetabel in surprise. "There are a whole lot of other ones in that room, but not one that can hold a candle to it, if I do say it who shouldn't. I heard lots of people say the same thing. You ought to have heard what the women said about that corner, Sophia. They said—well, I'd be ashamed to *tell* you what they said. I declare if I wouldn't!"

Mr. Elwell asked, "What did you think of that big ox we've heard so much about?"

"I didn't look at the stock," returned his sister indifferently. She turned to one of her nieces. "That set of pieces you gave me, Maria, from your red waist, come out just lovely! I heard one woman say you could 'most smell the red roses."

"How did Jed Burgess' bay horse place in the mile trot?" asked Thomas.

"I didn't see the races."

"How about the preserves?" asked Sophia.

"I didn't see the preserves," said Mehetabel calmly.

Seeing that they were gazing at her with astonished faces she went on, to give them a reasonable explanation, "You see I went right to the room where the quilt was, and then I didn't want to leave it. It had been so long since I'd seen it. I had to look at it first real good myself, and then I looked at the others to see if there was any that could come up to it. Then the people begun comin' in and I got so interested in hearin' what they had to say I couldn't think of goin' anywheres else. I ate my lunch right there too, and I'm glad as can be I did, too; for what do you think?"—she gazed about her with kindling eyes. "While I stood there with a sandwich in one hand, didn't the head of the hull concern come in and open the glass door and pin a big bow of blue ribbon right in the middle of the quilt with a label on it, 'First Prize.' "

There was a stir of proud congratulation. Then Sophia returned to questioning, "Didn't you go to see anything else?"

"Why, no," said Mehetabel. "Only the quilt. Why should I?"

She fell into a reverie. As if it hung again before her eyes she saw the glory that shone around the creation of her hand and brain. She longed to make her listeners share the golden vision with her. She struggled for words. She fumbled blindly for unknown superlatives. "I tell you it looked like—" she began, and paused.

Vague recollections of hymnbook phrases came into her mind. They were the only kind of poetic expression she knew. But they were dismissed as being sacrilegious to use for something in real life. Also as not being nearly striking enough.

Finally, "I tell you it looked real *good*," she assured them and sat staring into the fire, on her tired old face the supreme content of an artist who has realized his ideal.

Almera
Hawley Canfield

b. 1787; m. 1808; d. 1874

&O f course I never saw her. She died years before I was born. But she left behind her a portrait so full of her personality that no living figure is more human to me than my great-grandmother.

I do not at all refer to the portrait over the dining room mantelpiece, showing her as a withered old woman in a frilled cap, which is now the only tangible sign of her existence left in her old home. No; that might have been any withered old woman in a frilled cap.

There is another portrait of my great-grandmother not done on canvas with oils. Here are some of the strokes which one by one, at long intervals, as if casually and by chance, have painted it for me.

When I was about eight years old, I went out one day to watch old Lemuel Hager, who came once a year to mow the grass in the orchard back of the house. As he clinked the whetstone over the ringing steel of his scythe, he looked down at me and remarked: "You favor the Hawley side of the family, don't you? There's a look around your mouth sort o' like Aunt Almera, your grandmother —no—my sakes, you must be her great-granddaughter! Wa'l—think of that! And it don't seem more'n yesterday I saw her come stepping out same's you did just now; not so much bigger'n you are this minute, for all she must have been sixty years old then. She always was the *littlest* woman. But she marched up to me, great lummox of a boy, and she said, 'Is it true, what I hear folks say, Lemuel, that you somehow got out of school without having learned how to read?' And I says, 'Why, Mis' Canfield, to tell the truth, I never did seem to git the hang of books, and I never could seem to git up no sort of interest in 'em.'

"And she says back, 'Well, no great boy of eighteen in the town *I* live in is a-goin' to grow up without he knows how to read the Declaration of Independence,' says she. And she made me stop work for an hour—she paid me just the same for it—took me into the house, and started teaching me.

"Great land of love! If the teacher at school had 'a' taught me like that, I'd 'a' been a minister! I felt as though she'd cracked a hole in my head and was just pouring the l'arning in through a funnel. And 'twa'n't more'n ten minutes before she found out 'twas my eyes the trouble. I'm terrible nearsighted. Well, that was before the days when everybody wore specs. There wa'n't no way to git specs for me; but you couldn't stump Aunt Almera. She just grabbed up a sort of multiplying-glass that she used, she said, for her sewing, now her eyes were kind o' failing her, and she give it to me. 'I'll take bigger stitches,' says she, laughing; 'big stitches don't matter so much as reading for an American citizen.'

"Well, sir, she didn't forgit me; she kept at me to practice to home with my multiplying-glass, and it was years before I could git by the house without Aunt Almera come out on the porch and hollered to me, that bossy way she had, 'Lemuel, you come in for a minute and let me hear you read.' Sometimes it kind o' madded me, she had such a way o' thinkin' she could make everybody stand 'round. Sometimes it made me laugh, she was so old, and not much bigger'n my fist. But, by gol, I l'arned to read, and I have taken a sight of comfort out of it. I don't never set down in the evening and open up the Necronsett *Journal* without I think of Aunt Almera Canfield."

One day I was sent over to Mrs. Pratt's to get some butter, and found it just out of the churn. So, munching on a cookie, I sat down to wait till Mrs. Pratt should work it over, and listened to her stream of talk—the chickens, the hailstorm of the other day, had my folks begun to make currant jelly yet? and so on—till she had finished and was shaping the butter into round pats. "This always puts me in mind of Aunt Almera," she said, interrupting an account of how the men had chased a woodchuck up a *tree*—who ever heard of such a thing? "Whenever I begin to make the pats, I remember when I was a girl working for her. She kept you right up to the mark, I tell you, and you ought to have seen how she lit into me when she found out some of my butter pats were just a little over a pound and some a little less. It was when she happened to have too much cream and she was 'trading in' the butter at the store. You'd have thought I'd stolen a fifty-cent piece to hear her go on! 'I sell those for a pound; they've got to *be* a pound,' says she, the way she always spoke, as though that ended it.

" 'But land sakes, Mis' Canfield,' says I, all out o' patience with her, 'an ounce or two one way or the other—it's as likely to be more as less, you know! What difference does it make? *Nobody* expects to make their pats just a pound! How could you?'

" 'How could you? How could you?' says she. 'Why, just the way you make anything else the way it ought to be—by keeping at it till it *is* right. What other way is there?'

"I didn't think you could do it. I *knew* you couldn't; but you always had to do the way Mis' Canfield said, and so I began grumbling under my breath about high-handed, fussy old women. But she never minded what you *said* about her, so long as you did your work right. So I fussed and fussed, clipping off a little, and adding on a little, and weighing it between times. It was the awfulest bother you ever saw, because it spoiled the shape of your pat to cut at it, and you had to start it over again every time.

"Well, you wouldn't believe it, how soon I got the hang of it! She'd made me think about it so much, I got interested, and it wasn't any time at all before I could tell the heft of a pat to within a fraction of an ounce just by the feel of it in my hand. I never forgot it. You never do forget that kind of thing. I brought up my whole family on that story. 'Now you do that spelling lesson just exactly *right*,' I'd say to my Lucy, 'just the way Aunt Almera made me do the butter pats!' "

I was sitting on the steps of the Town Hall, trying to make a willow whistle, when the janitor came along and opened the door. "The Ladies' Aid are going to have a supper in the downstairs room," he explained, getting out a broom. I wandered in to visit with him while he swept and dusted the pleasant little community sitting room where our village social gatherings were held. He moved an armchair and wiped off the frame of the big portrait of Lincoln. "Your great-grandmother gave that, do you know it?" he observed, and then, resting on the broom for a moment and beginning to laugh,

"Did you ever hear how Aunt Almera got folks stirred up to do something about this room? Well, 'twas so *like* her!

"The place used to be the awfulest hole you ever saw. Years ago they'd used it to lock up drunks in, or anybody that had to be locked up. Then, after the new jail was built in the shire-town, the sheriff began to take prisoners down there. But nobody did anything to this room to clean it up or fix it. It belongs to the town, you know, and nobody ever'll do anything that they think they can put off on the town. The women used to talk a lot about it—what a nice place 'twould be for socials, and how 'twould keep the boys off the streets, and how they could have chicken suppers here, same as other towns, if this room was fixed up.

"But whose business was it to fix it up? The town's of course! And of course nobody ever thinks that he and his folks are all there is *to* the town. No, they just jawed about it, and kept saying 'wa'n't the Selectmen shiftless because they didn't see to it!' But of course the Selectmen didn't have the money to do anything. Nothing in the law about using tax money to fix up rooms for sociables, is there? And those were awful tight times, when money came hard and every cent of tax money had to be put to some good plain use. So the Selectmen said *they* couldn't do anything. And nobody else would, because it wasn't anybody's business in particular, and nobody wanted to be put upon and made to do more than his share. The room got dirtier and dirtier, with the lousy old mattress the last drunk had slept on right there on the floor in the corner, and broken chairs and old wooden boxes, and dust and dry leaves that had blown in through the windows when the panes of glass were broken—regular dumping ground for trash.

"Well, one morning bright and early—I've heard my mother tell about it a thousand times—the first person that went by the Town Hall seen the door open and an awful rattling going on. He peeked in, and there was little old Aunt Almera, in a big gingham apron, her white hair sticking out from underneath a towel she'd tied her head up in, cleaning away to beat the band. She looked up, saw him standing and gaping at her, and says, just as though that was what she did every day for a living, 'Good morning,' she says. 'Nice weather, isn't it?'

"He went away kind of quick, and told about her over in the store, and they looked out, and sure enough out she come, limping along (she had the rheumatism *bad*) and dragging that old mattress with her. She drug it out in front to a bare place, and poured some kerosene on it and set fire to it; and I guess by that time every family in the street was looking out at her from behind the window shades. Then she went back in, leaving it there burning up, high and smoky, and in a minute out she came again with her dustpan full of trash. She flung that on the fire as if she'd been waiting all her life to have the chance to get it burned up, and went back for more. And there she was, bobbing back and forth all the fore part of the morning. Folks from the Lower Street that hadn't heard about it would come up for their mail, and just stop dead, to see the bonfire blazing and Aunt Almera limping out with maybe an old broken box full of junk in her arms. She'd always speak up just as pleasant and gentle to them—*that* made 'em feel queerer than anything else. Aunt Almera talking so mild! 'Well, folks, how are you this morning?' she'd say. 'And how are all the folks at home?' And then *slosh!* would go a pail of dirty water, for as soon as she got it swept out, didn't she get down on her creaking old marrow-bones and scrub the floor! All that afternoon every time anybody looked out, splash! there'd be Aunt Almera throwing away the water she'd been scrubbing the floor with. Folks felt about as big as a pint-cup by that time, but nobody could think of anything to do or say, for fear of what Aunt Almera might say back at them, and everybody was always kind o' slow about trying to stop her once she got started on anything. So they just kept indoors and looked at each other like born fools, till Aunt Almera crawled back home. It mighty nigh killed her, that day's work. She was all crippled up for a fortnight afterwards with rheumatism. But you'd better believe folks stirred around those two weeks, and when she was out and around again there was this room all fixed up just the way 'tis now, with furniture, *and* the floor painted, and white curtains to the windows, and all. Nobody said a word to her about it, and neither did she say a word when she saw it—she never was one to do any crowing over folks—once she'd got her own way."

The hassocks in our pew began to look shabby, and my aunt brought them home from church to put fresh carpeting on them. They suggested church, of course, and as she worked on them a great many reminiscences came to her mind. Here is one: "I used to love to ride horseback, and Grandmother always made Father let me, although he was afraid to have me. Well, one summer evening right after supper I went for a little canter and didn't get home till about half-past seven. As I rode into the yard I looked through the open windows, and there was Grandmother putting her bonnet on; and it came to me in a flash that I'd promised to go to Evening

Prayer with her. I was a grown-up young lady then, but I was scared! You did what you'd promised Grandmother you would, or something happened.

"So I just fell off my horse, turned him out in the night pasture, saddle and all, and ran into the house. Grandmother was putting on her gloves, and, although she saw me with my great looped-up riding skirt on and my whip in my hand, she never said a word nor lifted an eyebrow; just went on wetting her fingers and pushing the gloves down on them as though I was ready with my best hat on. That scared me worse than ever.

"I tore into my room and slipped off my skirt. Women rode side-saddle, those days, and the way the pommels were set, you had to wear under your long skirt something like riding trousers to keep from chafing a sore place under your knee. But I didn't have time to take those off. The last bell was ringing from St. James tower. I snatched a regular skirt out of the closet (they were all long and full, then) and put it on right over my riding trousers, slammed on a hat, threw a long cape around me, and grabbed my gloves. As the bell began to ring its last stroke, and Grandmother stepped out of the house, I stepped out beside her, all right as to the outer layer, but with the perspiration streaming down my face. I'd hurried, and those great thick riding trousers were hot under my woolen skirt! My! I thought I'd die!

"It was worse in the church! Over in our dark, close corner pew there wasn't a breath of air. It must have been a hundred by the thermometer. I was so hot I just had to do something! There weren't but a few people in the church, and nobody anywhere near our corner, and it was as dark as could be, back in our high pew. So when we knelt down for the General Confession I gathered the cape all around me, reached up under my full skirt, unbuttoned those awful riding trousers, and just cautiously slipped them off. My! What a relief it was! Grandmother felt me rustling around and looked sharp at me, to see what I was doing. When she saw the riding trousers, she frowned; but I guess I must have looked terribly hot and red, so she didn't say anything.

"Well, I knew it was an awful thing to do in church, and I was so afraid maybe somebody *had* seen me, although old Dr. Skinner, the rector, was the only one high enough up to see over the pew top, and he was looking at his Prayer Book. But I felt as mean as though he'd been looking right at me. Well, he got through the Remission of Sins, and we stood up for the Psalms, and sat down for the First Lesson. It was something out of the Old Testament, that part about how the Jews went back and repaired the broken walls of Jerusalem, each one taking a broken place for his special job. And then how they got scared away, all but a few, from the holes in the walls they were trying to fix up.

"Dr. Skinner always read the Lessons very loud and solemn, as though he were reading them right *at* somebody, and he'd sort of turn from one to another in the congregation with his forefinger pointed at them, as if he meant that just for them. What *do* you suppose I felt like when he turned right towards our corner, and leaned 'way over and shook his finger at me, and said in a loud, shaming tone, 'But Asher continued and *abode* in *his* breaches!' I gave a little gasp, and Grandmother turned towards me quick. When she saw the expression on my face (I guess I must have looked funny), she burst right out into that great laugh of hers—ha! ha! ha! She laughed so she couldn't stop. Actually she had to get up and go out of church, her handkerchief stuffed into her mouth. We could hear her laughing as she went down the walk outside!

"You'd have thought she'd be mortified, wouldn't you? I was mortified almost to death! But she wasn't a bit. She laughed every time she thought of it, for years after that. It was just like her! She did love a good laugh! Let anything happen that struck her as funny, and she'd laugh, no *matter* what!"

Later on, as we carried the hassocks back to the church and put them in our pew, my aunt said, reflectively, looking around the empty church: "I never come in here that I don't remember how Grandmother used to say the Creed, loud and strong—she always spoke up so clear: 'From thence he shall come to judge the quick and the dead. I believe in the Holy Ghost; the Holy Catholic Church; the Communion of saints; the Forgiveness of sins—' and then she'd stop dead, while everybody went on, 'the Resurrection of the body:' and then she'd chime in again, 'and the Life everlasting. Amen.' You couldn't help noticing it, she took the greatest pains you should. But if anybody said anything about it she always snapped back that she didn't believe in the resurrection of the body, and she wasn't going to *say* she did. Sometimes the ministers would get wrought up, especially the young ones, and one of them went to the Bishop about it, but nobody ever did anything. What *could* you do? And Grandmother went right on saying the Creed that way to the day of her death."

On the hundredth anniversary of the organization of our parish there were, of course, great doings in the way of centenary celebra-

tions. Many of the old rectors came back to visit, to make after-
dinner talks, and to preach at special services. One of the most interesting of these old men was the Reverend Mr. Jason Gillett, who
had been rector for a year shortly after the Civil War, when he was
a young man just out of the theological seminary. He had since
become well known, one might say famous (in church circles at
least) for his sermons of a fervor truly evangelical (so it was said),
delivered in a voice noted for its harmony and moving qualities.
We had often read about his preaching, in the church papers. He
had brought up from decay several old parishes and had founded one
of the finest and most thriving in Chicago.

There was a stir when his return for a day was announced, and
the morning when he preached, the church was crowded to the doors.
He proved to be a spiritual-faced, white-haired, handsome old man,
equipped with fine eyes and beautiful hands as well as his famous
voice. He preached a sermon which held everyone in the church
breathlessly attentive. I noticed that his stole was exquisitely worked
in gold thread, and after the service, when the Altar Guild were
in the vestry folding and putting things away, we saw that his surplice
was of extremely fine material, with a deep band of embroidery about
the hem. "Loving lady-parishioners," conjectured one of the Guild,
holding it up.

"They say the women are always crazy about him, everywhere,
and no wonder!" said another. "Such a fascinating personality."

"How did you like his sermon?" I asked. Personally I had found
it rather too dramatic for my taste. It rubs me the wrong way when
I feel that somebody is trying to work on my emotions, although
I always feel a little ashamed of this natural ungraciousness, which
is labeled in the talk of the old people of our locality as "Canfield
cussedness."

One of my companions answered me, "Why, the tears ran right
down my cheeks, towards the end of that sermon!"

Another added, "Such a power for good as he has been, all his life.
Think of his having begun his wonderful work right here in our
little parish."

The door opened and the preacher himself entered in his black
cassock, followed by a group of people. He was a little flushed from
the handshaking reception he had been holding in the vestibule
and still wore the affable smile which had gone with the handshaking. The men and women who had followed him in were still
talking two or three at once, trying to get his attention, still fixing

their eyes on him, unwilling to leave him, moved evidently by his
mere presence.

"It's a renewal of my youth to be here again in this dear old
parish," he said genially, using a set of inflections of his fine voice
quite different from those of the sermon. "I find it all comes back
to me with the utmost freshness. Ah, youth! Youth!"

He broke off to say in still another tone, "I know none of you
will object to my saying also that it is an immense relief to find the
parish rid of that detestable incubus, Mrs. Almera Canfield. You
must all breathe a happier air, since she took her mocking cynicism
into another world."

A quick shifting of eyes, lifted eyebrows, and suppressed smiles
told him that he had been indiscreet. He faced the uncomfortable
little situation with a well-oiled ease of manner. "Have I offended
someone here?" he asked, instantly, turning towards us. Then, seeing by my expression that I was the one involved, he said gallantly,
"It's not possible that so very young a lady can have any connection
with a generation so long since passed away."

"Mrs. Almera Canfield was my great-grandmother," I said, perhaps
rather drily. Not that I cared especially about Great-grandmother,
of whom at that time I knew very little, and who seemed as remote
from my life as Moses. But that same contrary streak in my nature
was roused to resentment by his apparent assumption that a smile
and a word from him could set anything straight.

He found the fact of my relationship and of my knowledge of it
very amusing. "Where, oh, where out of Vermont could you find a
modern young person who even knew the name of her great-grandmother? I'm sure, my dear, that family loyalties are outlawed by
such a long interval of years. And I'm also sure by one look at you,
that you are not at all like your great-grandmother."

He seemed to think, I reflected, that I would be sure to take that
as a compliment. She must have been an old Tartar.

I could think of nothing to answer, and he turned away again,
to go on chatting with the people who continued to hang on his
words, laughing when he said something playful, nodding a grave
concurrence in his more seriously expressed opinions, their eyes fixed
on his.

They all moved away, out into the church and down the aisle,
and I did not see him again till that evening, when, quite unexpectedly, he appeared beside me in the break-up of the company after
the large public dinner.

"I feel that I owe you an apology," he began persuasively and courteously, "for having let slip that chance remark about a relative of yours, even so very far distant. I would not have said it, of course, if I had dreamed that any member of her family . . ." Up to this point he had used the same sort of gracious voice that he had employed after church that morning, but now unexpectedly his tone had an edge. I had a divination that it was not only quite different from any inflection he had used, but also not at all what he had intended. "I try to be fair . . . to be tolerant . . . to be *forgiving,* but really I can never forget the . . ." (It was as if a wave of lava had burst up out of the smiling pleasantness of his agreeable manner.) "I simply can't express to you the blighting, devastating effect she had on me, young, sensitive, ardent as I was at that time!"

He started at the violence of his own voice and glanced quickly around him as if to see whether anyone else had heard it. Then he looked intensely annoyed by his own gesture.

"You are probably assuming that I refer," he went on more quietly, but still pressingly (it was as if for some reason he quite cared to influence my unimportant opinion), "that I refer to her dictatorial assurance that she knew better than anyone else how things ought to be run. Of course you must have heard plenty of stories of her overbearing ways. But that is not the point; no, although she was a hard parishioner on that account for a young clergyman struggling with the administration of his first parish. What came back to me, in a wave of bitterness as I stood up to preach today, was the remembrance of the peculiarly corrosive vein of irony with which she withered and dried to the root any play of poetry or emotion in those about her. So far from feeling any natural, human sympathy with ardent youth, she had a cold intolerance for any nature richer or more warmly colored than her own. She made it her business to drop an acid sneer upon any expression of emotion or any appeal to emotion, and a life-long practice in that diabolical art had given her a dreadful skill in that technique, guaranteed to hamstring any spontaneity of feeling, any warmth of personality. I could quote you dozens of such poisoned shafts of hers. . . . Here's one that came into my mind as I stood again in that pulpit, where I first dedicated myself to the service of God.

"I can never forget her comment on the first sermon in which I let myself go into the fervor which was given me by nature. It was an appeal for foreign missions, a cause always dear to my heart. I was carried away by my feelings, and fairly poured out my soul to my listeners. I have always considered that to be my first real sermon, the first time I felt sure of my Vocation. Afterwards, as I stood in the robing room, faint with the reaction after my emotion, I heard someone just outside the door say, 'Well, Aunt Almera, what did you think of the sermon?' You won't believe what her answer was! She said, 'Oh, I *like* to see anybody enjoy himself as much as that young man did.' "

This unexpected conclusion brought to me a sudden, horrifying desire to laugh. But it was essential not to let this be seen. For he had wound himself up again to a heat which astonished me. It was as if his intention had been casually to show me an old scar, and he had found to his surprise that the wound was unhealed, as raw as ever.

"Why," he cried, "she all but drove me out of preaching, at the very outset of my career, sitting there as she did, Sunday after Sunday, fixing that cynical, aged eye on me. You can't know . . . I hear that you have been brought up, luckily for you, outside of this deadly New England atmosphere. . . . You can't *imagine* how it kills and freezes all the warmth and color and fire out of life to have such a . . . if I hadn't escaped out of it to . . ."

"I'm afraid I've been brought up mostly in a New England atmosphere," I said. I was beginning to feel inexplicably cross and prickly.

As if struck by something in my tone, he now looked at me very hard. I don't know what he saw in my face . . . perhaps a family resemblance. He said sharply, "I can't think what in the world made me bring all this up," and turned his back on me with a noticeable lack of suavity and grace of manner.

Once I was taken to see an old woman who had come from Ireland as a young girl, just after the great famine in '47, and had gone to work for Grandmother, who was then only sixty-three years old. She told me this story, in her thick, early-nineteenth-century brogue, which I will not try to reproduce here: "There was a pretty girl, young and happy-looking, that lived up the road with her father, a poor weak rag of a man with a backbone like a piece of string. He'd married for his second wife a hard, hard woman. And when they found out the girl was in trouble, and her sweetheart that was the cause of it off up in the North Country for the winter to work as a lumberjack, didn't the stepmother turn the poor girl out—yes, out like a dog. And old Mrs. Canfield—that was some kin to you, I forget what— where I was working, she went right out and brought her in, and kept her there safe all winter, treating her as nice as anybody, letting her sew to pay for her keep, and helping her make the baby clothes. She'd go with her to church every Sunday, the girl right on her arm, and nobody daring to say a word, for fear of old Mrs. Canfield's tongue. 'For,' she used to say, 'let 'em say a word if they dare, and I'll tell a few things I know about some folks in this town, which ones had to be married in a hurry, and which ones' babies came into the world ahead of time.' You see, she was so old she knew everything that had happened from the beginning almost. She'd say, 'There's lots worse things done every day in this town than anything Margaret's done,' she'd say, and nobody to answer her back a word.

"But everybody was thinking it very certain that the man would never come back, and if he did, he'd never own the child, nor have anything to do with Margaret, poor girl! You see, in those days there weren't any mails that were carried 'way back off in the woods, and she neither had any word of him nor he of her. Well, old Mrs. Canfield knew what people were saying all right, and I could see that she was troubled in her mind, though she never lowered her high head by an inch. Margaret's time drew near, and no sign from John Dawson that was away. But Margaret never lost her faith in him a minute. 'When John is back,' she'd say, just as sure of him as though they'd been married by the priest; but I could see old Mrs. Canfield look queer when she'd hear Margaret talking that way.

"And then one morning, in April 'twas, and we'd all the doors and windows open for the first time, Margaret had gone down the walk to look at the lilac bush to see if there were any buds on it, and around the corner came John Dawson!

"Her back was to him and he hadn't any idea she was there, so when she turned round, they stared at each other for a minute, as if they'd never seen each other. Now he had come, Margaret stood there frozen, waiting, like a little scared, helpless—I had the half of me hanging out the kitchen window to see what would happen, and I'll never forget it—never—never—never—the look on his face, the astounded look on his face, so strong with pity and love. 'Margie! *Margie!*' he said in a loud voice, and threw his sack off his back and his ax from his hand, and ran, ran to take her in his arms.

"Well, when I could see again, I went off to tell old Mrs. Canfield, and there was the old lady in her own bedroom, standing bolt upright in the middle of the floor, and crying at the top of her voice. Her wrinkled old face was just a-sop with tears. Faith, but it was the grand cry she was having! And the good it did her! When she came to, she says to me, 'Well,' says she, 'folks aren't so cussed as they seem, are they?'

"And then we went downstairs to get out the fruitcake and the brandied peaches; for the minister married them in our parlor that afternoon."

One day old Mr. Morgan, the one-armed Civil War veteran, took me along with him, to get out of the buckboard and open gates, on the back road along the river. He was going up to a hill pasture to salt his sheep. It took forever to get there, because his horse was so slow, and he had time to tell me a great many stories. This was one of them: "When I was a boy at school, I worked at Aunt Almera Canfield's doing chores night and morning. I remember how she used to loosen herself up in the morning. She was terribly rheumaticky, but she wouldn't give in to it. Every morning she'd be all stiffened up so she couldn't stand up straight, nor hardly move her legs at all; but she'd get herself dressed somehow, and then two of her sons came in to help her get started. She'd make them take hold of her, one on each side, and walk her around the room. It was awful to hear how she'd yell out—yell as though they were killing her! They'd stop, the sweat on their faces, to see how much it hurt her, and then she'd yell at them to go on, go on, *she* hadn't asked them to stop! They were over sixty, both of them, with grandchildren themselves, but they didn't dare not do what she said, and they'd walk her round again. She'd kick her poor legs out in front of her hard, to get the joints limbered up, and holler with the pain, and kick them out again, till by and by she'd get so she could go by herself, and she'd be all right for the day. I tell you, I often think of that. Yes, lots of times, it comes back to me."

Up in the sheep pasture, as we sat to rest the horse, he told me this: "I always thought Aunt Almera knew all about the John Brown raid before most folks did—maybe she sent some money to help him. She wasn't a bit surprised, anyhow, when she heard of it, and all through the whole business she never thought of another thing, nor let anybody else. He was caught—any of us that lived in that house those days will never forget a one of those dates—and put in jail on the 9th of October, and his trial lasted until the 31st. Aunt Almera made us get together in the evenings, me and the hired girl and one of her grandsons and her daughter, all the family, and she'd read aloud to us out of the *Tribune* about what had happened that day at his trial. I never saw her so worked up about anything—just like ashes her face was, and her voice like cold steel. We got as excited about it as she did, all of us, especially her grandson, that was about my age. The day of his execution—December 2nd, it was—Aunt Almera came at dawn to wake me up. 'Put on your clothes,' says she, 'and go over to the church and begin to toll the bell.' I didn't need to ask her what for, either. I'll never forget how awful she looked to me.

"Well, we tolled the bell all day long, one or the other of the family, never stopped a minute. You never heard anything so like death. All day long that slow, deep clang—and then a stillness—and then *clang!* again. I could hear it in my head for days afterwards. Folks came in from all around to find out what it meant, and Aunt Almera called them all into her parlor—she sat there all day and never ate a mouthful of food—and *told* them what it meant, so they couldn't ever get the sound of her voice out of their ears. Between times she'd read out of the Bible to whoever was there, 'Avenge thou thy cause, O Lord God of battles,' and 'It is time for thee, O Lord, to lay to thy hand, for they have destroyed thy law,' and 'Let there be no man to pity them; nor to have compassion of their fatherless children.' It was the darndest thing to hear her!

"You'd better believe when Abraham Lincoln sent out the first call for men there wasn't a boy of military age in our town that didn't enlist!"

An aged cousin had just died, and as we sat downstairs talking with the doctor, he said to my aunt, who had been taking care of the sick woman: "She took it hard! She took it hard!"

They both frowned, and my aunt looked rather sick. Then the doctor said, "Not much like your grandmother, do you remember?"

"Oh, yes, I remember," said my aunt, her eyes misty, her lips smiling.

The doctor explained to me: "Your great-grandmother was an old, old woman before she ever was really sick at all, except for rheumatism. And then she had a stroke of paralysis that left her right side dead. She lived four days that way—the only days she'd spent in bed in years, since she was a young woman, I suppose. Her mind wasn't very clear, she couldn't talk so that we could understand her, and I don't think she rightly knew anybody after her stroke. I guess she went back, 'way back, for we saw from what she did that she thought she had a little baby with her. I suppose she thought she was a young mother again, and that was why she was in bed. We used to see her spread out her arm, very gentle and slow, the only arm she could move, so's to make a hollow place for a little head, and then she'd lie there, so satisfied and peaceful, looking up at the ceiling with a smile in her eyes, as if she felt a little, warm, breathing creature there beside her. And sometimes she'd half wake up and stretch out her hand and seem to stroke the baby's head or snuggle it up closer to her, and then she'd give a long sigh of comfort to find it there, and drop off to sleep again, smiling. And she'd always remember, even in her sleep, to keep her arm curved around so there'd be room for the baby; and even in her sleep her face had that shining new-mother look—that old wrinkled face, with that look on it! I've seen lots of death-beds, but I never—" He stopped for a moment.

"Why, at the very last—do you remember?"—he went on to my aunt, "I thought she was asleep, but as I moved a chair she opened her eyes quickly, looked down as if to see whether I had awakened the baby, and put her finger to her lip to warn me to be quiet. 'Sh!' she whispered.

"That was the way she died."

The Heyday
of the Blood

The older professor looked sharply at his assistant, fumbling with a pile of papers. "Farrar, what's the *matter* with you lately?" he asked, brusquely.

The younger man started, "Why—why—" his face twitched. He went on desperately, "I've lost my nerve, Professor Mallory, that's what's the matter with me."

"What do you mean—nerve?" asked Mallory, challenging impatience in his tone.

The younger man started, "Why—why—" His face twitched. He went trembling so that the papers he held fell on the floor. "I worry—I forget things—I take no interest in life. The psychiatrists tell me to relax, to rest. I try to but it's no good. I never go out—every evening I'm in bed by nine o'clock. I take no part in college life beyond my own work. I turned down that chance to organize a summer seminar in New York, you know—I'll never have such a splendid professional opportunity again!—If I could only sleep! Heavens, what nights I have! Yet I never do anything exciting in the evening. I keep seeing myself in a sanitarium, dependent on my brother—why, I'm in hell—that's what's the matter—"

Professor Mallory interrupted him, patiently now, as if he were quieting a frightened saddle-horse. "But don't your psychiatrists do more than just advise you to take it easy? What do they tell you about your case?"

The young man's face drew together in a spasm. "That's just it," he cried. "They won't tell me the truth. Not one. They won't speak right out. They pretend to believe that a little rest and quiet is all I need. But I've read enough case histories to know I'm doomed by the craving for defeat. I've heard about the 'will to—' " He choked and stopped.

The older man looked at him speculatively. When he spoke again his voice was neither challenging nor patient. It had a relaxed, offhand quality. "Well, well," he said, "let's leave it at that. I can't advise you. All this is no field of mine. I don't know anything about psychiatry except what I read in the papers. I do know from there that psychiatrists pay a lot of attention to childhood impressions, and I should say they show their good sense in that. I've had childhood experiences of my own." He paused, hesitated, swung around in his swivel chair from his desk and said as if on an impulse, "I'd sort of like to tell you about one. You're not too busy?"

"Busy! I've forgotten the meaning of the word! I don't dare to put any pressure on myself."

"Very well, then; I mean to carry you back to the stony little farm in the Green Mountains, where I had the good luck to be born and raised. You've heard me speak of Hillsboro. The story is all about my great-grandfather, who came to live with us when I was a little boy."

"Your great-grandfather?" protested the other. "People don't remember their great-grandfathers!"

"Oh, yes, they do, in Vermont. There was my father on one farm, and my grandfather on another, without a thought that he was no longer young, and there was 'Gran'ther' as we called him, eighty-eight years old and just persuaded to settle back, let his descendants take care of him. He had been in the War of 1812—think of that, you mushroom!—and had lost an arm and a good deal of his health there. He had lately begun to get a pension of twelve dollars a month. For an old man he was quite independent financially, as poor Vermont farmers look at things; and he was a most extraordinary character. His arrival in our family was an event.

"He took precedence at once over the oldest man in the township, who was only eighty-four and not very bright. I can remember bragging at school about Gran'ther Pendleton, who'd be eighty-nine come next Woodchuck Day, and could see to read without glasses. He had been ailing all his life, ever since the fever he took in the war. He used to remark triumphantly that he had now outlived six doctors who had each given him but a year to live, 'and the seventh is going downhill fast, so I hear!' This last was his never-failing answer to the attempts of my conscientious mother and anxious, dutiful father to check the old man's reckless indifference to any of the rules of hygiene.

"Our parents had never been stern or harsh with us, but we children never dreamed of questioning their firm decisions. Neither did Gran'ther Pendleton question them. He ignored them, this naughty old man, who would give his weak stomach frightful attacks of indigestion by stealing out to the pantry and devouring a whole mince pie because he had been refused two pieces at the table—this rebellious, unreasonable, whimsical old madcap brought a high-voltage electric element into our quiet, orderly life. He insisted on going to every picnic and church sociable, where he ate all the indigestible dainties he could lay his hands on, stood in drafts, tired himself to the verge of fainting away by playing games with the children, and returned home, exhausted, animated, and quite ready to pay the price of a day in bed, groaning and screaming out with pain as heartily and unaffectedly as he had laughed with the pretty girls the evening before.

"The climax came, however, in the middle of August, when he announced his desire to go to the county fair, held some fourteen miles down the valley from our farm. Father never dared let Gran'ther go anywhere without going with the old man himself, but he was perfectly sincere in saying that it was not because he could not spare a day from the haying that he refused pointblank to consider it. The doctor who had been taking care of Gran'ther since he came to live with us said that it would be crazy to think of such a thing. He added that the wonder was that Gran'ther lived at all, for his heart was all wrong, his asthma was enough to kill a young man, and he had no digestion; in short, if Father wished to kill his old grandfather, there was no surer way than to drive fourteen miles in the heat of August to the noisy excitement of a county fair.

"So Father for once said 'No,' in the tone that we children had come to recognize as final. Gran'ther grimly tied a knot in his empty sleeve—a curious way he took to express strong emotion—put his one hand on his cane, and his chin on his hand, and withdrew himself into that incalculable distance from the life about him where very old people spend so many hours.

"He did not emerge from this until one morning toward the middle of fair-week, when all the rest of the family were away—Father and the bigger boys on the far-off upland meadows haying, and Mother and the girls blackberrying in the burnt-over lot, across the valley. I was too little to be of any help, so I had been left to wait on Gran'ther, and to set out our lunch of bread and milk and huckleberries. We had not been alone half an hour when Gran'ther sent me to extract, from under the mattress of his bed, the wallet in which he kept his pension money. He counted it over carefully, sticking out his tongue like a schoolboy doing a sum. 'Six dollars and forty-three cents!' he cried. He began to laugh and snap his fingers and sing out in his high, cracked old voice:

" 'We're goin' to go a skylarkin'! Little Jo Mallory is going to the county fair with his Gran'ther Pendleton, an' he's goin' to have more fun than ever was in the world, and he—'

" 'But, Gran'ther, Father said we mustn't!' I protested, horrified.

" 'But I say we *shall!* I was your gre't-gran'ther long before he was your feyther, and anyway I'm here and he's not—so, *march!* Out to the barn!'

"He took me by the collar and pushed me ahead of him to the stable, where old white Peggy, the only horse left at home, looked at us amazed.

" 'But it'll be twenty-eight miles, and Peg's never driven over eight!' I cried, my established world of rules and orders reeling.

" 'Eight—and—twenty-eight!
But I—am—*eighty*-eight!'

"Gran'ther improvised a sort of whooping chant of scorn as he pulled the harness from the peg. 'It'll do her good to drink some pink lemonade—old Peggy! An' if she gits tired comin' home, I'll git out and carry her part way myself!'

"I thought this the funniest idea I'd ever heard and laughed loudly as together we hitched up, I standing on a chair to slip the check-rein in place, Gran'ther doing wonders with his one hand. Then, just as we were—Gran'ther in a hickory shirt not very clean, an old hat flapping over his wizened face, I bare-legged, in my faded everyday old clothes—we drove out of the grassy yard, down the steep, stony hill that led to the main valley road. Along the hot, white turnpike, deep with dust, we joined the farm teams on their way to the fair. Gran'ther exchanged hilarious greetings with the people who constantly overtook old Peg's jogging trot. Between times he regaled me with spicy stories of the hundreds of thousands—they seemed no less numerous to me then—of county fairs he had attended in his youth. He was horrified to find that I had never been even to one.

" 'Why, Joey, how old be ye? 'Most eight, ain't it? When I was your age I had run away and been to two fairs an' a hangin'.'

" 'But didn't they lick you when you got home?' I asked shudderingly.

" 'You *bet* they did!' cried Gran'ther with gusto.

"I felt the world expanding into an infinitely larger place with every word he said.

" 'Now, this is somethin' *like!*' he exclaimed, as we drew near to Granville and fell into a procession of wagons all filled with country people in their best clothes, who looked with friendly curiosity at the ancient, shriveled cripple, his face shining with sweat and animation, and at the small boy beside him, his bare feet dangling high above the floor of the battered buckboard, overcome with the responsibility of driving a horse for the first time in his life, and filled with such a flood of new emotions and ideas that he must have been quite pale."

Professor Mallory leaned back and laughed aloud at the vision he had been evoking—laughed with so joyous an abandon and relish in his reminiscences that the face of his listener relaxed a little.

"Oh, that was a day!" went on the professor, still laughing and wiping his eyes. "Never will I have another like it! At the entrance to the grounds Gran'ther stopped me while he solemnly untied the knot in his empty sleeve. I don't know what kind of harebrained vow he had tied up in it, but with the little ceremony disappeared every last trace of restraint, and we plunged head over ears into the saturnalia of delights that was an old-time county fair.

"People had little cash in those days, and Gran'ther's six dollars and forty-three cents lasted like the widow's cruse of oil. We went to see the fat lady, who, if she was really as big as she looked to me then, must have weighed at least a ton. My admiration for Gran'ther's daredevil qualities rose to infinity when he entered into free-and-easy talk with her, about how much she ate, and could she raise her arms enough to do up her own hair, and how many yards of velvet it took to make her gorgeous, gold-trimmed robe. She laughed a great deal at us, but she was evidently touched by his human interest, for she confided to him that it was not velvet at all, but furniture covering; and when we went away she pressed on us a bag of peanuts. She said she had more peanuts than she could eat—a state of unbridled opulence which fitted in for me with all the other superlatives of that day.

"We saw the dog-faced boy, whom we did not like at all; Gran'ther expressing, with a candidly outspoken cynicism, his belief that 'them whiskers was glued to him.' We wandered about the stock exhibit, gazing at monstrous oxen, and hanging over the railings where the prize pigs lived to scratch their backs. In order to miss nothing, we even conscientiously passed through the Woman's Building, where we were very much bored by the serried ranks of preserve jars.

"'Sufferin' Hezekiah!' cried Gran'ther irritably. 'Who cares how gooseberry jell *looks*. If they'd give a felly a taste, now—'

"This reminded him that we were hungry, and we went to a restaurant tent, where, after taking stock of the wealth that yet remained of Gran'ther's hoard, he ordered the most expensive things on the bill of fare."

Professor Mallory suddenly laughed out again. "Perhaps in heaven, but certainly not until then, shall I ever taste anything so ambrosial as that fried chicken and coffee ice cream! I have not lived in vain that I have such a memory back of me!"

This time the younger man laughed with the narrator, settling back in his chair as the professor went on:

"After lunch we rode on the merry-go-round, both of us, Gran'ther clinging desperately with his one hand to his red camel's wooden hump, and crying out shrilly to me to be sure and not lose his cane. The merry-go-round had just come in at that time, and Gran'ther had never experienced it before. After the first giddy flight we retired to a lemonade-stand to exchange impressions, and finding that we both alike had fallen completely under the spell of the new sensation, Gran'ther said that we 'sh'd keep on a-ridin' till we'd had enough! Nobody could tell when we'd ever git a chance again!' So we returned to the charge, and rode and rode and rode, through blinding clouds of happy excitement, so it seems to me now, such as I was never to know again. The sweat was pouring off from us, and we had tried all the different animals on the machine before we could tear ourselves away to follow the crowd to the race track.

"We took reserved seats, which cost a quarter apiece, instead of the unshaded ten-cent benches, and Gran'ther began at once to pour out to me a flood of horse talk and knowing race track aphorisms, which finally made a young fellow sitting next to us laugh superciliously. Gran'ther turned on him heatedly.

"'I bet-che fifty cents I pick the winner in the next race!' he said sportily.

"'Done!' said the other, still laughing.

"Gran'ther picked a big black mare, who came in almost last, but he did not flinch. As he paid over the half-dollar he said: 'Everybody's likely to make mistakes about *some* things; King Solomon was a fool in the head about women-folks. I bet-che a dollar I pick the winner in *this* race!' and 'Done!' said the disagreeable young man, still laughing. I gasped, for I knew we had only eighty-seven cents left, but Gran'ther shot me a command to silence out of the corner of his eyes, and announced that he bet on the sorrel gelding.

"If I live to be a hundred and break the bank at Monte Carlo three times a week," said Mallory, shaking his head reminiscently, "I could not know a tenth part of the frantic excitement of that race or of the mad triumph when our horse won. Gran'ther cast his hat upon the ground, screaming like a steam calliope with exultation as the sorrel swept past the judges' stand ahead of all the others, and I jumped up and down in an agony of delight which was almost more than my little body could hold.

"After that we went away, feeling that the world could hold nothing more glorious. It was five o'clock, and we decided to start back. We paid for Peggy's dinner out of the dollar we had won on the race—I say 'we,' for by that time we were welded into one organism— and we still had a dollar and thirty-seven cents left. 'While ye're about it, always go the whole hog!' said Gran'ther, and we spent twenty minutes in laying out that money in trinkets for all the folks at home. Then, dusty, penniless, laden with bundles, we stowed our exhausted bodies and our uplifted hearts into the old buckboard, and turned Peg's head toward the mountains. We did not talk much during that drive, and though I thought at the time only of the carnival of joy we had left, I can now recall every detail of the trip—how the sun sank behind Indian Mountain, a peak I had known before only through distant views; then, as we journeyed on, how the stars came out above Hemlock Mountain—our own home mountain behind our house, and later, how the fireflies filled the darkening meadows along the river below us, so that we seemed to be floating between the steady stars of heaven and their dancing, twinkling reflection in the valley.

"Gran'ther's dauntless spirit still upheld me. I put out of mind doubts of our reception at home, and lost myself in delightful ruminatings on the splendors of the day. At first, every once in a while, Gran'ther made a brief remark, such as, ' 'Twas the hind-quarters of the sorrel I bet on. He was the only one in the hull kit and bilin' of 'em that his quarters didn't fall away'; or, 'You needn't tell *me* that them Siamese twins ain't unpinned every night as separate as you and me!' But later on, as the damp evening air began to bring on his asthma, he subsided into silence, only broken by great gasping coughs.

"These were heard by the anxious, heartsick watchers at home, and, as old Peg stumbled wearily up the hill, Father came running down to meet us. 'Where you be'n?' he demanded, his face pale and stern in the light of his lantern. 'We be'n to the county fair!' croaked

Gran'ther with a last flare of triumph, and fell over sideways against me. Old Peg stopped short, hanging her head as if she, too, were at the limit of her strength. I was frightfully tired myself, and frozen with terror of what Father would say. Gran'ther's collapse was the last straw. I began to cry loudly, but Father ignored my distress with an indifference which cut me to the heart. He lifted Gran'ther out of the buckboard, carrying the unconscious little old body into the house without a glance backward at me. But when I crawled down to the ground, sobbing and digging my fists into my eyes, I felt Mother's arms close around me.

" 'Oh, poor, naughty little Joey!' she said. 'Mother's bad, dear little boy!' "

Professor Mallory stopped short.

"Perhaps that's something else I'll know again in heaven," he said soberly, and waited a moment before he went on: "Well, that was the end of our day. I was so worn out that I fell asleep over my supper, in spite of the excitement in the house about sending for a doctor for Gran'ther, who was, so one of my awe-struck sisters told me, having some kind of 'fits.' Mother must have put me to bed, for the next thing I remember, she was shaking me by the shoulder and saying, 'Wake up, Joey. Your great-grandfather wants to speak to you. He's been suffering terribly all night, and the doctor thinks he's dying.'

"I followed her into Gran'ther's room, where the family was assembled about the bed. Gran'ther lay drawn up in a ball, groaning so dreadfully that I felt a chill like cold water at the roots of my hair; but a moment or two after I came in, all at once he gave a great sigh and relaxed, stretching out his legs, laying his one good arm down on the coverlet. He looked at me and attempted a smile.

" 'Well, it was wuth it, warn't it, Joey?' he said, and closed his eyes peacefully to sleep."

"Did he die?" asked the younger professor, leaning forward.

"Die? Gran'ther Pendleton? Not much! He came tottering down to breakfast the next morning, as white as an old ghost, with no voice left, his legs trembling under him, but he kept the whole family an hour and a half at the table, telling them in a loud whisper all about the fair, until Father said really he would have to take us to the one next year. Afterward he sat out on the porch watching old Peg graze around the yard. I thought he was in one of his absent-minded fits, but when I came out, he called me to him, and, setting his lips to my ear, he whispered:

" 'An' the seventh is a-goin' downhill fast, so I hear!' He chuckled to himself for some time over his familiar battle-cry, wagging his head feebly, and then he said: 'I tell ye, Joey, I've lived a long time, and I've larned a lot about the way folks is made. The trouble with most of 'em is, they're 'fraid-cats! As Jeroboam Warner used to say—he was in the same regiment with me in 1812—the only way to manage this business of livin' is to give a whoop and let her rip! If ye just about half-live, ye just the same as half-die; and if ye spend yer time half-dyin', someday ye turn in and die all over, without rightly meanin' to at all—just a kind o' bad habit ye've got yerself inter.' Gran'ther fell into a meditative silence for a moment. 'Jeroboam, he said that the evenin' before the battle of Lundy's Lane, and he got killed the next day. Some live, and some die; but folks that live all over die happy, anyhow! Now I tell you what's my motto, an' what I've lived to be eighty-eight on—' "

Professor Mallory stood up and, laying a hand on the younger man's shoulder, said: "This was the motto he told me: 'Live while you live, and then die and be done with it!' "

Men, Women—and Children

The
Forgotten Mother

~§I t was one of Dr. Burrage's sayings that neither he
nor his son—his adopted son, that is—knew anything at first hand
about mothers. "Dr. Wright's died at his birth. And I lost mine when
I was between four and five. Can't remember her at all. Well, yes, I
do have a dim picture of someone with brown hair, rather soft and
light, with a lock that often fell over her forehead. I can remember
how she used to brush it back with her hand. Queer, how a meaningless gesture like that should stick in a child's memory. Then there's
something connected with her in a recollection I have of walking
along a beam laid on the ground. You know how kids love to do
that. She was there at the time, I presume."

Once, four or five years after his beloved adopted son had gone into
practice with him, another faint memory of her emerged into visibility
from nowhere, as things from the past do come back to people approaching old age. The two doctors had been sitting late before the
fire in a sociable silence. They often ended their days by such a quiet
time together. The bond between them was so close that they scarcely
needed words to share each other's thoughts. The clock striking midnight aroused them from this silent communion of comradeship.
"Well, son, we must get to bed," said Dr. Burrage, heaving himself
up from his armchair. He added, "Odd! Just now, I seemed to be

way back in the past . . . back to some time when I sat quiet like this with my mother."

"I thought you couldn't remember her," remarked Dr. Wright, winding his watch.

"Well, of course I can't. Not really," admitted the older man. "I was too young when she died to remember her."

He was repeating what people always say about children whose mothers die young; what had been said in his hearing a great many times when he was a little boy of five. "No, he won't remember her. He's too young." Especially had this been said by the handsome, energetic young woman who, when he was six, became his stepmother, and who from that time on ran the family life so competently that his father, from earning very little, made constantly a bigger and bigger income and blew his brains out in a fit of jealousy and drunken melancholia when he was forty-two. His handsome stepmother soon married again and went away to live in the Philippines. From then on Henry Burrage—but he was twenty then—had to manage by himself without any parents at all. For the few recollections of his mother, vivid at the time of her death, had long ago been blurred to nothingness by time and by his stepmother.

Naturally some memories endured longer than others. Not until he had lived four or five years without her did the hawk episode fade out of his mind. Odd that it persisted so long. There was nothing much to it anyway, and it happened when he was quite small. His mother—his own mother—had taken him to spend the day on a farm—he never knew whose, nor why. Probably it belonged to a cousin or uncle of hers. There were other children there, older than he, good-natured country children used to playing with all ages, who carried him out to a game of tag in the back yard.

He had not liked that back yard from the moment he set eyes on it. Even before, he had not liked being taken away from his mother by strangers, although the strangers were only boys and girls bigger than he. A back yard that did not have his mother in it, might have—he didn't know what. The first thing he saw as he looked suspiciously around was an apple tree between the house and the barn, and he didn't like that, either. A dead limb on it pointed stiffly off towards a grove of old oaks set so thickly that he could not see what was in the darkness under them. Only a strip of plowed field lay between the yard and the darkness under the trees. It was too narrow to suit Henry. He wished his mother had come along. Without her, everything in this

new world held a menace. The kind, masterful older children sent
him to and fro in the game. His feet trotted docilely wherever he was
told to go; but in his heart a dark pool of uneasiness brimmed slowly
up towards fear. The dead branch kept pointing so.

After a time the big little girl who was directing proceedings sent
him to hide behind the lilac bush, next the house. It was close to an
open window. As he squeezed himself down into his hiding place he
heard through the window two grown-up voices speaking in dark
secret tones. The game was blindman's buff. It was the first time he
had ever played it, and he found it terribly exciting. His heart rose
sickeningly into his throat every time the hooded "it" came near, grop-
ing dreadfully with those blind clutching hands. Once they grasped
and shook the thin branches of the bush that were his only poor
shelter. His throat drew together convulsively into a knot. When the
game's center shifted to the other side of the yard, he sank down on
his heels, worn out with tension, trying to get his breath through
that knot. But now behind him, a man's bass voice, rumbling ominously, said, "Hand me my gun, will you, Ella? I want to have it handy
if I see that hawk in the woods."

A hawk. A hawk! What was a hawk, the little city boy asked himself feverishly, that a man—big he must be to have a deep voice like
that—should be so afraid of it that he must take his gun with him.
He stood up to peer fearfully through the twigs of the bush over at the
dark trees, hiding something so dreadful that great grown-up men
were frightened of it, and covered his face in his arms. If a *man* was
frightened of it— Henry's legs gave way under him. A hawk! What is a
hawk? He whispered the evil-sounding word over to himself, crouching behind the lilac bush. Fear oozed out of the woods, as out of a
cracked bottle, and, thick, clammy, black, flowed sluggishly across the
field towards Henry. The other children had stopped playing, and
were talking. He had forgotten them. The vague menace that had
darkened the air ever since he had left his mother, grew blacker. He
could not stop whispering to himself, "A hawk. A hawk—" although
he could feel how every repetition of the evil word drew towards him
the unknown danger out from the darkness under the oak trees. Cold
sweat burst from his pores, trickling down his back like ice water.
Never again in all his life from that moment on to his dying hour,
did Henry Burrage feel such strangling terror.

And now the older children turned and ran back to the little guest,
putting out their hands, dragging him out, saying kindly, cheerfully,
"Come on! We're going over to the woods to play. Come on!"

This saved the little boy's reason. For the shock pierced through the numb nightmare helplessness in which he had been crouching, frozen, silent, crazed, and awoke his instinct for self-preservation. Here was no dangerous unknown that muffled a little boy in blackness without showing anything against which he could fling himself in resistance. Here were real arms and legs and bodies he could fight. Here was good flesh and blood which he could bite and kick and scratch. They would never take him to the woods where the hawk would get him. Never. Never. He would kill them every one before he would go to the woods.

He was seized and held high in the air. The grownups had run out of the house, rushing to the struggling, screaming children. The farmer, his rifle still in one hand, with the other had torn the little boy from his murderous attack. Through his own frantic sobbing, Henry could hear that everyone was loudly talking, the bewildered, frightened children protesting, "No, we were *not* teasing him. We weren't even anywhere *near* him. We had only—" the elders saying, "If he were *my* child, I know what I'd do!"

He heard a man's voice say, gloatingly, "You've *got* to punish him, Mary, this time. You've *just got* to *whip* him. If *you* don't, I will."

A woman cried out, "Look what he's done to poor little Ella's dress. He ought to be spanked till he can't—"

Then his mother's voice—*his mother's voice!* He had forgotten that he had a mother. "Give him to me, Ed. Don't you touch him, Aunt Ella, he's *my* little boy. You leave him to me. Leave him alone, I say!"

He was in her arms now, in his mother's arms, he was clutching at her with all his might, she was carrying him around to the other side of the house, away from the forked tongues of anger licking hotly around them.

She sat down on the ground in the shade of a big currant bush and took him on her lap, in her arms. She put her cheek against his and let him cry and cry and cry, holding him close till—could it be true, could it be true!—he felt that if he could keep on crying only a little longer, he would have wept away the dreadfulness that had seemed the end of life. With his every sob, he could feel it going away. The muscles of his clenched hands began to loosen. The relief made him cry harder than ever.

When the last wild burst of sobs was over, he was himself, not a fear-crazed maniac, just Henry, sitting on his mother's lap and feeling something smooth and soft in his hand. It was the ribbon at her throat on which his hand had been clenched so tautly that he could not, when he first tried, open his fingers. That ribbon was blue, wasn't it?

Seems as though it had been blue when he saw his mother tying it before the mirror, this morning, ages ago, before they had come to this place. He opened his hand and lifted his head to look at the ribbon. His eyes were still swimming, he was still drawing long convulsive breaths that sounded like sobs. They did not feel like sobs. They felt like coming up into the air where you could breathe, after having been held a long time under water. His breathing slowed down. He began to finger the crumpled blue ribbon with grimy little hands.

At this his mother smiled at him and set him down on the ground beside her. "What do you say we lay out a pretend farm?" she proposed. She cleared a space on the earth with a sweep of her hand and began to make a wall of pebbles around it. "Where do you think the road ought to go?" she asked him.

He showed her where he thought the road should be. She leaned forward to draw the line of it as he pointed, and a lock of her soft brown hair fell down over her eyes. She put it back with her hand. Henry reached for a bit of old shingle that would make a bridge. "Let's have a brook," he said. He had meant to go on to say, "I like brooks, don't you?" but his voice was so shaky he didn't try. "Yes, brooks are sort of nice," his mother answered.

They worked together, making fields and the barnyard, looking for stones small enough and flat enough to be steppingstones. The little boy's breathing and pulse gradually slowed down till they were nearly all right. His mother did not ask him—she never asked him—what had made him act so naughty. But presently he asked her something. In a trembling whisper, and keeping his head bent very low, he asked, "Mother, what is a hawk?" She told him, and added a story from her own country childhood about a brave mother hen who had fought off a hawk from her baby chicks.

He sank his head still lower. "It's not a—a—a dragon?" he breathed.

"No, oh, no," she told him quietly, "only a bird, not as big as that rooster over there." As she told him this, she sat up, and put back her hair from her forehead with her hand.

He lifted his head then and looked into her eyes, deeply into his mother's honest eyes.

They went on making the play-farm, the little boy moving pebbles here and there, his mother making a rail fence out of twigs. They scooped out a place for a pond, and put moss around the sides. He said, "I'm going to make the road go a long, long way, clear off to town."

All the while there was flowing into him the knowledge that he was safe, that there was nothing to fear, that a hawk is only a bird no bigger than a rooster. He had been filled to the last smallest cell of his body with terror. Now terror was gone, and into the empty little Henry that was left poured confidence and courage. Flooding rich and warm, this tide of faith in life began to circulate in his every vein and artery. It did not come from his mother. It came from his having learned what the things you are afraid of, really are. Those old oak trees—they were nothing but trees. The stiff evil pointing branch—it was only a piece of dead wood. A hawk is only a bird.

The knot that had been strangling him loosened, loosened, fell away.

Presently his young mother saw that her little boy had fallen asleep, so soundly asleep that he did not wake up till they were at home again.

He never spoke of that day. Nor did his mother. During the next year he learned so many new things—trains and telephones and how to go to the grocery store alone, and how to tie his own shoelaces—that when he remembered his mistake about the hawk he was quite ashamed that he had ever been such an ignorant baby. So he forgot it.

There was no such reason for his forgetting the time he walked the beam, and all his life he kept a few shreds of memory about that. About a year before his mother died, a long squared timber—perhaps left behind by the builder who had just finished a new cottage next door—lay for a day or two across the front yard of the little one-story brown house that was Henry's home. One morning when Henry's young father came out on the front porch after breakfast, a gust of the boyishness such a short time behind him blew him up on it to run lightly from one end to the other, setting his feet down on the narrow beam with nimble precision, and leaping off at the other end with a pirouette of triumph. So of course little Henry must do this also. He stepped happily up on the end, as his father had. But when he lifted one foot to put it in front of the other, he fell off. The grass was soft. He was not hurt at all, but very much surprised. He rose at once and tried it again more cautiously. Again, before he could set down his advancing foot he lost his balance and tumbled off on the grass. His father laughed good-naturedly at the clumsy child, looked at his watch, kissed his wife goodby, pulled down his vest, and went off to the factory office to work. But halfway down the street he turned and came leaping back to kiss his wife goodby again. "You look like sunshine," he told her. This was because she wore a yellow dress with ruffles, she said. He shook his head, put his hand gently on her hair, and went away again. She stood on the porch, looking after him and smiling.

Henry had been thinking hard about walking that beam. He felt that his two falls were due to his not having really put his mind on it, and with great care he stepped up once more. He fell off at once. At this he lost his temper, scrambled up to his feet, and kicked the beam with all his might. It was very hard, and Henry's foot was soft. He hurt his toes dreadfully and gave a yell of rage.

"What's the matter?" asked his mother, turning her head towards him. She was still smiling although by this time Henry's father had turned the corner and was out of sight.

"I want to walk this thing the way Father did," he told her, frowning and sticking his lower lip very far out.

"Well, why don't you?"

"I ca-a-an't!" he complained in a nasal whine.

"Yes, you can if you want to." She stopped smiling, gave her attention seriously to her son's problem, and stepped down from the porch to where he stood. "You can do anything—if you want to enough to learn how," she told him.

"How do you learn things?" he asked dubiously.

"You keep trying to."

So he began to try and she to keep him trying. He was soon ready to give up, but she reminded him a good many times what fun it would be to know how to run along as his father had, so after resting and eating another piece of bread and butter, he tried some more. It went better. He took two steps without falling. His mother clapped her hands and looked proud. He learned that it helped to wave his arms around as he stepped cautiously forward. His mother brought out a basket of mending and sat on the edge of the porch, watching him as he took those two steps over and over—and fell. Presently he took three before he fell. "Goody!" said his mother. "Try again."

But he was hot and tired, and sorry that he had ever begun this stupid business. What did he care about it! He turned around to his sand pile and went on with a mountain he had started there yesterday. His mother said nothing. A little anxiously, he called her attention to the bigness of the mountain he was making. She nodded and smiled pleasantly. But she did not clap her hands or look proud. "Oh, dear!" thought little Henry crossly. He went on patting and poking at his mountain, but he did not see it. "Oh, *dear!*" he said. Presently he went back to the beam.

"That's fine," said his mother.

But it wasn't fine at all. It wasn't a bit of fun any more. It was just work. Yet somehow, it didn't seem quite so hard to do. By and by, he had taken six tottering steps before falling. And then seven, and then eight. He and his mother looked at each other proudly.

After lunch and his nap, when he went out on the front porch the tiresome thing was still lying across their yard, as he felt it lying across his mother's mind. Yielding to this pressure, he went back languidly and practiced some more. His mother came out beside the beam to watch. "You're getting along *well*," she said. He tried harder.

"Why," said his mother, holding out her hands to show, "you've only so much more to go, to do it all."

Then it came to Henry. Before he had even once shakily teetered his way from one end to the other of the beam, he was not shaky any more. Something in his head that had been holding out against his wanting to do it, gave way. Something in his legs that had been wavering and uncertain, straightened and steadied. Henry knew how. Straight and true he trotted to the far end of the beam and jumped off. He was tired, quite tired, but happy. "Watch me!" he told his mother, and stepping up, trotted all the way back. Whatever had made him think it was hard to do?

"Well, *Henry!*" said his mother.

Henry knew by the way she said this that she was just as proud of him as she could be. It was not the first time his mother had been proud of him, but it was the first time he had known she was. It was glorious! His heart shone. He ran to her to hug her knees with all his might. She was a Friend, Henry's mother was, so she had quiet Quaker ways and did not squeal and call him darling and honey-bunch and such things. But Henry knew what she meant.

There were no other Friends in the town where Henry's father had taken his young bride, so she had no Meetings to go to. But sometimes she and little Henry had Meeting by themselves. Once in a while of a winter afternoon, before the stove (his parents were poor as well as young and had only a stove, not a furnace), once in a while in summer, out in the side yard under the very old oak tree that overhung the tiny cottage, Henry's mother would say, "What do you say we have Meeting?"

Henry liked Meeting pretty well, although there wasn't much to it. All you did was just to sit quiet. Sometimes when he was still very small, he sat on his mother's lap. Sometimes he sat beside her and held her hand. She let him do whatever he felt like doing, so long as he was quiet. Sometimes, when they had Meeting out-of-doors, he slid down and lay on his back on the ground, looking up into the strong, crooked, rough branches of the old oak tree, and through them at the blue, blue sky. Once or twice he dozed off into a nap. Once or twice his mother prayed. Always the same prayer, "God please make my little boy strong and good." The first time, "What is 'God'?" he asked her curiously, but shyly, for a string inside him had been softly plucked by the sound of her voice when she said the word. She answered him, "When a little boy wants to do what's right, that's God in his heart."

But mostly there was no talk at all. Just a stillness, and Mother's face so quiet and calm that it made Henry feel quiet and calm to look at it.

Then she died and he began to forget her. It did not take long. He was so young, four and a half years old. And his stepmother was so devoted to him. She was the daughter and only child of the rich man who owned the factory where Father went to work in the office, so of course after she married Father he got a better job, and after that a better one yet. There was soon plenty of money, instead of too little. They moved to a new home. It was so large and so different from the little brown cottage, that his stepmother told his father the plain old furnishings just wouldn't do. So everything was bought fresh and new. There was nothing, not a chair, not a picture, nor a scarf, nor so much as a handkerchief that could remind little Henry of his mother who had died.

"You're *my* little boy now, honey-bunch!" his pretty stepmother often told him, hugging him hard. "And *I'm* going to give you *a . . . good . . . time!*" She never said anything to him about his mother, but, bit by bit, one time or another, he overheard how she talked to other people—how she pitied him because his mother had deprived him of the toys and candy and clothes every child needs to be happy. "Think of it! He had *never* been to the circus! And he had never had a toy with wheels—not so much as a little express wagon! Nor any fun either. His mother was a Quaker. She didn't know *how* to have a good time!"

Henry's stepmother, whom he was taught to call by her pet name of Tulip—knew all about having a good time. She saw to it that Henry's father did, too. They were always dressing to go out in the evening, to dinner, to a country club dance, to a restaurant in a city forty miles away, to the theater—or perhaps for a week end in New York. Henry learned to dodge them for a few days after a New York week end because they had headaches and were cross. "I can't ever make up to my poor husband," Henry heard her say to other people, "for those poky moldy years of his first marriage."

Once a visitor asked her, idly, "Did you ever know his first wife?" Tulip's face darkened. "Yes, I did! That is, I met her once or twice. I remember her very well." Her voice was sharp.

"What was she like?"

"I always hated her!" cried Tulip. "She was one of those horrid women who are satisfied no matter what they have! She was always smiling. I hated her."

Another time, some years later, one evening after a good many cocktails, when talking to a man who excited her, she said she didn't care *who* knew that she fell dead in love with Henry the first time she saw him, a young employee in her father's office, and had nearly died of jealousy of the plain, dowdy Quakeress he was married to. "It runs in our family," she said proudly, "to have strong feelings. No Quaker blood in *us!*" And sure enough, by and by, her feeling for the man who excited her grew so strong that Henry's father shot himself.

But that was later, after Henry had grown up, or almost, and was in college.

Nobody had ever thought of such a thing as his going to college— Tulip because it seemed to her a hideous waste of time for anybody to bother with books; Henry because he was lazy, spoiled, and ignorant; Henry's father because he always thought just what Tulip did. As to the rest of the people who knew Henry and his father and Tulip, half of them were sure the kid would be in the reform school by the time he was old enough for college, and the other half couldn't see any more sense in book-learning than Tulip did.

Eight or nine years after her marriage, Tulip began to get tired of Henry. It was just about the time when she had finally succeeded in killing and completely burying his mother. Perhaps she knew this. Perhaps it was because he had all of a sudden stopped being a cute kid with cute ways and had grown into a gangling, clumsy, long-legged boor with the worst manners in this world. So Tulip told his father that though it simply broke her heart to be separated from the dear boy, she felt he ought to be in a good military school where he would be handled by *men*. Of course his father felt so too, as soon as Tulip told him to.

From that time on, Henry had no home and no mother and no father. In June he went from his prep school into a summer camp, and in September back to prep school, staying in Tulip's house only

a few days in between times. The first year he was at school was one
long horror to him. Badly trained, badly taught, badly spoiled as he
was, nobody liked him, and he hated everybody. The school was what
is called "well run," that is, run so that on the surface nothing could
be seen of what was really going on in any boy's life. Setting-up
exercises, cold showers, meals, drill, classes, study-hall, drill, hikes,
cold showers, chapel, games, drill, meals—every minute of the day
was spent in doing something active—*left!* right! *left!* right!—under
the eye of a supervising officer, and plenty of them, one to every six
boys. All that was Henry (and a good deal of him had accumulated
by this time) lay festering in the dark, far beneath the school's flaw-
less varnish.

His first summer camp began in the same way—why not, the camp
being run to make extra money by three of the officer-teachers on
the school faculty. But it was worse, because by this time adolescence—
whatever we mean by that—had come to him. In the well-run school
it meant that when those strong qualities which were to make Henry
a man of power, for good or evil, came violently into life, they found
him shut up in solitary confinement in a lightless cave. Like waves
from an ocean immeasurably greater than Henry, they thundered
along under the low rocky roof of the cavern which was now the
only place the real Henry had to live in—flooding over him, lifting
him off his feet, half drowning him, battering him against the sides
of his prison till he was all one bruise. At the meeting where the
officer-teacher-counselors of camp put their heads together about
how to keep the boys in order, "Watch out for that Henry," they said.
"He's got bad blood in him." So the guard set on Henry redoubled.
To the right and to the left of him, wherever he was, stretched ranks
of other boys, under the same discipline as he—they called it discipline—a watchful teacher-officer at each end of the row. It was a
very well-run camp. His mother, quite forgotten, lay in her grave far
away.

But one of the teachers liked to go fishing. One morning in July,
he felt like having a day on the lake and needed a boy to help
him with the other oar of the heavy lake boat. Henry, because he
was big for his age and because nobody else wanted him around,
was told off for this duty. After they were well out on the water,
the teacher, guided by those unseen weather signs legible to fisher-
men, decided that he would have better luck if he fished from an
island at the other end of the lake.

By the time they had landed there, the teacher had thought of

a way to get rid of the disagreeable hulking fellow who would certainly make a noise if he stayed near. He said in a tone of imitation
geniality, "Wouldn't you like to try your hand too? Take this rod,
and go around to the cove at the other end of the island, and see
how you make out with casting." He added indulgently, longing
for a whole day of quiet for his own fishing, "Take your lunch
along so if you have good luck you won't need to stop."

Henry, fishing rod in hand, clumped heavily on his big feet through
the woods to the other end of the island. It was not more than
a mile away from the fisherman-teacher. But every step of that
distance took Henry into a realm where since his little boyhood
he had not in a waking moment set foot, not once—into quiet, solitude,
and silence. A huge weather-beaten granite rock, shaded by an age-
scarred oak tree, lay like a fallen giant, half in the water of the
cove, half on the beach. Henry climbed up on it and hung his
feet over the edge, his huge clumsy feet that made him awkward
and showed he was to be great in stature among men. He fastened
the imitation fly on his line as he had seen his teacher do, and
made a few casts, with no success. It was not very interesting. Presently his arm tired. Having no watchful supervising teacher near
him to keep him active, he laid his rod down.

It was great, he thought, not to have anybody around to spoil
his sitting and doing nothing, if he wanted to. He looked down
idly at his feet. Funny how light it made a person feel not to be
slogging along, *left,* right, *left,* right, hammering down hard and
heavy on the earth. It must make your feet surprised to be floating,
nothing but air under them. He swung them idly to and fro to
feel their lightness. Then, forgetting this, he let them hang down
and stared at the sunlit water, brim-brim-brimming up on the beach
of the little cove where he sat, quiet and still for the first time since—
he could not remember when he had ever sat so still as this. Back
of him a bird dropped a sleepy summer note into the woods. After
a while he slid down on the warm rock, stretched himself out and
put his arms under his head. Strange, as he looked up into the strong,
crooked, rough old oak branches, strange how light he began to feel,
all of him, not just his feet. The rock was so strong. It bore him
up as though his heavy, overgrown body that was too big for him
weighed no more than that of a little tiny boy on his mother's lap.

He lay thus a long time. An hour? Two hours? Once, looking up
at the arch of the sky, bent over the lake, he thought that it was as
blue as a piece of blue ribbon.

He had lain thus, motionless and relaxed, for most of the morning, when he shut his eyes, pinched them shut, with a shudder. He had felt surging towards him one of those frightful waves of feeling that left him battered and bruised to the bone. But this was not shut up and driven with savage force along a tortuous narrow channel deep in blackness. It had the whole universe to spread out in. It flooded over him from everywhere, from the sky, from the earth, the kind sun, the lake's calm stillness. He had been relaxed too long to stiffen himself against it, and when it reached him—soft, warm, mighty, gentle—it floated him off as light as air, up and up like a thistledown into the vast spaciousness above him where there was room for everything! Those terrific wants were only a part, a small part, of him, of living, of what was before him. There was room for them, for everything—sunny, limitless room in which life's different parts fitted together in their true proportions, made one shapely whole which a lonely big boy almost a man need not dread, need not fight, need not be ashamed of.

The knot that had been strangling him, loosened, loosened, fell away.

When he was dropped again, light as thistledown, on the strong sustaining rock, Henry, big overgrown boy though he was, rolled over on his face and began to cry. There was no one to hear him. He could cry as much as he wanted to.

When he had cried as much as he wanted to, and sat up again, he felt better—why, he could hardly believe it, he felt so much better. And, good gosh! was he hungry! He ate his lunch to the last crumb, strolling up and down the little beach. Then he tried seriously to fish and did catch two rock bass, little fellows. After that he went in swimming, and after that he just lazed around, playing with pebbles. Some, the flat ones, he skipped across the water. The pretty rounded ones he arranged vaguely in designs, stars and diamonds and things, thinking to himself how much better everything looked when it was arranged in a pattern.

When he heard the teacher coming, crashing through the woods, he was a little ashamed of being such a kid and brushed his hand back and forth to smooth out the designs he had made.

"Well—?" asked the fisherman-teacher. He looked at the two bass, small ones. It was four o'clock. They had been fishing for eight hours. He himself had nine pounds and a half of fish. His face told Henry what he thought of Henry as a fisherman. But he had passed examinations in pedagogic theory, remembered that a teacher must give his students plenty of encouragement and always think of something positive not negative to say, so he smiled and said in a cracked, imitation-cheery voice, "Pretty good, Henry. Pre-t-t-tty good, for the first time."

But Henry didn't hate his falseness and pretense, nor want to strangle him for it, as he would yesterday. He thought to himself with sympathy, "Gosh, it must be fierce to have a job like that."

After that most of Henry's leisure time was spent in fishing. He never became very expert at it, that is, he never brought back from his long solitary days of angling any very big catches. But he continued to go. And fishing is such a right masculine sport that nobody at school, or camp, or even in Tulip's house, interfered with it. They interfered with him less anyhow after that first summer. There was less need to. "He was," they said proudly at faculty meetings, "coming out all right after all." As with so many other troublesome boys, the right school turned the trick, gave him just what he needed. He turned the corner of adolescence without disaster and became another person, a credit to their teaching. They were actually sorry to have him graduate.

When he did, he told his father and Tulip that he was going to study to be a doctor. They tried their best to dissuade him from this absurd idea. And so did everybody else who knew him. Tulip told him a thousand times, earnestly, "Now, Henry, don't be foolish! You *know* you'll never be able to stick it through! Don't you realize that it would take *eight years!* You'd simply die of boredom! You'd *never* have yourself a good time! Not once. Eight of the very best years of your life, when you might be having the best times, you'd be leaning over sick people and catching their diseases. Wherever in this world did you *get* such a crazy idea, anyhow?"

She repeated this with variations a good many times. Every time, when her breath gave out and she had to stop, Henry answered her sheepishly that he guessed he could stick it out all right. But he never told her wherever in this world he got such an idea, because he did not know.

Stick it out he did for those endless eight years, during five of which he had to support himself, his father dying and leaving no money. Tulip, of course, felt no call to spend her substance on another woman's son. Twice he had to drop out and get a business job to make enough money to go on with.

He was a big, grave, rather graceless man of twenty-seven when he finally had M.D. to put after his name, and began the practice that was to bring him such rich rewards, was to bring his patients help, protection, consolation. Old Dr. Hepplewaite took him in at once as assistant—"I don't say Henry's brilliant. But there's something—perhaps something about his character—that'll be useful to him in the practice of medicine."

There certainly turned out to be, although people differed as to what its name was. Some of his patients called it dogged persistence. "Dr. Burrage just *won't* let go of a patient," they said, comforted when he came lumbering into the sick-room. But others insisted it was his fearlessness. "You can feel it all over Dr. Burrage—he simply doesn't know what fear is," they said. And indeed when someone once asked him, he said he didn't know but that that was so, he really couldn't ever remember being seriously afraid.

He was a very fortunate man, one of those to whom the right things happen. Good luck seemed to be with him in all his personal relations, as well as in his professional work. He did not marry one of the stylish, lively, professionally-coifed society girls who fluttered around the young doctor as he began to succeed, any one of whom would have brought him money, social prestige, and influence. To their annoyance he married a quiet, brown-eyed little thing ("Not even neat! You should see her hair. It's always falling down!" they said scornfully) who brought him nothing but a heart so pure and loving that when she died young, it went on beating faithfully in the doctor's memory, making him happier than any flesh-and-blood woman he might have married to take her place.

All alone in life now, good luck . . . the greatest of good luck . . . led him to adopt the orphan who turned out such an ideal son. The quiet, undemonstrative love between the older and the younger man was so serene and steady that all who knew them saw their own paths more clearly in its light. Yet who else would have picked out that child, of all others! He had been a regular little demon, the doctor's older patients said when they told the story, as they often did. Left an orphan at four, he had been taken in by a family who did not want him—they had plenty of nice children of their own, older, and were dismayed by this passionate, bad little boy. But they were distant relations of his parents, and there seemed to be nobody else willing to give him a home. Dr. Burrage must have seen him, many's the time, as he came and went in that house, taking care of the old grandmother who was paralyzed and bedridden. And he knew of course, the way doctors know everything, that the little boy was not a welcome addition to the family. But he had never seemed to pay any attention to him till one day, stepping into the house, he found the children—the grownups too—in the midst of a frantic storm. The little fellow—the one who grew up to be Dr. Wright—was in a frightful tantrum, acting like a mad dog, screaming and kicking and scratching and biting the other children. The father rushed in just as Dr. Burrage arrived, and pulled the child away. The mother was crying and saying, "Just look what he's done to poor little Betty's face. *This* time he's got to be punished! If I have to do it myself he's going to be whipped till he—"

But the doctor had taken one long step forward and snatched the child into his own arms. "Leave him alone!" he said. "Don't you touch him. Leave him to me!"

No, he never claimed to have had any sort of prophetic divination about what the little boy's qualities really were. In later years, when people asked him, he always said honestly, "Why, I couldn't tell you what made me do it. I really haven't any idea. I just did."

Scylla
and Charybdis

*W*hen the elders of our family could think of nothing else to worry about they put in their time to good advantage on little Cousin Maria Pearl Manley. Yes—Maria Pearl—that was really the poor child's name, given in baptism. You can see that her troubles began early. That name was symbolical of what her life was to be, sharply divided between her mother's family (they were the ones who insisted on the Maria) and her father's folks, who stood out for the Pearl. Her father had died before she was born, and her mother lived only a few months after the baby came, and was so mortally ill that no one thought of naming the poor little girl. It was after her mother's death, when the two hostile families could collect themselves, that the long struggle over the child began by giving her that name.

Thereafter she was Maria for six months of the year, the period when she stayed with the Purdons; and Pearl the other half-year, when she was with her father's family, the Manleys. "The poor little tyke, not even a fixed name of her own," my grandmother used to say, pitying the child's half-yearly oscillations between those two utterly dissimilar houses "where there's nothing the way it should be in either one!" The circle of compassionate elders used to continue, "Dear, dear! What can the poor little thing ever learn, with such awful examples always before her eyes?"

Now, I don't deny that the elders of every tribe always are—always have been—and probably always will be, groundlessly alarmed by the upbringing of the rising generation. But in this case their forebodings seemed fully justified. Those two houses which formed the horizon of Maria Pearl's life were certainly extravagant examples of how not to conduct life. The Purdon grandfather and grandmother and aunt were the strictest kind of church people (the kind who make you want to throw a brick through the church windows), narrow, self-righteous, Old Testament folks, who dragged little Maria (the "Pearl" was never pronounced inside their doors) to church and Sunday school and prayer meeting and revivals and missionary meetings, and made her save all her pennies for the heathen. Not that she had many to save, for the Purdons, although more than well-to-do, were stingier than any other family in town. They loved money, it tore at the very fibers of their being to part with it, and they avoided this mental anguish with considerable skill. The dark, plain, well-fitting garments which clothed little Maria were never bought, but made over out of her grandmother's clothes; the soap which kept her clothes immaculately clean had cost no money, but was part of the amazing household economies in which old Mrs. Purdon was expert and into which she introduced Maria with conscientious care. The child learned to darn and patch and how to make soap out of left-over bits of fat, and how to use the apple culls for jelly and how, year after year, to retrim last season's hat for this.

From morning till night she lived in a close, airless round of intensive housekeeping and thrift. She spread newspapers down over the rugs, so the sun should not fade them; she dried every scrap of orange peel to use as kindling, she saved the dried beef jars to use for jams, she picked berries all day long instead of playing, and then sat up late with Aunt Maria and Grandmother, sorting them over and canning them on the stove in the woodshed, to avoid litter in the kitchen. She always wore gingham aprons, even to school, which no other child did, and she was treated as though she had offended against the Holy Ghost, if she forgot to wash her rubbers and put them in their place in the closet under the stairs. In the family housework she was held to a rigorous performance of her allotted share. She made her bed with the fear of the Lord in her heart lest a single wrinkle might not be smoothed out of the sheets. She poked desperately into the corners of every window she washed and polished. She ran anxious fingers over the dishes she wiped to be sure they had that glass-smooth surface which only repeated rinsings in very hot water can give. Then when all was done, her reward was to take her seat in their appallingly neat sitting room and, to the accompaniment of Aunt Maria's reading aloud out of a church paper, to set tiny stitches in the stout, unbleached cotton of which her underwear was made. They were really dreadful, the six months she passed with her mother's people.

But the other half-year was scarcely better, although she might have journeyed to another planet with less change in her surroundings. When the day came, the first of January, for her departure from the Purdon household, her solidly-constructed little trunk was filled with her solidly-constructed little clothes, her hair was once more re-braided to an even harder finish, her face was once more polished with the harsh, home-made soap, and her nails were cut to the quick. "It's the *last* time the poor child will have any decent care, till she comes back," Grandmother Purdon would say bitterly, but-toning up with exactitude the stout, plain warm little coat, and pulling down over Maria's ears the firmly knit toque of dark blue wool. They all went to the station to make sure she took the right train, and put her, each of them separately, in the hands of the Conductor. They kissed her goodby, all but Grandfather, who shook hands with her hard. It was at that moment that Maria's frozen little heart felt a faint warmth from the great protecting affection they had for her, which underlay the rigor of their training and which they hid with such tragic completeness.

The first day of the arrival at the Manleys' was always a dream of delight! To emerge from the silent rigidity of the Purdon house into the cheerful, easy-going noise of the Manley home, to exchange the grim looks of Grandmother Purdon for the exuberant caresses of Grandmother Manley; to leave behind all stringent admonitions to put your wraps on a certain hook, and to be allowed to drop them down on the floor where you stood . . . Little Pearl (she was never called Maria by the Manleys) felt herself rebounding into all the sunshine and good nature, as a rubber ball rebounds from a hard stone wall. She flung herself around Aunt Pearl's neck, and paid back with interest the "forty thousand kisses" which were the tradi-tion in that home. She flung herself into play with the innumerable little cousins, who cluttered up the floor; for there was always a married aunt or two back home, with her family, while an invisible uncle-by-marriage tried somewhere in a vague distance to get a hypothetical job. She flung herself into her bed at night joyfully reveling in the fact that the sheet corners were not turned squarely, and that the pillowcase had last seen the washtub on about the same date that Aunt Carry's husband had last had a job. It was a carefree dream to go to bed whenever she pleased—eleven o'clock if that suited her taste—with nobody to tell her to wash, or brush her teeth, or comb her hair; and to lie there watching Aunt Carry and Aunt Pearl, who always sat up till midnight at least, putting their hair in curlpapers and talking about the way the neighbor next door treated his wife. This was life!

But already the very next morning the dream was not quite so iridescent, as with no one to wake her, she opened her eyes at twenty minutes of nine, and knew that she had to be at school at nine! She sprang up, shivering in the cold room (Grandfather Manley never could manage the furnace, and also there were periods when there was mighty little money to buy coal), and started to claw herself into her clothes. But always just at first she forgot the Manley ways, and neglected to collect everything she had taken off, and put it under her pillow, the only spot in which you could keep things for yourself in that comfortably communistic family. Her shoes were gone, her nice new calfskin school shoes. She went flying out, comb in hand, tearing at the tangles in her hair, asking if anybody had seen her shoes. Aunt Carry, still in her nightgown, with a smeary baby in her arms, said, yes, she'd let her Elmer have them to run down to the grocery store to get some bread. Somehow they'd got out of bread and poor Aunt Pearl had had to go off to her work with only some crackers to eat. Surely little Pearl didn't grudge the loan of her shoes to her cousin. The bread was for all of them, and Elmer couldn't find his shoes, and anyhow one of them had a big hole in it and the snow was deep.

"But, Aunt Carry, how can I get to school? I'll be late!"

"Well, gracious, what if you are! Don't be so fussy! Time was made for slaves!" That was Aunt Carry's favorite motto, which she was always citing, and for citing which there were plenty of occasions in her life. Little Pearl thought somewhat resentfully, as she rummaged in her trunk for her other shoes, that if Aunt Carry had to enter the schoolroom late and get scolded, she'd think differently about time! But anyhow it was fun to wear her best shoes if she liked, and to watch their patent leather tips twinkling as she scurried about. They twinkled very fast during that quarter of an hour, as Pearl collected her wraps (her mittens she never did find after that day) and tried to scare up something for breakfast in the disordered kitchen, where the cat, installed on the table, was methodically licking the dirty plates clean. Pearl was not so lucky, and had to go off to school with a cracker in one hand and a piece of marshmallow cake in the other. The less said about her hair the better! Grandmother Manley's "forty thousand kisses" were not quite so wonderful this morning as they had been last night.

At noon Pearl ran home, her stomach in her heels, all one voracious demand for good food. Aunt Carry was crocheting by the window and there was no sign of any lunch. "Mercy me!" cried Grandmother Manley, "Is it noon? Why, how the morning has gone!" And then with the utmost compunction they both rushed out into the kitchen and began to hurry with all their might to get something for Pearl to eat. The kitchen fire was pretty low, and there were no potatoes cooked, and Aunt Carry had forgotten to order any eggs, and the milk bottle had been left outside and was frozen hard. Hurry as they might and apologize to Pearl almost with tears as they did, it was very little that Pearl had eaten when she went back to school, and she knew well enough that they would forget tomorrow, just as they had today. No, already Pearl felt that life could not be made *wholly* out of kisses and good nature. By nightfall, her thin kid shoes were rather scuffed and very wet, with a break in one of the patent leather tips where Cousin Tom had stepped on it, in a scuffle with his brother. Little Pearl nursed her sore toe and broken shoe with a weary feeling.

Always at the end of the six months with the Manleys, Pearl was nearly a nervous wreck. She was behind in her lessons, since there was not a quiet spot in the house to study, and even if there had been you couldn't escape from the noise of the trombone, which Aunt Carry's oldest was learning to play; she was underweight and anemic for lack of regular food and enough sleep . . . it wasn't much use to go to bed when nobody else did, and Aunt Pearl and Aunt Carry always visited in more than audible voices as they put up their hair in curlers; she had nothing to wear (since nothing had been renewed or mended) except a blue silk dress which Grandfather Manley had bought for her in a fit of affection, and some mostly-lace underwear which Aunt Carry had sat up till all hours making for her, so that "she should have something pretty like the other girls!" But for an active little girl, mostly-lace underwear soon was reduced to the quality of mosquito netting; and a blue silk dress in the Manleys' house was first cousin to Sir Walter Raleigh's cloak in the mud-puddle.

With all the family she had been night after night to the movies and not infrequently was kept up afterwards by the hysterics of little Nelly, Aunt Carry's nervous, high-strung five-year-old, who saw men with revolvers pointed at her, and desperadoes about to bind and gag her, till Pearl more than half saw them too, and dreamed of them afterwards. She had suffered the terrible humiliation of having the teacher send her home with a note saying that her hair must be washed and kept in better order, a humiliation scarcely lessened by the outraged affection of the Manleys, who had taken her into their loving arms, to moan over their darling's hurt feelings. She had thereafter made frantic efforts to keep her own hair in order, with what brush and comb she could salvage out of the jetsam in the room which was at once hers and the aunts' bedroom; but if she complained that her hair ribbons disappeared, or were crumpled in a corner of the drawer, she was told comfortably, not to be fussy. "For goodness' sakes, don't make such a fuss about things! Folks that do never have a minute's comfort in life, nor nobody else in the house either."

Yes, it was a rather pale, wild-eyed little Pearl, who on the first day of July scrambled together into her trunk what she could find, put on the hat which had been so bright and pretty when Aunt Pearl gave it to her at Easter, and which now after two months with the Manleys looked like a floor cloth. She did not put her hands over her ears to deaden a little the volume of noise as they all crowded about her in the station to say their vociferous goodbys, but that was only because she did not want to hurt their feelings. The instant she was in the train, she hid her face in her arms, quivering all over with nervous tension. Oh, the noise the Manleys always made over everything, and the confusion they were always in, when they tried to do anything, colliding with each other, and dropping things, and squealing and screaming! And it was all right for them to be warm-hearted and generous—but when they slathered money on ice cream, and then didn't have enough to pay for her ticket, till they'd borrowed it . . . !

Well, then there was the re-entrance into the Purdon house, the beautiful, fragrant cleanliness of everything, the dustless order, her own room, with smooth, white sheets, and her own safe closet into which nobody would ever plunge rummaging. And Aunt Maria so quiet and calm, with her nice low voice, and Grandmother Purdon so neat with her white lace collar, and her lovely white hair so well-brushed, and oh, the good things to eat . . . To sit down to a well-ordered table, with a well-cooked savory mutton stew, and potatoes neither watery nor underdone, and clear apple jelly quivering in a glass dish! And the clean, clean plates! Had Maria ever complained of having to rinse the dishes too often! She remembered the dried-on bits of food always to be felt on the Manley plates . . . !

The first evening too was always dreamlike, the quiet, deft despatching of the dishes, in the kitchen shining with cleanliness, and then all the evening free, and so quiet, so blessedly quiet, with no trombone, and no whoops of chatter or boisterous crying and laughing; no piano banging (except perhaps Aunt Maria softly playing a hymn or two), no children overturning chairs and slamming doors, no one falling up or downstairs, no crash of breaking crockery from the kitchen . . . little Maria sat on the well-swept porch behind the well-trained vines and soaked herself in the peace and quiet.

But by the next morning, the shine was a little off. When Aunt Maria came to wake her at half past six, *half past six* . . . why, no one at Grandfather Manley's thought of stirring till eight! And she was expected to wash and dress . . . not a button unbuttoned or a hair out of place under penalty of a long lecture on neatness . . . and "do" her room, even to wiping off the woodwork, and make her bed. Heavens! How fussy they were about those old corners! All this before she had a bit of breakfast. Then, breakfast with everybody's whole soul fixed on the work to be done, and nobody so much as dimly aware that it was a glorious, sunny, windy, summer day outside. Maria's heart sank, sank, sank, as she drank her perfectly made chocolate and ate her golden-brown toast, till it struck the dismal level where it usually lived during the Purdon half-year. "Come, Maria, don't loiter over your food. The only way to get the work done is to go right at it!"

"Oh, Maria, do you call that folding your napkin? I call it crumpling it into a ball."

"You forgot to put your chair back against the wall, Maria. If we each do faithfully our share of what is to be done, it will be easier for us all."

"No, the *spoons* go there . . . mercy, no! not the forks!"

"Don't twitch the curtain so as you go by. It takes all the fresh out of it. I only ironed them yesterday."

"Why, Maria, whistling! Like a little street boy!"

The July sun might shine and the wind blow outside, inside the house it was always gray, windless November weather. She felt herself curl up like a little autumn leaf, and, with a dry rattle, blow about the rooms before the chill admonitory breath of Grandmother Purdon and Aunt Maria.

Yes, the family elders were right in pitying her, as a child brought up just as badly as it was possible to be; and nobody was surprised or blamed her a bit, when she got out of both backgrounds as rapidly and as unceremoniously as she could, by making a very early marriage with an anonymous young man, somebody she had met at a high school dance. He seemed just like any young man, from the glimpse of him, which was all we had, before their marriage; but nobody knew a thing about his character or whether he would make a good husband. And, indeed, it seemed doubtful whether Maria Pearl would be any sort of wife or homemaker. How could she have learned anything about rational living, the poor little tyke, hustled from one bad example to another through all the impressionable years of her life? Suppose she kept house like the Manleys! Horrors! Or suppose she took after the Purdons! Her poor husband!

Nothing of the sort! There's not a happier home anywhere in the country than hers, nor a better housekeeper, nor a wiser mother. It's a perfect treat to visit in her cheerful, sunny, orderly house, or to talk with her well-brought-up, jolly children, or to see her well-fed, satisfied husband. And she herself is a joy to the eye, stout and rosy and calm. She is neither fussy nor slack, neither stingy nor extravagant, neither cold and repressed, nor slushy and sentimental.

How did it happen? Probably Maria Pearl doesn't know. But now, with the wisdom of hindsight, I can make a good guess. Those elderly crepe-hangers had reason enough to expect disaster . . . so far as their information and understanding went. What they did not allow for was the fact that every honeymoon voyage . . . every single one . . . has to battle head winds, treacherous crosscurrents, whirlpools . . . has to zigzag its way through a maze of hidden reefs. And yet a really astounding number avoid shipwreck. Perhaps it does a young pilot no harm . . . perhaps it helps . . . to have been warned beforehand that it won't do to lash the helm, lean over the taffrail and watch the sunlit waves go by. Evidently Maria Pearl has one of those fortunate natures which can learn from experience. This capacity does exist . . . occasionally . . . even in our poor dumb human race! The seesaw of her childhood, with its thrilling, soaring "ups" and its inevitable, spine-jarring "downs," did not throw her into a tail spin of frustration. Far from it. Somehow the shock treatment of those years roused her intelligence, taught her to steer a course.

Whenever the routine of her housekeeping begins to set too hard, and she feels like flying at muddy-footed, careless children with the acrimony natural to the good housekeeper, the memory of forlorn little Pearl among the Purdons softens and humanizes her words. And when the balance begins to swing the other way, when she tastes that first delicious, poisonous languor of letting things slide, when her Manley blood comes to the top, she has other memories to steady her. I have seen her, sitting at the breakfast table after the children are off to school, begin to sag in her chair and reach with an indolent gesture for a tempting novel; and I knew what was in her mind as she sprang up with a start and began briskly to clear off the table and plan the lunch.

The Rainy Day, the Good
Mother, and the Brown Suit

And yet she had done exactly what the books on child training assured mothers would ward off trouble on a stormy day. She had copied off the list of raw materials recommended by the author of "The Happy Child Is the Active Child": colored paper, blunt scissors, paste, pencils, crayons, plasticine—she had bought them all, well ahead of time, and had brought them out this morning after breakfast, when the rain settled down with that all-day pour. But, unlike the children in the books, Caroline and Freddy and little Priscilla had not received these treasures open-mouthed with pleasure, nor had they quietly and happily exercised their creative instinct, leaving their mother free to get on with her work. Perhaps her children hadn't as much of that instinct as other people's. At least, after a little listless fingering of colored paper Freddy turned away. "Say, Mother, I want to put on my brown suit," he said. Little did she dream then what the brown suit was to cost her. She answered casually, piling up the breakfast dishes, "I washed that suit yesterday, Freddy, and the rain came. So it's not dry yet."

He trotted back and forth after her as she stepped to and fro with the slightly nervous haste of a competent woman who has planned a busy morning. "But, Mother," he persisted, "I *want* to put it on. I *want* to." He raised his voice, "Mother, I want to put my brown suit on."

From the pantry where she had just discovered that the cream she had planned to use for the dessert was soured, she answered him with some asperity, "I told you it isn't dry yet!" But she reminded herself of the excellent rule, "Always make children understand the reasons for your refusals," and added, "It's hanging on the line on the side porch. Look out there, dear. You can see for yourself how wet it is."

He did as she bade him, and stood staring out, leaning his forehead on the glass.

Yet a little later as she stood before the telephone, grocery list in hand, he tugged at her skirt and as Central asked, "What number, please?" he said with plaintive obstinacy, "Mother, I *do* want to put on my brown suit."

She said with considerable warmth, "Somerset three six one. For heaven's sake, Freddy, that suit is WET. Is this Perkins and Larsen? How *could* you put it on! What price are your grapefruit today? Freddy, let go of my skirt. Grapefruit, I said. No, no— G for glory, r for run—"

But when she turned away from her struggle with the clerk, Freddy plucked at her hand and whimpered in the nasal fretting tone she had sworn (before she had children) no child of hers should ever use, "Mother, I waa-a-nt to pu-u-t my brown—"

"*Don't whine,*" she told him with a ferocity so swift and savage that he recoiled and was silent. She thought remorsefully, "Oh, dear, to scold is just as bad as to whine."

Going back into the pantry she recalled with resentment that psychologists of family life say that children's behavior—nine times out of ten—is only a reflection of their mother's moods. She did not believe a word of it. "Did *I* start this?" she asked herself unanswerably, and, "How can anybody help being irritated when they're so perfectly unreasonable!"

But she fervently wanted to be a very good mother. She remembered that the basis of child-rearing is to understand each child at all times, and went resolutely back into the other room, determined to understand Freddy, if it were her last act. Disconcertingly, it was not Freddy but Priscilla who ran to take her hand, who said pleadingly, timidly, as if appealing from the cruel decree of a tyrant, "Mummy, Fred *does* so want to have you let him wear his brown suit this morning!" The mother contained herself, collected the children—three-year-old Priscilla, five-year-old Fred, six-and-a-half-year-old Caroline—led them to the window and said, "Now just look at that suit! How could I let Freddy wear anything that's as wet as sop?"

At least that was what she thought she said. What the children distinctly heard was, "You're in the wrong, wrong, wrong. And I am right, right, right, as I always am. There's no use your trying to get around that!"

They stared gloomily out at this idea rather than at the wet clothes. Their mother went on, "What in the world does Fred *want* to wear his brown suit for, anyhow? What's the matter with the suit he's got on?"

What the children heard was, "No matter what Freddy said his reason was, I'd soon show you it was all foolishness." They attempted no answer, shaken as they were by wave after invisible wave of her impatience to be done with them and at something else. Indeed she was impatient. Why not, with her morning work all waiting to be done. She held her children for a moment with the bullying eye of a drill sergeant, and then said, challengingly, *"Well—?"* She meant, and they knew she meant, "I hope you realize that I have you beaten."

Something in Fred—it was something rather valiant, although his mother had another name for it—exploded with a crash. His round face grew grim and black. He looked savagely at his mother, thrust out his lower jaw and, keeping his eyes ragingly on hers, kicked a footstool, viciously, as if he were kicking her.

"Fred-*dy*," she said in a voice meant to cow him. But he was not cowed. He kicked again with all his might, looking at his mother and hating her.

And then—he was only a little boy—he broke. His hard defiant face crumpled up into despair. He crooked his arm to hide his suffering from his mother—from his mother!—and turned away to lean against the wall in the silent, dry, inexplicable misery which often ended what his mother called "Fred's tantrums." Little Priscilla began a whimpering. Caroline put her hands up to her face and hung her head.

Their mother thought, her nerves taut with exasperation, "I'd just like to see one of those child-specialists manage *my* children on a rainy day! They'd find out a thing or two!" But she loved her children. She loved them dearly. With her next breath she was ashamed of being angry with them. The tears came to her eyes and an aching lump into her throat. Bewildered, dismayed, she asked herself, in the purest surprise, "Why, how did we get into this dreadful state? What can the trouble be?"

She went back into the pantry, took a long breath, took a drink of water, tried to relax her muscles, cast her mind back to the book about what to do on a rainy day. But she could recall nothing else in it but that advice about appealing to the creative instinct. She had tried that, and it had failed.

She heard the front door open. The voice of a young cousin, no special favorite of hers, cried, "Ye gods and little fishes, what weather!"

He slammed the door behind him. Although he was nineteen, he still slammed doors as if he were twelve. He had come as he sometimes did when it rained, to wait in the living room for the bus that took him to college. One of its stopping places was their corner.

Priscilla, the literal, asked, "What does 'gods and little fishes' mean?"

"Mean?" said the freshman, laughing and flinging his books and his raincoat down on the floor. "What do you mean, mean? You mean too much, Prissy. What does this mean?" As she began to wash the dishes the mother could see that he had flung his heels in the air and was walking on his hands. "He's too old for such foolishness," she thought severely. And sure enough, out of the pockets of his adult suit of clothes, now upside down, little-boy junk rattled down around his hands. The children squealed and made a rush towards the bits of string, dirty handkerchiefs, knives, fishhooks, nails, pieces of cork, screws and pencils. "No you don't!" said he, returning his feet to the floor with a bang. "Everything there is a part of an important enterprise."

"What's a 'portant enter—" began Priscilla.

"Whatever I do," he told her coolly, "were it only to make a mouse-trap. If *I* made mousetraps there'd be a four-strip concrete road to my door in a week's time, you bet. No mousetrap of mine would ever have let out Uncle Peter's mouse, believe me."

"What? Who? What's Uncle Peter's mouse?" clamored the children.

"Oh, surely you know that story. No child of our family gets brung up without hearing that one. No? Well, one morning when Uncle Peter and Aunt Molly came down to breakfast—Priscilla, do *not* ask who they were and where they lived, it's no matter—they found a mouse in their trap. It was the kind of trap that catches the mouse alive, so they got the cat, and they all went out on the porch to open the trap and let the cat catch the mouse. Priscilla, do *not* say this was horrid of them, it was, and I can't help it, but that was the way it happened and it was so long ago probably they didn't know any better. So there they all were"—he illustrated how tensely they stood, stooping over an imaginary trap—"the two children and Uncle Peter and Aunt Molly. And the cat. She was scrooched right close in front of the cage"—he quivered and crouched with such vivacity of acting that the children began to laugh—"while Uncle Peter s-l-o-w-l-y, s-l-o-w-l-y lifted the door of the trap till it was open enough for the mouse to get out." He drew a long breath and made a dramatic pause. The children gazed at him, mouths open, eyes unwinking. "And then—!" He sprang into the air. "The cat jumped!" He clutched at Fred. "Uncle Peter hollered!" He ran to Caroline and seized her arm.

"The children yelled bloody murder!" He flung Freddy and Priscilla to right and left. "Aunt Molly shrieked!" He sank back on the floor. "But the mouse was gone!"

He gazed with enormous solemnity at his spellbound listeners. "The cat was prowling around, sniffing and lashing her tail"—he sniffed the air and getting up on his hands and knees lashed an imaginary tail—"but—there—was—no—mouse."

He sat cross-legged and earnest and went on, "Well, Aunt Molly was terribly afraid of mice, and she always had the idea that all a mouse wanted to do was to run up folks' clothes, so she was sure the mouse had done that to one of them. So she took one child and then the other, shook them till their teeth nearly dropped out"—he shot out a long arm and seized Priscilla, Caroline, and Freddy one after the other, shaking them hard and setting them into giggling fits—"and put first one and then the other inside the house and shut the door, quick! Then she shook herself hard. And went into the house and shut the door. Then Uncle Peter shook *him*self hard. And went in quick and shut the door. And then they had breakfast, wondering all the while where that mouse could have gone to. And after they'd finished breakfast, Uncle Peter stood up to go to the office and took hold of the lower edge of his vest to pull it down"—he seized the lower edge of an imaginary vest vigorously and stood appalled, a frantic expression of horror on his face—"*and there was the mouse!*" The children shrieked. "It had been under the edge of his vest and when he grabbed the vest he put his hand right around it, and when he took his hand away the mouse was in it, squirming." He showed them how it squirmed, and then, speeding up to express-train speed, finished the story all in one breath. "And he was so rattled he flung it right away without looking to see where, and it went spang into Aunt Molly's face and she fainted dead away—and the mouse beat it so quick they never did see it again."

He grinned down at the children, literally rolling on the floor, as pleased with the story as they. "Say, kids, what-d'you-say we act it out? I've got a few minutes before bus time. Let's. Who'll be what? I'll be Uncle Peter. Priscilla, you be one of the children. Caroline, you be Aunt Molly—that's a swell part! You must yell your head off when I throw the mouse in your face. Fred, you be—"

"I'll be the cat," said Fred, scrambling to his feet.

So they acted out the little drama, throwing themselves passionately into their roles, Caroline so magnificent with her scream and faint at the end that Priscilla said, "Oh, *I* want to be Aunt Molly."

So they did it over again, Priscilla screeching as though she were being flayed alive, and fainting with fat arms and legs outstretched.

"I'd kind o' like to be Uncle Peter," said Fred.

"Okay by me," said the student. "I'll be the cat."

By the time they had finished it again they were out of breath, what with screaming and running and laughing and acting, and sank down together on the floor. Little by little their laughter subsided to a peaceful silence. Freddy sprawled half over the knobby knees of the tall boy, Priscilla was tucked away under his arm, Caroline leaned against him. From the pantry where, unheeded, the mother went on washing dishes, she thought jealously, "What do they see in him? That story is nothing but nonsense." And then—she was really an intelligent person—it came over her, "Why, that is just what they like in it."

Out of the silence, almost as though she were thinking aloud, little Priscilla murmured, "Freddy was bad this morning." There was compassion in her tone.

"What was eating him?" asked the student, not particularly interested.

"He wanted to wear his brown suit. And it was wet, and he couldn't. So he kicked the footstool and was bad."

"What's the point about the brown suit, old man?"

The question was put in a matter-of-fact tone of comradely interest. But even so Fred hesitated, opened his mouth, shut it, said nothing.

It was Caroline who explained, "It's got a holster pocket at the back where he can carry his pretend pistol."

The mother in the pantry, astounded, remorseful, reproachful, cried out to herself, "Oh, why didn't he tell *me* that!" But she knew very well why he had not. She had plenty of brains.

"Oh, I see," said the student. "But why don't you sew a holster pocket on the pants you've got on, boy? On all your pants. It's nothing to sew on pockets. You girls, too. You might as well have holster pockets. When I was your age, I had sewed on dozens of pockets." He took a long breath, and began to rattle off nonsense with an intensely serious face and machine-gun speed: "My goodness, by the time I was fourteen I had sewed on five hundred and thirty-four pockets, and one small watch-pocket but I don't count that one. Didn't you ever hear how I put myself through college sewing on pockets? And when I was graduated, the President of the Pocket Sewing Union of America sent for me, and—"

"But you've only just got into college," Priscilla reminded him earnestly.

(In the pantry, her mother thought, with a stab of self-knowledge, "Why, is that *me*? Was I being literal like that . . . with my colored paper and crayons? How about *my* creative instinct? Did I show any when I insisted on sticking exactly to what the book advised? Why didn't I think up something else to try!")

"Priscilla," said the college student, sternly, "don't you know what happens to children who say 'go-up-bald-head' to their elders—oh, but—" He clutched his tousled hair, and said, imitating Priscilla's serious little voice, "Oh, but I'm not bald yet, am I?"

A horn sounded in the street. He sprang up, tumbling the children roughly from him, snatched his books. "There's my bus." The door slammed.

The children came running to find their mother. "Oh, Mother, Mother, can we have some cloth to make pockets out of?"

She was ready for them. "I've got lots of it that'll be just right," she said, telling herself wryly, "I can get an idea all right if somebody'll push it half way down my throat."

But for the rest of the morning, as the children sat happily exercising their creative instinct by sewing on queer pockets in queer places on their clothes, she was thinking with sorrow, "It's not fair. That great lout of a boy without a care in the world takes their fancy with his nonsense, and they turn their backs on me entirely. I represent only food and care—and refusals. I work my head off for them—and the first stranger appeals to them more."

Yet after lunch they put their three heads together and whispered and giggled, and "had a secret." Then, Caroline at their head, they trotted over to the sofa where their mother had dropped down to rest. "Mother," said Caroline in her little-girl bird-voice, "wouldn't *you* like to play Uncle-Peter-and-Aunt-Molly-and-the-mouse? You didn't have a single chance to this morning—not once—you were working so." They looked at her with fond shining eyes of sympathy. "Come on, Mother! You'll love it!" they encouraged her.

A lump came into her throat again—a good lump this time. She swallowed. "Oh, thanks, children. I know I'd like to. What part are you going to have me take?"

The secret came out then. They let Freddy tell her, for it had been his inspiration. He looked proudly at his mother and offered her his best. "Ye gods and little fishes! We're going to let you be the *mouse!*"

She clasped her hands. "Oh, children!" she cried.

From their pride in having pleased her, a gust of love-madness blew across them, setting them to fall upon their mother like soft-pawed kittens wild with play, pushing her back on the pillows, hugging her, worrying her, rumpling her hair, kissing her ears, her nose, whatever they could reach.

But Priscilla was not sure they had been clear. She drew away. "You don't have to get caught, you know," she reassured her mother earnestly. "The mouse wasn't caught—not—never!"

"*Vive Guignol!*"

ife in a military academy is no more regulated by authority than in a French school. Thus and no farther into the sacred precincts may parents penetrate when they lead the younger children to their classes in the morning. Here and nowhere else must they stand humbly and wait at closing hours till the children are released. It is as easy for a German or an Italian tourist to enter a French frontier fortress with a camera in his hand as for a mother to enter a French classroom to hear a recitation in arithmetic. In each case, if an authorization could conceivably be secured, it would come from no less a person than the head of a Ministry.

Everything in the school is foreordained by that distant potentate. His authority is steel-like and immutable. Minutely branching, it overlooks none of the minutiae of daily school routine. Every hour's work is laid out in advance: there is no appeal possible, no interruption of the schedule thinkable. How could a mere teacher in a little rural school reach the ear of the Minister of Public Instruction, and how presumptuous of her even to consider changing the program laid down by the highest and best of authorities!

And yet—those Basques! When their old traditions conflict with new ones, they just do as they like! Year after year the august Minister of Education has been flouted in every one of the little schoolhouses scattered about in the narrow Pyrenean valley that holds the canton of Midassoa, where very little (save this invention of public schools) has been altered in the last two hundred years. Two hundred, do I say? A thousand!

Twice or thrice a year some child looked up from Napoleon's campaigns, or from the question of how much profit the baker would make if he sold bread for one franc a kilogram, and had paid six hundred francs for a barrel of flour weighing . . . from this sort of consideration the child, raising his head, saw opening before him a radiant vista of forgetfulness. Down the road toward the school a gaunt old man was trudging, his shoulders stooped under a great wooden box, the black paint on which was as worn and thin as the wayfarer's frayed clothes. The first child to see him broke the penitentiary silence of the schoolroom with a shout, "Guignol! Here's Guignol!"—sprang to his feet, and rushed out of the door, followed by all his bullet-headed, black-aproned schoolmates, tearing down the road, capering as they ran, and shrieking joyfully, "Guignol! Here's Guignol!" Their gladness poured like sunlight about the dingy old man. His ancient, weary eyes brightened in that most ineffable of human joys, the certainty of being welcome—rare in most lives, but the very substance of his. As they swarmed toward him, children and grandchildren of those who had raced with the same cries of welcome to greet him years ago, he always set down his box and stood by it to wait for them, a tremulous smile on his lips. The children flowed about him, shouting shrilly, plucking at his hands, jumping up and down, the biggest boys trying to lift and carry the magic chest between them.

At the door of the schoolhouse stood the teacher, as forgetful of regulated routine as the children—forgetful too, for an instant, of her futureless life, living again in her childhood when she too had burst from the flat drab of everyday existence to race down the road toward Romance, shouting "Guignol!"

The old man looked no older to her now than he had then. He made her feel a little girl again, and it was a little girl's smile that wiped from her face the dark adult expression of conscientiousness.

If the day was fair the big box was set up and opened in the courtyard of the school, just as, years before there had been any schoolhouses in the Basque country, it had been set up in the public square of the village. If rain were falling, into the sacred classroom with it! Push back the teacher's desk, usually as inviolable as the Ark of the Covenant! Up with the creaking jointed supports which had held it high this half-century and more! "Children, sit down! Get yourselves settled. The show is about to begin."

The old man took his place behind the box, threw over the back of it and over his head and shoulders a greenish-black cloth, and instantly, by tradition, became invisible, in spite of legs clad in threadbare trousers, supported by thin feet in ragged brown canvas sandals.

A pause for arrangements within the theater; a pause filled with thrills and wriggles and long breaths from the waiting children—filled for the teacher with a gust of perfume from her youth. A long arm came from under the black cloth to pull a string which let down the front of the box, and a scene was disclosed to the eager eyes which recognized instantly the story that was to go with it.

Was it a mill wheel and some faded bushes painted on the flimsy canvas backdrop? The children began to laugh and clap their hands and shout out, "The Miller and the Devil!" Was it a pasteboard castle with battlemented walls? "Pampelune! Roland and the Saracens!" cried the boys. Did the backdrop show in dimmed colors a row of gray stone houses with mansard roofs and crudely painted ladies in crinoline promenading before them? "The new farce! The new comedy!" cried the children. It had been new when the father and mother of the teacher had sat cross-legged on the ground to watch Guignol.

When the curtain, rolling up, revealed on the crumpled canvas a mountain gorge with pasteboard rocks strewn about the stage, it was not applause that burst from the children, but the strains of the immortal tune, "There *was* an old soldier, and he *had* a wooden leg." They were silenced by the appearance of the jovial, unregenerately profane old veteran himself, stumping on and exclaiming with gusto as he caught sight of his audience, *"Agur!* Children of the Eskualdunak! *Agur!* Just the friends I needed to see!" Then, advancing to the front, leaning forward with a confidential whisper: "What scrape do you think I've got myself into now?" To which the enchanted children answered, "You've been poaching again!" And "How in the world could you guess that!" from the old rascal on the stage.

There were no favorites. They were all favorites. The backdrop showing a tropical scene consisting of three green reeds and a strip of blue representing the ocean, which meant "Polichinelle and the Crocodile" and gales of laughter, was no more noisily welcomed than the painted marble pillars, the background for the lamentable story of "The Countess and Her Lost Son." This drama always made the little girls cry. If there was a favorite it was perhaps "Polichinelle and the Gendarme," and this was natural, because in the last act Polichinelle with a knotty club beat the wooden head of the gendarme till the echoes resounded and the younger children (to whom it was almost new) nearly expired in their mirth.

In every piece—at least in all the funny ones—the forces of law and order and morality were joyously outgeneraled, outmarched, and out-witted by delightful scalawags. Like the story of the endless triumphs of Robin Hood over the Sheriff of Nottingham, they were the expression of a folk oppressed by lawgivers, forcing their cold, dry, logical morality hard upon the instinctive certainty of mankind that somehow you should be able to do as you wish without paying any penalty for it. The children's boisterous mirth laughed down, for a moment, the authority of the lawgivers who ruled their lives so heavily. How they loved the naughty rogues who gave them this breathing space! How heartily they scorned the stupidity of their victims! How idiotic of the rich old man who lent Polichinelle a bag of gold not to see the triumphant leer with which the latter favored the children, nor the limp stuffed forefinger laid cynically alongside the wicked red nose, nor to hear the hoarse chuckle with which the impenitent hero let his audience know that he never intended to pay back a penny! The gendarme who, following out the obnoxious traditions of his trade, was trying to arrest Polichinelle for the murder of his wife, fell into one trap after another, was beaten to a pulp in ambuscades, was drenched with slops, and finally in the last act, chittering in terror, retreated from a ghost (impersonated by Polichinelle in a sheet), not seeing the jaws of the crocodile gaping behind him.

The little children always took hard hold of someone's hand during this exciting scene; some of them even, still naïve, moved to pity even for a gendarme, used to warn him shrilly, "Look out! Right behind you! Take care!"

The children, in fact, always took part in the action. The plays could not have gone on without them. At a critical moment Roland, leaning in his tin armor over a prostrate foe, used to ask squeakingly, "Shall I spare his life?" And was always answered by a thunderous "No!"

"Which way did the rascal go?" the gendarme would gasp out, rushing upon the stage just as Polichinelle, the innkeeper's roast fowl under his arm, hid behind a chair. The children, in terror lest he discover their hero, cried out, "Out of the window into the garden!" or, "Down the street to the left!" After the baffled policeman had gone off on one of these false scents, how enchanting it was to have Polichinelle rise up slowly from behind his chair, waggle his head at them in triumph, and then, pirouetting madly with joy at his own duplicity, rush out to find the gendarme and play yet another trick upon him.

What lightness of heart filled the schoolroom during that hour of rest from the endless human struggle upstream toward its strange, hard, self-imposed ideals! What refreshment for those young souls as for an instant the grim insistence of civilization stopped grinding at them!

"I didn't suppose a little tap like that would kill her," remarked Polichinelle with no sign of regret, after having laid his wife low with a terrific blow from his club, "but" (carelessly) "she had a horrid voice and was always scolding; so it's just as well!"

Yes, yes, what a bright place the world seemed when one could get rid of people because they had horrid voices and scolded! Never, so long as the children could warn him in time, should the tiresome Law lay its talon on the defender of Freedom. When the hero, having thrown off pursuit, sat down in view of the audience to devour with champing, smacking, voluptuous relish the deliciously browned paste-board fowl he had stolen, the sympathetic children shared with him a primitive, restoring delight in food which was to add zest to their lives ever after.

It was soon over. Interludes of joy in the serious-minded gray of life are always short. It was increasingly short as the showman grew older and more asthmatic. He often looked very tired and always immeasurably ancient at the end, when he emerged from the black cloth, after Polichinelle had squeaked out his last thanks to the children for their sympathy and help, and he was often panting so that he leaned against the wall. But there was always a smile on his lips as he looked happily from one glowing child-face to another.

One of the bigger boys passed the hat around for the money every child had been saving in a corner of his desk, and the showman, after a bow, swept the few coppers into his pocket without looking at them. This was not through pride or decorum but because, compared to the children's applause, the money was of no consequence to him. What material needs, beyond a little food, an occasional bed, and enough ragged clothes to cover the skin, has one who, every day of his life, knows such satisfaction as his?

The children helped him pack up. One by one, the little figures of the comedies were rolled up in a ragged cloth, their battered wooden faces expressionless, their tinsled costumes threadbare, their stuffed arms and legs inert and limp, all quite unrecognizable as the sparkling personages of the plays. The bigger boys helped shut the box, un-jointed the supports, strapped them on, and lifted the whole to the thin shoulders which stooped more and more under it as the years went on. The children cried out as he turned to leave the schoolhouse, "Goodby, Guignol! Goodby!" and the old tramp was off on his way to the next schoolhouse, miles away, perhaps over a mountain pass where snow still lingered on the road.

How many years he had thus walked in and out of colorless narrow lives with his color and drama no one knew, the old showman least of all, for he was quite unlettered, could not so much as write his name and did not know his numbers. But only the oldest people in the mountain villages could remember a time before he had lived in a little one-room shack on the outskirts of Urona, the "county town," and had varied his daily puppet shows on a tiny stage there with these long tramps about the countryside. The children of Urona loved him as dearly as did the little mountaineers and watched as eagerly for his return from his pilgrimages. "Guignol is back!" they would announce prancingly to their mothers or nurses on seeing the old man pottering about his ramshackle little theater, or sitting in front of it on one of the low benches, eating the corn bread and onions which seemed to be his only food. The next day the audience assembled (no need to announce that there would be a performance), the mothers and nurses like giantesses on the diminutive benches set under the pollarded plane trees of the boulevard.

Of course he had no license from the municipality thus to occupy a part of the best (indeed the only) show street of the impecunious little city. But all the members of the municipal council had, in their time, sat on those low benches and screamed with delight when Polichinelle double-crossed the policeman. They no more thought of forbidding him to use their boulevard than of forbidding the sparrows which hopped about him, living lives as bright as his, as unburdened by possession and prosperity.

Indeed, as they came and went their anxious, responsible ways, the rulers of the community were as little conscious of the old man's gray presence as of the sparrows. Their eyes, clouded by successful calculations, were blind to the fact that the old showman was every day thinner and grayer and more bent. He had no one to think of him, and they had many other things to occupy their important thoughts, charged as they were with the welfare of the five thousand inhabitants of Urona, trying to keep up the pavements and keep down the beggars, to install sewers against the passionate protests of the older inhabitants, to hold their own against the Préfet, to shore up the crumbling walls of the twelfth-century church, to provide a monument to the war dead as imposing as that of other towns of their size—in general, to keep Urona sufficiently up to the mark so that visiting Parisians would not find too much to laugh at.

The historic storm of January, 1923, which swept in from the Bay of Biscay, wrecked all the harbors along the Basque coast, tore on into the interior with frightful wind and rain such as the oldest inhabitants could not remember and laid low structures which had withstood the storms for centuries. From four o'clock one afternoon, when after a sudden blackness the wind burst upon the town, the tempest shrieked and yelled up and down the defenseless streets of Urona. Nobody ventured abroad, not even the dogs. Heavy wooden shutters were barred tight, and the people sitting within shuddered to hear the roaring of the river as it rose higher and higher, and the banging of the chimney pots, scaffoldings, and street signs as the wind caught them and whirled them to destruction. At midnight the old stone bridge on the road to Spain went out with a crash, and in the same hour the enraged river, tearing its way over its embankments, flung huge blocks of stone from the ruined bridge up into the public square, where they lay for months thereafter.

But this marked the climax of the storm. By three o'clock the tempest had swept past, and when day broke the gray air lay still over the havoc wrought in the little city. The first calamity seen by the people who went cautiously out at dawn was that many of the beautiful plane trees, the pride of the region, were shattered to splinters. And the first sounds they heard were the sobs of the old showman who stood in the midst of a mass of wreckage, weeping bitterly.

A great tree had crashed down on his flimsy little theater, crushing it and the benches. All night the rain had beaten down on those of his little figures which had not been pulverized by the fall of the tree. There was nothing left. Nothing. He stood there sobbing aloud, now and then with a wail stooping to pick up from the ruins the sodden corpse of one or another of his lifelong little friends and comrades.

The municipal council held an emergency meeting at the emergency hour of eight o'clock that morning to take measures for the relief of the town. And what do you think was the first action taken by those middle-aged, material-minded business men with bags under their eyes and waistcoats grossly distended? It was to vote money—town money—sacred tax money—to build at once for Guignol a new theater and to stock it with as many marionettes as Paris could furnish that would fit the old showman's stories.

Yes, I know it sounds improbable. I can't help that. Just as I set it down here, that is what really happened.

With half the roof torn from the Town Hall, with bricks from every chimney strewing the streets, with trees lying crisscross on the boulevard, with the only bridge across the river gone, their first vote taken without a dissenting voice was for the old man weeping in the midst of his ruins—ruins which were theirs as well.

"He had the crocodile in his hands as I passed by—what was left of the crocodile," said the mayor, "all a shapeless mass of papier-mâché. Do you remember? The crocodile the gendarme backed into."

Did they remember!

"I saw something red on the ground off at one side," said the banker, "half trampled into the mud, and when I picked it up it was the red shirt of the miller. You know, the miller who fooled the devil."

"There lay the towers of Pampelune, splintered into matchwood," said the lawyer; "I could just make out what it had been. When I was a little boy, living up in the canton of Midassoa, how grand those towers looked to me! No real castle has ever seemed half so fine.

"I left my little grandson crying his heart out because he had been told he would never see again the old soldier who had a wooden leg."

From the clouded eyes of those representative men, heavy with their success, looked out for an instant the clarity of little boys' eyes; for an instant the flabby flesh of their overfed bodies was gone, and they were little, lithe sprites racing down a country road in the morning of life, shouting, "Guignol! Guignol!"

Yes, the best that money could buy—they voted it with a will, and telegraphed the order to Paris that very morning.

In a week everything they could buy had arrived, and the old showman, his face gray, his head shaking in a beginning of palsy, but with his old smile quivering on his lips, was reverently handling such actors as he had never seen before, nor dreamed of. Real satin, heavy shimmering reds and blues, clad the fine ladies; real gold lace adorned the broadcloth of the gendarme's uniform; the old veteran's wooden leg was hooped with shining copper; and oh, Polichinelle! What a hump! What a glorious red nose! What silver lace upon his peaked cap! What marvelously fashioned hands with finger nails painted on fingers and thumbs! There was, it is true, no Roland, no miller, no countess. The old showman had drawn those stories from traditions too ancient for the great world to remember. But clever artisans of Urona were already working to reproduce the missing figures, and other nimble fingers were sewing on the costumes, every seam and button and fold of which was familiar to everyone in town.

In a fortnight a new Guignol stood on the boulevard, superb in red paint picked out with gilt, and new rows of low benches stood before it. All day long the old showman hung about it, immaterial as a specter, but always with his tremulous smile—pulling on the cords running through patented arrangements of pulleys, so much better than anything he had ever had; or trying out the brightly painted scenery; or gloating over the finery of his actors.

When all was ready the gala performance was given. Marching down the boulevard, two by two, as on great fête days, shining silk hats on their bald heads, long-skirted frock coats on their corpulent bodies, the mayor with the broad red sash of his office girt about him, the *garde champêtre* in full uniform bringing up the rear, the municipal council arrived in a body and sat themselves down on the front benches, reserved for them, as for the family of the bride at a wedding, with heavy tasseled cords. Behind them, thick as they could sit, were children and children and children—prettily dressed little girls and ragged little boys, tiny gentlemen in fawn-colored gaiters and plain little girls in worn black cotton dresses, the only thing in common between them the dewy brightness of their young eyes. Behind them, row upon row, standing up, were their fathers and their mothers and their grandfathers and their grandmothers, dressed in their best black as for Sunday Mass, on their mature or withered faces a reflection from the light in the children's eyes.

Never was there such a show. When the curtain went up showing the familiar kitchen of the inn with the roast pasteboard fowl on the table, what a burst of applause! Such shouts of "Come in! Come in!" as at the little side door came the familiar knocking. As the door slowly, slowly opened, such expectant silence; and such enthusiasm when, thrust slyly around it, appeared the goggling eyes and great red impudent nose! *"Vive Polichinelle!"*

How eagerly they all called out the wrong directions to the pursuing gendarme as after the theft of the fowl he rushed about, trying to arrest the culprit! How magnificently did Polichinelle reward them with his great jovial bow and his shameless chuckle of joy!

The municipal council, sitting hunched on the low benches, their great paunches resting on their knees, laughed over the old jokes and over their being there, till they wiped their eyes. But they remembered to fall respectfully silent during the pathetic scene of the countess and her lost son, so silent that one could hear the little girls sniffing and using their handkerchiefs.

The last show was "Polichinelle and the Crocodile," the latter brilliantly varnished and savagely toothed, so that the littler children shuddered as the gaping jaws opened wide. One little fellow called out as naïvely as the mountain children, "Look out! Look behind you! Take care!"—only to have the others say, "Sh! Sh!" and remind him in whispers that it was only the gendarme in danger. The last act ended with Polichinelle's whirling dance of exultation in his own cunning and his thanks to the children for their help and sympathy. They cried as the curtain went down:

"Vive Polichinelle!"

"Vive Guignol!"

And before they went back to the world of duty and responsibility and cause and effect, they lingered to laugh and chat as the collection was taken up, the wonderful collection, with bank bills and silver in it.

The next morning the old showman did not appear. When at noon they went to his little shed to look him up they found him dead on his ragged mattress, the white marble of his lips set in a smile.

I know it sounds melodramatic. But just as I tell it to you, so it happened. His heart had probably been weak for some time, the doctor said.

"Goodby, Guignol!"

The Saint of
the Old Seminary

&School was over for the day. The children's little hemp-soled *espadrilles* padded softly on the floor as they filed out before Mlle Etchegaray. Her tired, kind eyes looked at each one in turn. Well-dressed pale French children from bourgeois homes, with intelligent, irregular faces; Spanish children, ragged, dirty, Murillo-beautiful, their heads crusted with filth from the dens of the Old Seminary; dark little Basques carrying their heads high with pride in being Basque—Mlle Etchegaray gave to each one the look that really sees. For twenty-five years parents in Mendiberria had counted on Mlle Etchegaray's ability to see what was there—and to report it. Did someone say, "Isn't your Jeanne getting stoop-shouldered?" the first defensive answer of Jeanne's mother would be, "Why, Mlle Etchegaray hasn't said anything to us about it!"

After the last bobbing head had vanished, the teacher set herself to straighten her desk before going wearily up the stairs to her lodging. But this afternoon—as usual—she was denied even a few minutes of restful solitude. Footsteps approached. At the door Juanito Tuán's father appeared. Not happy and elated as he should have been. Not in the least. Could something have gone wrong with that scholarship for Juanito? After all the trouble she had taken with the inspector to get it!

The Tuáns were Spanish, but old Enrique left off, today, all his usual formalities of greeting.

"He won't go," he announced tragically.

He evidently expected the teacher to know the reason without being told. She did.

With the hot-blooded lack of moderation which endeared her to the Basques and Spaniards of Mendiberria she said intensely, "I wish that Tomasina had choked to death on her mother's milk!"

Enrique Tuán's deeply lined swarthy face took for an instant an appeased look.

But Mlle Etchegaray corrected herself conscientiously—characteristically: "No, I take that back. Tomasina is the only child I ever had in my classes whom I really couldn't endure. But perhaps I wouldn't hate her so much for her posing and lying if she weren't young and beautiful, while I am ugly and old and a spinster. No, I don't wish she had died, but I do wish to Heaven she would land her French sergeant, marry him, and have whatever it is she wants him for—leave off her mantilla, and wear hats, change her *espadrilles* for leather slippers, smoke cigarettes, be as French as she likes—only where we wouldn't have to see her—off in France somewhere." Officially, of course, Mendiberria became French territory several centuries ago, but the Basques refuse to take that annexation seriously.

Old Enrique, looking down at his blackened shoemaker's hands, said: "He'll never marry her. He's as ambitious as she. If only he could *get* his promotion and be stationed somewhere else along the frontier, and never show his face here again!"

"You mean—leave Tomasina for your Juanito? Tomasina for your daughter-in-law! You must be crazy! You know Tomasina!"

The old Spaniard fixed a somber gaze on her, his face working. In the silence she could hear his teeth grinding together.

"If Juanito wants her," he said finally, and leaned against the wall, wiping his forehead.

Emerging into the market place an hour later, Mlle Etchegaray turned toward the Tuán shop. Old Enrique sat at his bench, his hammer tapping fast, but the shop itself was empty. No customers sat on the brightly varnished benches which were the pride of the workman risen to proprietor; no foot pressed the strip of real carpet down the center; the pasteboard boxes of shoes on each side rose to the ceiling with no attendant to admire them. Mlle Etchegaray knew where to look, across the square at the Martinez vegetable stand. A tall slender boy leaned against the doorjamb there, gazing at a girl in a brightly flowered dress who was bending over a display of cabbages and to-matoes and with pretty, sinuous, self-conscious gestures rearranging them unnecessarily on the sloping boards of her stall. Old Enrique was watching them. His hands continued to tap blindly at the shoe he was resoling, but his blazing eyes cried, "Look out! Don't push me beyond what I can endure!"

Mlle Etchegaray stepped close to his open window and proffered hastily all she had to give.

"I came down to have a talk with Juanito. I thought it might do some good to make him understand what a marvelous opportunity this scholarship is, what a wonderful life he would have as a doctor, what a shame it would be to miss—"

Young laughter rippled through the air. Tomasina and Juanito were standing close together now, looking into each other's eyes, laughing. The girl's black hair glistened in the sun. She turned at the waist, flexible and firm, and leaned to tease a parrot, brooding mis-anthropically on his perch. With a grating scream he pounced at her finger. But she drew it away with a flash and now, holding her hand high above her head, shook it at him tauntingly as if she had castanets between her fingers. Then, curving her white neck, she turned her eyes again on the boy. The magnetism of that glance could be felt all across the square.

Steps sounded, heavy, leather-soled French steps. Mlle Etchegaray hastily looked another way, and moving forward, gazed through the dusty window of the pharmacist's shop at the familiar fly-specked bot-tles there. Presently she heard other steps behind her, not leather-soled, the soft scuff of *espadrilles*. Juanito walked slowly past, not see-ing her. He went into the shop without a glance at his father and sank down on one of the grand new benches, gazing at his feet.

Young laughter rippled through the air. Tomasina and Sergeant Brugnol were standing close together, looking into each other's eyes and laughing. The girl's black hair glistened in the sun. She poured her personality into her eyes so that once again it could be felt across the square. But Sergeant Brugnol, though his fair face wore a dazzled expression, was evidently able to remind himself that he had other things to do than to chat with the market-gardener's daughter. Lingering and turning back after several starts to leave her, he finally, in spite of her animation, lifted his cap in the citified French way, scorned and envied by wearers of tight-fitting berets, and went on down the street.

Tomasina's animation vanished. She watched him out of sight, her face dark and forbidding. The cobbler's hammer tapped away like an insistent, unwanted thought. When Mlle Etchegaray went into the shop, Juanito looked up at her, startled, with so wan an expression of misery that she only asked for a pair of shoestrings and went her way, passing, as she did so, a group of tourists in their outlandish clothes. A guide was talking to them in their outlandish language. A good many tourists came to Mendiberria. Their guides told them that Charlemagne—or was it Henry the Fourth?—had done something or other there, in the public square. Mendiberria people were of the opinion that the autobus company invented this unlikely story to get more trade.

Along with all the Basques and most of the Spanish in town, Mlle Etchegaray was indignant over the news of the discovery by the French of the secret path used by the Orthez smugglers and of the capture of their whole convoy in the night. As a schoolteacher she was a functionary of the French government, but she shared to the full the opinion of her high-spirited race that no government has a right to lay down a frontier across another people's territory. It was Basque on both sides, wasn't it? A pity it would be if a Basque couldn't walk over the mountain to his uncle and take him a twist of tobacco without having the top of his head shot off by murderous frontier guards. Of course, the four Orthez brothers did rather more than this, with their regular trips, loaded with bales of silks and tobacco and lace and what not; but their business was based on sound Basque principles. They were nice boys too, thought Mlle Etchegaray, fidgeting restlessly about her quarters over the schoolroom—steady, decent young fellows, real Basques. It was a horror to think of their being taken off to a French prison.

Another stick in the fire of her wrath was that Sergeant Brugnol must be delighted. It is part of the French campaign against smuggling to have the guards and their officers always from a distant part of France. Sergeant Brugnol, a big-boned Fleming from near the Belgian frontier, would have said confidently that the black-haired, neatly-made Southerners of Mendiberria were quite ignorant of him personally (all except that pretty little trick at the Martinez vegetable stand). But everybody in town knew that he was ambitious and joked about his burning desire to make a spectacular *coup* that would force his superiors to promote him. Mlle Etchegaray walked to the window to see if the guards and their prisoners were visible yet in the road down from the mountain and turned away quickly lest she should see what she was looking for.

As for the traitor who had given him the information—at the thought, the schoolteacher flung violently on the floor the book she chanced to have in her hand. A spy among them! It made her sick, as falsity always did. Who could it be? The Orthez boys had no enemies. She could imagine no one in Mendiberria capable of such treachery. The little shepherd boy who had run so fast down the mountain knew no more than that, as the Orthez band came along the path they always used, bent under their usual bales, suddenly the French frontier guards were all about them. From the pasture above he had heard men's voices shouting, scuffles on the stony path, Sergeant Brugnol's voice giving commands. He had run away then, all the way down to Mendiberria, knowing that certain people there would pay him well for a warning.

Mlle Etchegaray decided that a violent counter-irritant was what she needed. Little Maria Benevente was once more out of school. There was nothing for it but to go down to the Old Seminary again to see what the matter was. She had been putting it off—not that she was a timid woman. Quite the contrary. But the Old Seminary! She was the only respectable woman in town who ever went near it. "Oh, well, in broad daylight they wouldn't cut anybody's throat," she reassured herself. And as for dirt and germs, they could be washed off. "I'll just spray my nose and throat with a disinfectant and go."

But she did not see the Old Seminary that day, nor think of it for many days to come. As she stepped out of the schoolhouse door she saw the men with their drawn faces, hurrying to tell her. A boy from an upland farm, running fleetly by short-cut paths, had brought into town the news that Juanito Tuán, the only child of old Enrique, the widower, had been with the Orthez boys, had resisted arrest, had attacked the officer in command, and had been shot dead. They were bringing his body down on a stretcher. Someone must go to tell his father, so that his first intimation of the catastrophe should not be Juanito's dead body with a bullet hole through the temple.

Mlle Etchegaray broke in on their agitated story with frantic exclamations of unbelief—"But Juanito stopped going with the Orthez boys all of three years ago. Why should he join them now? It *must* be a mistake." The excited men cried her down: Yes, yes, it was Juanito. He had asked Pedro Orthez to let him make one more trip . . . people in the know had heard that much, before the party set out for Spain. And this second farm boy had picked up a little more from one of the guards: instead of surrendering with the others, Juanito had seemed to go crazy when he saw the French officer—had thrown off his bundle of lace and silk—had leaped straight at the sergeant, who shot in self-defense. There was no possible doubt.

Quick! She must go to tell old Enrique. Who else could? There was no other woman to whom the old cobbler ever spoke. He was a mad freethinker who would drive Father Casimiro out of the house if he tried to go. Quick! The guards with their prisoners and Juanito's corpse might arrive at any moment. She still cried out that it was too dreadful, it could not be true. The men, waving their arms, urged her to be quick. Some of them were weeping with rage and sorrow. They all talked at once, motioning her to hurry.

The clamor of their voices rose so loud that a group of tourists, passing in an autobus, looked out and smiled to see how those excitable Latins scream and gesticulate over nothing.

A few days after the funeral of Juanito Tuán, Mlle Etchegaray, going down to see if there was anything she could do for his father, found the Tuán shop still tight closed. But as she stood an instant before it the door opened and Enrique motioned her to come in quickly. He shut the door behind her, and shaking one fist in the air, dragged her to a long crack in one of the shutters and bade her look. She saw, coming across the square toward them, like a picture of Youth Triumphant brilliantly painted by the sun, the blond officer of the frontier guard, the man who had shot Juanito dead, arm in arm with Tomasina Martinez in her best flowered silk. Her splendid eyes were flashing, her small head held proudly under a gala white lace mantilla. Smiling, looking deep into the other's blue eyes, her smooth scarlet lips moving in low intimate talk, she came closer and closer, unconscious of the fierce gaze upon her. They passed, brushing against the closed shutters. The murmur of their young voices came into the darkness like the hum of bees. They were gone.

Mlle Etchegaray choked down her impulse to shout aloud her indignation at the sight of Tomasina flaunting on the arm of the man who had killed Juanito. First of all she must find some words to quiet the infuriated old man beside her. She reminded him hastily that Tomasina, now she was grown up, was just what she had been as a child—a lying, cheating, play-acting fraud, of too little account for decent people to bother with, adding dryly, "She's not worth even hating. She would have made Juanito miserable. She will make this Frenchman miserable."

Old Enrique cut her short.

"She will make no man miserable any more," he said solemnly.

Seeing the fear whitening the teacher's face, he said dryly, "No, I shall not need to touch her."

She was the last person to know what he meant to do. The examination for the *certificats d'étude* approaching now, everything else dropped from her mind.

It was said in Mendiberria that during the last fortnight before those examinations their teacher would not know if the house over her head were on fire. One after another, till late at night, she coached the children who were coming up. Everybody left her alone at such times, the honor of the town being involved. Sometimes mothers of the children with whom she was working came in silently to set down a covered dish of cooked food, but nobody stopped to gossip.

She had her usual success that year and emerged as usual to find everything in her two-roomed lodging in disorder and the supplies in her tiny kitchen almost exhausted. Basket on arm, she went down to the market place. Enrique Tuán was working quietly at his bench, deftly splitting a thick piece of leather with his thin sharp leather-cutting knife. He was as gray as a corpse, lean and gaunt, but collected and self-possessed. As she passed he looked up at her and nodded, his eyes tired and old, quite emptied of their frenzy. She went across to buy some vegetables and found there stout Mme Martinez, who waited on her silently, sighing heavily.

"Is Tomasina sick?" asked the schoolteacher.

"*Non!* oh, *non*, Mademoiselle!" cried her mother, putting both hands up to cover her face. Mlle Etchegaray said no more.

She usually stood on her professional dignity and waited till people told her local news of their own accord, but now she hurried into the bakeshop and asked the baker, point-blank, "Why isn't Tomasina at the Martinez stall?"

"She knows better than to show her face where we can see it," said the baker, folding his arms over his apron. And then, seeing her blankness, "Why, Mlle Etchegaray, hadn't you *heard?*"

No, she had heard nothing, she told him impatiently; he knew as well as she that it was the time of final examinations.

"Well, there was a letter from Tomasina to her darling Juanito . . . she'd never forget how sweet it was of him to go across the mountains once more and bring back the Spanish lace she simply yearned for. Only she couldn't bear the thought that he might be in danger and . . ." The baker half closed his eyes and went on in the monotonous singsong of a school child repeating a well-studied lesson, " 'Now, here is my plan for your safety. If you will tell me where the Orthez boys' secret path between the high peaks runs, I am sure I can drop enough hints to a certain blond booby . . . you know who . . . so that he will think he has solved the riddle, and will waste a cold night watching for you miles away from where you really are. Be sure to burn this letter, because if it should be found, both of us might get into trouble. Forever faithfully yours, Tomasina.' The dirty . . ." He spat, wiped his mouth on his hand and went on. "Juanito didn't burn the letter. The lovesick simpleton pinned it to his shirt right over his heart. That's where old Enrique found it . . . over the boy's dead heart. Enrique didn't waste any time passing it around so that every one of us could read it . . . pointing out every false, lying trick. We all knew every word of it . . . how she teased him into going, into telling her the path he would follow . . . and then sold him out to get a stand-in with Sergeant Brugnol." He stopped, out of breath, his face crimson with anger.

"Yes, it does look pretty dark," said the schoolteacher faintly. "But we must try to be fair. Have you thought that perhaps Tomasina really did her best to throw the sergeant off the track . . . to protect Juanito . . . only somehow her plan failed?"

"Her plan *didn't* fail," roared back the baker. "Enrique bribed Brugnon's housekeeper to pass out the seageant's map case through the shutters at two o'clock the next night. We looked it over—fourteen of us—at Enrique's home. It took only a few minutes to convince us. Then he returned it to the housekeeper. On that map there was a cross marked at the very spot of the ambush. And on the margin, the words, 'near midnight' and 'HERE' in exactly the same handwriting as 'Here is my plan for your safety' in Tomasina's letter to Juanito. Oh, her plan succeeded all right! And everyone knows about it. Why the very kids in the street, when they're caught cheating at knucklebones, just grin and say 'Forever faithfully yours!' "

Mlle Etchegaray found no words to answer. She was literally cold at the recollection of Tomasina as she had last seen her, triumphant on the arm of . . .

The baker was thinking of that too. He went on: "The first day after Enrique had told all this, she tried to come to the café with her Frenchman, dressed up the way she had been ever since, with her silk dress and leather slippers and white mantilla. It wasn't so white by the time she got out. We men did no more than turn our backs on them. But the boys, Juanito's friends, had rotten eggs in their pockets. She hasn't been seen out of the house since."

"She can't stay in the house the rest of her life," said Mlle Etchegaray.

"She might go jump off the cliff on Izcohébie hill then," suggested the baker, changing the position of some rolls on his counter.

"Does the French sergeant go to see her?"

"No, he's got his promotion and gone. But he'd dropped her before that, as soon as he heard the story. Even sneaking customs guards have *some* sense of decency, I suppose. Besides, Brugnon has been around. No doubt he figured that a bitch like that would sell *him* out as soon as she had a chance of catching a richer man. She's done for herself this time, Tomasina has. She's caught where not even she can find a way to wriggle out."

II

If Mlle Etchegaray had been the last to learn that Tomasina had done for herself, she was the first to know of the way out which Tomasina had found.

When she same back in the autumn after the two months of the summer vacation, she brought with her an old cousin from her home village to help her get through the rush of the first two weeks. Cousin Anna did the marketing, and so Mlle Etchegaray, never going down to *la place,* heard no more about Tomasina than from the babble of the children who told her that twice during the summer the girl had tried to return to her work on the square, "but a half an hour of what she got there sent her back to the house." Her father's hair was now quite white. Her mother began to cry if anyone spoke to her. The neighbors said that Tomasina had been like a wildcat at first: everybody on the street could hear her screaming at her parents. But since her last sortie there had been absolute silence. One little boy turned from his ball game a moment to say hopefully, "Maybe she's dead."

Little Maria Benevente was again not in school. "I'd better go to look her up while Cousin Anna is here," thought Mlle Etchegaray. "It's all very well not to be timid. But when a person has to make a visit to the Old Seminary, two are better than one."

As they went down the muddy, rutted lane, Cousin Anna asked, "I never happened to hear why they call that frightful old tenement house the 'Old Seminary.'"

"Because it is. It had been a seminary, crammed with boys learning how to be priests, from I don't know what date up to the time of the separation of Church and State. Then of course the Church had to vacate it."

"*Oh!*" said Cousin Anna, who was a good Clerical. "What a shame!"

"Guess again!" said the schoolteacher, stepping wide to avoid a pile of filth. "It was the best piece of good luck they ever had. All the sympathizers with the Church, oppressed by the wicked government, turned their purses inside out. Money just poured in—from as far as South America, a lot of it. They built themselves the New Seminary. You know it, that splendid big château on the West Road. Bathrooms they have now, and hot and cold water and a handball court of their own. They owe a vote of thanks to the government for getting them out of the medieval rookery where they'd been. Nothing succeeds like being oppressed."

Cousin Anna looked her disapproval, sternly. Presently she said: "But I don't see what call the Municipal Council had for letting the Old Seminary fall into such frightful neglect."

Mlle Etchegaray laughed grimly. "It was the old familiar story. The Municipal Council was split. You know how much bad feeling there always is. They never could get a vote to do anything. So year after year it stood idle, unguarded, open to the weather, doors unlocked, plundered of everything that could be torn loose. And little by little —I hope they're rejoiced to see it—it's been lived in by riffraff, toughs, bums, most of them Spanish, drifted over the frontier because Spain was too hot for them. By and by they began to bring their women-folks. You can imagine what they were like. It's their children I have at school."

Cousin Anna interrupted her here by an exclamation: "Heavens! What's that horrible smell!" She buried her nose in her handkerchief.

"The Old Seminary," said Mlle Etchegaray, fiercely. "A good many of the children in my class live in that smell and bring it with them when they come to school."

They were at the entrance and turned in now between tall, battered stone posts which had once been handsomely carved. From them hung a few splinters of what were once gates. The two women had been seen, and from out the long leprous, tumbledown building before them a crowd of children poured out to meet them. "Mademoiselle! Mademoiselle!" they shrieked, enchanted to see the revered ruler of the classroom come visiting. Around them eddied gusts of the fetid odor of sweaty, unwashed, excreting human beings, moldy rags, and decayed refuse.

Mlle Etchegaray said heatedly in Basque to her horrified old cousin, "Don't you dare show a thing of what you're feeling. And take that handkerchief down from your nose this instant!"

The children were all about them now, many even of the little ones drooping under baby brothers and sisters, all of them, babies and children alike, indistinguishably filthy, ragged, their heads matted with eczema sores, their hands and legs and feet and faces crusted with dirt and scabs of mange, their fingernails like black claws, their smiling lips and soft, brilliant eyes lovely as those of cherubim. Mlle Etchegaray's heart, as so many times before, dissolved in a wild, indignant tenderness. She looked more grenadier-like than ever. But the children knew her. They caught at her hands; they looked at her adoringly.

"I've come to see Maria Benevente," she said.

"The Beneventes live in the stable now," they cried, proud to be guides. "We will show you. And her mother had another baby just now."

The procession moved across the foul, garbage-strewn paving stones of the courtyard, under the eyes of sluttish black-haired women and rowdy-looking men dressed in grimy rags, leaning out of holes which had been window frames before the woodwork of the house had been torn out to make cooking fires.

"Here's where the Beneventes live," said the children, stopping before what looked like the entrance to a vegetable cellar.

Cousin Anna gasped and stepped back, but Mlle Etchegaray drew her firmly into the blackness. They found themselves standing on an earthen floor at one end of a long, narrow shed. At the far end a square hole in the stone wall let in rays of daylight that slanted down upon a woman lying on a mattress, the small round head of a tiny baby tucked into the crook of her arm. The same light showed, kneeling before a large wooden trough set on the ground, a woman washing clothes. The swish of the water as she lifted a cloth from it came to their ears. Hearing someone enter, she turned her head to peer into the dark, wringing out the cloth as she did so. Something about the gesture, very free, very graceful, was familiar to Mlle Etchegaray. She took a long step forward as if to see and stopped short with a smothered exclamation.

The other drew her hands quietly from the soapy water, rose to her feet, and wiping her hands on her apron with a servant's gesture, came forward, her large dark eyes fixed intently on the schoolteacher's.

"Yes, Mlle Etchegaray, it is Tomasina," she said in a humble, earnest voice. "God has been very good to me. Just when I thought the burden of my sin more than I could bear, He sent the blessed St. Teresa to me to show me how to expiate it. She told me to leave behind my great misery and led me here. I saw her stand—glorious!—in the courtyard here, beckoning me in."

"I'd have died without her this morning, and the baby too," said the woman from the bed. "See how clean she has made everything. Isn't it beautiful?" She put her hand on the coarse white sheet which covered her.

Tomasina stood before Mlle Etchegaray, her eyes dropped, her hands, reddened and swollen by washing, put together on her breast in the attitude of prayer. She was dressed like the poorest, in cheap black cotton, with an apron of coarse gray stuff. Her hair was hidden under a black cotton kerchief drawn tightly around her head.

Mlle Etchegaray looked at her in a stunned silence.

Cousin Anna's heart was outraged by such unresponsiveness. "I don't know what you've done that's wrong," she said warmly, laying her hand on Tomasina's shoulder, "but I'm sure it is glorious to do what you are doing now."

Tomasina's heavy white eyelids fluttered. She murmured, "God has been good to me, a sinner," but she did not look up.

Mlle Etchegaray, gazing at her in the twilight, still said nothing.

She kept the same silence before the flurry of talk that ran around town as the news spread. Everybody else exclaimed and speculated, but Mlle Etchegaray made no comments save by the shrugged shoulders and widespread hands of professed ignorance.

At first everybody echoed Enrique's contemptuous comments, "What's the girl up to *now?*"

"It's just another of her tricks. She'll soon get tired of it."

"Wouldn't it make you laugh to think of Tomasina Martinez being visited by the saints!" (The story of her vision was soon well known.) "Somebody in Heaven must have given St. Teresa the wrong address."

"Father Casimiro isn't any too enthusiastic, I hear. He asked her why she didn't go into a convent. She says she told him she needed a much harder penance. That's *one* way to put it! You couldn't get her into a convent! She wants to be the whole thing wherever she is!"

But as months went on, another note began to sound. First one, then another voiced a protest against Enrique's implacable bitterness.

"After all, Enrique, what more could anybody do for a penance? Nobody scrubs floors and washes children's heads and lays out the dead and takes care of old women with cancer just to show off. That's not play-acting!"

"You're being an audience for her this minute!" said Enrique sourly.

Later: "She has put a statue of St. Teresa up in a shrine on the wall of the courtyard just where she saw her vision. And after each piece of her work she goes out there to pray, rain or shine, kneeling on the paving stone."

"Where she can be seen," said Enrique.

Mlle Etchegaray never commented on such reports, but now she asked, "Where did she get a statue? I thought Father Casimiro didn't—"

"Oh, she doesn't have Father Casimiro for her confessor any more! She gets up at four o'clock in the morning and walks clear down the valley to St. Pé, to the priest there. He gave her the statue."

The next time the schoolteacher met Father Casimiro on the street she surprised the mild, absent-minded old priest by stopping to shake hands with him and in the most cordial manner to pass the time of day. He was not used to such friendliness from one of the anticlericals.

The tone of the general talk in town became more and more respectful: "Those people in the Old Seminary seem to think a great deal of Tomasina. They get her in to settle their quarrels, it seems, and have her take care of their money—the better ones, that is, with families. Some of the tough men use terrible language to her, they say. She never answers a word, just stops whatever work she is doing, puts her hands together on her breast, and begins to pray. Some of them were drunk the other day, I hear, and when she started to sweep the courtyard they began to yell foul words at her. She knelt down to pray for them, and one of them struck her over the head with his stick. They say when she fell the women burst out of the house, dozens of them, screaming like tigresses, and landed on the men as if they'd tear their eyes out. There was a free-for-all fight, about ten women to every man, and the men drunk. They ended by making the fellow who had struck her come to ask her pardon. But she wouldn't let him, took him out before St. Teresa's shrine, and bade him make his excuses there, on his knees, to the saint. She's had her head tied up ever since."

"She thinks a bandage looks like a halo," growled Enrique.

The winter wore on, and one day a mother bringing a child to school stopped to tell Mlle Etchegaray of a dramatic happening that was in everybody's talk: "A couple of drunks from the Old Seminary got to fighting with knives in the market place yesterday, and one of the children ran quick to get Tomasina. The moment the fighters saw her come up to them they stopped and looked foolish and went off, different ways. It was the first time she's been out on the street there since—you know when. Her face was as *white—!* they say, and shining! Like a lighted window, somebody told me. People stood back to let her pass, and some of the Frenchmen took off their hats. She didn't look at a soul, kept her head bent over her clasped hands, praying all the time."

"Did Enrique Tuán see her?" asked Mlle Etchegaray.

"Yes, she passed just in front of his shop. He looked at her like a demon. People didn't like it. It's about time he stopped saying those awful things about her anyhow. It's not Christian to keep up your grievance so long. Down in St. Pé they are all talking about her. Their priest says she is wonderful. They think it very queer, the people in her own town not appreciating her more."

Later: "Who do you think came today to our doors, begging, with a basket on her back, but Tomasina Martinez! She was begging for food and clothes for a poor family. My husband said, 'Tomasina! You begging!' She answered in a little voice as clear as a bird's, 'God is good to me, a sinner, to let me serve his poor.' Our Jeannot—you know what a tender-hearted little fellow he is—burst out crying and ran after her to ask her blessing."

She came thus to Mlle Etchegaray's door, begging for her poor. Mlle Etchegaray had always, ever since she had been in Mendiberria, given everything she could possibly spare, food, clothing, and money, to those of her school children who came from the Old Seminary. But she did not tell Tomasina this. After a moment's hesitation she said soberly she would see what she could do and went off to ransack the shelves of her tiny pantry. Tomasina, left alone, did not stir from where she stood in the middle of the floor. She bent her black coifed head over her clasped hands and began to pray.

Mlle Etchegaray, coming back, saw this picturesque tableau of piety and was unexpectedly set upon by an emotion which translated itself—before she could restrain it—into a small smile. Tomasina opened her eyes, caught the smile on the schoolteacher's lips. She closed her eyes more tightly and raised her prayers to a murmur. She never went again to the schoolhouse to beg.

But Juanito Tuán's father came. As spring approached and doors were opened, he sat many times of an evening on the doorstep of the schoolhouse, talking half to the schoolteacher, correcting arithmetic papers back of him, and half to the blackness before him.

"She is a devil, that girl, simply a devil. It must be Satan himself who tells her how to fool people. First she killed Juanito, and now she makes everybody forget him. Nobody but his poor old father remembers him, and what have I done? I am the one who has pushed her up to where she always wanted to be. My son is dead and done for, and his friends taking off their hats to the woman who killed him. This business of begging now—that she's invented to keep people thinking about her—I see them, man after man, stepping back to let her pass. And the Municipal Council giving in to her, when they never would even let you put the case to them!" (Tomasina had suddenly appeared before the Council, and speaking with such sweetness and devotion about her poor that even the most skeptical were moved, had prevailed on them to clean and repair the Old Seminary.) "Is Juanito any less dead because she puts on all these airs? He lies rotting in his grave, and his father has put his murderess where she gets what she wants. I did it! I!"

Sometimes the tired teacher, bending over the same mistakes in subtraction which she had corrected for a quarter of a century, heard him run wildly down the path in the darkness, weeping and crying, "I did it! I! I!"

But the next evening she would hear his voice again from the doorstep, moaning: "She says she is happy! That false, murdering woman says she is happier now than ever in her life. People who won't let me so much as say Juanito's name to them tell me, 'Look at her face as she goes along praying. Isn't that a beautiful happiness on it?' How did she get that happiness they all admire? By killing my boy. Yes, it was a fine thing for her and her soul when she killed Juanito. He lies in his grave so that she can be happy. 'Perhaps,' I tell people, 'you would like to have her murder *your* boy, so that she could repent even more gloriously.' "

Sometimes he interrupted his dreary muttering to call back: Mademoiselle, *you* know, don't you, that all this saint business is just because there wasn't any other way she could get out of her hole?" She took these questions as part of his monologue and did not answer, but once he got up and came into the lighted schoolroom, his bloodshot eyes blank with their long gaze into darkness, his gray hair shaggy with neglect, the dirt deep in the creases of his swarthy face, which he no longer remembered to wash. "See here!" he said challengingly. "You know as well as I, don't you, that all this is no more than just another way—the only way she had left—for Tomasina to go on being Tomasina?"

At first the gaunt schoolteacher only lifted her eyebrows and shoulders and spread out her hands in the gesture of professed ignorance. When she spoke, it was slowly, with long spaces between her three words: "I don't know," she said.

People began coming up from the village of St. Pé to pray for special favors before the St. Teresa of the Old Seminary and to ask Tomasina to pray with them. One woman had left her little girl very sick with a sore throat to come up to ask Tomasina to intercede for her. At the very hour—so the story went around—that Tomasina left the floor she was scrubbing and went down on her knees on the stones of the courtyard, the little girl in St. Pé smiled, said, "Oh, Grandmère, I feel so much better!" and when the mother reached home the fever had gone and the child was almost well.

"I know which book of pious stories that comes out of," growled Enrique. "It had a blue cover. That was the third story in it. I had it read to me when I was a boy, and so had she."

But fewer and fewer people would listen to Enrique. He might at least, they thought, not say such things to visitors who had come from another town all the way to a shrine in Mendiberria. They murmured, too, at Father Casimiro's passive, ungracious attitude. It was because he was getting old, they said. A younger priest would have helped Tomasina more, would have appreciated her, as the priest of St. Pé did. One day an autobusload of pilgrim excursionists drove all the way around from Lourdes, addressed themselves (naturally) to the priest of the parish, and said they would like to see the holy woman of whom they had heard and to pray with her before her shrine. Father Casimiro told them that he had not one but many holy women in his parish, and that he thought holiness was best practiced without too many spectators. And sent them away. Only think what a priest like the one at St. Pé would have done with such an opening!

The next autumn, when Mlle Etchegaray came back once more from her two months' vacation, she found the Tuán shop shut. Enrique paid so little attention to his work now, she heard, that people didn't give the cantankerous old man their custom. He scarcely seemed to notice whether he had work or not, going aimlessly up and down the streets as if he were looking for someone, sitting by Juanito's grave, his hand laid on it, and standing opposite the entrance to the Old Seminary, watching Tomasina.

Here for a time he was, by gusts, violent and abusive, calling out such jibes as "Tomasina! Tomasina! Why do you always choose the two times when the men are coming and going to work to be out sweeping the courtyard?" or accosting visitors with the suggestion that they go to Father Casimiro for an account of what was happening at the Old Seminary: "After all, *he* is the priest of this parish!" Or he shouted, the tears running down his cheeks, "Juanito! Juanito! Ask her who Juanito was!" Tomasina had once suddenly crossed the road, knelt in the mud before the dirty old man, and folding her hands in the gesture of prayer, her lovely face shining with the white fire of exaltation, said gently and humbly to him, "Punish me as you wish. It will be what I deserve." The old man had broken from his tears into dreadful laughter then, and looking from her to the deeply moved group of pilgrims back of her, cried out, "Always where there's somebody to see, my girl!"

But he had been made to understand not too gently by the authorities of the town that this sort of rowdyism would not be permitted. After this he stood silent, skeleton-thin and ragged, the incarnation of dirt and misery, tears running down his cheeks as though from a never-exhausted reservoir. When his half-starved old body could endure no more he shuffled back to Juanito's grave and sat beside it, resting, his hand laid across it as though to try to reach his son. And when he could stand again, he returned to his place across the road from Tomasina. Sometimes one of the many visitors to the shrine of the Old Seminary saw him standing thus, forlorn and emaciated, took him for a beggar, and offered him alms. Never more than once!

He seemed not to take his eyes from Tomasina. He saw her followed by adoring children, transformed by the cleanliness and care she gave them, kneeling with them before the statue of St. Teresa like their young spiritual mother; he saw her sweetly teaching the same children to play without the Stone Age ferocity that had been their habit; he saw the men and women in the tenement, lifted from their misery of poverty by the gifts of pilgrims to their shrine, consult and obey her; he saw many of the expressive, emotional Spanish women kneel to kiss her hand, although she always drew back with a pained look and motioned them to St. Teresa; he saw people coming to pray beside her, not only from St. Pé and the villages down the valley and beyond, but her own townspeople, women who had known and loved Juanito as a little boy, but who now, pale and anxious, thought of nothing but the sick person for whom they were praying. Exhausted, he went to sit by Juanito's grave and returned to see the young priest from St. Pé with a visiting priest come to look into Tomasina's story and listen to the girl, kneeling before the shrine, describe once more the vision that had brought her there. He saw an autobus of pilgrims from Lourdes, this time not consulting Father Casimiro, stop at the entrance of the lane and discharge a crowd of visitors who, after praying at the shrine, left Tomasina's hands full of offerings of which she kept not a penny for herself. He saw finally, one day, a delegation of students file into the courtyard and kneel before the shrine. Afterward the priest who was their leader asked Tomasina with deference if she could tell them of her vision. Old Enrique saw her leave the huge pan of potatoes she was peeling and come humbly forward, wiping her stained hands on her apron, her beautiful face like ala-baster under the severe folds of her black headkerchief. He saw her listeners absorbed, transported, their sensitive young lips parted. They were of Juanito's age at the time of his death, as big as men, as simple-hearted as boys. He saw Tomasina's eyelids raised once, only once, and saw her young audience thrill to the magnetism of her great eyes, deep with emotion.

After they went away, he walked steadily across the street and into the courtyard, drawing out his long leather-cutting knife, and without a word, without a change of expression on his sad old face, stabbed Tomasina to the heart.

III

Mlle Etchegaray was leaving Mendiberria. Not for the summer. For always. The day after Father Casimiro had departed for his new parish far up in the mountains, she had put in her application to be transferred to another school. She had gone to see the old priest off at the station, a great bouquet of flowers for him in her unbeliever's hand, and had, amazingly, asked him for his blessing. He had shown no surprise at this. He was perhaps too much broken by the shock of his transfer to a strange parish to have vitality enough left to be surprised at anything.

The day she was to leave town, Mlle Etchegaray set out on the road to the Old Seminary. It was marked from afar by a sun-gilded cloud which hung quivering over the crowd like dust at a fair. Like a fair it was lined with booths, selling souvenirs. Behind the booths were people she knew, old students of hers, very animated and active now, as they counted out change and called attention, leaning over their counters, to the attractions of their wares. Many of the booths were selling eatables too, for the crowds of pilgrims needed to be fed. She saw the baker bustling about, setting out hundreds of rolls fresh from the oven. His was one of the largest and finest of the booths.

As she came nearer the building the movement of the crowd be-came slower. They inched themselves forward slowly and stood for long periods without advancing at all. Visitors were being admitted to the courtyard by groups of forty at a time. Up and down the waiting line moved vendors of souvenirs on foot, some selling relics, although that was forbidden by both the Church and the municipal authorities. "A piece of wood from the broom used by the martyr the day of her death," a woman would say, drawing her relic furtively from under her shawl and speaking in a low voice, "guaranteed authentic." Everyone now crowded to one side to allow an excited group to pass, returning from the shrine. The news flew about, pervasive as the dust: "A cure! That woman in the middle hadn't walked for ten years!" Some well-tailored North American women with loud voices laughed and called back and forth to each other as they took snapshots.

A smartly dressed young man fought his way down the line, asking, "Which is Mlle Etchegaray? I was told the schoolteacher was here." When he reached her he said, speaking in her ear in a furtive tone like that of the vendors of relics, that he was a reporter from a left-wing newspaper in Paris, sent down to make an investigation, and to report along modern scientific lines on all this furore. He looked at her knowingly, with a smile of secret understanding. "I've been told that you—a highly intelligent, thinking person—can give me the real inside facts of the matter, and I'd like to make an appointment to get some stuff from you that will—"

"The facts?" said Mlle Etchegaray, breaking in on his whispering with her natural tone. "So far as that goes, I can tell you the facts right here. A girl of this town who had done a great wrong gave the rest of her life to self-inflicted penance for it, devoting herself to the poorest miserables, from whom the rest of us held aloof. She served them to the hour of her death, and since then has been serving them and all other poor by her example, which has caused the founding of a national organization of girls of good family to give part of their superfluities and time to the needy. She was killed by an insane man who died in prison shortly after. There have been many authentic cures made on the place where she died, and people love her memory for them. She has brought much prosperity to her townspeople, as you can see for yourself. The former priest of the parish was too old and too infirm to take charge of the complex situation always caused by a sudden influx of pilgrims, and has been sent to a smaller parish more within his powers. Those are the facts, if facts are what you are looking for." She added conscientiously, "I have forgotten to say that she was very beautiful."

"But—but—" The smart young man was disconcerted. "I was told that you knew all about—"

Mlle Etchegaray lifted her shoulders and spread out her hands. "I know nothing whatever about anything," she told him, passing forward with the crowd into the courtyard.

When she came out, half an hour later, she turned away from the crowd, off into the waste country covered by gorse, its thorny, graceless branches hung with yellow bloom. She walked a long time there, following aimlessly one after another of the wandering sheep-tracks through it, her head sometimes bent, sometimes lifted to look up at the mountain where Juanito was killed, sometimes turned to look back at the Old Seminary. Presently, picking a few of the harsh, spiky sprays of blossoming gorse, she went to lay them on the neglected, unmarked grave of old Enrique.

Gold
from Argentina

&ᵹUp the steep slope to Mendigaraya toiled an automobile, and this was remarkable, for Mendigaraya lies high in the Pyrenees, is geographically fifteen miles from a railroad, spiritually two centuries from the modern world, and does all of its business by oxcart. The only contact with the twentieth century known to that region is through the occasional departure of one of the poorest boys, starved out, who emigrates to South America, and through the very infrequent return of one years later, either as a ragged failure or as a pot-bellied, well-to-do man in store clothes and suspenders, accompanied by a heathenish wife with a hat on her head. (Any Basque woman used to covering her sleek black hair with a mantilla would as soon go out on the street in her chemise as in a hat. And no Basque mountaineer, his lean, agile body sashed in red, ever gets enough to eat or can stop work long enough to acquire corpulence.)

Unless they come back to visit their old homes the emigrants are seldom heard of after their departure. Basques poor enough to be driven to emigrate can rarely read and write. Even if they could their families could not read their letters. For the most part they disappear forever, the strong, handsome young men, despairing at the grinding narrowness of the lives before them, who pluck up courage to take the plunge, and, hiding their homesick panic under a pale bravado of gaiety, set off down the long stony road leading to St. Jean-de-Luz and the railroad.

But of course one never knows; this car might be bringing a returned "American," as Basques who have lived in Argentina are always called. What other possible reason could an automobile have for coming to Mendigaraya? The little boys in blue berets, playing *pelota* up against the wall of the church, halted their nimble sandaled feet and stared at the strange vehicle panting into the far end of the village street. The girls, drawing water at the fountain, stopped their chatter and turned their long, lustrous eyes toward it in wonder.

The automobile turned the one corner of the street and stopped short, stalling with a grunt of astonishment, for it found itself in an impasse, low, whitewashed, red-beamed houses before it, set thick all around a small public square of beaten earth, shaded by pollarded plane trees. There was no way out between the houses, not even an alleyway. Mendigaraya is at the end of the road and does not mind admitting it.

The door of the car opened, and a man stepped out, instantly known, by all the Basque eyes looking at him, to be a foreigner. He had stiff leather shoes on his feet, and his stumping, wooden-legged gait was that of a city-dweller. He looked about him, saw that one of the houses announced by a faded sign that it was both the city hall and the post office, and knocked on its door.

The elderly postmaster, who was also the town clerk and who had, like everybody else in town, been staring from a window at the automobile, lost no time in opening the door. The stranger stepped in and introduced himself as a lawyer from St. Jean-de-Luz, come to get some legal information from the town records of Mendigaraya. The two men sat down together after the town clerk had shut the upper half of the door at the back of his office, through which a too-friendly cow was thrusting a pretty head. The questioning began. Was anything known in Mendigaraya about the Yturbe and the Haratz families? Of course, there were Yturbes everywhere. What were those in this town?

Well, everything was known about them—two landless, moneyless, unimportant clans, not very bright, not very honest, not very clean, not very industrious—good-natured, easy-going, with never a penny's worth of property between them, and extremely prolific, as such clans are apt to be the world around. They were not bad people, seldom got into prison for anything, and were rather convenient to have around, as they furnished the necessary hired men and domestic servants for other people with more energy and brains. They were, in short, the kind of people who, since the fantastic invention of universal suffrage, can be counted on to vote for the candidate with the loudest voice.

The lawyer from St. Jean-de-Luz listened attentively to this piece of town lore and asked if two of the grandmothers in the clan had not been sisters.

Yes, that was true; two Bidaranty girls they had been, from a scrub family, exactly like the ones they had married into. Yes, they were both still living, although very old now. There was one now, this minute, over across the square. The lawyer turned in his chair, settled his glasses on his nose, and looked hard through the window at an old crone, her head tied up in a rusty black handkerchief, creeping feebly about, stooping to pick up fallen twigs and putting them in a gunny-sack which she dragged along with one hand. That was Granny Haratz, about seventy-seven now, useful for gathering fuel for the cooking fire, and for nothing else. Her sister, Grandmother Yturbe, spent her time in the pastures, watching the cows to see that they did not wander, the usual work given to members of the community whose time was worth nothing.

And had those sisters ever had a brother?

Ah, that the town clerk did not know. He was a newcomer to Mendigaraya, having lived there only thirty-seven years. But the town records would show. They did. Yes, there had been an elder brother, Jean Manuel Bidaranty, who, sixty-two years ago, at the age of nine-teen, had gone to South America. Here was the record of his birth, his baptism, all the data about his securing his passport.

The lawyer pulled from his black leather portfolio a packet of documents, compared names, dates, ages. Evidently—he remarked after a time—evidently the same man.

He folded his documents together and returned them to his serviette, remarking that he had just received word from a lawyer in Buenos Aires that M. Bidaranty was dead.

How strange, thought the town clerk, to hear one of such a tribe as the Bidarantys called a *monsieur!*

The lawyer went on to say that, dying, M. Bidaranty had willed what property he had to his two sisters. Now that the identification was complete, there were only some legal formalities to be finished. They would take perhaps a month—perhaps two—possibly as long as three. Inheritances were long in getting themselves settled. And then he would transfer the property to the two heiresses.

The town clerk had listened to this, open-mouthed, his eyes wider and wilder with every breath he drew. He now asked in a faint voice if it would be indiscreet to inquire whether M. Bidaranty had left much?

No, the lawyer told him, it would not be in the least indiscreet. No secret about it. Quite a tidy little sum. About three million dollars.

He reached for his hat and stepped toward the door.

The town clerk sat stricken, numb to his marrow.

"Good day," said the lawyer pleasantly, opening the door, "and many thanks for your assistance."

He stepped out.

The town clerk came to life with a convulsive shudder and cried after him in a cracked voice, "Did you say dollars? Or francs?"

"Dollars," said the lawyer, conversationally, and, stepping into his car, disappeared.

The town clerk never was the same man again.

Mendigaraya reeled from the shock. The news flared up and down the narrow valley like fire in dry weeds, and in a twinkling burned away a number of false ideas about the Yturbe and Haratz families. Everybody saw now what he had not chanced to note before, that the Yturbes had great natural distinction of manner, and that the younger Haratz girls had wonderful hair and eyes. Everybody remembered what respected citizens they had always been, and there was a universal feeling among the better people of the town that it was not suitable for members of such good old families to be in menial positions. Generous friends, whose fathers were—now—reported to have been the intimate friends of their fathers, rushed to help them out of their temporary difficulties. Before long one of the grandsons was taken into partnership by the village grocer. Three of the granddaughters, servant girls, were sought in marriage by sons of well-to-do farmers who worked their own land and owned many head of cattle. Another grandson, who had been stableboy for the doctor in the next town—the doctor who had once been almost elected to the Chamber of Deputies—was taken into the doctor's family on the most familiar terms and was already a great favorite with the doctor's marriageable daughter. An Yturbe boy! Think of it!

The two old ladies, now dressed in black silk presented to them by friendly neighbors, were removed from the earth-floored huts in which they had always lived and borne their numerous children, into salubrious new quarters in an elegantly furnished house, with sheets on the beds, wax flowers in glass bells on the mantelpieces, and actually—almost the only one in the village—a cast-iron two-holed cookstove in the kitchen. Of course the bewildered, docile old women never did any cooking on the stove, the fire on the hearth being so much handier.

This house was thrown open to them in a burst of humanity by the only landed proprietor thereabouts, a wealthy Frenchman who owned four of the houses in town and had three farms to rent. He was on the point of settling, rent free, on one of his farms, a widowed daughter of Mme Yturbe, when a sudden thought struck him, waking him up in the night, piercing to his vitals.

By dawn the next morning his son, a well-to-do horse-trader, as shrewd as himself, was dispatched down the road to St. Jean-de-Luz with instructions to see that lawyer in person and find out the truth about this wild story, which, after all, as the proprietor had suddenly remembered, rested on nothing more than the uncorroborated say-so of the town clerk, who, judging from the state of extreme agitation in which he had been found after the visit of the lawyer, might easily have misunderstood the whole business.

The horse-dealer left at six one morning. By nine, everybody in the village (with the natural exception of the Yturbe and Haratz families) knew why he had gone. They were all shuddering at the danger they had unwittingly been in and were thanking Providence that they had for a townsman so sagacious a person as the proprietor. During the two days of his son's absence the village went into a trance of suspended animation.

On the evening of his return the village notables assembled at his house to hear his report. It threw them into an ague. He had not, it is true, been able to see the lawyer, who had gone to Bordeaux and would not be back for a fortnight more. And, shrewd son of a worldly-wise Gallic father, he had been far too knowing to confide in a mere jackanapes of a lawyer's clerk. But he had heard—what had he not heard!

All St. Jean-de-Luz was talking of it. He had heard from everybody that the whole story was a hoax, an infamous practical joke. Jean Manuel Bidaranty had returned from South America years ago, a poor vagabond, like all the other Bidarantys, had earned a scanty living in a fishing village farther up the coast, and when he died, had not left enough money to bury him. Everybody knew all the details of the true story—had heard in just which cemetery his poor wooden cross was to be found, had been told the full name of the fisherman who had employed him. Three million dollars nothing! Of all the preposterous tales! Nobody but backwoods simpletons would have believed for an instant such a preposterous story.

The assemblage of village notables, headed by the almost-Deputy himself, who had gathered to hear the news, turned with one accord to rush out and denounce the wretched impostors. But the well-to-do Frenchman called them back in an agonized voice. They had no more *proof* of this last story than of the first. Suppose the Yturbes and Haratz families were not wretched impostors at all, but really valid heirs to three million dollars. It would not do to be in too great haste. The story did sound madly impossible, and thanks be to God and all the saints, there was still time to draw back. But *suppose it should be true!*

The group of notables glared upon each other with tortured faces. Superior, upper-class people as they were, they expected as a matter of course to dominate any situation in which they found themselves and to extract from it whatever profit there might be, naturally the due of the refined and cultivated. But this situation—! Until the lawyer came back, what would be safe for them to do? To *do?* How could they even know what to feel, utterly at sea as they were, with no data on which an intelligent person could form a judgment? Were those Haratz girls really handsome, or were they common slatterns? Were the Yturbe boys promising lads or the scum of the earth? How could anybody know? Were ever human beings put into so hideous a situation as the townspeople of those two families?

Shut into this suspense, in the intolerable position of having nobody to blame, their nerves gave way, and they turned on each other. Before that first meeting had broken up, they had begun to quarrel fiercely, twitting each other with old scandals, raking up forgotten family skeletons, which, by the customary conspiracy of silence among gentry, had been kept dark lest the lower classes learn of them. Their exasperation found a real relief in this wrangling, which, after the fashion of wrangling, rose in intensity and fury from day to day. What else could they do to fill those long slow days of waiting?

The apoplectic French proprietor, meeting Mme Haratz in her black silk dress on the street, put up his hand to doff his hat to her, snatched it down again indignantly, put it up again falteringly, and glared upon her in an uncertainty so violent that he felt something give way in his brain and fell to the ground in the first of the paralytic seizures which finally carried him off. People were as tense as fiddle strings. If wheels sounded in the street everyone leaped to his window and was enraged to see that it was only the miller with an oxcart loaded with bags of corn.

Even in their confusion, however, there was one thing which was almost at once obvious to them all. Whatever happened, they could prevent the others from exploiting those dumb ignorant peasants.

They were revolted by each other's sordid calculations. Secretly, one by one, they went to warn the Yturbe and Haratz families. It was a Christian duty, they told Mme Haratz, to let her know that the doctor's mother had died in an insane asylum and that the doctor often showed signs of the same malady, homicidal mania. Did Mme Yturbe perhaps know that the proprietor of their house had been accused of poisoning his first wife? And did the Haratz girls know that the young men who had shown such mercenary haste in seeking them out after it was known they were heiresses were not at all what they should be—were drunkards—thieves—had illegitimate families in other villages—had served terms in prison—walked in their sleep? And had the Yturbes happened to hear that it was the persecutions of the grocer that had driven his former partner to suicide?

To these revelations of the criminal, diseased, and depraved character of their neighbors, the Yturbe and Haratz families listened, pale-cheeked, panic-struck, credulous. They doubted not a word of it. It fell in perfectly with their conception of life, founded on tremulous notions of witchcraft and black art. Never, never had they dreamed that the people around them were so dangerous, so savage, so adroit—but now that they knew it, it seemed quite understandable.

They held a council of their own, at night, behind locked doors—cowering together, starting at every sound, constantly sending one of the boys to make sure no one was listening at the windows. What could they do? How could they escape from the perils around them? How could they, poor, ignorant, bewildered, helpless folk as they were, hold their own against these upper-class, highly educated assassins, crooks, robbers, and maniacs who surrounded them, as they had all seen a flock of sheep surrounded by wolves?

No idea of resistance crossed their minds. Never in the memory of man had any one of them been able to defend himself against property owners, who could read and write and cipher, and knew how to get the law on you if you didn't do as they wished. Open resistance would not have the faintest shadow of success. And even if fighting could have saved them, there was not a drop of fighting blood in the lot of them.

But—like an inspiration it came to them—there are other ways of escape for creatures who dare not fight. With a huddled, sheeplike rush, once the idea was conceived, they made their plans. The night was a dark one. There were plenty of strong arms to carry the children. They could be far, far on their way before dawn. For at least twenty-four hours, perhaps longer, no one could guess where to look for them. And it would take a good day, after that, to find them. Fifteen miles, while long and hard for the soft feet of well-to-do folk, does not seem far to people used to working hard for their living. And it was all downhill to St. Jean-de-Luz.

Four days later the son of the proprietor once more came back from a trip to St. Jean-de-Luz. He was gray with fury. They had gone. The whole tribe. To Buenos Aires. To where Jean Manuel had lived. They had found the lawyer just returned to his office, and had asked him, so he said, if they had the right to go? If there was money enough to pay for their tickets? If anyone could get the law on them if they did go? Would they inherit that money if they went to South America as well as if they stayed here?

The lawyer had said yes to all these questions. He would, he told them, send all necessary identification to the Buenos Aires lawyer who had the matter in hand. He had bought their tickets for them and helped them get off. After all, why not, he had said impudently to the man from Mendigaraya, if that was what they wanted?

No, it had not been a hoax about the money. All solid fact. Just as the lawyer had said at first. Incredible. True.

The Apprentice

The day had been one of those unbearable ones, when every sound had set her teeth on edge like chalk creaking on a blackboard, when every word her father or mother said to her or did not say to her seemed an intentional injustice. And of course it would happen, as the end to such a day, that just as the sun went down back of the mountain and the long twilight began, she noticed that Rollie was not around.

Tense with exasperation—she would simply explode if Mother got going—she began to call him in a carefully casual tone: "Here, Rollie! He-ere, boy! Want to go for a walk, Rollie?" Whistling to him cheerfully, her heart full of wrath at the way the world treated her, she made the rounds of his haunts; the corner of the woodshed, where he liked to curl up on the wool of Father's discarded old windbreaker; the hay barn, the cow barn, the sunny spot on the side porch—no Rollie.

Perhaps he had sneaked upstairs to lie on her bed where he was not supposed to go—not that *she* would have minded! That rule was a part of Mother's fussiness, part too of Mother's bossiness. It was *her* bed, wasn't it? But was she allowed the say-so about it? Not on your life. They told her she could have things the way she wanted in her own room, now she was in her teens, but—her heart raged against unfairness as she took the stairs stormily, two steps at a time, her pig-

157

tails flopping up and down on her back. If Rollie was on her bed, she was just going to let him stay right there, and Mother could shake her head and frown all she wanted to.

But he was not there. The bedspread and pillow were crumpled, but not from his weight. She had flung herself down to cry there that afternoon. And then she couldn't. Every nerve in her had been twanging, but she couldn't cry. She could only lie there, her hands doubled up hard, furious that she had nothing to cry about. Not really. She was too big to cry just over Father's having said to her, severely, "I told you if I let you take the chess set you were to put it away when you got through with it. One of the pawns was on the floor of our bedroom this morning. I stepped on it. If I'd had my shoes on, I'd have broken it."

Well, he *had* told her to be sure to put them away. And although she had forgotten and left them, he hadn't forbidden her ever to take the set again. No, the instant she thought about that, she knew she couldn't cry about it. She could be, and she was, in a rage about the way Father kept on talking, long after she'd got his point, "It's not that I care so much about the chess set," he said, just leaning with all his weight on being right, "it's because if you don't learn how to take care of things, you yourself will suffer for it, later. You'll forget or neglect something that will be really important, for *you*. We *have* to try to teach you to be responsible for what you've said you'll take care of. If we . . ." on and on, preaching and preaching.

She heard her mother coming down the hall, and hastily shut her door. She had a right to shut the door to her own room, hadn't she? She had *some* rights, she supposed, even if she was only thirteen and the youngest child. If her mother opened it to ask, smiling, "What are you doing in here that you don't want me to see?" she'd say—she'd just say—

She stood there, dry-eyed, by the bed that Rollie had not crumpled, and thought, "I hope Mother sees the spread and says something about Rollie— I just hope she does."

But her mother did not open the door. Her feet went steadily on along the hall, and then, carefully, slowly, down the stairs. She probably had an arm full of winter things she was bringing down from the attic. She was probably thinking that a tall, thirteen-year-old daughter was big enough to help with a chore like that. But she wouldn't *say* anything. She would just get out that insulting look of a grownup silently putting up with a crazy unreasonable kid. She had worn that expression all day; it was too much to be endured.

Up in her bedroom behind her closed door the thirteen-year-old stamped her foot in a rage, none the less savage and heart-shaking because it was mysterious to her.

But she had not located Rollie. Before she would let her father and mother know she had lost sight of him, forgotten about him, she would be cut into little pieces. They would not scold her, she knew. They would do worse. They would look at her. And in their silence she would hear droning on reproachfully what they had repeated and repeated when the sweet, woolly collie-puppy had first been in her arms and she had been begging to keep him for her own.

How warm he had felt! Astonishing how warm and alive a puppy was compared to a doll! She had never liked her dolls much, after she had held Rollie, feeling him warm against her breast, warm and wriggling, bursting with life, reaching up to lick her face—he had loved her from that first instant. As he felt her arms around him, his beautiful eyes had melted in trusting sweetness. And they did now, whenever he looked at her. "My dog is the only one in the whole world who *really* loves me," she thought passionately.

Even then, at the very minute when as a darling baby dog he was beginning to love her, her father and mother were saying, so cold, so reasonable—gosh! how she *hated* reasonableness!—"Now, Peg, remember that, living where we do, with sheep on the farms around us, it is a serious responsibility to have a collie dog. If you keep him, you've got to be the one to take care of him. You'll have to be the one to train him to stay at home. We're too busy with you children to start bringing up a puppy, too." Rollie, nestling in her arms, let one hind leg drop awkwardly. It must be uncomfortable. She looked down at him tenderly, tucked his dangling leg up under him and gave him a hug. He laughed up in her face—he really did laugh, his mouth stretched wide in a cheerful grin.

All the time her parents kept hammering away: "If you want him, you can have him. But you must be responsible for him. If he gets to running sheep, he'll just have to be shot, you know that."

They had not said, aloud, "Like the Wilsons' collie." They never mentioned that awfulness—her racing unsuspectingly down across the fields just at the horrible moment when Mr. Wilson shot his collie caught in the very act of killing sheep. They probably thought that if they never spoke about it, she would forget it—*forget* the crack of that rifle, and the collapse of the great beautiful dog! Forget the red red blood spurting from the hole in his head. She hadn't forgotten. She never would. She knew as well as they did, how important it was to train a collie-puppy about sheep. They didn't need to rub it in like that. They always rubbed everything in. She had told them, fervently, indignantly, that of *course* she would take care of him, be responsible for him, teach him to stay at home. Of course, of course. *She* understood!

And now, this afternoon, when he was six months old, tall, rangy, powerful, standing up far above her knee, nearly to her waist, she didn't know where he was. But of course he must be somewhere around. He always was. She composed her face to look natural and went downstairs to search the house. He was probably asleep somewhere. She looked every room over carefully. Her mother was nowhere visible. It was safe to call him again, to give the special piercing whistle which always brought him racing to her, the white-feathered plume of his tail waving in elation that she wanted him.

But he did not answer. She stood still on the front porch to think.

Could he have gone up to their special place in the edge of the field where the three young pines, their branches growing close to the ground, made a triangular, walled-in space, completely hidden from the world? Sometimes he went up there with her. When she lay down on the dried grass to dream, he too lay down quietly, his head on his paws, his beautiful eyes fixed adoringly on her. He entered into her every mood. If she wanted to be quiet, all right, he did too.

It didn't seem as though he would have gone alone there. Still— She loped up the steep slope of the field rather fast, beginning to be anxious.

No, he was not there. She stood, irresolutely, in the roofless, green-walled triangular hide-out, wondering what to do next.

Then, before she knew what thought had come into her mind, its emotional impact knocked her down. At least her knees crumpled under her. Last Wednesday the Wilsons had brought their sheep down to the home farm from the upper pasture! She herself had seen them on the way to school, and like an idiot had not thought of Rollie. She had seen them grazing on the river meadow.

She was off like a racer at the crack of the starting pistol, her long, strong legs stretched in great leaps, her pigtails flying. She took the short cut down to the upper edge of the meadow, regardless of the brambles. Their thorn-spiked, wiry stems tore at her flesh, but she did not care. She welcomed the pain. It was something she was doing for Rollie, for her Rollie.

She was tearing through the pine woods now, rushing down the steep, stony path, tripping over roots, half-falling, catching herself just in time, not slackening her speed. She burst out on the open knoll above the river meadow, calling wildly, "Rollie, here, Rollie, here, boy! here! here!" She tried to whistle, but she was crying too hard to pucker her lips. She had not, till then, known she was crying.

There was nobody to see or hear her. Twilight was falling over the bare knoll. The sunless evening wind slid down the mountain like an invisible river, engulfing her in cold. Her teeth began to chatter. "Here, Rollie, here, boy, here!" She strained her eyes to look down into the meadow to see if the sheep were there. She could not be sure. She stopped calling him as if he were a dog, and called out his name despairingly, as if he were her child, "Rollie! oh, *Rollie,* where are you!"

The tears ran down her cheeks in streams. She sobbed loudly, terribly. Since there was no one to hear, she did not try to control herself.—"Hou! hou! hou!" she sobbed, her face contorted grotesquely. "Oh, Rollie! Rollie! Rollie!" She had wanted something to cry about. Oh, how terribly now she had something to cry about.

She saw him as clearly as if he were there beside her, his muzzle and gaping mouth all smeared with the betraying blood (like the Wilsons' collie). "But he didn't *know* it was wrong!" she screamed like a wild creature. "Nobody *told* him it was wrong. It was my fault. I should have taken better care of him. I will now. I will!"

But no matter how she screamed, she could not make herself heard. In the cold gathering darkness, she saw him stand, poor, guiltless victim of his ignorance, who should have been protected from his own nature, his soft eyes looking at her with love, his splendid plumed tail waving gently. "It was my fault. I promised I would bring him up. I should have *made* him stay at home. I was responsible for him. It was my fault."

But she could not make his executioners hear her. The shot rang out, Rollie sank down, his beautiful liquid eyes glazed, the blood spurting from the hole in his head—like the Wilsons' collie. She gave a wild shriek, long, soul-satisfying, frantic. It was the scream at sudden, unendurable tragedy of a mature, full-blooded woman. It drained dry the girl of thirteen. She came to herself. She was standing on the knoll, trembling and quaking with cold, the darkness closing in on her.

Her breath had given out. For once in her life she had wept all the tears there were in her body. Her hands were so stiff with cold she could scarcely close them. How her nose was running! Simply streaming down her upper lip. And she had no handkerchief. She lifted her skirt, fumbled for her slip, stooped, blew her nose on it, wiped her eyes, drew a long quavering breath—and heard something! Far off in the distance, a faint sound, like a dog's muffled bark.

She whirled on her heels and bent her head to listen. The sound did not come from the meadow below the knoll. It came from back of her higher up, from the Wilsons' maple grove. She held her breath. Yes, it came from there.

She began to run again, but now she was not sobbing. She was silent, absorbed in her effort to cover ground. If she could only live to get there, to see if it really were Rollie. She ran steadily till she came to the fence and went over this in a great plunge. Her skirt caught on a nail. She impatiently pulled at it, not hearing or not heeding the long sibilant tear as it came loose. She was in the dusky maple woods, stumbling over the rocks as she ran. As she tore on up the slope, she heard the bark again, and knew it was Rollie's.

She stopped short and leaned weakly against a tree. She was sick with the breathlessness of her straining lungs, sick in the reaction of relief, sick with anger at Rollie, who had been here having a wonderful time while she had been dying, just dying in terror about him.

For she could now not only hear that it was Rollie's bark. She could hear, in the dog language she knew as well as he, what he was saying in those excited yips—that he had run a woodchuck into a hole in the tumbled stone wall, that he almost had him, that the intoxicating wild-animal smell was as close to him—almost—as if he had his jaws on his quarry. Yip! Woof! Yip! Yip!

The wildly joyful quality of the dog-talk enraged the girl. She had been trembling in exhaustion. Now it was indignation. So that was where he had been—when *she* was *killing* herself trying to take care of him. Plenty near enough if he had paid attention to hear her calling and whistling to him. Just so set on having his foolish good time, he never thought to listen for her call.

She stooped to pick up a stout stick. She would teach him. She was hot with anger. It was time he had something to make him remember to listen. She started forward on a run.

But after a few steps she stopped, stood thinking. One of the things to remember about collies, everybody knew that, was that a collie who had been beaten was never "right" again. His spirit was broken. "Anything but a broken-spirited collie"—she had often heard a farmer say that. They were no good after that.

She threw down her stick. Anyhow, she thought, he was really too young to know that he had done wrong. He was still only a puppy. Like all puppies, he got perfectly crazy over wild-animal smells. Probably he truly hadn't heard her calling and whistling.

All the same, all the same—she stood stock-still, staring intently into the twilight—you couldn't let a puppy grow up just as he wanted to. It wouldn't be safe—for *him*. Somehow she would have to make him understand that he mustn't go off this way, by himself. He must be trained to know how to do what a good dog does—not because *she* wanted it, but for his own sake.

She walked on now, steady, purposeful, gathering her inner strength together, Olympian in her understanding of the full meaning of the event.

When he heard his own special young god approaching, he turned delightedly and ran to meet her, panting, his tongue hanging out. His eyes shone. He jumped up on her in an ecstasy of welcome and licked her face.

She pushed him away. Her face and voice were grave. "No, Rollie, *no!*" she said severely. "You're *bad*. You know you're not to go off in the woods without me! You are—a—*bad—dog*."

He was horrified. Stricken into misery. He stood facing her, frozen. The gladness went out of his eyes, the waving plume of his tail slowly lowered to slinking, guilty dejection.

"I know you were all wrapped up in that woodchuck. But that's no excuse. You *could* have heard me, calling you, whistling for you, if you'd paid attention," she went on. "You've got to learn, and I've got to teach you."

With a shudder of misery he lay down, his tail stretched out limp on the ground, his head flat on his paws, his ears drooping—ears ringing with the doomsday awfulness of the voice he loved and revered. To have it speak so to him, he must have been utterly wicked. He trembled, he turned his head away from her august look of blame, he groveled in remorse for whatever mysterious sin he had committed.

As miserable as he, she sat down by him. "I don't *want* to scold you. But I have to! I have to bring you up right, or you'll get shot, Rollie. You mustn't go away from the house without me, do you hear, *never*."

His sharp ears, yearning for her approval, caught a faint overtone of relenting affection in her voice. He lifted his eyes to her, humbly, soft in imploring fondness.

"Oh, Rollie!" she said, stooping low over him, "I *do* love you. I do. But I *have* to bring you up. I'm responsible for you, don't you see."

He did not see. Hearing sternness, or something else he did not recognize, in the beloved voice, he shut his eyes tight in sorrow, and made a little whimpering lament in his throat.

She had never heard him cry before. It was too much. She sat down by him and drew his head to her, rocking him in her arms, soothing him with inarticulate small murmurs.

He leaped in her arms and wriggled happily as he had when he was a baby; he reached up to lick her face as he had then. But he was no baby now. He was half as big as she, a great, warm, pulsing, living armful of love. She clasped him closely. Her heart was brimming full, but calmed, quiet. The blood flowed strongly, steadily, all through her body. She was deliciously warm. Her nose was still running, a little. She sniffed and wiped it on her sleeve.

It was almost dark now. "We'll be late to supper, Rollie," she said, responsibly. Pushing him gently off she stood up. "Home, Rollie, home."

Here was a command he could understand. At once he trotted along the path towards home. His tail, held high, waved plumelike. His short dog-memory had forgotten the suffering just back of him.

Her human memory was longer. His prancing gait was as carefree as a young child's. She plodded behind him like a serious adult. Her very shoulders seemed bowed by what she had lived through. She felt, she thought, like an old woman of thirty. But it was all right now, she knew she had made an impression on him.

When they came out into the open pasture, Rollie ran back to get her to play with him. He leaped around her in circles, barking in cheerful yawps, jumping up on her, inviting her to run a race with him, to throw him a stick, to come alive.

His high spirits were ridiculous. But infectious. She gave one little leap to match his. Rollie took this as a threat, a pretend play-threat. He planted his forepaws low and barked loudly at her, laughing between yips. He was so funny, she thought, when he grinned that way. She laughed back, and gave another mock-threatening leap at him. Radiant that his sky was once more clear, he sprang high on his steel-spring muscles in an explosion of happiness, and bounded in circles around her.

Following him, not noting in the dusk where she was going, she felt the grassy slope drop steeply. Oh, yes, she knew where she was. They had come to the rolling-down hill just back of the house. All the kids rolled down there, even the little ones, because it was soft grass without a stone. She had rolled down that slope a million times—years and years before, when she was a kid herself, six or seven years ago. It was fun. She remembered well the whirling dizziness of the descent, all the world turning crazily over and over. And the delicious giddy staggering when you first stood up, the earth still spinning under your feet.

"All right, Rollie, let's go," she cried, and flung herself down in the rolling position, her arms straight up over her head.

Rollie had never seen this skylarking before. It threw him into almost hysterical amusement. He capered around the rapidly rolling figure, half scared, mystified, enchanted.

His wild frolicsome barking might have come from her own throat, so accurately did it sound the way she felt—crazy, foolish—like a little kid, no more than five years old, the age she had been when she had last rolled down that hill.

At the bottom she sprang up, on muscles as steel-strong as Rollie's. She staggered a little, and laughed aloud.

The living-room windows were just before them. How yellow the lighted windows looked when you were in the darkness going home. How nice and yellow. Maybe Mother had waffles for supper. She was a swell cook, Mother was, and she certainly gave her family all the breaks, when it came to meals.

"Home, Rollie, home!" She burst open the door to the living room. "Hi, Mom, what'you got for supper?"

From the kitchen her mother announced coolly, "I hate to break the news to you, but it's waffles."

"Oh, *Mom!*" she shouted in ecstasy.

Her mother could not see her. She did not need to. "For goodness' sakes, go and wash," she called.

In the long mirror across the room she saw herself, her hair hanging wild, her long bare legs scratched, her broadly smiling face dirt-streaked, her torn skirt dangling, her dog laughing up at her. Gosh, was it a relief to feel your own age, just exactly thirteen years old!

The Murder
on Jefferson Street

With its low, bungalow-style, stucco cottages, and its few high, old-fashioned, clapboarded houses, Jefferson Street looked like any side street in the less expensive part of any American large-town, small-city. And it was just that. Like all collections of human habitations everywhere, its roofs sheltered complex and unstable beings, perilously feeling their way, step by step, along the knife-edge-narrow path of equilibrium that winds across the morasses and clings to the precipitous cliffs of life.

Mrs. Benson, the slender, middle-aged, well-bred widow who had moved to Jefferson Street because it was cheap, was the only one of them—as yet—whose foot had slipped too far from that path for recovery. With her every breath since her husband's death, she had slid down towards that gray limbo of indifference in which nothing seems worth struggling for. She was lost and she knew it, yet even she, stumbling and faltering, did her best to walk forward a little longer . . . until her daughter grew up. At fourteen, Helen, plain, virtuous, intelligent, charmless, needed all the help she could get, if she were to have even a small share of the world's satisfactions.

Although Mrs. Benson went through the normal maneuvers of life, speaking, smiling, asking and answering questions, her secret aloofness from what other people prized was, of course, obscurely felt by the people around her. It was both felt and feared by the Warders, who were her next-door neighbors. It was one of many dark shadows which menaced the security of their Jefferson Street life. They felt everything, feared everything, started back at the snapping of a twig, all their senses strained like those of nervous explorers cautiously advancing, hand on cocked trigger, into an unknown jungle. For they were undertaking a hazardous feat compared to which hunting big game or living among hostile savages is sport for children. They were moving from one social class to the one above it.

Their family (as far as Jefferson Street knew it) was made up of Bert Warder, his wife, their daughter Imogene and a brother Don, employed in a bank in Huntsville. But this presentable floe, visible above the white-collar surface, was the smallest part of the tribe. Below it was a great substructure, sunk deep in the ocean of manual work—overalled uncles who were factory hands, drab, stringy-necked aunts who "worked out," brothers who were garage mechanics, sisters who sold over the counters of ten-cent stores. Only Bert and his bank-clerk brother Don sat at desks with pens in their hands. Bert, like most of the men who lived on Jefferson Street, was an employee of the great Stott McDevitt Electric Company. His desk there felt to him like a pedestal. His bungalow home was another. To the occasional Packard car which, trying to locate a dressmaker or a trained nurse, sometimes purred into it and rolled noiselessly out, Jefferson Street looked plebeian and small-employee-ish enough. For Bert Warder and his wife, brought up in tenement houses in a black brutally industrial city, Jefferson Street was patrician with its small lawns, its shade trees, its occasional flowerbeds, above all, its leisure-class tennis courts on the two vacant lots at the end. They could hardly believe that Bert's night-school-educated brains had lifted them to such a height. The watchful tips of their antennae soon told them that in the class into which they were transferring themselves it was considered no notable feat to live in a home with a yard, so they took care to speak of the street as other people did, with amused condescension for its humbleness; but in reality they all three worshiped it, admired, feared and tried to imitate its inhabitants, lived in dread that something from their past might cast them out from it, and did what we all do, passionately collected their neighbors' weak points as potential ammunition with which to resist attacks on their own. They would have fought to the death against a threat to their social standing on the street—as indeed they did, quite literally, when they felt themselves so threatened.

Tautly on the lookout as they were, they naturally suspected that Mrs. Benson's preoccupied good manners were intended as a reflection on their own. They even wondered whether the Tuttles (neighbors on the other side) might not be looking down on them and on Jefferson Street. There was nothing definite in Francis and Mary Tuttle around which this suspicion could crystallize. It was everything. In their every contact with the Tuttles, the Warders uneasily felt the need to make an effort towards more ease, pleasantness, reticence and quietness than was natural to them. It was fatiguing. And they were never sure they had quite caught the new tune.

Yet, as a matter of fact, the Tuttles did not look down on Jefferson Street but were as glad to live there as the Warders. And, exactly like the Warders, had escaped to it from a life they shuddered to look back on. It was true, as Bert Warder's quiveringly suspicious nose for class differences told him, that both Francis and Mary his wife had been brought up in a house grander than any Bert had ever set foot in, and that Francis' youth (which he mentioned as little as Bert mentioned his) had been spent not with hired girls and factory hands but with Senators and Bank Presidents. But his past had something else in it—misery and failure, and a period of total black eclipse such as the vigorous Bert had never dreamed of. Francis thought of his past as seldom as possible. Till Mary had dragged him up out of the morass of self-contempt in which he lay, already half drowned, and set his feet beside hers on the knife-edge-narrow path of equilibrium, he had taken for granted that his failure in life was inevitable, was because he was an all-around misfit. Living with her, he had begun to hope that perhaps it was only his family he did not fit. He said—he thought—"family." What he meant was "brother." Away from Roger there might be a place for him in the world, after all, he began to hope.

When Mary thought of that past, as wretched for her as for Francis, it was to Francis' mother not his brother, she cried, "Shame on you! Shame!" His mother had long been dead but no tombstone could hide her from Mary's wrath. In the old bad days when both sons were little boys, and the mother's favoritism was at its maddest worst, people used to say, if they noticed Francis at all, "It's hard on an ordinary boy, and rather a weakling at that, to have such a successful older brother. Doesn't give him a chance, really." But Mary knew that Roger was not the one to blame for the tragedy of their relation. She had thought him stub-fingered and tiresome, the sort of successful person who bores sensitive and intelligent ones; but living as she did—mouselike invisible poor relative—close to both of them, she had always known that Roger felt wistful and clumsy beside Francis' accurate rightness of taste, and that he had even a dim divination of

Francis' exquisite undeveloped gift. No, part of Roger's exasperating rightness was that he had never accepted his mother's overvaluation. The older brother had steadily tried to be friendly; but Francis' mother had early conditioned the younger to see in any friendliness from anyone only a contemptuous pity for his own ineptitude. "You, *you!*" cried Mary ragingly to the woman in her grave. "Before your little poet-son could walk alone, you had shut him into the black vault with your stupid admiration of Roger's commonplace successes, your stupid notion that Francis' fineness was weakness. And every year you added another padlock to the door. What strange hateful mania possessed you, you wicked woman, with your mean perverted bullying . . ." Whenever another bitter adjective came into her mind she said all this and more to Francis' dead mother, ending triumphantly, "But *I* know what he is and I've always known—a poet, a spirit so fine and true that just to breathe the air with him lifts an ordinary human being to nobility! I, the little poor young cousin-drudge you never noticed, I married a broken man, and he's a whole man now —or will be soon. I've given him children who adore him, *who depend on him!* And I depend on him. He earns their living and mine. He's escaped from the role of defeated weakling you bullied him into. He creates happiness and knows it! He's coming to life. And every day I bury *you* a little deeper, thank God!"

Never a word of this did she say to Francis. He did not recognize personal resentment as one of the permissible elements in life. Not in his life. It belonged in a lower, meaner world than his. Mary had found the key to his vault, had triumphantly thrown open the door and led him out to happiness, without letting him hear a single reproach to his mother or brother at which his magnanimity could take fright. She knew magnanimity to be the air he must breathe or die. It was part of what she adored in him, part of what she loved in the world he shared with her. But she did not practice it in her own thoughts. Francis, she knew, would have cut his hand off before he would have admitted even to himself that the smallest part of his passionate delight in the twins came from the knowledge that Roger's brilliant marriage was childless, and that he had—at last—something that Roger envied. She felt no such scruples. Hugging her babies to her, she often reveled, unabashed, in happy savagery, "You dumb conspicuous go-getter, you haven't anything like *this* in your expensive empty house!" Sometimes in reaction from the loftiness of Francis' ideals she thought, "Why can't he *be* unfair like anybody, and hate Roger, even if Roger's not to blame? It's nature. Who but Francis could feel guilty—not over *being* unfair, but over the mere temptation to be not angelically just? It'd do him good to let himself go."

But she did not believe this. "He couldn't let himself go into unfairness like just anybody," she thought, "for he's not just anybody. He's a poet with a poet's fineness of fiber. And about the only civilized being on the globe."

So there was Jefferson Street: its low bungalows, its awkward high older houses with their jigsaw ornamentation, filled with people who day by day set one foot before the other along the knife-edge-narrow path that ran—for the Warders across a treacherous black bog, for the Tuttles along the face of a cliff with crashing breakers below, for the others here and there, high and low, as Fate decreed. Nothing happened. Mrs. Benson was the only one who had lost the path. And she sank but slowly towards her final fall. Three years went by. Her daughter was a Senior, getting high marks; unnoticed by the boys. Bert Warder had held his job, not yet realizing that he would never do more than hold it, would never get any higher; only beginning to feel aggrieved because other men were stepped up over his head. He had also, with what sweating pains and secret study nobody would know, learned to play tennis without betraying that he had never before held a racket in his hand. Imogene Warder had passed her examinations—well, nearly all—and was, with some conditions, a Senior in the high school, intensively noticed by a certain kind of boy. Francis Tuttle had not only held his job and had two raises in salary, but had learned to grow roses. His June garden now made him catch his breath. And he had written a little shy and beautiful poetry. Poetry, not verse. "Give me three years more," cried Mary his wife to Fate. "Give me only *two* more, and he'll be safe." The exquisite happiness Francis gave her and gave their children even softened her heart towards his mother. Once she thought—just once!—"Why, perhaps she was a victim too. Someone may have hurt her in childhood as she hurt Francis, hurt her desperately, so that her will to live was all warped into the impulse to hurt back."

Yes, just once, Mary had a moment of divination and guessed that the will to hurt comes by subterranean ways from pain and fear, not from malignancy.

It was but a flash. A partial guess, so weak and newborn a beginning of understanding that it had no more than an instant's universal life before Mary, frightened by a glimpse at the vicious circle of the human generations, seized it and made it personal, "Oh, yes—horrors!— of course, if Francis were still sick with that self-hating Roger-obsession, mightn't he, one way or another, pass his own wretchedness on to the children? And when they grew up, they would pass it on to their children. . . ."

She looked across the room at Francis and the twins, wrestling together on the couch, wildly, happily, breathlessly laughing, and thought contentedly, "Well, there's *one* misery that won't be handed on. His hurt is all but healed."

Leaning on her sword she stood, negligently smiling, at the gate of the garden where Francis grew poetry and roses, from which she had walled his demon out.

II

And then, one day four years after the Warders had moved to Jefferson Street, Fate, unheeding Mary's appeal for only a little longer respite, rode in on the bicycle of the evening newspaper boy, flinging up on each front porch the usual hard-twisted roll of trivial and ugly news. But this time, among the ugly items was a headlined statement about the arrest of one Donald Warder in Huntsville. He had been stealing from the bank he worked for, it seemed; had been playing the races; spending money on fancy women; he would probably get a long term in the penitentiary.

When Bert Warder walked across his front porch on his way home from the office that April afternoon, he was wondering resentfully why dumbbells like Frankie Tuttle got one raise after another, while he with three times Frankie's pep just barely held his own, with frequent callings-down. "But I can beat hell out of him at tennis, anyhow." He applied his tried-and-true old remedy to his soreness and felt the pain abating. The evening paper was still lying in front of the screen door. He stopped, picked it up, glanced at the headlines.

Although the news took him so by surprise as to leave him stunned, his body acted as bodies do when left to themselves, in obedience to the nature of the soul dwelling in them. He rushed into the house, shut the front door, locked it and jerked down the shades of the front windows. His wife and daughter stared at him, surprised. "Look here! Look here!" he said in a strangled voice, and beckoned them to read the headlines.

They read the news together, dropped the paper, looked at each other in despair. The same thought was in them all—if only they need never open that door, if only they could leave town that night, never again be seen by anybody on Jefferson Street. For they knew that as they stood there, all their neighbors up and down the street were opening screen doors, taking in the paper. And, knowing what their own exclamations would have been, had those headlines referred to someone's else brother, they cowered before the gloating, zestful comments they could almost literally hear, "Say, that must be Bert Warder's brother, Don. What-do-you-know-about-that? Well, *well*— maybe we'll have a little less kidding from Bert about our Harvey's being suspended from high school." "Why, look here, I see in the paper where Bert Warder's brother is jailed for stealing. What kind of low-down folks are they anyhow? And Bert being so snooty when he found out that your mother was divorced."

Imogene drowned out the twanging of these poisoned arrows by a sudden outcry, "I can't *ever* go back to school. Those mean kids'll just razz me to death. Helen Benson's so jealous of me about the boys, she'll be tickled pink to have something terrible like this on me. Oh, I think Uncle Don ought to be *shot!*"

Her father and mother too had been thinking that Don deserved to be shot for wrecking their lives. For of course they could not run away from this disgrace. Of course they must, and the very next morning, appear before their neighbors with a break in their armor far worse than anybody's. Harvey Starr's suspension from high school, Joe Crosby's not getting his raise, Mary Seabury's divorced mother, Frankie Tuttle's weak tennis, Helen Benson's unattractiveness to boys —they had been held up by the Warders as shields against possible criticism of slips in their manners. But against the positive disgrace of a brother in the penitentiary! And of course, now everybody would find out about their folks—the aunt who was somebody's hired girl, the old grandmother who couldn't write her name. All that would be in the newspapers, now. "If I had Don Warder here, I'd . . ." thought his sister-in-law vindictively. But Don of course was in jail. "Safe in jail!" thought his brother bitterly. "*He* won't have to walk into an office tomorrow morning, and all the mornings, and face a bunch of guys that'll . . ." Like his wife, his mind was full of foreseen descriptions by newspaper reporters of his illiterate tenement-house relatives. He held the newspaper up to go on reading it. It rattled in his shaking hands. Imogene flung herself on her mother's shoulder, sobbing, "Mamma, you *got* to send me to boarding school. Every kid in school will be picking on me."

Behind the newspaper her father gave a choked roar of rage. Lowering the sheet, he showed a congested face. His jaws were set. "Boarding school! More likely you'll have to get out of high school and go to work." They looked at him, too stunned to ask what he meant. Still speaking between clenched teeth he told them, "Our savings were in Don's bank and I see in the paper here where it says the bank's on the rocks because of the money he stole."

With a wringing motion of his hands as if they had a neck between them, he crushed the paper, flung it to the floor, and turned on his weeping wife and daughter as if he would like to wring their necks too. "What's the good of standing there hollering?" he shouted at them. "Haven't you got any guts? Don't take it lying down like that! Stand up to them! Get back at them before they begin!"

He tramped into the next room and they heard him locking doors and windows.

It was true, just as the Warders thought, that the neighbors began to talk about them as soon as the headlines were read. Helen Benson had taken her mother over to the Tuttles' garden to look at the newly opened tulips. Mrs. Tuttle, newspaper in hand, came out of their shabby tall old house, read out the news to them and they all said how hard it was on the Warders. "Oh, I bet there's some mistake," said Francis Tuttle. "The paper just says he's accused of it. There's no proof he's done it, you notice. I remember Don Warder very well, the time he came to visit Bert last summer. He's not that kind at all. I bet when they get to the bottom of it that they'll find somebody's double-crossed him. Maybe one of the other men in the bank. I'm going to tell Bert Warder I bet that's what happened, the first time I see him." Thinking intently of the accused man's probable innocence, he was absent-mindedly fingering his sandy hair which, he had noticed for the first time that morning, had begun to thin a little.

Mrs. Benson said, "It'll be a terrible blow to the Warders. We must be sure to show our sympathy for them. Helen, couldn't you think of something specially nice to do for Imogene?" She had by now slipped so far from the narrow path trod by those who still cared what happened, that this like all news was no more than a murmur in her ears. But, that Helen might learn what is correct, she brought out the right formula in the right voice.

"Yes, indeed," said Mary Tuttle, in her warm eager way. "People's friends ought to stand close around them when trouble comes."

Mrs. Murray across the street, seeing the four of them standing close together, not looking at the flowers, knew what they were talking about and came over to say compassionately, "I could cry when I think of poor Emma Warder! She'll take this hard."

Helen Benson was awed by her first contact with drama. "My! Imogene must be feeling simply terrible," she said. "I wonder if she wouldn't like to be Vice President of our class. I'd just as soon resign.

Mother, how would it be if I went right up now to the Warders and told Imogene . . ."

But Helen's mother said, her sorrow salt in her heart, "No, when people have had a blow it's better to leave them to themselves a little at first. Don't you think so, Mrs. Tuttle?"

Mary, annoyed to see Francis once more passed over as if he were not present, said resolutely in a formula she often used, "Yes, that is what my husband always advises in such cases, and I have great confidence in his judgment."

But Francis had turned away. How like Mary it was to try even in little things to make it up to him for being a nonentity! But sometimes he thought she only drew attention to the fact that he was. A little nettled, as any man might be (no, considerably more than a man who had had in his past no nightmare nervous collapse), he walked along in the twilight towards the house. On the other side of Mary's wall his exiled demon kept pace with him, trying hard to reach him with old dark associations of ideas, thinking longingly how easy it would be to tear open that nearly healed wound if only these passing relapses could be prolonged. He succeeded in starting a familiar train of thought in Francis' mind, like a brackish taste in his mouth. "And now to grow bald!" he meditated moodily. "What Bert Warder calls my 'moth-eaten' look will be complete." His fingers strayed up to his head again to explore the thinning hair. Deep under the healthy scar-tissue forming over his inner wound, an old pulse of pain began to throb. Roger was getting bald too, he remembered, but of course baldness gave Roger dignity and authority, would actually add to his prestige. Francis, bald, would drop to a lower insignificance. "To him that hath, and from him that hath not—the motto of my life," thought Francis. His demon's eyes glittered redly in hope.

But Mary had built her wall high and strong. And inside its safe protection Francis' roses had struck down deep roots. The gardener came to himself with a smile at his absurdity that sent his demon scurrying away into outer darkness.

"Good gosh, only a thin place in my hair, and seeing myself bald a'ready!" he thought, amused. It had been through that mental habit as through a secret back door, he reflected, that many a dose of poison had been smuggled into his life. He stooped to straighten a drooping tulip. As he stood up, the evening star shone brightly pale in the eastern sky. The inner eye of his intelligence focused itself to a finer accuracy: the world stood before him in its true, reassuring proportions. "Suppose I do get bald—bald as an egg—what of it!" he thought; and, loose, at ease, forgot himself to admire a young pear tree, its

myriad swelling buds proclaiming with pride that, mere humble living cellulose that it was, its roots had found the universal source of
growth. "And all amid them stood The Tree of Life," thought Francis,
his eyes deeply on the miracle.

"Da-d-d-dy," came cautiously from the sleeping porch. The bars
of the railing there were high and set close together because of the
dangerous three-story drop to the cement-floored basement entrance
below, but Francis could make out the twins in their pajamas like
little bears in a cage. "How about a sto-o-ory?" they called down.

"With you in a sec," called Francis, running into the house.

The twins rushed out on the landing to meet him, hopping, twit-
tering, and as he snatched them up, planting loud kisses on his cheeks,
his ears, his nose. "Praise be to God who gave me life!" sang Francis'
heart as he had never dreamed it could. On the swelling tide of this
joy, this thankfulness, he rode up with a surge to the highest point—
but one—of his long struggle with himself. Quite effortlessly, quite
naturally, he thought, "Too bad that Roger's wife can never give him
children," and went warm with delight that he had wished his brother
well.

III

Francis had meant to tell Bert Warder when he next saw him that
he was sure Don had never stolen a cent, that somebody had double-
crossed him. But the next time he saw Warder, he did not tell him
that or anything else.

The morning after the newspapers had announced the arrest of
Bert's brother, Francis stepped out to the border along his front-
yard path to get some tulips for Mary to take to Emma Warder,
Bert's wife. But there was something so beautiful on the first one he
cut that he stood still to look at it, marveling, forgetting the errand
his sympathy had sent him on. Dew-drops clung to the flower, every
tiny globe a magic mirror reflecting all the visible universe. Francis
smiled dreamily down on the extravagance of this beauty. At first
he remembered with amusement that he was the man who only last
night had thought life hard to bear because his hair was getting
thin. Then he forgot himself in contemplation of the divine play-
fulness that shrinks the great far blueness of the sky, the nearby in-
tricacy of trees, immeasurable space itself, to ornament the white
perfection of a flower. The doors of his heart swung softly open, as
they do when a poem knocks and asks to be written.

Another door opened, the door of the next house. Through it—
because he must—Bert Warder came resolutely out from the safety

of his home to face the arena full of enemies waiting to spring upon him. The odds were against him now. He knew that. But he was no coward. He was no man to take things lying down. He was worn with sleeplessness, and half sick with dread of this first impact with a world echoing to his disgrace. But he did not lose his head. Grimly he fixed his mind on the plan for defense he had worked out in the long dark: to get in the first punch and make it hurt. But would he be able to carry out this plan? Cornered by Fate as he was, how could he reach anyone with a first thrust? He had no hope that he could, no hope at all; but he bared his teeth savagely with the desperation of the trapped, and would not give up. The instinct of self-preservation, feeling him appeal as if for his very life, responded with a wild rush of its inordinate stimulants to action. His eyes fell on Frankie Tuttle in the garden next door. He was mooning over a flower he held in one hand, while the other hand in a mechanical gesture drew up the sandy hair over a spot at the top of his head. When a man's hand does that without his realizing it, he fears baldness. The instinct of self-preservation, as it can when driven hard by fear, rose to genius, and showed the endangered man how to strike, in all safety, a first blow to ward off the attack which would be too much for him. He took off his hat, put his hand up to his head and walked rapidly along the sidewalk towards the Avenue, keeping his eyes on Frankie.

When Francis, his heart still unguardedly opened to its very depths by ecstasy, looked up from his tulip, he saw Bert Warder passing by on his way to the trolley, holding his hat in one hand. With the other he was ostentatiously patting and ruffling his abundant dark hair in uncouth caricature of Francis' unconscious fumble. As their eyes met, Bert let fly his arrow with all his might. His words were but trivial and a little common, but his panic tipped them well with the poison of the wish to hurt, and he put his back into the bending of his bow, his broad beefy back. Long before the meaning of the vapid pleasantry had penetrated to Francis' mind, the malignity of its intention was quivering deep in his opened, softened heart. "That's the way to do it, Frankie!" called Bert in a loud coarse tone, his fingers leaping about grotesquely in his hair. "You've *got* a clearing up there. Scratch 'em up into it where you can get at 'em. Scratch 'em up into the clearing."

For a nightmare second, Francis, like a man who dreams he sees a friend run on him sword in hand, felt not pain so much as a wild incredulity. His eyes widened, his dumbfounded face was blank, his up-raised arm and fumbling fingers froze foolishly where they were. From his confusion a gleam of light shone into the other's darkness.

The constriction around Bert's heart loosened. It might really work then, the system of attacking first. He'd sure knocked old Frankie cold, his first try. No man who looked like that could collect his wits for taunts about jailbird brothers. After the hours of helpless dread that lay back of Bert, his relief was exquisite. And the hope it gave! Hope! He might, after all, be able to defend himself. Drinking in greedily Francis' stunned expression and grotesque attitude, he burst into a yelling haw! haw! of triumph and clutching hope to his breast, ran on courageously to where a fellow-worker stood waiting for the trolley.

By that time the meaning of his words reached Francis' mind. He snatched his hand down from his thinning hair with a betraying jerk. Through the quiet morning air Bert's voice came, loudly repeating his joke to Joe Crosby, who remarked, turning back to look at Francis, "Why, I never noticed he has a bald spot." The trolley roared along the tracks and carried the two men away to the office where Francis was at once to follow them.

By the end of that day everybody over in the Stott McDevitt works and out on Jefferson Street knew that the Warders didn't want to have anything said to them about their bad news. "Some folks take trouble that way," said their neighbors with sympathy.

So, since that was the way the Warders took it, nobody did say anything about it to them. And since it was never mentioned nobody knew exactly what was happening. People naturally took for granted that Bert's first thought had been of his brother's innocence, and that like Joe Crosby at the time of his sister's divorce, he was spending his last cent to pay defending lawyers. Since his face grew steadily more haggardly anxious, they supposed that his efforts were all in vain. They sympathized silently, and read without comment day after day the abbreviated accounts of his brother's trial in the local newspapers.

For they were both brief and colorless. Huntsville was far away in another state; one more revelation of the doings of a dishonest bank employee was hardly news; the reporters apparently found Don too obscure a thief to be interesting. No revelations about a grubby working-class family were ever printed. But the Warders saw in every newspaper mention of Don's trial plenty of other material for malicious satisfaction on the part of their neighbors. When finally Don was found guilty and sentenced to fifteen years in prison Bert Warder said wildly to his wife, "Nobody need tell *me* what they're saying to each other. By God! I'd like to knock the words down their dirty throats."

Drunk first with shame and then with anger—for two weeks after

Don's conviction, the bank did fail and the Warders did lose their savings—he had a drunken man's glowering readiness to take offense at nothing. He snarled and hit out in response to harmless greetings; he started every conversation with an unprovoked verbal aggression; be protested every decision made against him at the North Side Tennis Club—as Jefferson Street people called the two vacant-lot courts; he took every happening in the office as flagrant and unfair discrimination against him. His neighbors, his fellow-workers knew that his snarls were cries of pain, and for a time—a short time—said to each other tolerantly, "Poor old Bert, no wonder he's got a grouch." But they had tempers of their own, grievances of their own, their tolerance soon wore thin, his unprovoked attacks began to strike sparks. Two could play as well as one, they reminded him forcibly, at being offensively personal. He was not the only one who knew how to give a nasty dig. Nobody of course dreamed of sinking so low as to throw his brother up to him, Don now in stripes behind prison bars. In fact that story soon passed out of their minds. They had seen Don only once or twice. They were full of their own affairs, their own secret troubles and hidden disgraces. They did not mention the convicted thief, or remember him. But the convict's brother had not forgotten. He imagined in the turn of every exasperated retort a reminder that they had something on him, a threat that he would hear a thing or two about jailbirds if he went too far. So he did not go too far—with them. Every rough rejoinder to a brutal sally from him frightened him into choking down his ill-nature. A sort of approximate balance was found. After a week or so, a Jefferson Street maxim ran, "Anybody can get along with Bert Warder—all you got to do is to tell him to go to hell once in so often."

But there was one among them foolishly unable to return evil for evil. Or to defend himself from boorishness by being boorish. And Bert's first handful of mud had told him where he could fling more without having it flung back on him. Mary, annoyed to have Bert's ragging increasingly center on Francis, used to think, "If Francis only had more vanity! He'd get mad then at teasing instead of feeling ashamed that he's bothered by it; and he'd defend himself." But she was wrong. Against the blackguardism of the wish to cause pain, Francis now as in his youth could devise no defense that he was willing to use. The others on Jefferson Street and in the office snatched up whatever weapon came to hand, dirty or not. If a hit below the belt was what reached Bert's sensibilities most sharply, all right—sure— they'd hit below the belt—why not? But to Francis a choice between committing an ignoble act or suffering from one, was no choice at all. For him only one of those two alternatives was conceivable.

When in an idiotic pleasantry that became threadbare that summer, Bert came suddenly behind him, blew hard on the thinning spot in Francis' hair, rattling off with a noisy laugh, "Let-the-air-*blow*-on-the-head-the-hair-will-*grow*-on-the-head," Francis only jerked away in a gesture of nervous annoyance, and then grinned apologetically for feeling sore. He was incapable of hitting back as the others did, with a jibe about Bert's pendulous paunch, any mention of which, it was an open secret, made him wince, or about his big flat feet, or his bulging eyes, or his occasional bad grammar. He could not understand the idea the men around him had that hurting Bert Warder's feelings eased their own. Rather the contrary, it seemed to him. To find a festering wound in Bert's life and to press on it hard with a word well chosen for its power to cause him pain—how could that do anything but make a bad matter worse? A good deal worse. For Bert's uncouth tormentings caused him only discomfort and annoyance. But it would be shame, as at a real disgrace, which he would feel, to spy upon another's unhealed sores and dash his fist into the one that looked as though it would hurt the most. From his shadowed childhood on, Francis Tuttle had never understood why, with all the unavoidable pain in the world, anyone should wish to add to it.

So he could do no more than try to hide under an apologetic grin the annoyance which, in spite of himself, he found rankled more and more when week after week Bert rang the changes about his looking moth-eaten, twitted him with his poor tennis, his mistakes in gardening, his inability to carry a tune. He even managed a grin, though a faint and weary one, over a new stunt of Bert's which emerged in June, a burlesque imitation of Francis' tennis serve, winding up with grotesquely strenuous contortions to deliver at the end a ball of a lamentable young-ladyish feebleness.

But it was his watchful demon, not he, who grinned, when Bert in a chance remark, stumbled on one of the two secrets in Francis' life he was ashamed of. This was the lesser secret, the one he had thought he had quite outgrown. One Saturday afternoon in June, at the end of some doubles, as they were pulling on their sweaters, Bert Warder chanced to comment on the election of his daughter Imogene to be Vice President of her class in the high school— ". . . right over the head of Helen Benson, I understand. She's all right, Helen is, but kind o' slow. No S. A. as the boys say." The other men all knew that Helen had resigned to make place for the Warder girl and had insisted on her election. A self-conscious silence fell on the group. Sensitive to silences as a sick man to draughts, Bert went hot and cold with his usual reflex of panic—were they thinking that because Imogene was a convict's niece—he backed into his corner and bared his teeth.

But Joe Crosby thought of something to turn the conversation. "I never heard that sex appeal is what swings elections," he said.

The casual quality of the remark blew away Bert's suspicion. But his nerves had been shaken. They needed an outlet. A safe one. His eyes fell on Francis Tuttle. "Sure, S. A. is what settles elections!" he cried at random, giving Francis a great dig in the ribs. "That's why our own Valentino gets elected to all the fat offices in town."

Francis was astonished to feel a sharp twinge from old bitterness. He had not, then, not even yet, left behind the boyish chagrin over all those elections in school, in college, when Roger again and again had been chosen to any office he would accept, and Roger's dead loss of a brother had never been so much as thought of. It was absurd that he still cared anything about that. But an involuntary quiver had passed over his face, just one. It was enough for his tormentor. "Why for fair, Frankie! There's more truth than poetry in what I say. You never do get elected to anything, do you? Were you *ever*?"

This was the time, of course, for Francis to tell him to mind his own damn business. But he could never tell anybody that, and now could think of nothing but a sorry shame that he felt even a last throb of that trivial adolescent hurt. He kept his eyes on the racket he was putting into its case; he fumbled with its fastenings; he was silent. He felt diminished and looked it.

As half-asphyxiated lungs strain joyfully to draw in a life-giving gush of fresh air, Bert felt his own painfully diminished self expanding in the other's discomfort. What suffocating man would hold his hand from the one window he can open? "Poor old Frankie!" he cried gloatingly. "Never had no luck with 'lections. Let's 'lect him to something right now. I nominate him to be Honorary Fly-Swatter to the Ladies' Aid Society. Haw! Haw!"

As they walked down the street together, he composed variations on this new theme. Mary, coming out to meet Francis, heard his horse-laugh, heard him as he turned in at his front walk bawl out, "I nominate Mr. Francis Tuttle to be scorekeeper in the One-legged Men's Athletic Meet. Who will second my motion?"

"What's he talking about?" she asked.

Francis answered, "Oh, nothing."

Sitting that evening over her accounts, Mary chanced to glance up at Francis, reading, and was startled to see an old shadow on his face. He wore the shrunken look that had always frightened her. She had not seen it for a long time now. His relapses in the last years had come seldom and were short; but they still made her almost as miserable as he. Adding up a total and transferring it to the next page she thought, "It is like an old tubercular lesion. Doctors tell you that even when they are healed—or almost—they feel strains that are nothing to normal tissue." Looking down fixedly at her column of figures but not seeing it, she fell for the hundredth time into a puzzled wonder at the inexplicable difference between what people think about bodily and mental sickness. "If it had been a temporary breakdown in a normal lung, acquired in childhood by direct infection from the outside, now almost but not quite healed—why, we'd have told everybody about it, sure of their sympathy. We'd have given it as the natural explanation for the things Francis isn't quite well enough to do yet. There'd have been nothing to hide. Everybody would be interested, and sort of proud and encouraged when Francis recovered. But because it's a temporary breakdown of a personality he's recovering from—and yet that was forced on a sensitive mind by a direct infection from the outside as much as any disease germ!—we have to hide it as though it were a disgrace. He and I can't even talk it over together, and plan what's best to do."

More than by anything else, she was worn by the need to appear unconscious of what was the center of her thoughts. Now, for instance, to be forced to cast about in the dark for a possible explanation of the recurrence on Francis' face of that old look of sickness. Not even to be sure she was not imagining it. What strain could have come into their safe Jefferson Street refuge that was just the same now as ever? Nothing had happened there to change anything. She did give one fleeting thought to Bert Warder's joshing. But he had always been a boor. And anyhow, he was only teasing. Teasing. The word brought up recollections of child play. And child play was always unimportant. The thought reassured her. She began to emerge from her concentration, set her pen down to the paper again, added 23 to 44, and thought in the phrase she had heard her elders let drop so often, "Oh, teasing's nothing." She shot a sidelong look at Francis again. He was reading. His face looked quiet. Yes, she must have been mistaken. It could be no recurrence of his old trouble, vague and dimmed as that was now. Perhaps his tennis had tired him. Presently the idea occurred to her that he might have a real worry, a present one, something at the office perhaps. No matter how bad that was, it would be less dangerous.

IV

She was right. It was a present worry. About a real danger. But not in the office. In his past, close to the foolish weakness uncovered by Bert's random thrust, lay his other secret—the base and bad one. The two were woven together by a thousand connecting nerves. Bert's hammering on one had set the other a-quiver. Suppose, he thought, horrified, that some day, with a reflex reaction like this, some involuntary quiver of his face should betray his feeling about Roger. That he had such a secret to hide was his shame. That Mary might learn it was his terror. Great-hearted as she was, she would never go on sharing life with him if she knew of his mean jealousy of Roger—fiercely suppressed, always festering in the dark hollow of his heart. He thought, as he had a thousand times in his boyhood, that there could be no depravity so low as this vicious ill-will towards his unconscious, blameless brother. He told himself once again that he was cheating Mary—he knew why she overlooked his personal insignificance, his poverty—it was because she had the illusion that he was true-hearted, above baseness. If she should learn that he was capable of this obscene resentment against the kind and generous Roger's superiority—she would turn away from him forever. Was there any real difference— no, there was not—between such a feeling towards a brother and the up-raised arm of Cain?

But Mary was looking at him! She had lifted her eyes from her account book! He had not seen when. How long had she been watching him? A man with a guilty secret is always terrified to be watched. Had she guessed? Had she read this thought in his face? He froze. And waited.

But Mary smiled. The room shone. The golden light around him brought Francis with a start out of his nightmare.

"Why, you've been asleep," said Mary.

"Yes, I must have dropped off for a moment." He thought he had been having a bad dream. What a relief to be waked up!

Before he lay down to sleep that night, he stepped over to the twins' little cribs. Through the high railing of the sleeping porch the barred moonlight shone on their round faces, bland in sleep. How safe they looked. And it was he who made them safe, their father. His heart grew great with love.

But after he was in bed Mary heard him draw the long sighing breath of disheartenment. "What is it, dear?" she murmured. He did not answer. Probably he was already asleep, she thought.

He was awake. His sigh had been of disheartenment. He had perceived that his love for his little boys was tarnished by satisfaction in
his brother's childlessness.

The tide that had been sweeping in so strongly had begun to ebb.
The two vacant-lot courts had never been so busy as that summer.
Bert Warder made them the center of Jefferson Street life as much as
he could. For there he knew success. By concentrating fiercely on his
game, he had made himself one of the best players in the group, and
looked forward all through his uneasy days to the hour between
quitting-time and supper when his racket brought him almost his
only respite from misery. His big unused workingman's body grunted
with satisfaction in the hard physical effort and the copious sweat;
the strain of his fixed idea relaxed in a momentary forgetfulness of
Don in jail; and his perpetual doubt of his equality with those about
him fell with the ravening zest of starvation on the chance to inflict
defeat.

He steered clear cunningly of the two or three men who could beat
him; and naturally played a good deal with Frankie Tuttle. They
did not work in the same department of Stott McDevitt, but he
scarcely let a day go by without hunting up Francis, inviting him to
play, and saying facetiously that he did hope *this* time he might get by
Francis' cannon-ball serve and maybe score a few points against him:
promising if he did, to campaign for Frankie's election to be town
dog-catcher, or chief reader-aloud at the Sewing Society. Day by day
he scored more points.

Mary went up to watch the play once and afterwards said, "See
here, Francis, why don't you give up tennis for the rest of the summer?
You're wearing yourself out." But the turn of her phrase, the quality
of her voice, showed Francis how pitiful he looked on the courts,
going to pieces under Bert's ragging, trotting about, broken-kneed,
like a futile old woman, unstrung, unable to command even his usual
modestly competent strokes. If he stopped playing now after such
exhibitions of feebleness there would be no limit to the joshing he
would get at Bert's hands.

And by this time Bert's joshing did not so much annoy as frighten
him. He was terrified at the thought that another chance lunge in the
dark might lay open to Bert's rough handling the secret shame he was
trying to leave behind. Bert had, so far, never twitted him with Roger,
but at any moment he might try that line; certainly would if he
guessed that to be a sore point. Francis' nerves tautened in vigilance
if he even caught sight of Bert from afar. He seemed to feel Roger in
the air, whenever Bert was present.

He was right in feeling that Roger's name was often in Bert's mind. The contrast between Francis' brother, distinguished, wealthy, well-known, and his disgraced convict brother was one of the sorest of Bert's stripes, the worst of all his envies. Glaring across the net at Francis, going forlornly and hopelessly through the complicated wind-up for his serve, he often thought (as he called out in his witty way, "Play ball, bald head"), "There's one sure thing, 'bo . . . you'll never know from *me* I ever heard of that big stiff!"

Mary was rather troubled by the way Francis seemed to feel the heat that summer. But the hot weather would soon be gone. And wasn't he growing thinner? She'd have to start the evening hot chocolate and crackers again. He didn't seem to have the interest in his garden of other summers. Perhaps only that he hadn't much time left over from tennis. He hadn't written a line of poetry for weeks. But of course the wind of poetry blew fitfully. Was he enjoying the twins as much as he did? Or was that only a fancy of hers?

It was no fancy of hers. Coming in to his children after his daily defeat in tennis, worn out with standing guard over his threatened secret, it was soon borne in on him that he had been in a fool's paradise. Now, while his little sons were babies, yes, of course, they were his, as other men's children were theirs. But they grew so fast. Over and over he lived helplessly through in imagination, as if it had already happened, how they would turn from him. They would soon naturally be asked to visit their Uncle Roger. They could not but be struck by the difference between the two homes. They would begin to compare their father with his brother. And then they would see how their father always took a back seat, never was consulted, never elected to any office, had no influence. As they grew, they would note people's surprise that a Senator—Roger would probably be a Senator by that time—had such a queer singed-cat of a brother. . . . "And now—" Francis often thought, his fingers fumbling with his thinning hair—"now a mangy singed-cat."

Twenty times a day it seemed to him, he was startled to find that without knowing it he was nervously drawing his hair up over the crown of his head.

He was even more startled to discover that he was not the only one to notice this involuntary reflex. "Have you hurt the top of your head lately, Mr. Tuttle?" Mrs. Benson once asked him. He was shocked, and turned on her such a darkening face that she hurriedly excused herself, "I just noticed that you often put your hand up to it."

He snatched down his hand—to his amazement it had been once more lifted to his head—and told her shortly, "No. I'm all right." As he moved away a strange thought came to him, one that soon became familiar by repetition. "It would be better if all the hair on my head would come out. And have it over with!" Sometimes he imagined for an instant between sleep and waking that this had happened. And it was a relief. He was sickened to find that he could not control himself even in such a little matter as fumbling with that thin place. How could he hope to hide his secret vice? Every time he found his fingers in his hair he thought anew, disheartened at his own weakness, that he would never be quick enough to hide what would come leaping up to his eyes at a mention of Roger.

v

But until now he had had Mary. As long as Mary was there . . .

Then early in August a tragic telegram took Mary away for a time. Her delicate sister, now a young wife, was lying at the point of death, her baby prematurely born. "Come at once. Florence calling for you," the telegram read. She telephoned the news to Francis who looked up the hour of the next train for her and hurried to draw the money from the savings bank to cover her expenses. Mary, wild with sorrow and alarm, began to pack, interrupted herself to run over to ask Mrs. Benson to keep a neighborly eye on Francis while she was away, tried to think what clothes the twins would need, stopped to telephone the cleaning-woman about getting Francis' meals, stood still in the middle of the floor and wrung her hands. When Francis came with the money, he was startled to see her so distraught. "If it were only time for my vacation, so I could go along to take care of the twins," he said.

"Oh, if you only could be there to take care of *me!*" cried poor Mary, weeping on his shoulder. "I'm scared to death to go by myself. I don't know how to face anything without you now!"

The memory of this cry of Mary's, the thought of her need for him, Mary's real and actual need for *him* hung like incense around Francis as he stood on the station platform that evening looking after the train from which the twins' handkerchiefs still fluttered. It was a sweetness in the night air as he let himself into the empty house. He was breathing it in as he fell asleep, his arm on the pillow sacred to Mary's dear head. Mary had not yet wholly gone.

The next day, the first day since his marriage that he had wakened alone, he arrived early at the office. To his surprise Bert Warder was at a desk farther down the same room, among the apprentices. Francis wondered if this meant that Bert had been definitely put out of the drafting room. There had been some gossip about his mistakes there. Bert's eyes were roving about unhappily. He saw the surprise in Francis' glance. "You, damn you, with your rich brother and your pull! Of course you get on!" he thought, savage over the injustice of the world. To say something he called out foolishly, "Hey there, Francis, I got special orders to report here to keep the air blowing through your clearing." As Francis took out the papers from his drawer he heard Bert's loud unmodulated voice explaining the joke about "the clearing." "Have I got to go all through that again?" thought Francis, shrugging his shoulders wearily. But the men near Bert thought the joke a flat one, found Bert's noise about it tiresome, and took no pains to conceal their impression. Smarting, humiliated, apprehensive, resentful, Bert drew glumly back into himself, waiting bodefully for a chance to pay Francis out for his rebuff.

At lunch he went out of his way in the cafeteria to sit at the same table with Francis, ostentatiously familiar with him, and after work he let trolley after trolley go by the corner where he waited till Francis arrived. Knowing that he had been punished for being too fresh, he was impelled by the fatality that hangs over people who have struck a false note, to strike it yet more loudly. Francis had never found him harder to endure. As they walked up Jefferson Street together, he said peremptorily, "Run on in and get your tennis things on, Frankie. We'll have a set before supper. Maybe if I try *hard* I can score a point or two on you."

"It's gosh-awful hot for tennis," protested Francis.

Bert's heavy eyebrows lifted ironically over his bulging eyes, he began a certain menacing one-sided smile which was the introduction to his worst joshing. It was uglier than usual, ominous and threatening. There was but one threat that Francis feared. It came instantly into his mind. He lost his head, "This is the time he is going to bring Roger up—and I have not yet thought what to say or how to look!" and said in a hurried panic, "All right, all right. Yes, let's play. It may do us good."

A couple of hours later he came in. He had lost one love set after another to Bert. Too tired to bathe and change, he sank down in a chair. The cold supper that was to be left for him every evening by Mary's cleaning-woman faced him on the table. After a time he ate a little of it, and went stiffly to bed. But for a long time not to sleep. Out of the darkness white balls hurtled towards him. Every time he began to doze, he saw one like a bullet, driving straight towards his eyes, and starting to one side to avoid it woke up to find himself sweating, his heart beating fast, all his muscles taut.

The cleaning-woman, come in early by Mary's instructions to get Mr. Tuttle's breakfast, told him, "You don't look so good, Mr. Tuttle."

"It was hot last night," he told her, pushing his uneaten breakfast away.

It was hot all that day too. But in spite of it he lingered in the furnace-like office till the 5:20 trolley. To no avail. As soon as he stepped off the trolley Bert and a couple of others shouted at him to come and make a fourth at doubles. They played set after set, shifting partners in all the possible combinations. But defeat always came to the side that Francis was on. He could have told them that beforehand, he thought, playing more and more feebly.

When he went home he found two letters waiting for him in the hot shut-up living room. One from Mary. One from Roger. What could Roger be writing for? Avoiding that envelope with apprehension he opened Mary's. The twins were well, she wrote, her sister had recognized her but was not expected to live. The rest was love. ". . . Take care of yourself, darling, *darling!* I miss you so! I need you, dearest. I love you. I love you." A murmur as from Mary's voice rose faintly from the paper, but died away in the silence coldly breathed out from the letter he had not read. He sat a long time looking at it, forgetting his dinner. But it had to be read. He tore it open.

Roger wrote to give Francis the news everybody was to see in the newspaper the next day, that through a new business combine, he was now one of the Vice Presidents of the Stott McDevitt Company, as well as of his own. "We'll see to it that this means some well-deserved advancement for you too, Francis, old man," wrote Roger pleasantly. His letters were always kind. "It'll be fine to see more of you and Mary. We may even decide to become neighbors of yours. Nothing holds us here. And I certainly would enjoy getting acquainted with my splendid little nephews."

The darkness fell slowly around Francis holding the letter in a clutch he could not relax. He had not eaten since noon. His old inner wound opened slowly, gaping here and there, and began to bleed. No, no, he told himself, shamed to the heart, it was nothing so clean and wholesome as bleeding; it was the drip of pus from a foul old ulcer. Well, a man was a leper, who could feel nothing but mortal sickness over his own brother's success.

The blackness deepened. Out of it, one after another, there hurtled towards him bullet-like revelations of his own pitiful abjectness. He had always known he was a dub at business, a dub at tennis, a dub at life—everybody's inferior in everything! But till now he had hoped he might at least grow into a harmless dub. But he was not even that. He was incurably vicious, with the mean vice of feebleness. The beast in his heart would not die, starve it though he might. It snarled and gnashed its teeth over every new triumph of Roger's and sprang up from its lair, rattling its chain in sordid hope every time a faint shadow came over Roger's life. He would rather die, oh, infinitely rather die, than have Mary learn that her husband could not kill that beast, tighten his hold as he might around its filthy throat.

Through the darkness a voice in a loud snarl came to Francis' ears, "He'll never have any children. And I have two sons." Francis leaped to his feet. Who was there in the dark with him? He had thought he was alone. He snapped on a light and looked wildly around the empty room. He was alone.

Had *he* said that? Or had he only thought it so fiercely that it rang in his ears like a cry? His knees shook. Suppose Mary had been there? Suppose Bert Warder had heard him? Why, he was likely to betray himself wholly at any moment, even without the dreaded mention of Roger's name. How it would be mentioned tomorrow at the office, after everyone had seen the announcement in the morning paper! And he who could control his voice no more than his fingers—he found them again fumbling involuntarily at the crown of his head!

He turned off the light, undressed and sat down on the edge of his bed to think, to plan, to prepare himself for tomorrow's ordeal. Everyone would speak of Roger to him, not Bert only, everybody. And he had only this one night in which to find the right look, the right intonations, the right answers.

Yet when it happened he was somehow equal to it. Tense and careful as a man handling a bomb, he thought he had come through safely. Everybody had said the proper thing about what good luck it was to have his brother one of the Company's Vice Presidents, and he had made the proper answers. At least they had sounded all right when he said them. Why did he still have this terrified uneasiness? Then he realized that his apprehension came from the fact that Bert Warder alone had not said a word to him. He, alone of all the men, had only nodded with a sardonic smile, and sat down silently to work. Francis' heart gave a frightened leap. Bert knew something. Somehow he had found out. Perhaps spying on him from a distance as he had doggedly answered the congratulations of the other men Bert had seen through the mask he had tried to keep closely clamped over his face.

All that morning Bert stuck closely to his desk. But Francis knew that he was not thinking of his work. As the hot morning went on, and Bert said nothing, did not so much as look at him, Francis was surer and surer that somehow he knew. But how could he have found out?

A few moments before lunch time Bert took his hat and without a word went out by himself. He was not at the cafeteria at all. In the alarm over this inexplicable variation from routine Francis suddenly knew how Bert had found out. He had been standing outside the open windows last night listening in the dark, and had heard that cry of evil joy in Roger's childlessness. Yes, of course, that was what had happened.

All that afternoon Francis covertly watched Bert. It was strange how easy it was to watch him without seeming to. Even when his back was squarely turned, he could see Bert continually leaving his desk to go from one man to another, whispering in their ears. And then not knowing that Francis could see them even though his back was turned, the listener would stare at him, nodding, nodding his head with pursed-up lips, as Bert went on whispering, whispering, telling about the shameful secret he had heard as he stood eavesdropping in the dark.

Through the breach in Mary's wall the demon had stepped softly in, bringing blackness with him.

VI

Bert said nothing about tennis that day and went home early. Francis got off the trolley at Jefferson Street alone. Forgetting to look in the mailbox, he let himself into the unaired empty house. He did not go about to open windows. He sat down heavily, alarmed to feel his legs shaking under him. He could not afford to be agitated. He must collect himself. His only hope lay in not losing his head. The situation was grave. Bert might even now be coming up the walk to . . . He looked out to reassure himself, and saw not Bert, but a shining limousine drawing up in front of the house.

Before he knew that he had recognized it as Roger's, his trembling legs had carried him in a wild rush of panic to the back of the house. The locked kitchen door halted him. If he went out there he would be seen. Where could he hide? Glaring around, he saw the closet where the mops and cleaning-cloths were kept. He flung himself into it. He was just in time. He had no more than drawn the door shut when the front doorbell rang, and it came to him sickeningly that he could not remember whether he had locked the front door when he came in. He had not breathed till now, when, his lungs almost collapsing, he gasped deeply and drew in to his last capillary the stench from the dirt on the damp mops, decomposing in the heat. The bell rang again. The noise found out his hiding place so accurately that for an instant he felt he was discovered, and gave up hope. He tightened his clutch on the doorknob. Even if they found him out he would hold the door shut, no matter how they pulled on it. He braced himself. A long silence. Had they stepped into the house? He tried to listen. The drumming of his pulse was the only sound. He stood rigid, clutching the doorknob to him, breathing the fetid air deeply in and out of his lungs. Presently from the street the sound of a starting motor came dimly through the closed door.

He waited a long time before he ventured to come out. This might be a trap to make him think they had gone. If he opened the door he might see someone's cold contemptuous eyes fixed on the door, waiting for him. But when he finally did cautiously turn the knob and look out, the kitchen was empty. He tiptoed to the front door, found he had locked it, that he had been safe all the time.

And then, coming to himself for a moment's respite, he turned so faint in a revulsion of feeling that he could not stand. What in God's name had he been doing? But was it possible! It was so remote from anything he wished that he thought for an instant he must have dreamed it. He, Francis, had had no intention of hiding from Roger! Why should he? There was no reason. Suppose Mary had been there? What possible reason could he have given her?

The respite was over . . . *suppose someone had seen him!* A cold sweat drenched him. Someone had seen him, of course. Everyone! They all must have known what he had done. Everyone on the street must have seen him leave the trolley and go into the house. They all knew Roger by sight. They must all have been looking from their windows, saying to each other, "But he's there. I saw him go in just now." Perhaps they had gone out to the street to tell Roger that. Tomorrow they would say to him, suspicious eyes boring into his, "Why in the world didn't you let your brother in yesterday?" What could he answer?

He wrung his hands. "What can I say? What can I say?" Then he thought of a way out. It was simple. He could say he had gone at once to sleep, that he had not heard the bell. He would hurry up to the sleeping porch now and lie down so that if anyone came in he would be found there, his eyes closed. He raced up the stairs and flung himself down on the bed, clenching his eyelids shut. It was essential that he should seem to be asleep. Then he remembered that nobody could come in because the doors were locked. He opened his eyes. He tried to get up.

But he was by now exhausted. He fell back, his wide-open eyes facing a new danger. He imagined Bert Warder asking him the next morning, "What were you up to yesterday that you didn't want your brother to catch you at?" He must think of an answer to that question. Perhaps if he went over it all now in anticipation, question and answer, he might be able to . . . Suppose Bert said suddenly, "What did you get into the mop-closet for yesterday, when your brother . . ."

Oh, horror! He had forgotten to keep his eyes shut to prove to people who came in to spy on him that he really had been asleep when Roger rang the bell. He shut them hard. Then slowly remembered, no, no, that was not necessary. The front door was locked. No one could come in. He opened them again and stared out through the high railing of the sleeping porch.

He had been trying to think what he could answer Bert Warder tomorrow. But how could he hope to control his face to hide his secret when he had no control over his fingers—he snatched his fumbling hand down from his head—over his body—he felt himself cowering again in front of the foul-smelling mop. His desperate thoughts of how to ward off tomorrow's danger were cut short by a sudden cold divination of the present peril. Danger was stealthily closing in on him now, this instant. He felt it creeping up on him from behind. He had known what that danger was. He tried wildly to remember. Oh, yes. He was to keep his eyes closed so that people would think him asleep. He had forgotten that. He shut them tightly, and weak with relief, felt that he had been just in time.

He opened them in the morning, rose and under the cleaning-woman's eyes went through the motions of eating breakfast. He and Bert happened to walk into the office together. He was incapable of speech, all his vitality concentrated on being on his guard. Bert looked pale and out of sorts and said he hadn't been feeling very well yesterday. But he was all right today, he said, goggling his eyes, "And how about some tennis?" Francis saw through this trick instantly. He knew Bert was lying, and why he was lying . . . to throw Francis off his guard. His plan was to wait till Francis was exhausted at the end of the tennis that afternoon and then suddenly to shoot his question like one of his cannon-ball serves . . . *"Why didn't you let your brother in yesterday?"* Yes, it would come to him like one of those fiercely driven balls he could not return.

All day he tried to invent a way out of the trap laid for him. But it was not till he was on the trolley with Bert that his inspiration came to him. The ride home was triumphal. He told Bert with a happy smile that he was going to change his clothes for tennis, and ran into the empty house. He stepped lightly, exultantly, into the kitchen and putting all his weight against it, tipped the heavy refrigerator to one side. As it toppled he stooped, still smiling, and held his right hand under it.

VII

But of course the bandaged hand that could not hold a racket could not hold a pen or run a typewriter either. When he went to the office, he was sent home on sick leave. This pleased him. It meant he could lie on the bed all day, his eyes tightly shut to prevent the discovery that threatened him, that threatened Mary through him. The moment he opened them—as he must if he went downstairs to eat— Mary was in danger again, might at any moment be dragged in the filth of knowing what kind of man her husband was. But he had grown very clever in thinking of ways to protect Mary from that discovery. "I seem to be very sleepy," he said cunningly to the cleaning-woman. "The doctor who took care of my hand told me the accident might have that effect and wanted me to sleep as much as I could. Just keep some food on a tray for me, will you, outside the door. When I wake up I will eat it."

After this he need not open his eyes. He could lie, hour after hour, reveling in the pain of his mangled hand, glorious anguish with which he was buying security for Mary. He could, waiting till black night, grope his way into the bathroom, find scissors and razor blades by feel, and use them without looking. Without opening those tightly shut eyelids he could find the food left for him on the tray, and empty it out in the corner of his closet so that the cleaning-woman would think he ate it. Mostly he lay rigidly still, as still as if he were in his coffin. Now that there was no longer any reason to raise his hand to his head, his arms lay quiet at his side. What a heavenly rest! He was resting almost as well as if he were dead. And Mary was as safe as if he were dead. He was very tired, but infinitely proud of knowing how to protect Mary.

Sometimes his tense eyelids relaxed and he really slept. That was the best. Oh, that was the best . . .

VIII

Since he no longer knew whether it was night or day he could not judge of time. How long had he lain there keeping Mary safe? A day . . . a week . . . a year? The silence of the empty house seemed to be broken by voices. The cleaning-woman's. And—could it be—it sounded like Mary's! It couldn't be Mary's, could it, come back into danger when he was so sure he had made her safe? Not *Mary!* This must be a ruse of his enemies to frighten him into opening his eyes.

He sat up in bed, staring into the red blackness of his closed lids. Horrified, he strained his ears and recognized the children's voices. And that was Mary's step in the hall downstairs. His heart beat in time with it as with no other. Mary had come back, walking straight into mortal peril.

Once more he had failed. He had not saved her after all. For a moment he was undone with defeat, and trembling from head to foot sat dumb with stupid panic.

He heard the dear remembered step start up the stairs. With an effort greater than any in all his life, he summoned his soul to rise on the wings of love and be strong. And saw how even now it was not too late. Even now, though Mary's dear step was mounting the stairs, unsuspecting . . . Now, now was the time to play the man, once for all.

He flung himself on his love for Mary, and with one beat of its mighty wings it bore him beyond Destiny that thought to have him vanquished. Weak he might be—his love, immortal and divine, made him, at the last, mightier than Fate.

IX

Only after the excitement of the clearing of Don's name was all over, when the Warders were on the train going home from their exhausting week in Huntsville did they begin to understand all that the proving of Don's innocence meant to them. Their days in Huntsville after the melodramatic discovery of the real thief, were so crammed with raw emotion they had been bewildered. They had passed without a pause from their first incredulous excitement to incredulous joy and then indignant sympathy for their brother with all those months of undeserved wretchedness back of him. What a nightmare they had all lived through, they said over and over to each other. They had wept together, and the tears had washed the poison out of their wounds so that now, in the train on their way home, they were faint in the sweet weakness of convalescence. Bert's heart that had been crushed shut by shame and fear, softened, opened and let him out from the bitter desolation of self-pity. His imagination that had been smothered under the consciousness of disgrace drew breath again. He forgot what he had suffered; his thoughts were for his brother. "Poor Don!" he said over and over. "Poor *Don!*" After what he had lived through, it was like dying and going to heaven, to feel love and compassion. He was proud with a noble and new pride that the loss of all his savings weighed as nothing with him compared to his brother's vindication.

The news had been in the newspapers. With headlines. Everybody must have read it. The Warders almost expected a congratulating delegation of neighbors to meet them at the station. But when they climbed heavily down from the dusty train and saw that the platform was empty, they thought at once that it was only uneducated working-class people who made a fuss in public, and laid the lesson humbly to heart.

There was no one to be seen on Jefferson Street when they stepped from the trolley at the home corner. They set their suitcases down with a long breath, to look. There was their street! It was theirs, with its genteel lawns, its ornamental useless flower-gardens, its dignified park-like shade trees. There it stood brooding dreamily in the blue summer twilight, and welcomed them back.

"I'll carry the bags, both of them," said Bert to his wife, chivalrously. They trudged along towards their home, their own home, redeemed, shining, safe. They belonged here, they thought, with deep content. They were accepted by these refined people who took lawns and trees and flowers for granted. Their purged hearts swelled with thankfulness, with friendliness, with good resolutions. They must be worthy of their good fortune.

As they approached the Benson house they saw that Helen was standing on the front porch, looking at the newspaper. What a nice girl Helen was, they thought fondly. Imogene called, "*Ooh*-hoo, Nellie!" and skipped up the front walk. Stricken by Helen's face she fell back, shocked. "Oh . . . why . . . what's the *matter?*"

Two or three short sentences were all Helen had to say. Her news, whining ominously like a loaded shell, flew over her listeners' blanched faces, not exploding till long after it had passed.

They stood like stocks, stupidly listening to the sound of the words they could not understand. Then Bert said in a flat voice, "Not Frankie Tuttle! You didn't say it was *Frankie Tuttle!*" He took the newspaper from Helen's hand. Through the brooding summer twilight the headlines shrieked.

JEFFERSON STREET MAN GOES SUDDENLY INSANE LEAPS FROM THIRD STORY TO DEATH

NO MOTIVE IS KNOWN FOR THE ACT

The paper fell from his hand.

"This very morning," said Helen.

"That deep cement-covered entrance to the basement," began Mrs. Benson. "Right over the high railing around the sleeping porch. Mary had come home—you knew she'd been away with a sick sister— and she just started up the stairs."

The Warders, stunned, sank down on their suitcases. Bert's mouth hung slackly open.

Joe Crosby came over from across the street. His lips twitched. His eyes were red. He shook Bert's hand without a word. The Warders had been only bludgeoned into stupefaction by the headlines. They had not believed them. But this silence told them what had happened. Mrs. Warder and Imogene began to cry. A film came over Bert's bulging eyes. He got out his handkerchief, blew his nose, and took his hat off, holding it on his knee and looking fixedly down at it.

After a time when they could, they asked the usual questions. And had the usual answers. No, it just doesn't make sense. His accounts in perfect order. His health all right—he'd hurt his hand of course, but that was not serious; the doctor said it was healing without any sign of infection. And everything going extra well with him, seems though— his brother just made Vice President of the company, the luckiest kind of a break, his brother thinking the world and all of him—came right over the minute he heard of this and took Mary and the children back. To make their home with him. Always. Said he'd always wanted children in his home. No, everything in the business end of his life was fine, couldn't be better. His brother kept saying there wasn't *anything* he wouldn't have done for him. And no trouble at home, Lord, *no!* He and Mary were the happiest couple on the street. Suspicious of their good faith, Bert said it seemed as if there *must* have been some warning. "No, there wasn't. He was just exactly the same as ever, the last time anybody saw him. He'd hurt his hand, you know—was that before you went to Huntsville? No, I guess it was afterwards— and that kept him away from the office for a while. It must have been while he was at home with that, that he . . . ."

Bert Warder was shocked at a glimpsed possibility of unneighborly neglect. "For the Lord's sake, hadn't anybody gone in to see that he was all right?" he asked sternly.

Mrs. Benson defended herself hastily, "Oh, yes, yes. Before she left Mary had asked me to look after him, and I went over there every day. Sometimes twice. But the cleaning-woman always said he was asleep. She told me the doctor had given him something to deaden the pain in his hand and make him drowsy."

Joe Crosby confirmed this. "Yes, every time I went in too, he was asleep. I went clear up to his room several times. The shades were pulled down and it was dark. But I could see he was asleep all right." He answered the stubborn question in the other's face. "Yes, I know, Bert, I felt just the way you do, as if we might have done *something*, if we'd been any good. But you know there isn't anything *any*body can do when it's a case of . . ." he drew in a long breath before he could pronounce the word, "it was just plain insanity, Bert."

"Frankie wasn't insane!" rapped out Bert, indignant. "He was a *swell* fellow!"

Joe lowered his voice and with a dark shamed intonation and yet with a certain relish of the enormity he was reporting, said, "Bert, when they picked up his body they found he'd shaved his head. All over. Every spear of hair shaved off. Down to the skin. The way you shave your face."

This did stagger the questioner. He said feebly, "You don't *say* . . . ! Good gosh, his *head!* Why, what in the . . . what ever would make anybody do *that?*" and fell back into his stockish uncomprehending blankness.

Mrs. Benson murmured an explanation, "The doctors told his brother that's one of the signs of religious mania—the tonsure, you know. They told his brother that sometimes insane . . ."

"Oh, they make me tired!" cried Joe Crosby in angry sorrow. "They don't know anything about it. Why don't they keep still!"

Bert Warder agreed sadly, "I guess nobody knows anything about what causes insanity."

It came over him that this was no waking nightmare, was fact. But he could not admit it as fact. "It just don't seem *possible* to me!" he told them, his voice breaking grotesquely in his pain. "Why, Frankie and me . . . why, I never *had* a better pal than Frankie Tuttle!"

The Biologist
and His Son

The older children had gone noisily and cheer-
fully off to kindergarten and school. Upstairs the baby was making
half-grumbling, half-cheerful remarks, giving notice to any ear acquainted with babies that he had now been a long time awake after
his nap, that he was feeling blithe and refreshed, but that he would be
seriously displeased if one of his servitors did not soon give him
some attention.

"What do you say we bring him down for a few minutes?" suggested the mother. "I don't have to start clearing up the table this
minute."

With the habitual, only half-conscious gesture of the twentieth-
century man, the scientist father glanced at his watch. So the mariner
glances at his compass. For the same purpose. To learn the exact
spot to which the moment had brought him. The glance reassured
him. "Sure," he answered, "I have half an hour before I must start
for the laboratory. I'll go get him." He pushed back his chair and went
upstairs.

The mother relaxed in her chair. Unheard of, she thought, to have
a pause between one and another of the tasks which trod fast on each
other's heels, from her waking hour to the falling-into-bed end of
her day.

A door opened upstairs. The baby, seeing his father coming towards his crib, cried out joyfully in his own lingo, quite intelligible to both his parents, that he was pleased at the prospect of being picked up by one of the two pickers-up he most approved of.

The mother heard her two menfolks coming down the stairs. She had given her youngest child his bottle just before his nap, not two hours before. But she turned her face towards the door as eagerly as though she had been separated from him for days or months. The baby rode through the door, high in his father's arms. The mother's eyes (only a few years before they had been the shallow pretty eyes of a pretty girl, fixed exclusively on her skin, her lipstick, her hair-do, her boy-friends, her own affairs) shone in a passion of love. She had forgotten how marvelous her little son was, how miraculous it was to have a new baby. The same astonished delight that he and his mother were in the same world brightened the baby's round face to a glow. He opened his mouth in a toothless grimace of joy, grotesque and exquisite.

"Hello there, Toots!" said his American mother, undramatically.

The father sat down at the table, holding his small son on what for a father corresponds to the lap of a mother. The baby was still so young that he could not sit up without support. At the times when he was out of his crib, somebody held him. This procedure is passed by the latest baby-books as psychologically acceptable, so the parents enjoyed without reservations the rich sensuous pleasure given them by this contact with the warm, firming jelly of the small body. The baby liked it too.

But the table was still cluttered with dishes, silver, glass from the luncheon. With that array of glittering and shining objects before him on the table, *within reach*, the baby forgot his mother, he thought no more of his father. He lunged far forward—much farther than any adult seeing his tininess could have dreamed possible—and in a fiercely energetic sweep, gathered towards him an armful of—of everything. Water-glass, plate, spoons, fork, butter-dish, together with a wisp of the tablecloth clutched firmly in one hand. In a commanding gesture of power, he drew it all towards him, tipping over, clattering.

"Mercy on us!" cried the mother, laughing, dismayed. She sprang up with the steel-spring speed and controlled accuracy of her thirty-two years. She pushed all those breakable objects to one side and the other, tucked the tablecloth back out of the baby's reach, and left a bare expanse of wood before him.

But rapid as her action had been, her mind had remembered an axiom of those excellent baby-books: "Don't take away from children things they can't have, without substituting something they can have. No vacuums!"

"I'll get him a pot-lid to play with," she said; "Mitsy used to like pot-lids when she was little. Perhaps he's old enough now for that." She stepped quickly into the kitchen and brought out a tin lid. It was round, with a black knoblike handle in the middle. She laid it on the table in front of the baby, knob down, tilted to one side.

It did not look as interesting to the baby as the glass and china which had been taken away. But he felt too comfortable to resent the affront. His spine braced against his father's warm solid body gave him a delicious sensation of security. He gave the pot-lid an amiable look and put out a fat small hand to see what it felt like.

The lid was balanced unevenly on the knob. It tilted down at one side under the weight of the baby's hand. The tin edge made a little click as it struck the table.

The baby was surprised. He lifted his hand and put it down again on the other side of the lid. The lid tilted again, and clicked more loudly on the table. The baby liked clicks. But he did not understand what made the thing move. He had not told his hand to make it move.

His hand rose again and came down more heavily. His purpose was to make that thing stay put. But it did not stay put. His muscles were, as yet, by no means under the control of his brain. His hand struck the metal circle a slanting wavering blow. Now the lid did not tilt. It spun part way around on its knob—a quarter-turn before coming to rest. At this unexpected circular motion, the little face took on an expression of astonishment, so extreme that the mother began to laugh. He did not notice this. His eyes were fixed, so intently that they crossed a little, on the phenomenon he was exploring. He had handled other objects. But they had all moved to and fro, bang! Or up and down, bang! But not around in this new circular spinning motion.

Visibly and purposefully he took thought, and set his hand tentatively to the lid. It swung part way around a circle, its rim clicking irregularly on the table as the wobbling little hand moved it.

The baby had wanted it to lie flat. The other things he knew, like a block, or a stick, or a spoon, all lay flat. What was this unruly idea of waveringly going around in a circle? The faintly marked eyebrows drew into a straight line, the little mouth clamped shut on the resolve to make the thing do what he wanted it to do, not what it wanted to. He looked much older than he was. For the time between two heartbeats his parents saw to their incredulous astonishment that he looked exactly as his doctor-grandfather, now gray-haired and be-spectacled, looked when confronted with a complicated surgical case.

His face was dark with determination. He frowned, focusing his will power on the problem before him. And for the first time in his life, he stretched out both his hands in a co-ordinated gesture.

"*Oh—!*" cried his mother in surprise and delight.

The scientist had followed the baby's doings with an accurate professional knowledge. It was as though he could look through the gold-down-covered skull at the developing brain and see, visibly enacted, the inner drama of growth, development, increasing mastery of nerve-centers and muscles. He smiled at his wife as proud as he would be when their son graduated from college with high honors.

The scientist's wife thought back and said aloud, "That's much earlier than any one of the others could control both hands at once."

Silently she thought forward, "He is going to be very bright. Very strong. Fine co-ordination." In one leap, her imagination soared years ahead, saw him conquering in football, in hockey. Or perhaps that good muscular co-ordination would make him a world-famous pianist. Or perhaps—foreboding blew coldly across her dream—there may be in him some of Uncle Jerry's moral slipperiness, and this muscular dexterity may tempt him into cheating at cards.

All this at the time-annihilating speed of feeling and thinking, between two breaths, between two heartbeats. She looked back at the baby as he was now. He looked like any other baby. He was not doing anything at all remarkable. His short, short human ability to give his attention to anything had come abruptly to an all too human end. He had forgotten that he had wanted to make that tilting thing lie flat. His interest in it had sprung suddenly to life. It was gone as quickly, like a light snapped off at the switch. He cared no more about it. As idly as a monkey, still bleeding from his fight over a bright piece of tin, lets it fall from his hand to scratch himself and look blankly around with his shallow, hard simian eyes, the baby had forgotten the existence of the pot-lid, challenging his powers. Like the adult voter at the polls, forgetting—what was so agonizingly present to his heart when his son was on the front line in battle— the life-and-death need for a strong international organization to keep the peace, the baby saw no point in making any effort to go on mastering a problem which, a moment before, had passionately interested him.

His face sagged into vacancy. He looked younger than he was, looked as he had when he was a passive, month-old cocoon. He leaned his head, that great human bone-box crammed with the raw material of intelligence, peacefully against his father's chest, and took his ease within the support of his father's encircling arms. He slumped down, he let his hand—antenna of his personality—stray aimlessly over the surface of the pot-lid. He yawned the startlingly human yawn of his age.

His mother gave the modern's look of unquestioning submissiveness at her master, the watch on her wrist. "About time to put his next feeding on to warm," she thought.

In the baby's inattentive tactile exploring of the new object before him, his tiny fingers grasped the edge of the lid. It was a gentle meaningless reflex. From his birth, his fingers had closed on anything they touched. But it happened that at the same moment, the muscles of his arm chanced to contract a little, so that the hand grasping the lid lifted it slightly from the table. Since he did not know he had done this, he let it fall. The resultant noise was no mere click. It was a clash, a metallic bang.

His hand halted dead to ask his brain what this noise was. His eyes, which had begun to float sleepily to and fro, opened wide and focused with a snap on the hand and the lid. He had learned to focus his eyes so many weeks ago that he could now control and give the necessary orders to the complicated set of nerves and innumerable tiny muscles involved, instantly, with as automatic a skill as a master-violinist rips off a two-octave run, or a star batter lines out a home run over the scoreboard. He was trying to bring his brain into a focus as clear. What had happened to his hand? To the lid?

His fingers were still curved around the edge of the lid. He set those muscles, flexed the bigger muscles of his arm and lifted his hand. The tin object rose with it. Why, it wasn't the shape he thought it was! The baby's face took on an expression of epic intentness—so perhaps did Madame Curie's in the laboratory. Or Benjamin Franklin's, when he touched his knuckle to the key.

Up, up, up! When the lid stood straight up, one side towards him, the baby saw it no longer as a round flat object, but tall and thin. How could it be utterly different from what it had been? He gazed at it in a wild surmise—so Columbus may have gazed over the railing of his caravel at the wavering shore light in the night's blackness.

Of course the untutored muscles of his arm could not hold themselves steady more than an instant. They wavered. The lid slid down, knob uppermost this time, and clashed with its whole metal surface on the wood.

Oh, what a glorious sound was that! The baby's ears transmitted the rolling sound waves to his brain as, to ours, comes the clash of cymbals in an orchestra. His nerves, quivering to the stimulation of the clatter, swept him away from those capacities for logic and intellectual deduction which for a single instant had been stirred into dawning life. Deep, primitive, sensory reflexes shook his little being to the core. That mighty crash! Had he himself made it? How? He leaned forward, panting. He would do it again. He had done it once.

But now what was involved was not an old reflex gesture for his hand, like closing around an adult finger. This was new, and there were several parts to it. His fumbling baby-brain tried to bear in mind the several complicated movements to be made. In years to come, learning to check his speed on the beginner's slope of the skier's practice field, he would recite his directions to himself, "Knees bent! Toes turned in equally from both sides! Weight well forward!" trying to think and perform a number of things in the same instant. As manfully he now wrestled with the complex maneuver of tensing some muscles and loosing others.

At his first try he failed. Once he failed. Twice he failed. His smooth round face that had been so bland became savagely taut. Strange to see his little jaw set hard.

His parents watched him intently. They held their breath. He had forgotten that they were in the room with him. He had forgotten that they existed. He was alone with the effort that was to be life-long with him, as with all his ancestors, all his descendants—to master and direct the forces of the material world around him.

On this he concentrated all that he could control of the forces he found within him.

And then—why, it was easy. His brain perceived which orders to issue to muscles and nerves. As soon as he knew what orders to give, mere brute matter, like tin and wood, became his slave. In a gesture wild and uncertain but not random, using far more energy than was needed, he lifted the lid high from the table and dashed it down. Again that marvelous exciting clatter. And then again. And again. His face blazed. His nerves tingled in delicious spasms as the agitated air waves beat on his eardrums. Bang! Clash! Bang! Clash!

His mouth fell open in animal gratification like that of a primitive man dancing his heart out to the frenzy of rattle and drum. Bang! Clash! He could do it as often as he wanted. Clash! Bang! On his face sat might and power. Bang! Clash! Clatter! Glory! Glory! Bang!

During his struggle to go beyond what till then had been possible to him, his parents' young faces had been almost as tense as his.

Their well-disciplined brains analyzed accurately the meaning of the moment for him. They followed him in thought to the last nerve-center. But their eardrums, like his, had been violently assaulted by the unexpectedly loud clang of metal on wood. For them, as for the baby, this jar had snapped the thread of the effort to understand. It summoned their nerves, as it did his, to a reaction that was purely, wildly sensory. The little boy gloriously clashing a tin pot-lid on the table suddenly seemed to them the funniest thing they had ever seen. They burst into laughter. Tears ran down their cheeks. They laughed like crazy things. They did not look at all like serious young intellectuals. They looked like hilarious children playing with a toy.

But through the rhythmic clang of the little Maenad's cymbal, the kitchen clock now made a remorselessly reasonable sound, striking the half hour. It said but one syllable in a small, self-contained voice. To the parents it was like the stentorian "—'SHUN!" of a drill sergeant. Docile, obedient, unquestioning, they snapped to attention, wheeled and marched as they were ordered.

The mother took the lid away from the baby and went out to the kitchen to put the milk for his next feeding on to warm. The father carried him upstairs to his crib.

The baby made no protest. He was tired. He had lived deeply with all he had. He had adventured forward beyond his age. He had reached out from the simple manageable mechanisms of babyhood to grasp some of the complexity of being human. And he had had enough—for a while. He yawned, rubbed his eyes with his fists, relaxed all his muscles, sagged limply in his father's arms till, as when he had been newborn, his weight seemed twice what it was.

His father laid him down in his crib. His fingers clutched mechanically around the big masculine thumb. But he did not care when his father gently unloosed the five pink petals. He drew in a deep breath and turned his head to one side till he could see the particular wall-lamp which was his landmark for being sure he was in his own bed.

He had used up an unheard-of sum of nervous, muscular, intellectual energy. He needed food. He slid back to an age far below his own and gazing vacantly at the ceiling, waited with the idiotic simplicity of a one-celled organism for someone to put the food he needed into his mouth.

Sex Education

It was three times—but at intervals of many years —that I heard my Aunt Minnie tell about an experience of her girlhood that had made a never-to-be-forgotten impression on her. The first time she was in her thirties, still young. But she had then been married for ten years, so that to my group of friends, all in the early teens, she seemed quite of another generation.

The day she told us the story, we had been idling on one end of her porch as we made casual plans for a picnic supper in the woods. Darning stockings at the other end, she paid no attention to us until one of the girls said, "Let's take blankets and sleep out there. It'd be fun."

"No," Aunt Minnie broke in sharply, "you mustn't do that."

"Oh, for goodness' sakes, why not!" said one of the younger girls, rebelliously, "the boys are always doing it. Why can't we, just once?"

Aunt Minnie laid down her sewing. "Come here, girls," she said, "I want you should hear something that happened to me when I was your age."

Her voice had a special quality which, perhaps, young people of today would not recognize. But we did. We knew from experience that it was the dark voice grownups used when they were going to say something about sex.

Yet at first what she had to say was like any dull family anecdote; she had been ill when she was fifteen; and afterwards she was run down, thin, with no appetite. Her folks thought a change of air would do her good, and sent her from Vermont out to Ohio—or was it Illinois? I don't remember. Anyway, one of those places where the corn grows high. Her mother's Cousin Ella lived there, keeping house for her son-in-law.

The son-in-law was the minister of the village church. His wife had died some years before, leaving him a young widower with two little girls and a baby boy. He had been a normally personable man then, but the next summer, on the Fourth of July when he was trying to set off some fireworks to amuse his children, an imperfectly manufactured rocket had burst in his face. The explosion had left one side of his face badly scarred. Aunt Minnie made us see it, as she still saw it, in horrid detail: the stiffened, scarlet scar tissue distorting one cheek, the lower lip turned so far out at one corner that the moist red mucous-membrane lining always showed, one lower eyelid hanging loose, and watering.

After the accident, his face had been a long time healing. It was then that his wife's elderly mother had gone to keep house and take care of the children. When he was well enough to be about again, he found his position as pastor of the little church waiting for him. The farmers and village people in his congregation, moved by his misfortune, by his faithful service and by his unblemished character, said they would rather have Mr. Fairchild, even with his scarred face, than any other minister. He was a good preacher, Aunt Minnie told us, "and the way he prayed was kind of exciting. I'd never known a preacher, not to live in the same house with him, before. And when he was in the pulpit, with everybody looking up at him, I felt the way his children did, kind of proud to think we had just eaten breakfast at the same table. I liked to call him 'Cousin Malcolm' before folks. One side of his face was all right, anyhow. You could see from that that he *had* been a good-looking man. In fact, probably one of those ministers that all the women—" Aunt Minnie paused, drew her lips together, and looked at us uncertainly.

Then she went back to the story as it happened—as it happened that first time I heard her tell it. "I thought he was a saint. Everybody out there did. That was all *they* knew. Of course, it made a person sick to look at that awful scar—the drooling corner of his mouth was the worst. He tried to keep that side of his face turned away from folks. But you always knew it was there. That was what kept him from marrying again, so Cousin Ella said. I heard her say lots of times that he knew no woman would touch any man who looked the way he did, not with a ten-foot pole.

"Well, the change of air did do me good. I got my appetite back, and ate a lot and played outdoors a lot with my cousins. They were younger than I (I had my sixteenth birthday there) but I still liked to play games. I got taller and laid on some weight. Cousin Ella used to say I grew as fast as the corn did. Their house stood at the edge of the village. Beyond it was one of those big cornfields they have out west. At the time when I first got there, the stalks were only up to a person's knee. You could see over their tops. But it grew like lightning, and before long, it was the way thick woods are here, way over your head, the stalks growing so close together it was dark under them.

"Cousin Ella told us youngsters that it was lots worse for getting lost in than woods, because there weren't any landmarks in it. One spot in a cornfield looked just like any other. 'You children keep out of it,' she used to tell us almost every day, '*especially you girls*. It's no place for a decent girl. You could easy get so far from the house nobody could hear you if you hollered. There are plenty of men in this town that wouldn't like anything better than—' She never said what.

"In spite of what she said, my little cousins and I had figured out that if we went across one corner of the field, it would be a short cut to the village, and sometimes, without letting on to Cousin Ella, we'd go that way. After the corn got really tall, the farmer stopped cultivating, and we soon beat down a path in the loose dirt. The minute you were inside the field it was dark. You felt as if you were miles from anywhere. It sort of scared you. But in no time the path turned and brought you out on the far end of Main Street. Your breath was coming fast, maybe, but that was what made you like to do it.

"One day I missed the turn. Maybe I didn't keep my mind on it. Maybe it had rained and blurred the tramped-down look of the path. I don't know what. All of a sudden, I knew I was lost. And the minute I knew that, I began to run, just as hard as I could run. I couldn't help it, any more than you can help snatching your hand off a hot stove. I didn't know what I was scared of, I didn't even know I *was* running, till my heart was pounding so hard I had to stop.

"The minute I stood still, I could hear Cousin Ella saying, 'There are plenty of men in this town that wouldn't like anything better than—' I didn't know, not really, what she meant. But I knew she meant something horrible. I opened my mouth to scream. But I put both hands over my mouth to keep the scream in. If I made any noise, one of those men would hear me. I thought I heard one just behind me, and whirled around. And then I thought another one had tiptoed up behind me, the other way, and I spun around so fast I almost fell over. I stuffed my hands hard up against my mouth. And then—I couldn't help it—I ran again—but my legs were shaking so I soon had to stop. There I stood, scared to move for fear of rustling the corn and letting the men know where I was. My hair had come down, all over my face. I kept pushing it back and looking around, quick, to make sure one of the men hadn't found out where I was. Then I thought I saw a man coming towards me, and I ran away from him—and fell down, and burst some of the buttons off my dress, and was sick to my stomach—and thought I heard a man close to me and got up and staggered around, knocking into the corn because I couldn't even see where I was going.

"And then, off to one side, I saw Cousin Malcolm. Not a man. The minister. He was standing still, one hand up to his face, thinking. He hadn't heard me.

"I was so *terrible* glad to see him, instead of one of those men, I ran as fast as I could and just flung myself on him, to make myself feel how safe I was."

Aunt Minnie had become strangely agitated. Her hands were shaking, her face was crimson. She frightened us. We could not look away from her. As we waited for her to go on, I felt little spasms twitch at the muscles inside my body. "And what do you think that *saint,* that holy minister of the Gospel, did to an innocent child who clung to him for safety? The most terrible look came into his eyes—you girls are too young to know what he looked like. But once you're married, you'll find out. He grabbed hold of me—that dreadful face of his was *right on mine*—and began clawing the clothes off my back."

She stopped for a moment, panting. We were too frightened to speak. She went on, "He had torn my dress right down to the waist before I—then I *did* scream—all I could—and pulled away from him so hard I almost fell down, and ran and all of a sudden I came out of the corn, right in the back yard of the Fairchild house. The children were staring at the corn, and Cousin Ella ran out of the kitchen door. They had heard me screaming. Cousin Ella shrieked out, 'What is it? What happened? Did a man scare you?' And I said, 'Yes, yes, yes, a man—I ran—!' And then I fainted away. I must have. The next thing I knew I was on the sofa in the living room and Cousin Ella was slapping my face with a wet towel."

She had to wet her lips with her tongue before she could go on. Her face was gray now. "There! that's the kind of thing girls' folks ought to tell them about—so they'll know what men are like."

She finished her story as if she were dismissing us. We wanted to go away, but we were too horrified to stir. Finally one of the youngest girls asked in a low trembling voice, "Aunt Minnie, did you tell on him?"

"No, I was ashamed to," she said briefly. "They sent me home the next day anyhow. Nobody ever said a word to me about it. And I never did either. Till now."

By what gets printed in some of the modern child-psychology books, you would think that girls to whom such a story had been told would never develop normally. Yet, as far as I can remember what happened to the girls in that group, we all grew up about like anybody. Most of us married, some happily, some not so well. We kept house. We learned—more or less—how to live with our husbands, we had children and struggled to bring them up right—we went forward into life, just as if we had never been warned not to.

Perhaps, young as we were that day, we had already had enough experience of life so that we were not quite blank paper for Aunt Minnie's frightening story. Whether we thought of it then or not, we couldn't have failed to see that at this very time, Aunt Minnie had been married for ten years or more, comfortably and well married, too. Against what she tried by that story to brand into our minds stood the cheerful home life in that house, the good-natured, kind, hard-working husband, and the children—the three rough-and-tumble, nice little boys, so adored by their parents, and the sweet girl baby who died, of whom they could never speak without tears. It was such actual contact with adult life that probably kept generation after generation of girls from being scared by tales like Aunt Minnie's into a neurotic horror of living.

Of course, since Aunt Minnie was so much older than we, her boys grew up to be adolescents and young men while our children were still little enough so that our worries over them were nothing more serious than whooping cough and trying to get them to make their own beds. Two of our aunt's three boys followed, without losing their footing, the narrow path which leads across adolescence into normal adult life. But the middle one, Jake, repeatedly fell off into the morass. "Girl trouble," as the succinct family phrase put it. He was one of those boys who have "charm," whatever we mean by that, and was always being snatched at by girls who would be "all wrong" for him to marry. And once, at nineteen, he ran away from home, whether with one of these girls or not we never heard, for through all her ups and downs with this son, Aunt Minnie tried fiercely to protect him from scandal that might cloud his later life.

Her husband had to stay on his job to earn the family living. She was the one who went to find Jake. When it was gossiped around that Jake was in "bad company" his mother drew some money from the family savings-bank account, and silent, white-cheeked, took the train to the city where rumor said he had gone.

Some weeks later he came back with her. With no girl. She had cleared him of that entanglement. As of others, which followed, later. Her troubles seemed over when, at a "suitable" age, he fell in love with a "suitable" girl, married her and took her to live in our shire town, sixteen miles away, where he had a good position. Jake was always bright enough.

Sometimes, idly, people speculated as to what Aunt Minnie had seen that time she went after her runaway son, wondering where her search for him had taken her—very queer places for Aunt Minnie to be in, we imagined. And how could such an ignorant, homekeeping woman ever have known what to say to an errant willful boy to set him straight?

Well, of course, we reflected, watching her later struggles with Jake's erratic ways, she certainly could not have remained ignorant, after seeing over and over what she probably had; after talking with Jake about the things which, a good many times, must have come up with desperate openness between them.

She kept her own counsel. We never knew anything definite about the facts of those experiences of hers. But one day she told a group of us—all then married women—something which gave us a notion about what she had learned from them.

We were hastily making a layette for a not especially welcome baby in a poor family. In those days, our town had no such thing as a district-nursing service. Aunt Minnie, a vigorous woman of fifty-five, had come in to help. As we sewed, we talked, of course; and because our daughters were near or in their teens, we were comparing notes about the bewildering responsibility of bringing up girls.

After a while, Aunt Minnie remarked, "Well, I hope you teach your girls some *sense*. From what I read, I know you're great on telling them 'the facts,' facts we never heard of when we were girls. Like as not, some facts I don't know, now. But knowing the facts isn't going to do them any more good than *not* knowing the facts ever did, unless they have some sense taught them, too."

"What do you mean, Aunt Minnie?" one of us asked her uncertainly.

She reflected, threading a needle, "Well, I don't know but what the best way to tell you what I mean is to tell you about something that happened to me, forty years ago. I've never said anything about it before. But I've thought about it a good deal. Maybe—"

She had hardly begun when I recognized the story—her visit to her Cousin Ella's Midwestern home, the widower with his scarred face and saintly reputation and, very vividly, her getting lost in the great cornfield. I knew every word she was going to say—to the very end, I thought.

But no, I did not. Not at all.

She broke off, suddenly, to exclaim with impatience, "Wasn't I the big ninny? But not so big a ninny as that old cousin of mine. I could wring her neck for getting me in such a state. Only she didn't know any better, herself. That was the way they brought young people up in those days, scaring them out of their wits about the awfulness of getting lost, but not telling them a thing about how *not* to get lost. Or how to act, if they did.

"If I had had the sense I was born with, I'd have known that running my legs off in a zigzag was the worst thing I could do. I couldn't have been more than a few feet from the path when I noticed I wasn't on it. My tracks in the loose plow dirt must have been perfectly plain. If I'd h' stood still, and collected my wits, I could have looked down to see which way my footsteps went and just walked back over them to the path and gone on about my business.

"Now I ask you, if I'd been told how to do that, wouldn't it have been a lot better protection for me—if protection was what my aunt thought she wanted to give me—than to scare me so at the idea of being lost that I turned deef-dumb-and-blind when I thought I was?

"And anyhow that patch of corn wasn't as big as she let on. And she knew it wasn't. It was no more than a big field in a farming country. I was a well-grown girl of sixteen, as tall as I am now. If I couldn't have found the path, I could have just walked along one line of cornstalks—*straight*—and I'd have come out somewhere in ten minutes. Fifteen at the most. Maybe not just where I wanted to go. But all right, safe, where decent folks were living."

She paused, as if she had finished. But at the inquiring blankness in our faces, she went on, "Well, now, why isn't teaching girls—and boys, too, for the Lord's sake don't forget they need it as much as the girls—about this man-and-woman business, something like that? If you give them the idea—no matter whether it's *as* you tell them the facts, or as you *don't* tell them the facts, that it is such a terribly scary thing that if they take a step into it, something's likely to happen to them so awful that you're ashamed to tell them what—well, they'll lose their heads and run around like crazy things, first time they take one step away from the path.

"For they'll be trying out the paths, all right. You can't keep them from it. And a good thing too. How else are they going to find out what it's like? Boys' and girls' going together is a path across one corner of growing up. And when they go together, they're likely to get off the path some. Seems to me, it's up to their folks to bring them up so when they do, they don't start screaming and running in circles, but stand still, right where they are, and get their breath and figure out how to get back.

"And anyhow, you don't tell 'em the truth about sex" (I was astonished to hear her use the actual word, taboo to women of her generation) "if they get the idea from you that it's all there is to living. It's not. If you don't get to where you want to go in it, well, there's a lot of landscape all around it a person can have a good time in.

"D'you know, I believe one thing that gives girls and boys the wrong idea is the way folks *look!* My old cousin's face, I can see her now, it was as red as a rooster's comb when she was telling me about men in that cornfield. I believe now she kind of *liked* to talk about it."

(Oh, Aunt Minnie—and yours! I thought.)

Someone asked, "But how *did* you get out, Aunt Minnie?"

She shook her head, laid down her sewing. "More foolishness. That minister my mother's cousin was keeping house for—her son-in-law—I caught sight of him, down along one of the aisles of cornstalks, looking down at the ground, thinking, the way he often did. And I was so glad to see him I rushed right up to him, and flung my arms around his neck and hugged him. He hadn't heard me coming. He gave a great start, put one arm around me and turned his face full towards me—I suppose for just a second he had forgotten how awful one side of it was. His expression, his eyes—well, you're all married women, you know how he looked, the way any able-bodied man thirty-six or -seven, who'd been married and begotten children, would look—for a minute anyhow, if a full-blooded girl of sixteen, who ought to have known better, flung herself at him without any warning, her hair tumbling down, her dress half unbuttoned, and hugged him with all her might.

"I was what they called innocent in those days. That is, I knew just as little about what men are like as my folks could manage I should. But I was old enough to know all right what that look meant. And it gave me a start. But of course the real thing of it was that dreadful scar of his, so close to my face—that wet corner of his mouth, his eye drawn down with the red inside of the lower eyelid showing—

"It turned me so sick, I pulled away with all my might, so fast that I ripped one sleeve nearly loose, and let out a screech like a wildcat. And ran. Did I run? And in a minute, I was through the corn and had come out in the back yard of the house. I hadn't been more than a few feet from it, probably, any of the time. And then I fainted away. Girls were always fainting away; it was the way our corset strings were pulled tight, I suppose, and then—oh, a lot of fuss.

"But anyhow," she finished, picking up her work and going on, setting neat, firm stitches with steady hands, "there's one thing, I never told anybody it was Cousin Malcolm I had met in the cornfield. I told my old cousin that 'a man had scared me.' And nobody said anything more about it to me, not ever. That was the way they did in those days. They thought if they didn't let on about something, maybe it wouldn't have happened. I was sent back to Vermont right away and Cousin Malcolm went on being minister of the church. I've always been," said Aunt Minnie moderately, "kind of proud that I didn't go and ruin a man's life for just one second's slip-up. If you could have called it that. For it *would* have ruined him. You know how hard as stone people are about other folks' letdowns. If I'd have told, not one person in that town would have had any charity. Not one would have tried to understand. One slip, *once*, and they'd have pushed him down in the mud. If I had told, I'd have felt pretty bad about it, later—when I came to have more sense. But I declare, I can't see how I came to have the decency, dumb as I was then, to know that it wouldn't be fair."

It was not long after this talk that Aunt Minnie's elderly husband died, mourned by her, by all of us. She lived alone then. It was peaceful October weather for her, in which she kept a firm roundness of face and figure, as quiet-living country-women often do, on into her late sixties.

But then Jake, the boy who had had girl trouble, had wife trouble.

We heard he had taken to running after a young girl, or was it that she was running after him? It was something serious. For his nice wife left him and came back with the children to live with her mother in our town. Poor Aunt Minnie used to go to see her for long talks which made them both cry. And she went to keep house for Jake, for months at a time.

She grew old, during those years. When finally she (or something) managed to get the marriage mended so that Jake's wife relented and went back to live with him, there was no trace left of her pleasant brisk freshness. She was stooped and slow-footed and shrunken. We, her kins-people, although we would have given our lives for any one of our own children, wondered whether Jake was worth what it had cost his mother to—well, steady him, or reform him. Or perhaps just understand him. Whatever it took.

She came of a long-lived family and was able to go on keeping house for herself well into her eighties. Of course we and the other neighbors stepped in often to make sure she was all right. Mostly, during those brief calls, the talk turned on nothing more vital than her geraniums. But one midwinter afternoon, sitting with her in front of her cozy stove, I chanced to speak in rather hasty blame of someone who had, I thought, acted badly. To my surprise this brought from her the story about the cornfield which she had evidently quite forgotten telling me twice before.

This time she told it almost dreamily, swaying to and fro in her rocking chair, her eyes fixed on the long slope of snow outside her window. When she came to the encounter with the minister she said, looking away from the distance and back into my eyes, "I know now that I had been, all along, kind of *interested* in him, the way any girl as old as I was would be in any youngish man living in the same house with her. And a minister, too. They have to have the gift of gab so much more than most men, women get to thinking they are more alive than men who can't talk so well. I *thought* the reason I threw my arms around him was because I had been so scared. And I certainly had been scared, by my old cousin's horrible talk about the cornfield being full of men waiting to grab girls. But that wasn't all the reason I flung myself at Malcolm Fairchild and hugged him. I know that now. Why in the world shouldn't I have been taught *some* notion of it then? 'Twould do girls good to know that they are just like everybody else—human nature *and* sex, all mixed up together. I didn't have to hug him. I wouldn't have, if he'd been dirty or fat and old, or chewed tobacco."

I stirred in my chair, ready to say, "But it's not so simple as all that to tell girls—" and she hastily answered my unspoken protest. "I know, I know, most of it can't be put into words. There just aren't any words to say something that's so both-ways-at-once all the time as this man-and-woman business. But look here, you know as well as I do that there are lots more ways than in words to teach young folks what you want 'em to know."

The old woman stopped her swaying rocker to peer far back into the past with honest eyes. "What was in my mind back there in the cornfield—partly anyhow—was what had been there all the time I was living in the same house with Cousin Malcolm—that he had long straight legs, and broad shoulders, and lots of curly brown hair, and was nice and flat in front, and that one side of his face was good-looking. But most of all, that he and I were really alone, for the first time, without anybody to see us.

"I suppose, if it hadn't been for that dreadful scar, he'd have drawn me up, tight, and—most any man would—kissed me. I know how I must have looked, all red and hot and my hair down and my dress torn open. And, used as he was to big cornfields, he probably never dreamed that the reason I looked that way was because I was scared to be by myself in one. He may have thought—you know what he may have thought.

"Well—if his face had been like anybody's—when he looked at me the way he did, the way a man does look at a woman he wants to have, it would have scared me—some. But I'd have cried, maybe. And probably he'd have kissed me again. You know how such things go. I might have come out of the cornfield halfway engaged to marry him. Why not? I was old enough, as people thought then. That would have been nature. That was probably what he thought of, in that first instant.

"But what did I do? I had one look at his poor, horrible face, and started back as though I'd stepped on a snake. And screamed and ran.

"What do you suppose *he* felt, left there in the corn? He must have been sure that I would tell everybody he had attacked me. He probably thought that when he came out and went back to the village he'd already be in disgrace and put out of the pulpit.

"But the worst must have been to find out, so rough, so plain from the way I acted—as if somebody had hit him with an ax—the way he would look to any woman he might try to get close to. That must have been—" she drew a long breath, "well, pretty hard on him."

After a silence, she murmured pityingly, "Poor man!"

A Family
Alliance

She had never read Thomas à Kempis's axiom that temptation can do no more than show what stuff you are made of. For that matter she had never heard of Thomas à Kempis or any other literary classic not included in the required reading-list of the Blue Falls High School. So far but not one rung higher up the educational ladder had her country coaxed the reluctant Jigger. (Her name was really Gladys, but that along with many other things about her was not known to the young crowd she ran around with in New York. The first evening, before Dora Warren had a chance to introduce her, one of the boys several inches shorter than she had asked ironically, "Who's the cute little jigger with the cock-eyed bob?" And Jigger she remained thenceforward.) But if she ever had heard that axiom she would have called the worthy Thomas a darned old liar. For she was convinced that her troubles were to be laid to temptation alone, and that the stuff she was made of had nothing to do with the matter.

Temptation's name was Dora Warren. Like every insidious danger Dora seemed harmless. She wanted nothing for herself but to think that everything Jigger did was cute. They had met only a few months after Jigger had clawed her way to the New York job she had set her heart on from the time she could read *Vogue*. During those months Jigger had not gone very far, but she was on her way. She had found out that her clothes were impossible, where to get others, where to have her hair done and where to buy shoes, and in general to get her New York legs under her, when Dora, who had broken into the big town all of a year before, dropped in one night to see if the food in that "residence club" was any better than in hers. It was not; but she thought Jigger marvelous. They had about the same kind of job and made about the same salary. They both came from small places and were crazy about New York. Dora proposed that they join forces, rent a studio apartment, and have some decent eats. Not to speak of latchkeys.

They were different enough to get on well together. Dora worked in a publisher's office, and Jigger in that of a silk importer. Dora was rather plain—that is, she was pretty in an old-fashioned way, plump and little and smiling, with curly hair, amiable blue eyes, rosy cheeks, and regular features. The kind our forefathers thought "looked good enough to eat." With that 1880 aspect, the poor girl had learned early, of course, to expect little in the way of admiration and to take thankfully what she got. Jigger was plain in the way that is pretty now—long-legged, flat-hipped, sleekhaired, with thin dark face and high cheekbones. Along with her clothes she had picked up the weary, slightly sinister expression that went with them, and successfully gave the desired effect of being something that would poison you in no time if you ate it.

They settled down very soon into the roles to which, according to today's standards, they were destined by their looks, Dora the one who did the kissing, Jigger extending the cheek. Jigger, introduced by Dora to her crowd, instantly took precedence over her, in virtue of slinky hips, irregular features and a snugly fitting aura of bad medicine. Dora, humble through long practice, took up the second fiddle without resentment, and fell into the role of satellite, doubled with that of press agent. Accustomed to getting her limelight by reflection, and being really very warmhearted, she enjoyed nothing more than telling people nice things about Jigger and her family.

How could anybody expect Jigger, inexperienced in life as she was, to foresee the danger lurking in Dora's pleasant little puffs? She had hardly noticed them at first. She certainly never encouraged Dora's propaganda, although she had not rushed to contradict her with priggish accuracy every time she heard a Dora-ized version of the facts floating around. For that matter she couldn't have contradicted her. When Dora let fall the statement that the Pratts, Jigger's people, "were one of the old land-owning families in the upper Hudson Valley," she was telling the truth. And so she was when she told the crowd that "Jigger is running up to spend the week end at her people's country place." You couldn't object to that. Jigger didn't, anyhow. Nor to "Jigger's mother is a professional woman too. A musician—pianist." You couldn't object, not what you'd call *object,* when she said, "Her father is at the head of a business." Every word of it was so. What could Jigger have done about it?

As far as that goes (just as a person who constantly hears a foreign language comes to think in it) she slid into using Dora's lingo herself. She not only said but thought, "I'm just running up for the week end to my people's country place." She was, wasn't she? And on the first evening she met Spike Hunter it was she herself, not Dora at all, who let fall that her people were one of the old land-owning families in the upper Hudson Valley, and that her mother was a professional pianist.

But she was so flustered that night she would have said anything. If she had thought it might make a better impression on Spike, she would have said she was an orphan, or a Hungarian countess. She mentioned her folks only because someone had just told her young Hunter was a Yale graduate, son of a fine old Ohio family, and she hoped a hint that she too had A Family might attract his attention. For she wanted him to like her from the minute she saw his queer dark face with its fuzzy funny eyebrows and its black eyes and its bulging forehead. "Don't tell me that I look like a Russian!" he stopped her first exclamation. "You would be the three thousand and sixty-fifth to say that and I want to keep you in the one and only class where you belong."

She liked his line. She liked his eyebrows. She liked his voice. She was also a little afraid of him, which did no harm. It was not because she was getting awfully tired (though she was) of living in one room and pretending it wasn't the bedroom; and of delicatessen food; and cooking over a hot plate; and dressing as though she earned more than she did; and talking about things she didn't know anything about; and making the same old rackety noise whether she felt like it or not; and in general living according to a pattern that fitted her looks better than it did her. She was twenty-four years old now, Jigger was, had lived with Dora in one or another studio apartment for longer than she ever admitted, and there were moments when she panted like a hart after a kitchen with a full-size electric range with an OVEN. She seldom allowed herself to think of that, because when she did her mind was almost instantly out of control. Before she could open the copy of the *New Yorker* on her knee, she was swept from the airy kitchen in which the dream-range stood, out to a breeze-swept, vine-shaded, back porch on which sat a non-poisonous Jigger shelling peas out of her own garden, and from there to a real dining room not an alcove, and upstairs to a bedroom with a real bed in it. A double bed.

But this was not why she was crazy about Spike Hunter, any more than spring is why seeds sprout. They wouldn't sprout if it weren't springtime of course. But there have to be seeds before springtime can do anything with them.

Whether it was the mention of her family or something else, Spike liked her all right. She hardly dared believe he did as much as he seemed to. Before long they stopped going around with the crowd and went around together. A striking couple they were, who might have stepped right out of the advertisements of a transatlantic steamship line—you know, the spiffy quietly upper-class couple who play shuffleboard; lean over the rail; lounge around the A-deck swimming pool; and on the dock are not cringingly ashamed but in a well-bred way proud of their luggage. Jigger knew they looked like that, but it didn't seem so important to her as it would have five years ago. In fact it seemed less important to her with every minute. Sometimes, when she and Spike were with astonished awe discovering yet one more idea or feeling they had in common that nobody else had ever shared, she forgot all about how she looked for half an hour at a time. This was a great rest to her.

Spike had made no secret of the fact that he had taken to Jigger on sight, and getting off to a fast start he kept on burning up the track. Before long, a paltry two months, he was adoring her, and telling her so and Jigger was so happy that she ached, and might have lost the discontented sullen expression that made her look so distinguished, if a secret uneasiness gnawing at her heart had not fastened it still more firmly on her face. But then, defying convention in the courageous way that made her love him so, Spike asked her to marry him —not just propositioned her to try sleeping in his flat till they had found out whether they could make a satisfactory sex adjustment to each other, but actually legally get married to him, even though he wasn't making much money yet. Just as her father had asked her mother; and Jigger cried heartily for joy just as her mother had, and said, yes, sure, she couldn't think of anything she'd like better and she didn't give a damn about the money. (This sentiment if not the turn of the phrase was also like her mother.)

And then—they went to tell Dora, and she said, "Oh, how marvelous! You'll have the wedding at your people's country place, of

course." And Spike, who had been impatiently listening to yards and
yards of Dora's line, said, "Sure, where else?"

But it was not then she heard the breakers crashing. She was still
in too shining a cloud of glory to look ahead. She said, "Oh, *yes!*"
and sank into a dream at the very idea of her wedding day.

It was the letter from Spike's father and mother that gave Jigger
her first intimation of the trouble Dora had made for her. She and
Spike had written the news of their engagement to their families the
same day. But the answer from Jigger's parents, living much nearer,
came first. Naturally they wrote to Jigger as they always did only
more so, and Jigger being in an emotional state, shed some more
happy tears over their motherly and fatherly love and anxiety and
hopes for her happiness. They each had written a note to Spike too,
enclosing them in the same envelope with her letter. "Sweet!" Jigger
thought these notes. But Spike was out in Ohio on business and was
taking advantage of the trip to visit his parents. She couldn't hand
her own parents' greetings over to him at once. They too, of course,
looked forward to her being married from her own old home.
"Mamma says wait till June when the peonies will be out," wrote her
father, "and if you do, I'll get the barn and chicken-houses painted."
It was one of the family jokes—getting the barn and chicken-houses
painted. Wait until June? Jigger shuddered at the thought of those
weary weeks. Not much!

Two days later came the letter from Spike's family, the Hunters of
Ohio. Jigger opened the big square envelope, and read the well-turned
phrases (there was a marked family likeness to Spike's style in them)
written in very black ink on thick creamy linen paper, and although they gracefully expressed welcome to her as their son's fiancée,
her face was very grave. She took out her parents' letters. They had
been written on sheets torn off the family pad, and she guessed by the
looks the ink had partly dried down in the bottle and her mother
had added a little water to make it run better.

After office hours that day a tall, dark, sophisticated-looking Park
Avenue girl with a worried expression went into a chic shop to buy a
box of the most expensive cream linen paper in stock and a bottle of
the blackest ink. And that evening Jigger sat down to write her father
and mother. She said she was sending them some New York letter
paper, and would they mind using this when they wrote Spike. And
perhaps—she consulted Spike's parents' letter—she'd just write out a
few phrases that they might care to use. She tore that beginning up
and started again. This time she wrote that she had told them so far

only about Spike himself, but of course parents would be interested in his family too. The Hunters were an old Ohio family, more or less in politics like all Ohio people. Spike's mother's family were Southerners. "I'll probably have to endure a good deal of Big House, Charm of the Old South . . . always remember to call it The War Between the States," she wrote, putting it in New Yorkese so that it wouldn't sound like boasting. "His father is owner and editor of the largest daily newspaper in the place where they live—it was his father's before him. He is Trustee of one of the Ohio universities. Spike's sister is married and she and her husband are now living in Paris." She hesitated, wrote, "France, you know," was ashamed and tore up that letter. The next time she began boldly by asking them right out if they would mind not referring to each other as Mamma and Papa when they wrote Spike because he . . . She started again, saying she knew they would take it just as a joke as she meant it if she . . . She started again.

To make a long story short, Jigger wrote letters to her parents all night long and in the morning tore them all up and burst into tears. Not of joy, either! If she'd been there at home *with* them, she might perhaps have made them understand. But you couldn't write that kind of a letter to your father and mother. At least Jigger couldn't. Not to *her* father and mother. I haven't spoken about it before—it was something she would have blushed to have the gang suspect—but Jigger was rather a nice girl.

She decided the simplest thing was not to show their letters to Spike when he came back but to tell him they had sent all kinds of good wishes to him and their commiseration of his hard luck and so forth and so on. When he actually saw her again, Spike was so astounded to find that Jigger was still there, still engaged to him, that he hadn't dreamed her, that nobody else had run away with her yet, that he never noticed about her parents' letter one way or the other.

He had a raise in salary that spring (an upturn of business coming just at the right time for him) and so much encouragement from his boss (he was on the selling end for a big firm of wholesale druggists) that they fell to calculating minutely the cost of life in the suburbs. Rebels against accepted conventions as they were, they found it amusing to startle their crowd by the quaint plan of living in a house with a yard around it. Then Jigger went to her boss (the silk importer) and told him cheerfully that she was going to get married and that she would be leaving next week to go home and get her things ready. As for the boss, he went through the typical reaction of an employer in such a situation. Choking down a hot wave of resentment at youth's ingratitude—"So that's the way it is! The empty-headed little doll has been working me for a meal ticket all those weeks and weeks when she wasn't worth a nickel, and now when she's just beginning to be some help in the office, she gads off with the first boy who makes a pass at her"—he accepted the inevitable, forced his lips to a smile, wished her good fortune, and added ten dollars to her final pay check as a wedding present.

You must know by this time what kind of folks Jigger's father and mother were, and can imagine just how they looked as they got out of their Ford at the station at Blue Falls, well ahead of time because Mr. Pratt wanted to ask the station agent about a new sprayer which should have arrived before this, and Mrs. Pratt wanted to speak to him seriously about his small daughter's practicing. "If Laura can't get in at least her hour a day, Mr. Elmore, it's a waste of time for her to take. I'd feel I was getting your dollar a lesson under false pretenses," said Mrs. Pratt. She spoke firmly. She did not like false pretenses of any kind.

The train came chugging around the curve, and they hurried out on the platform. The tears were in Mrs. Pratt's eyes, a lump in Mr. Pratt's throat. Their little girl was coming back home for the last time—at least the last time she would still be theirs.

Some of the New York make-up and a good deal of the New York expression had evaporated from Jigger's face during the trip from Manhattan to Blue Falls, and when she saw her father and mother waiting there, with their muddy country rubbers on their feet and that steady loving look in their eyes, she ran to them on her high heels and flung her arms around their necks and shed a few more tears.

But all the same, all the same . . . ! When she got into the three-seasons-ago station wagon, smelling slightly of sulphur spray, and drove over rutted roads to her "people's country place" and saw the square clapboarded dark-brown house with the mansard roof and the jigsaw work under the eaves; the bay window filled with geraniums and wandering Jew; the golden oak dining room set; the front parlor with its long lace curtains draped back from the windows and its comfortable furniture upholstered in brown rep; and her mother's battered black upright piano and round piano stool screwed high for the children who "took" of Mrs. Pratt—there was something queer about her smile. They had a surprise for her, they told her, something done in honor of the wedding. Proudly watching her face they drew her into the front hall.

A brand-new maple floor had been laid there, and new paper was on the walls. "Well, Sister, what do you say to that?" asked Mr. Pratt. (For at home Jigger was not even Gladys, but Sister.) Sister-Jigger, feeling their eyes on her, looked at the shiny varnish on the light yellow floor and at the pretty little sprigs of flowers on the new wall paper and cried out with enthusiasm that it was *perfectly mar*-velous! Knowing her every inflection from babyhood up and having the advantage of twenty-five years more of life's battering than she, they perceived at once that something was very wrong. And they were very much afraid they knew what it was.

They had tried to put out of their minds the uneasiness they had felt when they read their daughter's letter about the University-Trustee, newspaper-owner, living-in-Paris family she was marrying into. But it came coldly back now, filling the newly done-over front hall with dismay. So they all began to talk in loud cheerful voices and moved on to take Jigger to her own room. They left her there to unpack and went downstairs together, heavy-hearted.

Looking around the fresh new hall, "Gosh, I wish it was over!" said Mr. Pratt, plucking at the loose skin on his brown weather-beaten neck.

"Now, Papa, don't get nervous. The father of the bride is always fit to be tied, they say. It'll be all right." This was what Mrs. Pratt said. They both agreed that one look at Sister's face showed her young man was what she wanted, and what else mattered. But after her husband had put on his overalls and had gone out to boss the spraying of the far orchard, Mrs. Pratt stood a long time by her old piano looking fixedly at the cover of "The Mulhausen Album for Beginners," although she must have known every word and letter in it by heart. She was thinking so deeply that she did not notice the arrival of a little boy till he was there behind her. Coming to herself she caught sight of her face in a mirror opposite and was startled to see how somber and foreboding she looked. "I'll have to do better than that," she thought, and said with an artificial cheerfulness that alarmed the little boy, "Oh, how are you, sonny? Let's start our five-finger exercises today with *both* hands. Don't you think that will be *nice?*"

Jigger had taken off her city shoes and put on a pair of sneakers, had changed her dress for the old slacks and sweater she always left hanging in her closet, and was now in the side yard under the grape arbor. A wild idea had occurred to her that perhaps they could have an outdoor garden-party wedding, with a striped tent for refreshments and a banked-flower altar, and not have to go inside the house at all. But one look was enough. The side yard was just the side yard, no more. There were, it is true, lilac bushes, clumps of tulips in bloom, the big bush of snowball and a hydrangea showing green bursting leaves; but there were also big rhubarb plants in the corner, and a line of currant bushes at one side; and from it you saw the *outside* of the house! Also the barns and chicken-houses, which had not been painted. Jigger stood still to look at the outside of her father's old house standing sturdily high and square on its green grass, the new leaves on its locust trees throwing a pattern of shadow on its shingled roof. From the open windows came the sound of five-finger exercises, stumblingly played. A hen with some chickens wandered around the corner of the side porch. Some clean dish towels fluttered from a line by the back door. Jigger clenched her fists and said stormily, "I'll be darned if any snooty Ohio people are going to make me ashamed of my own home!"

This did not prevent her from having, during the three weeks before her wedding, a great many crazy ideas about how not to go through with what she (and Dora) had started. Every day she said fiercely to herself, "Let them think what they will. It's nothing to me!" And every day she knew that what they thought would be a good deal to her, might easily be a handicap to her all her married life. Every day she reminded herself that it would unendurably hurt her father and mother if now she just ran away with Spike around the corner in New York somewhere and got married by a justice of the peace or the County Clerk or whoever married people; and every day she thought they might easily be even more hurt if she was married at home under the eyes of those hateful Ohio eyebrow-lifters. It seemed too awful to expose her parents and her home to such supercilious eyes, when, if that one contact between the two families could be avoided, the Ohio people need never, never see the old Pratt place and its owners. You can imagine how crazy were some of her plans for escape when I tell you that one of them was to pretend that she was nuts—simply ga-ga—on the idea of being married in an orange grove, and to insist on carrying both families off to Florida. Another was to have a church wedding and the wedding breakfast in the hotel and never go near the house at all. If you had only seen the Blue Falls church and the Blue Falls hotel you'd know that this idea was the last superlative of craziness.

After each of those wild fluttering beatings of her wings against the bars, she managed to come back to her senses and went on discussing with her mother how many chickens would be needed for the salad, and whether the ice cream freezers they had already arranged to borrow would be enough or whether one more wouldn't be safer.

The unspoken accompaniment in her mind to all these preparations was an outraged, "If I could just get back at that goof Dora!"

She put on a grimacing cheerfulness to hide the existence of this undercurrent and she was, naturally, about as successful in hiding it as in her childhood when she had tried to hide from her mother that she had broken a plate and hidden the pieces. Mrs. Pratt grimaced cheerfully back, her heart as heavy as lead. When Mr. Pratt called her to come see how high the peas were sprouting, or to tell him where she wanted the clothesline hung and getting her there all to himself, asked in a low anxious voice, "Don't you think maybe Sister kinda hates to have those folks from Ohio come here for—" or, "Wouldn't it be better if we could somehow—" Mrs. Pratt always cut him short, "Mercy, no! Fred! What an idea! She's just a little nervous about getting married. All girls are." She wasn't going to have *any*body, no matter if he was Trustee of a University, make her Fred feel apologetic about not having made more money. He'd made enough! Then the two parents would look at the peas or the clothesline and go back to make more cheerful answers to their daughter's cheerful remarks, and say how nice it was they were going to meet her family-in-law.

Then the fateful day came. Not the wedding day. The day the Hunters from Ohio were to arrive. They had decided not to drive, Spike wrote. His mother's back wasn't strong and long drives tired her. They were due on the late afternoon the day before the wedding and Spike with them. The cheerful grimaces had worn pretty thin by that time, and none of the three Pratts even tried to keep them up as they made the last preparations at the house and donned their new street clothes to go to the station. There was little talk of any kind, and what there was, on a note of open nervous uncertainty. "Sister, would you rather have me wear my overcoat?" "Which tie would you like to have me put on?" "Oh, Mother, *do* you think I look all right in this jersey?" "Will this hat do, Sister? Or shall I go without any?"

In the car, Mrs. Pratt and her daughter on the back seat plucked at each other's neck arrangements, smoothed down each other's hair, put on their gloves and took them off and put them on again. On the front seat Mr. Pratt was thinking sadly, "I ought to have got on better. Other men do." On the platform, hearing the train whistle, they arrayed themselves in a row, thought that looked silly, stood back of each other, thought that looked worse, and held their ground despairingly just where they chanced to be. The train stopped. The brakeman came running down the steps, set a stool and turned to give a hand to an undeniably Fifth Avenue traveling costume, surmounted by a severe perfectly-fitting little dark hat which proclaimed negligently that it had been made in Paris. Back of this came a tan camel's hair overcoat accompanied by tan gloves, and topped by a marvelously fine and supple felt hat, the brim turned dashingly down in front. Yes, there were people inside those clothes, but Jigger did not see them. Behind the Fifth Avenue costume with the Paris hat and the camel's hair overcoat was a tall young man with soft black eyebrows and bumps on his forehead. He was just as well dressed as the others but Jigger was so amazed to see who it was, she did not notice his clothes at all. It was Spike! Why, there was *Spike!* She gave a shriek of pure astonishment, echoed by one like it from the young man who ran rapidly towards her. Forgetting all her plans for well-bred mannerly self-control she sped as fast as she could into his arms.

When they came back to this life, which took them rather longer than they realized, the Fifth Avenue costume and the tan overcoat had stiffly shaken hands and exchanged formal greetings with Mr. and Mrs. Pratt. Spike and Jigger were presented now and nervously shook hands with all. Spike's father and mother did nothing whatever to put their son's fiancée at her ease. They merely murmured a few guarded cool words which she could hardly hear.

"I hate them!" thought Jigger. "They don't like me! I'll hate them always! I'll take Spike away from them if it's my last act."

Then Mr. Pratt said what had been agreed on beforehand (after the livery car idea had been abandoned in a tacit resolution to get it over once and for all) as the best thing to say. He didn't do very well with it, did not use the jaunty accent his daughter had tried (trying not to seem to try) to suggest to him as the best way to carry it off. But he said it—"Well, our good faithful old family car awaits us at the back. I guess we can all squeeze into it . . . unless the young people would rather walk." The young people indicated that they *would* rather walk.

Jigger, aware at once of suppressed surprise from the Paris hat and the expensive overcoat, ground her teeth and thought, "If I can only live through it!" which is not a desirable way to look forward to your wedding day. Nobody thought of anything to say, so they all went around to the back of the station. As Jigger and Spike were helping to get the sophisticated, expensive, going-to-Europe luggage into the car, didn't Spike have to rest the heavy pigskin kit bag on the rusty rear fender so that it sagged and cracked and threatened to fall right off!

The four elders took their places. Spike shut the doors. "All right. We'll expect you when we see you," said Mr. Pratt, being overjaunty now to make up for having boggled his speech about the car. They drove away, leaving Jigger and Spike to manage somehow to use up two hours walking the two miles to the old Pratt place.

The first thing that happened after the car started was that Spike's father pulled off his gloves. "I see you don't wear 'em," he remarked to Mr. Pratt at the wheel. When he had taken them off, he stretched his hands and wriggled his fingers and murmured, "Gosh! That feels good!" He then hunched himself out of his overcoat, tossed it over the back of the seat, ran his fingers around his collar, and took a long breath.

His wife might have had something to say to this if her attention had not been fully engaged by Mrs. Pratt's answer to her first question. She had asked, in a guarded voice, "Have you been away on tours a good deal this winter, Mrs. Pratt?" Jigger's mother had not the faintest idea what this meant, but having a lifelong habit of counting on plain truth-telling in all situations, answered, "Oh, no, I never go away from home. I couldn't leave Mr. Pratt. And he can't ever get away for more than a day or so. You know how it is with a farm and orchards. There's always something that has to . . ." She did not finish her sentence. Her eye had fallen on the elegant camel's hair overcoat which hung over the back of the front seat. It was folded so that the inside was out. Inside the collar was a forgotten price tag, very new and clean.

Mrs. Pratt glanced from this to the expensive suitcases. She now saw that they were new, brand-new. And so was the pigskin kit bag. She looked around full into the face of the woman next her, and saw under the perfectly fitting French hat a face like her own, frankly middle-aged, rather worn, with honest somewhat anxious eyes.

From the front seat came the voice of Jigger's father, making conversation if it killed him, "I understand you are much interested in education, Mr. Hunter." Spike's father looked around at his wife, got no help from her and answered uncertainly, "Not so specially. Newspaper work is my line. I run the little daily my father started. I haven't time for much else. We can't afford much help in the office or the press room on our subscription. And there's the job printing, too. That's what keeps us out of the red. I do a lot of it myself, write editorials, read proof. I take my turn at everything from office boy to bill collector . . ."

"Why, I understood from Sister—our daughter, I mean—that you are a Trustee of one of the Ohio universities."

"Oh, *that!*" said Mr. Hunter, laughing. "They call it a university. There are seventeen of them, somebody told me once, or was it twenty-seven? It's just a local school, a Methodist institution—only a hundred and forty-seven students. They were having a hard time to get anybody to take a vacant place on the Board and Mother wanted me—m'wife, I mean . . ."

He went no farther. Mrs. Pratt leaned forward over the new price mark on the overcoat to ask intensely, "Do you mean to say you are *Methodists?*"

"Yes," they said. "Why?"

"Why, so are we!" cried Mrs. Pratt.

They were as struck by this as she. "You don't say so!" said Spike's father, turning his head to look at Mrs. Pratt as if he saw her for the first time. "Kenneth never told us that!" said Mrs. Hunter.

"Kenneth!"

"Perhaps Gladys hadn't happened to tell him about it."

"Gladys!"

"Well, anyhow," said Mrs. Pratt, "I've played the organ in our church for twenty-five years."

Over his shoulder Mr. Hunter said, "Mother was Epworth League leader when I first knew her. That's where we got acquainted."

"Well . . . !" said the mother of the bride.

"Well . . . !" said the mother of the bridegroom.

A thoughtful silence followed. Presently Mrs. Hunter asked, "How did your daughter ever happen to *go* to New York?"

"Well, she *wanted* to," explained Mrs. Pratt apologetically.

"Yes, I know." The other mother understood perfectly.

"It's better to let them," wisely commented the Ohio father from the front seat. "They have to get it out of their systems."

There was another reflective silence. This was broken by Mrs. Hunter's putting her hands up to her head, "Would you mind if I took this hat off? It's so tight it gives me a headache. Kenneth would have me buy it."

"It's very stylish," said Mrs. Pratt, looking at it on the other woman's knee.

"Oh, stylish!" said Mrs. Hunter impatiently. "I never had such a thing on my head before. *I* think it makes me look perfectly ridiculous."

Mrs. Pratt now asked her acutely, "Did you come by way of New York or straight here?"

"We've been in New York with Kenneth three whole days," said the other.

"You must be tired."

From the front seat Mr. Hunter cried out, "Tired? *Dead!* Once is enough for me. I wouldn't live there if you gave me the town."

"That's what I always say!" agreed Mr. Pratt.

They were now arrived. "Here we are," said Mr. Pratt, setting the hand brake. He had stopped at the side porch and when they got out they faced the row of currant bushes. "My, aren't they far along!" said the lady with the Paris hat in her hand. "They'll be ready to do up before long, won't they?"

"I hope they'll last till some of our early raspberries are ripe," said Mrs. Pratt.

"Yes, I put up mine with raspberries too," said the Fifth Avenue traveling costume.

"Well, well, come on *in*, folks," said Mr. Pratt heartily. "We're awfully glad to have you here."

They all went in and shut the door. And it was not opened again till two hours later when Spike and Jigger appeared, and Jigger, bracing herself and looking discontented and repellent, pushed it open and led her fiancé inside her home. This is what she saw. In the living room sitting with her father—who was in his shirt sleeves—sat a fatherly looking bald-headed man, also in his shirt sleeves. Both men were smoking pipes. "Hello, Sister," said her father. "Hunter and I have been swapping yarns about the tough sledding during the depression." He turned from her, back to the other man. "We certainly were down to the low-water mark around here."

The Ohio man nodded. "You're telling *me*. I couldn't collect a worn dime for ads or subscriptions. Had to take anything they gave me in exchange . . . stovewood, potatoes . . . or nothing at all. The bank could have foreclosed on me any day." He stopped to draw on his pipe.

Mr. Pratt, casting his eyes back to the same past, broke in reflectively. "You couldn't open a newspaper—do you remember?—without reading about big shots jumping out of skyscraper windows. Well, we little fellows had our troubles, too. Of course we *did* have the orchards. But who was buying apples those days . . . ! I got out and plowed between the rows and raised . . . oh, anything we could eat . . . vegetables . . ." He shook his head. "Had some rabbits, too. I hope I never have to eat fried rabbit again as long as I live."

The two fathers looked at each other in a comradely intimacy of shared memory—as if they had been in the same regiment at Verdun or Bastogne. The Ohio newspaper man went on, "Yeah, the depression sure had us down." He paused. "But it couldn't knock us out."

"No sir, we didn't quit," said the New York farmer with pride. "And here we are!"

"Yeah, here we still are."

Jigger and Spike turned, looking deeply into each other's eyes, and stepped out into the front hall, shutting the door behind them. They were not alone there. Voices sounded from the top of the stairs. Someone was starting down. Looking up, Jigger say a pleasant-faced, gray-haired, comfortable-looking woman in one of her mother's wraparound blue aprons. She was saying over her shoulder to Mrs. Pratt on the landing above, "But she's never liked it at all over there. Nor he either. They're crazy to get back to Akron." Seeing her son's fiancée staring up at her, she explained, "I was just telling your mother about Kenneth's married sister, Carrie. He's probably told you her husband works for a company that makes vacuum cleaners and when they thought they'd try to sell some in France, they wanted somebody over there that understood all about the way it works. He's a very good hand with machinery, Carrie's husband is."

Having now come to the bottom step, she looked around her and said, "My, I wish my front hall was as fresh as this. We haven't had it done over since Kenneth was in the seventh grade. But I simply can't get Mr. Hunter to admit how terrible it looks." She looked shyly and kindly at the girl before her and said, smiling, "You must make Kenneth mind you better than I ever have his father." She had a very sweet smile.

"Oh, I love her!" thought Jigger emotionally. "I must be sure not to hurt her by keeping Spike all to myself—not *all* the time."

A roar of laughter came from the living room. "What a good time those boys are having," said Mrs. Hunter, indulgently.

The two mothers passed on to the kitchen, Mrs. Pratt saying, "We thought it would be nice to have baking-powder biscuits with the salad —little tiny ones, you know."

"Yes, I cut mine out with a napkin ring," said Mrs. Hunter.

Alone in the front hall, gazing into each other's eyes, were a couple of distinguished young cosmopolites, just stepped out of their expensive stateroom on an ocean greyhound. Dreamily, almost absently, as if they did not know what they were doing, they put their arms around each other and laid their cheeks close together.

"Do you know, Kenneth," breathed the girl in his ear, "we've got a long way to go to live up to our parents."

"Amen, Sister."

As Ye Sow—

Casually, not that she was especially interested, just to say something, she asked as she handed out the four o'clock pieces of bread and peanut butter, "Well, what Christmas songs are you learning in your room this year?"

There was a moment's pause. Then the three little boys, her own and the usual two of his playmates, told her soberly, first one speaking, then another, "We're not going to be let to sing." "Teacher don't want us in the Christmas entertainment." Their round, eight-year-old faces were grave.

"Well—!" said the mother. "For goodness' sakes, why not?"

Looking down at his feet, her own small David answered sadly, "Teacher says we can't sing good enough."

"Well enough," corrected his mother mechanically.

"Well enough," he repeated as mechanically.

One of the others said in a low tone, "She says we can't carry a tune. She's only going to let kids sing in the entertainment that can carry a tune."

David, still hanging his head humbly, murmured, "She says we'd spoil the piece our class is going to sing."

Inwardly the mother broke into a mother's rage at a teacher. "So that's what she says, does she? What's she *for*, anyhow, if not to teach children what they don't know. The idea! As if she'd say she would teach arithmetic only to those who are good at it already."

The downcast children stood silent. She yearned over their shame at falling behind the standards of their group. "Teachers are callous, that's what they are, insensitively callous. She is deliberately planting an inferiority feeling in them. It's a shame to keep them from going up on the platform and standing in the footlights. Not to let them have their share of being applauded! It's cruel."

She drew in a deep breath, and put the loaf of bread away. Then she said quietly, "Well, lots of kids your age can't carry a tune. Not till they've learned. How'd you like to practice your song with me? I could play the air on the piano afternoons, after school. You'd get the hang of it that way."

They brightened, they bit off great chunks of their snacks, and said, thickly, that would be swell. They did not say they would be grateful to her, or regretted being a bother to her, busy as she always was. She did not expect them to. In fact it would have startled her if they had. She was the mother of four.

So while the after-school bread-and-butter was being eaten, washed down with gulps of milk, while the November-muddy rubbers were taken off, the mother pushed to the back of the stove the interrupted rice pudding, washed her hands at the sink, looked into the dining room where her youngest, Janey, was waking her dolls up from naps taken in the dining room chairs, and took off her apron. Together the four went into the living room to the piano.

"What song is it your room is to sing?"

"It came upon the midnight—" said the three little boys, speaking at once.

"That's a nice one," she commented, reaching for the battered songbook on top of the piano. "This is the way it goes." She played the air, and sang the first two lines. "That'll be enough to start on," she told them. *"Now—"* she gave them the signal to start.

They started. She had given them food for body and heart. Refreshed, heartened, with unquestioning confidence in a grownup's ability to achieve whatever she planned, they opened their mouths happily and sang out.

> "It came upon the midnight clear,
> That glorious song of old."

They had evidently learned the words by heart from hearing them.

At the end of that phrase she stopped abruptly, and for an instant bowed her head over the keys. Her feeling about Teacher made a rightabout turn. There was a pause.

But she was a mother, not a teacher. She lifted her head, turned a smiling face on the three bellowing children. "I tell you what," she said. "The way, really, to learn a tune, is just one note after another. The reason why a teacher can't get *every*body in her room up to singing in tune, is because she'd have to teach each person separately— unless they happen to be naturally good at singing. That would take too much time. A teacher has such a lot of children to see to."

They did not listen closely to this. They were not particularly interested in having justice done to Teacher, since they had not shared the mother's brief excursion into indignation. But they tolerated her with silent courtesy. They were used to parents, teachers, and other adults, and had learned how to take with patience and self-control their constantly recurring prosy explanations of things that did not matter.

"Listen," said the mother, "I'll strike just the two first notes on the piano— 'It came—' " She struck the notes, she sang them clearly. Full of good will the little boys sang with her. She stopped. Breathed hard.

"Not quite," she said, with a false smile, "pret-t-ty good. Close to it. But not quite, yet. I think we'd better take it *one* note at a time. Bill, *you* try it."

They had been in and out of her house all their lives, they knew her very well, none of them had reached the age of self-consciousness. Without hesitation, Bill sang, "I-i-it—" loudly.

The mother, as if fascinated, kept her eyes fixed on his still open mouth. Finally, "Try again," she said. "But first, *listen*." Oracularly she told them, "Half of carrying a tune is listening first."

She played the note again. And again. And again. Then, rather faintly, she said, "Peter, you sing it now."

At the note emitted by Peter, she let out her breath, as if she had been under water and just come up. "Fine!" she said. "Now we're getting somewhere! David, your turn." David was her own. "Just that one note. No, not *quite*. A little higher. Not quite so high." She was in a panic. What could she do? "Wait," she told David. "Try just breathing it out, not loud at all. Maybe you can get it better."

The boys had come in a little after four. It was five when the telephone rang—Bill's mother asking her to send Bill home because his Aunt Emma was there. The mother turned from the telephone to say, "Don't you boys want to go along with Bill a ways, and play around for awhile outdoors? I've got to get supper ready." Cheerful, relieved to see a door opening before them that had been slammed shut in their faces, yet very tired of that one note, they put on their muddy rubbers and thudded out.

◄§

That evening when she told her husband about it, after the children had gone to bed, she ended her story with a vehement "You never heard anything like it in your life, Harry. Never. It was appalling! You can't *imagine* what it was!"

"Oh, yes I can too," he said over his temporarily lowered newspaper. "I've heard plenty of tone-deaf kids hollering. I know what they sound like. There *are* people, you know, who really *can't* carry a tune. You probably never could teach them. Why don't you give it up?"

Seeing, perhaps, in her face, the mulish mother-stubbornness, he said, with a little exasperation, "What's the use of trying to do what you *can't* do?"

That was reasonable, after all, thought the mother. Yes, that was the sensible thing. She would be sensible, for once, and give it up. With everything she had to do, she would just be reasonable and sensible about this.

So the next morning, when she was downtown doing her marketing, she turned in at the public library and asked for books about teaching music to children. Rather young children, about eight years old, she explained.

The librarian, enchanted with someone who did not ask for a light, easy-reading novel, brought her two books, which she took away with her.

At lunch she told her husband (there were just the two of them with little Janey; the older children had their lunch at school), "Musical experts say there really is no such thing as a tone-deaf person. If anybody seems so, it is only because he has not had a chance to be carefully enough trained."

Her husband looked at her quickly. "Oh, all right," he said, "all *right!* Have it your own way." But he leaned to pat her hand. "You're swell," he told her. "I don't see how you ever keep it up as you do. Gosh, it's one o'clock already."

During the weeks between then and the Christmas entertainment, she saw no more than he how she could ever keep it up. The little boys had no difficulty in keeping it up. They had nothing else to do at four o'clock. They were in the indestructible age, between the frailness of infancy and the taut nervous tensions of adolescence. Wherever she led they followed her cheerfully. In that period of incessant pushing against barriers which did not give way, she was the one whose flag hung limp.

From assiduous reading of those two books on teaching music she learned that there were other approaches than a frontal attack on the tune they wanted to sing. She tried out ear-experiments with them, of which she would never have dreamed without her library books. She discovered to her dismay that sure enough, just as the authors of the books said, the little boys were musically so far below scratch that, without seeing which piano keys she struck, they had no idea whether a note was higher or lower than the one before it. She adapted and invented musical "games" to train their ears. The boys, standing in a row, their backs to the piano, listening to hear whether the second note was "uphill or downhill" from the first note, thought it as good a game as any other, rather funnier than most because so new to them. They laughed raucously over each other's mistakes, kidded and joshed each other, ran a contest to see who came out best, while the mother, aproned for cooking, her eye on the clock, got up and down for hurried forays into the kitchen where she was trying to get supper.

David's older brother and sister had naturally good ears for music. That was one reason why the mother had not dreamed that David had none. When the two older children came in from school, they listened incredulously, laughed scoffingly, and went off to skate or to rehearse a play. Little Janey, absorbed in her family of dolls, paid no attention to these male creatures of an age so far from hers that they were as negligible as grownups. The mother worked alone, in a vacuum, with nobody's sympathy to help her. Toilsomely, she pushed her heavy stone uphill, only to see it, as soon as she took away her hand, begin to roll rapidly back.

Not quite in a vacuum. Not even in a vacuum. Occasionally the others made a comment, "Gee, Mom, those kids are fierce. *You* can't do anything with them." "Say, Helen, an insurance man is coming to the house this afternoon. For heaven's sake keep those boys from screeching while he is here. A person can't hear himself think."

So, she thought, with silent resentment, her task was not only to give up her own work, to invent and adapt methods of instruction in an hour she could not spare, but also to avoid bothering the rest. After all, the home was for the whole family. They had the right to have it the background of what *they* wanted to do, needed to do. Only not she. Not the mother. Of course.

She faltered. Many times. She saw the ironing heaped high, or Janey was in bed with a cold, and as four o'clock drew near, she said to herself, "Now today I'll just tell the boys that I can *not* go on with this. We're not getting anywhere, anyhow."

So when they came storming in, hungry and cheerful and full of unquestioning certainty that she would not close that door she had half-opened for them, she laid everything aside and went to the piano.

As a matter of fact, they *were* getting somewhere. She had been so beaten down that she was slow to notice the success of the exercises ingeniously devised by the authors of those books. Even with their backs to the piano, the boys could now tell, infallibly, whether a second note was above or below the first one. Sure. They even thought it distinctly queer that they had not been able to, at first. "Never paid any attention to it, before," was their own accurate surmise as to the reason.

They paid attention now, their interest aroused by their first success, by the incessant practicing of the others in their classroom, by the Christmas-entertainment thrill which filled the schoolhouse with suspense. Although they were allowed no part in it, they also paid close attention to the drill given the others, and sitting in their seats, exiled from the happy throng of singers, they watched how to march along the aisle of the Assembly Hall, decorously, not too fast, not too slow, and when the great moment came for climbing to the platform how not to knock their toes against the steps. They fully expected to climb those steps to the platform with the others, come the evening of the entertainment.

It was now not on the clock that the mother kept her eye during those daily sessions at the piano, it was on the calendar. She nervously intensified her drill, but she remembered carefully not to yell at them when they went wrong, not to screw her face into the grimace which she felt, not to clap her hands over her ears and scream, "Oh, horrible! *Why* can't you get it right!" She reminded herself that if they knew how to get it right, they would of course sing it that way. She knew (she had been a mother for sixteen years) that she must keep them cheerful and hopeful, or the tenuous thread of their interest and attention would snap. She smiled. She did not allow herself even once to assume the blighting look of patience.

Just in time, along about the second week of December, a gleam shone in their musical darkness. They could all sound—if they remembered to sing softly and to "listen to themselves"—a note, any note, within their range, she struck on the piano. Little Peter turned out, to his surprise and hers, to have a sweet clear soprano. The others were—well, all right, good enough.

They started again, very cautiously, to sing that tune, to begin with "It ca-ame—" having drawn a deep breath, and letting it out carefully. It was right. They were singing true.

She clapped her hands like a girl. They did not share her overjoyed surprise. That was where they had been going all the time. They had got there, that was all. What was there to be surprised about?

From now on it went fast; the practicing of the air, their repeating it for the first skeptical, and then thoroughly astonished Teacher, their triumphant report at home, "She says we can sing it good enough. She says we can sing with the others. We practiced going up on the platform this afternoon."

Then the Christmas entertainment. The tramping of class after class up the aisle to the moment of footlighted glory; the big eighth graders' Christmas pantomime, the first graders' wavering performance of a Christmas dance as fairies—or were they snowflakes? Or perhaps angels? It was not clear. They were tremendously applauded, whatever they were. The swelling hearts of their parents burst into wild hand-clapping as the first grade began to file down the steps from the platform. Little Janey, sitting on her mother's lap, beat her hands together too, excited by the thought that next year she would be draped in white cheesecloth, would wear a tinsel crown and wave a star-tipped wand.

Then it was the turn of the third grade, the eight- and nine-year-olds, the boys clumping up the aisle, the girls switching their short skirts proudly. The careful tiptoeing up the steps to the platform, remembering not to knock their toes on the stair-treads, the two lines of round faces bland and blank in their touching ignorance of—oh, of everything! thought David's mother, clutching her handbag tensely.

The crash from the piano giving them the tone, all the mouths open,

"It came upo-on the midnight clear,
That glorious song of old."

The thin pregnant woman sitting in front of the mother leaned to the shabbily-dressed man next to her, with a long breath of relief. "They do real *good*, don't they?" she whispered proudly.

They did do real good. Teacher's long drill and hers had been successful. It was not howling, it was singing. It had cost the heart's blood, thought the mother, of two women, but it was singing. It would never again be howling, not from those children.

It was even singing with expression—some. There were swelling crescendos, and at the lines

> "The world in solemn stillness lay
> To hear the angels sing"

the child-voices were hushed in a diminuendo. She ached at the thought of the effort that had gone into teaching that hushed tone, of the patience and self-control and endlessly repeated persistence in molding into something shapely the boys' puppylike inability to think of anything but aimless play. It had taken hours out of her life, crammed as it was far beyond what was possible with work that must be done. Done for other people. Not for her. Not for the mother.

This had been one of the things that must be done. And she had done it. There he stood, her little David, a fully accredited part of his corner of society, as good as anybody, the threat of the inferiority-feeling averted for this time, ready to face the future with enough self-confidence to cope with what would come next. The door had been slammed in his face. She had pushed it open, and he had gone through.

The hymn ended. The burst of parental applause began clamorously. Little Janey, carried away by the festival excitement, clapped with all her might—"learning the customs of *her* corner of society" thought her mother, smiling tenderly at the petal-soft noiselessness of the tiny hands.

The third grade filed down the steps from the platform and began to march to their seats. For a moment, the mother forgot that she was no longer a girl who expected recognition when she had done something creditable. David's class clumped down the aisle. Surely, she thought, David would turn his head to where she sat and thank her with a look. Just this once.

He did turn his head as he filed by. He looked full at his family, at his father, his mother, his kid sister, his big brother and sister from the high school. He gave them a formal, small nod to show that he knew they were there, to acknowledge publicly that they were his family. He even smiled, a very little, stiffly, fleetingly. But his look was not for her. It was just as much for those of his family who had been bored and impatient spectators of her struggle to help him, as for her who had given part of her life to roll that stone uphill, a part of her life she never could get back.

She shifted Janey's weight a little on her knees. Of course. Did mothers ever expect to be thanked? They were to accept what they received, without bitterness, without resentment. After all, that was what mothers worked for—not for thanks, but to do their job. The sharp chisel of life, driven home by experience, flaked off expertly another flint-hard chip from her blithe, selfish girlhood. It fell away from the woman she was growing to be, and dropped soundlessly into the abyss of time.

After all, she thought, hearing vaguely the seventh graders now on the platform (none of her four was in the seventh grade)—after all, David was only eight. At that age they were, in personality, completely cocoons, as in their babyhood they had been physical cocoons. The time had not come yet for the inner spirit to stir, to waken, to give a sign that it lived.

It certainly did not stir in young David that winter. There was no sign that it lived. The snowy weeks came and went. He rose, ravenously hungry, ate an enormous breakfast with the family, and raced off to school with his own third graders. The usual three stormed back after school, flinging around a cloud of overshoes, caps, mittens, windbreakers. For their own good, for the sake of their wives-to-be, for the sake of the homes which would be dependent on them, they must be called back with the hard-won, equable reasonableness of the mother, and reminded to pick up and put away. David's special two friends came to his house at four to eat her cookies, or went to each other's houses to eat other cookies. They giggled, laughed raucously, kidded and joshed each other, pushed each other around. They made snow-forts in their front yards, they skated with awkward energy on the place where the brook overflowed the meadow, took their sleds out to Hingham Hill for coasting, made plans for a shack in the woods next summer.

In the evening, if the homework had been finished in time, they were allowed to visit each other for an hour, to make things with Meccano, things which were a source of enormous pride to the eight-year-olds, things which the next morning fell over at the lightest touch of the mother's broom.

At that age, thought the mother, their souls, if any, were certainly no more than seeds, deep inside their hard, muscular, little-boy flesh. How do souls develop, she wondered occasionally, as she washed dishes, made beds, selected carrots at the market, answered the telephone. How do souls develop out of those rough-and-ready little males? If they do develop?

David and Peter, living close to each other, shared the evening play-hour more often than the third boy who lived across the tracks. They were allowed to go back and forth by themselves, even though the midwinter blackness had fallen by seven o'clock. Peter lived on the street above theirs, up the hill. There was a short cut down across a vacant lot, which was in sight of one or the other house, all the way. It was safe enough, even for youngsters, even at night. The little boys loved that downhill short cut. Its steep slope invited their feet to fury. Never using the path, they raced down in a spray of snow kicked up by their flying overshoes, arriving at the house, their cheeks flaming, flinging themselves like cannon balls against the kitchen door, tasting a little the heady physical fascination of speed, on which, later, as ski-runners, they would become wildly drunken.

"Sh! *David!* Not so *loud!*" his mother often said, springing up from her mending at the crash of the banged-open door. "Father's trying to do some accounts," or "Sister has company in the living room."

Incessant acrobatic feat—to keep five people of different ages and personalities, all living under the same roof, from stepping on each other's feet. Talk about keeping five balls in the air at the same time! That was nothing compared to keeping five people satisfied to live with each other, to provide each one with approximately what he needed and wanted without taking away something needed by one of the others. (Arithmetically considered, there were of course six people living under that roof. But she did not count. She was the mother. She took what she got, what was left. . . .)

That winter, as the orbits of the older children lay more outside the house, she found herself acquiring a new psychological skill that was almost eerie. She could be in places where she was not, at all. She had an astral body which could go anywhere. Anywhere, that is, where one of her five was. She was with her honey-sweet big daughter in the living room, playing games with high school friends (was there butter enough, she suddenly asked herself, for the popcorn the young people would inevitably want, later?). She was upstairs where her husband sat, leaning over the desk, frowning in attentiveness at a page of figures—that desk light was not strong enough. Better put the floodlight up there tomorrow. She was in the sunporch of the neighbor's house, where her little son was bolting Meccano strips together with his square, strong, not-very-clean hands—his soul, if any, dormant far within his sturdy body. She floated above the scrimmage in the high school gym, where her first-born played basketball with ferocity, pouring out through that channel the rage of maleness constantly gathering in his big frame which grew that year with such fantastic rapidity that he seemed taller at breakfast than he had been when he went to bed. She sent her astral body upstairs to where her little daughter, her baby, her darling, slept with one doll in her arms, and three others on the pillow beside her. That blanket was not warm enough for Janey. When she went to bed, she would put on another one.

She was all of them. First one, then another. When was she herself? When did *her* soul have time to stretch its wings?

One evening this question tried to push itself into her mind, but was swept aside by her suddenly knowing, as definitely as if she had heard a clock strike or the doorbell ring, that the time had passed for David's return from his evening play-hour with Peter. She looked at her watch. But she did not need to. A sixth sense told her heart, as with a blow, that he should before this have come pelting down the hill, plowing the deep snow aside in clouds, hurling himself against the kitchen door. He was late. Her astral self, annihilating time and space, fled out to look for him. He must have left the other house some time ago. Peter's mother always sent him home promptly.

She laid down the stocking she was darning, stepped into the dark kitchen, and put her face close to the window to look out. It was a cloudless cold night. Every detail of the back yard world was visible, almost transparent, in the pale radiance that fell from the stars. Not a breath of wind. She could see everything: the garbage pail at the woodshed door, the trampled snow of the driveway, the clothes she had washed that morning and left on the line, the deep unbroken snow beyond the yard, the path leading up the hill.

Then she saw David. He was standing halfway down, as still as the frozen night around him.

But David never stood still.

Knee-deep in the snow he stood, looking all around him. She saw him slowly turn his head to one side, to the other. He lifted his face towards the sky. It was almost frightening to see *David* stand so still. What could he be looking at? What was there he could be seeing? Or hearing? For as she watched him, the notion crossed her mind that he seemed to be listening. But there was nothing to hear. Nothing.

She did not know what was happening to her little son. Nor what to do. So she did nothing. She stood as still as he, her face at the window, lost in wonder.

She saw him, finally, stir and start slowly, slowly down the path. But David never moved slowly. Had he perhaps had a quarrel with Peter? Had Peter's mother been unkind to him?

It could do no harm now to go to meet him, she thought, and by that time, she could not, anxious as she was, not go to meet him. She opened the kitchen door and stepped out into the dark, under the stars.

He saw her, he came quickly to her, he put his arms around her waist. With every fiber of her body which had borne his, she felt a difference in him.

She did not know what to say, so she said nothing.

It was her son who spoke. "It's so still," he said quietly in a hushed voice, a voice she had never heard before. "It's so still!"

He pressed his cheek against her breast as he tipped his head back to look up. "All those stars," he murmured dreamily, "they shine so. But they don't make a sound. They—they're *nice*, aren't they?"

He stood a little away from her to look up into her face. "Do you remember—in the song—'the world in solemn stillness lay'?" he asked her, but he knew she remembered.

The starlight showed him clear, his honest, little-boy eyes wide, fixed trustingly on his mother's. He was deeply moved. But calm. This had come to him while he was still so young that he could be calmed by his mother's being with him. He had not known that he had an inner sanctuary. Now he stood in it, awe-struck at his first sight of beauty. And opened the door to his mother.

As naturally as he breathed, he put into his mother's hands the pure rounded pearl of a shared joy. "I thought I heard them singing —sort of," he told her.

Married
Children

The young wife:

    Goodby! *Goodby!*" She turned the golden brown of her tanned face up towards the two pale, indoor, middle-aged faces at the open window. "It's been *won*derful to have you!" The train began slowly to move. Walking along on the platform beside it, she clasped her father's clean wrinkled hand, and said affectionately, "Dear old Dad!" Her mother's, a little knotted with arthritis, but carefully kept, she kissed. The train picked up speed. She let them go. "*Goodby!* Come again!" she shouted, waving her hand. They were gone. A flurry of dust settled down to stillness. She stood a moment looking after the train, the smile still on her face. She was thinking with satisfaction, "Well, the first visit went off all right."

She walked home at a brisk pace, smiling all the way, and let herself into the living room. It looked empty and deserted. Elated, she stood a moment to expand into the roominess left by departing guests and, stepping into the kitchen, *her own kitchen,* began cheerfully to wash the dishes left from lunch.

As she worked her eyes roamed regally around her domain. "I love it all, *all!*" she thought. Every object she touched had been part of a happy hour. She set a washed bowl down on the drainboard and remembered how Christopher's eyes had shone the day he came in with it under his arm. He had been making it himself in odd moments to surprise her. It had come over her all of a sudden how *grand* he was

—she thought of some of the girls back home who had married awful poker-playing boys—men who prided themselves on being sports and went right on spending their money on the races the way they had before they were married, grudging every cent for housekeeping, husbands who wanted to live in one room and go out to dance in a roadhouse every evening.

"Oh, Chris! How did I ever have the good luck to get you!" she had cried, and had fallen into his arms so hard they both went down on a chair—and it had gone to pieces! And there they had sat on the floor in each other's arms—in the midst of scattered chair-rounds and legs—laughing and laughing. "Like a couple of silly kids!" thought the wife. In the memory of it her face bloomed with gaiety. What good times they had had together! "No matter how rich we ever get, or how many children we have, or *anything*, nothing can ever be lovelier than this first winter." She could have kissed the very door through which Christopher came in from work, always cheerful, not only always loving her, but always *liking* her, no matter what she did. Dad was the salt of the earth, of course. But he always found something sharp and sarcastic to say if anybody unfolded the newspaper before he did, and the way he looked at his plate if the breakfast sausage wasn't cooked to suit him certainly did take away everybody else's appetite. She hadn't known but that all men were like that at home. Christopher, who took everything so easily, who thought it was too wonderful of her to cook his meals at all, anyhow; Chris —always tickled to death all over again every time he came back to the house to find he really was married to her and had a home— well, Christopher simply took her breath away.

She had finished the dishes now. Singing at the top of her voice, *"Mister and Missus is the name!"* she began to get the wash ready for old Maria Half-Wolf when she came loping up on her pinto, her black braids flying. If that old redskin wasn't exciting to have around —like a movie—compared to Hennessey's Steam Laundry delivery wagon! How romantic and picturesque and interesting every bit of the life here was anyway! As she came and went, sorting over and gathering up the laundry, her eyes were often on the magnificent golden spaciousness outside. Those miles of sunlight! That clear strong tireless wind! Compare what she was seeing out of her window to the postage stamp of lawn, the smothering heavy-leaved trees, the crowded, commonplace suburban houses that had shut in her life until now. "Honest, it makes a person feel like flying," she thought. "I could fly, I know I could, I feel so wonderful!" and stopped short, startled to realize that the reason she felt like flying was because Father and

Mother had gone away. And with them had gone the—the *weight* they put on her.

Why was it they always made her feel unsure of herself—like a child again? Was it because they had been grown up so long before she had? She had been dismayed to have that old doubt of herself, the wonder if she was doing things to suit them, come back in her very own home. "My! I'm glad we don't live next door!" she thought, and then, "I'm terrible! I'm simply awful!" she reproached herself, fixing her mind on how generous Father always was, how much Mother loved her. "They're sweet. They're swell. I owe them everything," she went on, but rebounded from this dutifulness into "But, oh, gosh! Does it seem good to do things the way *I* want them, not the way Mother thinks best. I'm going to make milk gravy for dinner, and *thicken it with flour and water!*" Laughing at the thought of how shocked her mother would be at this revolt from Law, she moved gaily to begin her cooking.

But as she worked alone, happily, free from criticism, from supervision, even from observation, in her very own kitchen, she felt, little by little, as if a cold draught had begun to blow, that, after having had somebody else there, it was queer to be alone by yourself in the place. Once she turned to say something to Mother and was daunted to see how empty the kitchen looked. Why, Mother was gone! Already far away. Her heart sank. Suppose something should happen! Suppose she should get sick! What could she do, if she got sick, all alone so far away from Mother!

Well, Mother would come, of course. Stooping to set her biscuits in the oven, she thought—almost as though it were for the first time —that goodness gracious, was she lucky to have a mother like that, somebody you could count on, *absolutely*. Let them be in China or Alaska, or Timbuctoo, Mother would be with them in thought, in love. And if there was trouble—she'd always taken it for granted, but really it was sort of wonderful to know that Mother would be with you as fast as travel could bring her, wanting nothing but what would be best for her children, ready to do anything to get it for them—*Mother!* "Gosh, I wonder will my children feel that way about me!" thought the young wife soberly, and asked herself with concern, "How do you suppose anybody gets that way?"

Chris burst in, Chris rushing off to wash and change his clothes before the ceremony of greeting her, and coming back in a hurry with open arms to kiss her a great many times all over her hair as well as her lips and cheeks and neck. "I simply adore your hair this way, Judy darling," he said. "You look like Garbo herself."

As they ate dinner they talked about their visitors. Christopher, as an orphan, was quite impressed with parents, quite taken with his wife's parents. She listened, pleased, to his appreciation of her father's geniality, uneasy to his praise of her mother's steadiness and competence. "Set that woman down anywhere, no matter where, and she'd take right hold and get things straightened out!" he said. His accent, his words, his admiration brought back to his young wife the shadow of her girlhood's dimmed jealous uncertainty of her own powers. She held her head down as she ate, and thought forlornly, "Nobody'd ever say that about *me.*"

"But," added Christopher thoughtfully, "she's not my kind of woman, of course."

His wife flung up her head. "What do you *mean?*" she asked, quickly.

He thought she was indignant at the criticism of her family, and quailed a little, but held his ground honestly, too. "I don't mean she's not fine. She is. As fine as they make 'em. But she's just not the kind of woman I'd ever take to. I don't know why. Too darned practical, maybe. I like 'em foolish—and young—and soft—and—" He put his hand over his wife's and looked at her fondly.

Before the young wife there opened a door, the door she had secretly feared would always be closed to her, the door that led to her place in life, her own place. There was a place for her then, a place that nobody of the overpowering older generation could fill. She stepped gladly through to take that place of her own, leaving her mother behind her.

And now she was safe, freed from that pervasive pressure. How she loved her mother! With all her heart. No silent reservations. "Yes, Mother is certainly *swell!*" she said earnestly, and put up her napkin to wipe her eyes.

The Father to his Secretary:

"Ready to take a letter, Miss Pratt?"

With decisive firmness the gray-haired stenographer laid down her notebook. "No, Mr. Underhill, I am not ready and I won't be until you give me the news about your daughter. Dear! dear! I can hardly believe she's really married. It seems only yesterday that Judy was galloping her fat little Shetland up and down Grove Street, screaming 'Hi-Yippi-Hi-Yea!'"

Her employer chuckled, "And snapping her cap-pistol at the trolley cars. Yes, I remember her that way, too. But it was quite a while ago. You and I have been working together better than eighteen years. Let's see. . . . There's nothing much to say about the children. I guess they're getting on all right. Well, no . . . they're having a pretty tough time financially. That's only to be expected, of course. The boy's insurance business doesn't amount to a whoop, I take it. He's had to hustle right out and find something to pay the grocer with. Got himself a filling station to run. I like his grit and push. It promises well for the future. But right now it's a case of pretty slim pickings for them all around. Not that it takes much to live on, the way they do, in half of one of those little shacks with three sticks of furniture." He stopped and pulled the pile of letters towards him.

"But that's not what I mean," persisted the secretary. "Most young couples have a hard time getting started. The big question is how do they take it? Are they good sports? Or is life getting them down?"

The father unhooked his spectacles from his ears and polished them thoughtfully on his handkerchief. "The nice kids!" he said in a tender tone. "So far as I can see, they don't even notice it."

He cleared his throat. She poised her pencil over her notebook. "T. C. Cook and Co.," he began, "Cleveland. You've got the street address in the files, Miss Pratt. We believe there is a market for your product in this territory and will be glad to handle same. You finish it, Miss Pratt—usual points: prices, discount, bank reference. I've got two weeks of back mail to plow through."

The Mother to the Grandmother:

"Well, all right, Mother, if you want to hear all about them, I'll try to tell you. But you'll hardly believe it if I do. I never was so shocked as when I got off that train and saw that forlorn town. A dozen cheap ramshackle bungalows set down anywhere on the desert. From Judy's letters you'd never *dream* what it's really like. Nor what kind of a house they live in! Only *half* of one of those miserable little wooden packing cases. Three bare rooms looking out into a desert of dust. That alkali dust! You eat it, you drink it—it took Charles and me three days after we left to get the gritty taste out of our mouths. And it didn't seem to . . ."

The older woman had been knitting. She now dropped her work in her lap, and looked with a little sharpness at her daughter. "Never mind about the dust, Etta. How is *Judy?*"

"Well, she *says* the climate and the altitude and everything agree with her. But you should see her skin. That rose-petal skin of hers!

All dried up and brown! I don't believe she half takes care of it. You never saw such a change in anybody's looks! She's had to have her hair bobbed, to make it easier to take care of. For there's not such a thing as a hairdresser within ten thousand miles of that place, I'm sure. The last of her permanent has grown out and been cut off—her hair's as straight as a string. She looks like a squaw. She runs the comb through it without so much as a glance at the mirror. Judith! You know how careful she used to be of her hair. It took her an hour to get every curl in place. But she has no time to think of her looks now. Nobody to notice them, either. Christopher would never know if she didn't even wash her face. He takes her for granted. And there's nobody in that town—*nobody*—who would know the difference. Or know anything else! I never saw such a place. Everybody looked to me as though they were just roosting for a while before they moved on. Why would anybody want to settle down in a desert?" Her tone was vehement now, "For it's a real *desert,* Mother, too dreary for words. No woman could keep house there—not what *we* think of as keeping house. Only Mexicans and Indians for help. You should see their *windows!* Judy has *no*body to come in except a dirty old half-and-half Mexican-Indian woman who does her washings. And how! But of course the water is stiff with alkali dust! Nobody could get anything clean."

The grandmother laughed. "Oh, goodness, Etta, how you do sputter! Who cares how they get their washings done? I want to hear about them. How'd you like Judy's husband now you've seen him at home?"

The mother looked off into the distance and said neutrally, "Well enough." She shifted in her chair and admitted, *"He's* all right." She swallowed, folded her lips and repeated, dryly, "I don't say he's not all *right*—a nice boy. Easy-going around the house. That sort of thing." She came to life, her eyes snapped, she leaned forward and asked with energy, "But will he ever be the provider Charles has been? That's the question! Do you know I don't believe he ever sells any insurance. As far as I can see, all he makes is out of a filling station they run. Yes, a regular roadside filling station, selling gas to automobilists! And when he has to be away, it has to be Judy who answers the bell, runs out and pumps it up for them and makes change and everything. What do you think of that?"

She flung the question out defiantly. Her mother asked rather dryly, "Does Judy mind?"

"Well, I wouldn't say she *minded.* She's always been protected—till now. She's like a child, about—she doesn't take in the meaning of such things. And you know what a sweet disposition she has. She'd never complain. Christopher is lucky to get her, if he did but know it. There are not many girls who'd be as cheerful as she is, in the life she had to lead."

Vehemence began to pulse hotly again in her voice, "Mother, you should see the furniture in that rattletrap little house. Cheap to begin with, and I suppose the glue all dried out by the heat. It falls apart if you look at it. Charles and I never sat our whole weight on a chair all the while we were there."

"Oh, well, daughter, you and Charles didn't have such a lot of furniture when you started in. The first time your father and I visited you, you were eating in the kitchen because there wasn't another table in the house—just two little stands."

The mother flashed a resentful look at the grandmother. "Why, I don't remember it that way at all," she said. Then, reluctantly, "Well, yes, perhaps. At the very beginning."

She looked hard at the older woman and said with heat, "You're just bringing that up to be contrary, Mother. This isn't the same thing at all. Times have changed—girls have a right to expect more—the home Judy came from was—" She shook her head, gave that up, appealed to her mother's deeper understanding. "Anyhow, it's not the furniture—it's the—it's the loneliness, the desolation of it all. She's absolutely isolated. Not a soul around that she can say a word to, not a real word. You know how she's always kept up with her music—in church, in the chorus here! I don't suppose there's a soul there who knows what good singing sounds like. Judy practically admitted she hasn't done a bit of practicing since she was married. No social life either—no club, no church—I don't suppose there's a book in the whole country except the Sears, Roebuck catalogue—no friends, nobody but a lot of— Well, all I can say is that any man who'll take a girl from a good home out to the middle of a desert and expect her to— Where's my handkerchief?"

The older woman said, in a sad murmur, "Etta, do you know why you're crying? It's not because Judy is having a hard time. It's because she isn't."

The other put down her handkerchief and cried out angrily, "I don't know what you're talking about!"

The grandmother went on, "Oh yes you do. Till now you've never *believed,* no matter what you said, that Judy could really be happy away from you. It's because you saw for yourself that she's through with you, that there's no need for you anywhere in her—"

"*Mother!* How *can* you say such a heartless thing! I'm *not* thinking of myself. I'd give my right hand for Judy's happiness, and you know it."

"Nobody's blaming you, Etta," said the grandmother dreamily, as if thinking of something else. "You're a good mother. Everybody knows that growing pains hurt."

"But, Mother, you've got this all wrong! Listen to me! I'm not jealous of Judy. I don't want to keep her for myself. *I love my daughter.*"

The grandmother sighed and said with profound sympathy, "My poor Etta, you've just got to learn to love her another way." She put her wrinkled hand on her daughter's.

There was a silence—then the younger woman said in a low faltering tone of pain, "Mother, at the station, when we were going away, Judy ran along beside the train, saying goodby—" she stopped to wipe her eyes and blow her nose, and, her lower lip trembling, murmured piteously—"and she looked so—so *cheerful!*"

An involuntary rueful laugh broke from her mother. "Well, daughter, so did you, twenty-four years ago."

They laughed. They clung to each other. They reached for their handkerchiefs.

The Washed Window

⇛Older people in Arlington have a special interest in the last house you pass as you leave our village to drive to Cambridge. It was built and lived in for many years by our first local skilled cabinetmaker. In the early days nearly every house had one good piece of professionally made furniture, brought up from Connecticut on horseback or in an oxcart. These were highly treasured. But the furniture made here was, for the first generation after 1764, put together by men who just wanted chairs, beds, and a table for the family meals—and those as fast as they could be slammed into shape.

For many years Silas Knapp lived in that last house practicing his remarkable skill. Nearly every house of our town acquired in those years one or two pieces of his workmanship. They are now highly prized as "early nineteenth-century, locally-made antiques."

He not only made many a fine chest of drawers and bedside stand there: he also brought up a fine family of children. You may never have noticed this house as you drove by, but once, some twenty or thirty years ago, a great American leader, who chanced to pass through Vermont, asked to be shown the old Knapp home. He had been delivering an important address to a large audience in Rutland. When he stood in front of the small low old house he took off his hat and bowed his gray head in silence. Then he explained to the person who had driven him down to Arlington, "For me it is a shrine."

This is the story back of his visit to the plain little early nine-teenth century artisan's house which to him was a shrine. Viola Knapp was one of the Vermont girls who "went South to teach," taking along with her the attitude towards life she had been brought up to respect. She married there—as the saying goes, "married well"— an army officer of good family. It was a happy, lifelong mating. Viola Knapp Ruffner and her husband, General Ruffner, lived here and there in various cities and towns and brought up a family of five children. It was while the Ruffners were living in West Virginia that—but I'll set the story down as I heard it in my youth, about sixty years ago, from the lips of the distinguished American educator who, as a boy, had been a student of Viola Knapp Ruffner. In his later years, he became one of my father's valued friends.

This is about as he used to tell it to us with many more details than I ever saw told in print. "I never knew exactly how old I was when I first saw Mrs. Ruffner, for in the days of slavery, family records— that is, black-family records—were seldom kept. But from what I have been able to learn, I was born, a slave, on a Virginia plantation, about 1858. In my youth, my home was a log cabin about fourteen by six-teen feet square. We slept on frowsy piles of filthy rags, laid on the dirt floor. Until I was quite a big youth I wore only one gar-ment, a shirt made out of agonizingly rough refuse-flax. We slaves ate corn bread and pork, because those foods could be grown on the plantation without cash expense. I had never seen anything except the slave quarters on the plantation where I was born, with a few glimpses of the 'big house' where our white owners lived. I cannot remember ever, during my childhood and youth, not one single time, when our family sat down together at a table to eat a meal as human families do. We ate as animals do, whenever and wherever an edible morsel was found. We usually took our food up in our fingers, sometimes from the skillet, sometimes from a tin plate held on our knees, and as we chewed on it, we held it as best we could in our hands.

"Life outside our cabin was as slovenly and disordered as inside. The white owners made no effort to keep things up. They really could not. Slaves worked; hence any form of work was too low for white people to do. Since white folks did no work, they did not know how work should be done. The untaught slaves, wholly ig-norant of better standards, seldom got around to mending the fences, or putting back a lost hinge on a sagging gate or door. Weeds grew wild everywhere, even in the yard. Inside the big house, when a piece of plastering fell from a wall or ceiling, it was a long time before anybody could stir himself to get it replastered.

"After the end of the Civil War, when we were no longer slaves, my family moved to a settlement near a salt mine, where, although I was still only a child, I was employed—often beginning my day's work at four in the morning. There, we lived in even more dreadful squalor, for our poor rickety cabin was in a crowded slum, foul with unspeakable dirt—literal and moral. As soon as I grew a little older and stronger, I was shifted from working in the salt mine to a coal mine. Both mines were then owned by General Lewis Ruffner.

"By that time I had learned my letters and could, after a fashion, read. Mostly I taught myself, but with some irregular hours spent in a Negro night school, after an exhausting day's work in the mines. There were no public schools for ex-slaves; the poor, totally unequipped, bare room where colored people, young and old, crowded in to learn their letters was paid for by tiny contributions from the Negroes themselves.

"About that time I heard two pieces of news, which were like very distant, very faint glimmers in the blackness of the coal mine in which nearly all my waking hours were spent. One was about a school for colored students—Hampton Institute it was—where they could learn more than their letters. The other was that the wife of General Ruffner was from Vermont and that she took an interest in the education of the colored people who worked for her. I also heard that she was so 'strict' that nobody could suit her, and that the colored boys who entered her service were so afraid of her, and found her so impossible to please, that they never stayed long. But the pay was five dollars a month, and keep. That was better than the coal mine —and there was also the chance that she might be willing to have me go on learning. I got up my courage to try. What could be worse than the way I was living and the hopelessness of anything better in the future?

"But I can just tell you that, great, lumbering, muscle-bound coal-mining boy that I was, I was trembling when I went to ask for that work. The Ruffners had just moved into an old house that had been empty for some time, and they were not yet established, their furniture not unpacked, the outbuildings not repaired. When I first saw her, Mrs. Ruffner was writing on an improvised desk which was a plank laid across two kegs.

"I falteringly told her I had come to ask for work. She turned in her chair and looked at me silently. Nobody had ever looked at me like that, not at my rags and dirt but as if she wanted to see what kind of person I was. She had clear, steady gray eyes, I remember.

Then she said, 'You can try.' After reflection, she went on, 'You might as well start in by cleaning the woodshed. It looks as though it hadn't been touched for years.'

"She laid down her pen and took me through a narrow side-passage into the woodshed. It was dark and cluttered with all kinds of dirty, dusty things. A sour, moldy smell came up from them. Great cobwebs hung down from the rough rafters of the low, sloping roof. Stepping back for a moment, she brought out a dustpan and a broom. A shovel leaned against the woodshed wall. She put that in my hand and said, 'Now go ahead. Put the trash you clean out, on that pile in the yard and we'll burn it up later. Anything that won't burn, like broken glass, put into that barrel.' Then she turned away and left me.

"You must remember that I never had done any work except rough, unskilled heavy labor. I had never cleaned a room in my life, I had never seen a clean room in my life. But I was used to doing as I was told, and I was dead set on managing to go ahead with learning more than I would in that poor beginner's schoolroom. So I began taking out things which anybody could see were trash, like mildewed rags, which fell apart into damp shreds the minute I touched them. There were also, I remember, some moldy heaps of I don't know what, garbage maybe, that had dried into shapeless chunks of bad-smelling filth. In one corner was the carcass of a long-dead dog, which I carried out to the pile of trash in the side yard. Glass was everywhere, broken and unbroken empty whiskey bottles, bits of crockery ware. These I swept with the broom and picking up my sweepings in my hands (I had no idea what a dustpan was for) carried them outside.

"The shed looked to me so much better that I went in to find Mrs. Ruffner. She was still writing. I told her, 'I cleaned it.' Pushing back her chair she went out to the woodshed with me.

"She made no comment when she first opened the door and looked around her with clear gray eyes. Then she remarked quietly, 'There's still some things to attend to. Those pieces of wood over there you might pile up against the wall in the corner. They would do to burn. Be sure to clean the floor well before you start piling the wood on it. And here's another pile of rotten rags, you see. And that tangle behind the door. You'd better pull it all apart and see what's there. Throw away the trash that's mixed with it.' She turned to go back, saying, 'Just keep on till you've got it finished and then come and tell me.'

"She didn't speak kindly. She didn't speak unkindly. I looked at the woodshed with new eyes and saw that, sure enough, I'd only made a beginning. I began to pull at the odds and ends in that dusty mess behind the door. And to my astonishment I felt I was perspiring. The work wasn't hard for me, you understand. It was like little boy's play compared to the back-breaking labor I had always done. And it wasn't that I minded carrying around in my bare hands things slimy with rot or having liquid filth drip on my ragged pants. I was used to dirt, and my hands were as calloused as my feet. What made me sweat was the work I had to do with my mind. Always before, when somebody had given me a piece of work to do, he had stood right there to do all the thinking. Here his orders would have been, 'Pull that piece of sacking out. That stick, put it on top of the woodpile. Those dried-up chicken bones, scrape them up from the dirt and throw them in the trash pile.' All I would have had to do was to plod along, doing what I was ordered. Now I was the one to give the orders.

"Now that I was really thinking about what I was doing, I was amazed to see how little I had done, how much more there was to do than I had seen.

"I stooped to pull apart the grimy, mud-colored tangle heaped up back of the door. As I stirred it, a snake crawled out from under it and wriggled towards the door. A big fellow. I wasn't surprised. I was used to snakes. I dropped a stone on his head and carried his long, black body out to the trash pile in the yard.

"Now I had come to a corner where chickens evidently roosted every night. Everything was covered with their droppings, like smearings of white paint. I thought nothing of handling them, and taking up the body of one I found lying still and dead in the midst of the rubbish. More rotted rags, a stained, torn pair of pants, too far gone even for me to wear, still smelling foul. Some pieces of wood, not rotten, fit for fuel. Everything I came to had first to be pulled loose from the things it was mixed up with, and enough of the dirt shaken off to let me make out what it was. And then I had to think what to do with it. No wonder that the sweat ran down my face. To see, I had to wipe my eyes with the back of my hands.

"Finally, the last of the refuse was taken apart and cleared away and the litter and filth which had dropped from it to the floor was swept together and carried out to the trash pile. I kept looking over my shoulder for somebody to make the decisions, to tell me what to do. 'Throw that away. Save that. Put it with the firewood. Toss that into the barrel with the broken glass.' But there was nobody there to give me orders. I went in to get Mrs. Ruffner. 'I got it done,' I told her.

"Laying down her pen, she came again to see. I felt nervous as, silent and attentive, she ran those clear eyes of hers over what I had been doing. But I wasn't at all prepared to have her say again, 'That's better, but there's a great deal still to do. You haven't touched the cobwebs, I see.' I looked up at them, my lower jaw dropped in astonishment. Sure enough, there they hung in long, black festoons. I had not once lifted my head to see them. 'And how about washing the window? Here, step in here and get a pail of water for that. Here are some clean rags. You'll have to go over it several times to get it clean.'

"She went back into the house and I stood shaken by more new ideas than I could tell you. I hadn't even noticed there was a window, it was so thick with dust and cobwebs. I had never had anything to do with a glass window. In the dark cabins I had lived in, the windows were just holes cut in the walls.

"I set to work once more, the sweat running down my face. Suppose she wouldn't even let me try to do her work. I never could get into Hampton! What if I just never could get the hang of her ways? Stricken, scared, I began again to clean that woodshed! I went over and over every corner of it. Once in a while I stopped stock-still to *look* at it, as I had never looked at anything before, trying really to see it. I don't know that ever in my life afterwards did I care about doing anything right, as much as getting that little old woodshed clean.

"When I came to what I thought was the end, I stopped to get my breath. I looked up at the slanting roof. The rafters were not only cleared of cobwebs but bare of dust; the floor was swept clean, not a chip, not a thread, not a glint of broken glass on it. Piles of firewood against the walls. And the window! *I* had washed that window! Five times I had washed it. How it sparkled! How the strong sunshine poured through it! Now the woodshed was no rubbish pile. It was a room. To me it looked like a parlor. I was proud of it. Till then I had never been proud of anything I had done.

"Then for the third time I went to call Mrs. Ruffner to inspect. Big boy as I was, twice her size, my hands were shaking, my lips twitching. I felt sick. Had I done it right this time? Could I ever do anything right?

"I watched her face as she passed my work in review, looking carefully up, down, and around. Then she turned to me and, looking straight into my eyes, she nodded and said, 'Now it's clean. Nobody could have done it any better.'

"She had opened the door through which I took my first step towards civilized standards of living."

He drew a long breath and went on, "For a year and a half I lived with those standards around me, working for Mrs. Ruffner. What I learned from her! It was like breathing new air. I could never say in words what she taught me, for it was not taught in words but in life. She never pronounced such abstract expressions as 'frankness' and 'honesty'—they radiated from her, like sunlight streaming silently through a clean window, as she spoke of the tasks she set me. They were so simple she took them for granted, but they were revelations to me. I have repeated ever so many times the story of what Mrs. Ruffner taught me by the way she lived in her home—lessons of as great a value to me as any education I ever had in all my life. To anybody seeing me from the outside, I would, I suppose, have seemed to be learning only how to clean a filthy yard, how to keep a fence in repair, how to hang a gate straight, how to paint a weather-beaten barn.

"And then how to study—how to learn from the books she helped me secure, the books she took for granted and which, for me, were revelations. She took my breath away by suggesting, casually, that I begin to have a library of my own. Me!

"It was an old dry-goods box. I knocked the boards out of one side, used them for shelves, and with Mrs. Ruffner's backing to steady me, began with incredulous pride to set up, side by side, one and another of the battered, priceless printed volumes which, under Mrs. Ruffner's roof, I had come to own. I owning books!

"And yet, after all, later on when the way ahead was darkly blocked, it was that woodshed which pushed open the door.

"It would take too long to tell you all the piled-up difficulties I had to climb over to reach my goal of a real school with real, full-time classroom study. All sorts of things happened as I made my way over the long distance which separated me from Hampton. And when I actually stood before that three-story, brick school building, it looked as though I would not be allowed to enter it as a student. My trip had been longer, harder, had cost more than I had dreamed it could. I was nearly penniless, footsore, dusty, gaunt, unwashed.

"The teacher who was in charge of admitting or turning away students gave me a long, doubtful look and told me to wait. Well, I waited. I saw her interviewing other students, better dressed, cleaner, ever so much more promising-looking than I, without a look at me. But I didn't go away. That solid, three-story brick building—all just to provide a chance to study for people who had never had a chance to study—how could I go away, even if I were not welcome? I waited. After several hours of watching that teacher admitting other students, she finally had an idea about me and told me briefly, dubiously, 'The classroom next to this one needs to be cleaned before the Institute opens tomorrow. Do you suppose you could sweep it out? There's a broom over there in the corner.'

"In all my life I never had an order which so uplifted my heart. Could I sweep it out? Oh, Mrs. Ruffner!

"I swept that classroom three times. I moved every piece of furniture and swept under each one. There was a closet. I swept that. Joyfully I swept every corner clean. I found a dust cloth. I dusted everything in the room, I turned the cloth and dusted everything again, and again. I was in the middle of my fourth dusting when the teacher opened the door and stepped in. She was a Yankee. She knew what to look for. She took a clean handkerchief from her pocket, shook it out, and passed it over the top of a desk. After one startled look at me, she rubbed the seat of a chair with it.

"I stood at ease, my head high, fearing nothing. I did not need anybody's permission to feel sure of myself. I had been asked to perform a task. I had done it.

"She passed her testing handkerchief over a window sill, and turned to face me. She was a Yankee and wasted no words. She put the handkerchief back in her pocket, and in a matter-of-fact voice said, 'You're admitted to Hampton.'

"I had been set an entrance examination. And thanks to Mrs. Ruffner I had passed it."

His name was Booker T. Washington.

War

"Through Pity
and Terror . . ."

       <big>**W**</big>hen the war broke out, Madeleine Brisman-
tier was the very type and epitome of all which up to that time had
been considered "normal" for a modern woman, a *nice* modern woman.
She had been put through the severe and excellent system of French
public education in her native town of Amiens, and had done so well
with her classes that when she was nineteen her family were about
to feed her into the hopper of the system of training for primary
teachers. But just then, when on a visit in a smallish Seine-et-Marne
town, she met the fine, upstanding young fellow who was to be her husband. He was young too, not then quite through the long formidable
course of study for pharmacists, who are in France next to being
doctors. It was not until two years later, when Madeleine was twenty-
one and he twenty-five, that they were married, and Madeleine left
Amiens to live in Madriné, the town where they had met.

Jules Brismantier's father had been the only pharmacist there all his
life, and Jules stepped comfortably into his father's shoes, his business,
and the lodgings over the pharmacy. If this sounds grubby and "working-class" to your American ears, disabuse yourself; the home over the
pharmacy was as well-ordered and well-furnished a little apartment as
ever existed in a "strictly residential portion" of any American suburb.
The beds were heirlooms, and were of mahogany, there were several
bits of excellent furniture in the small, white-paneled salon, and three

pretty, brocade-covered chairs which had come down from Madeleine's great-grandmother; there was a piano on which Madeleine, who had received a good substantial musical training, played the best music there is in the world, which is to say, German (Jules, like many modern young Frenchmen, had a special cult for Beethoven); and there was a kitchen—oh, you should have seen that kitchen, white tiles on the walls and red tiles on the floor and all around such an array of copper and enamel utensils as can only be found in well-kept kitchens in the French provinces where one of the main amusements and occupations of the excellent housewives is elaborate cooking. Furthermore, there was in the big oaken chests and tall cupboards a supply of bedding which would have made us open our eyes, used as we are to our (relatively speaking) hand-to-mouth American methods. Madeleine had no more than the usual number of sheets, partly laid aside for her, piece by piece, when the various inheritances from aunts and cousins came in, partly left there in the house, in which her mother-in-law had died the year before Madeleine's marriage, partly bought for her (as if there were not already enough!) to make up the traditional wedding trousseau without which no daughter of a respectable bourgeois family can be married. So that, taking them all together, she had two hundred and twenty sheets, every one linen, varying from the delightfully rough old homespun and home-woven ones, dating from nobody knew when, down to the smooth, fine, glossy ones with deep hemstitching on the top and bottom, and Madeleine's initials set in a delicately embroidered wreath. Of course she had pillow slips to go with them, and piles of woolen blankets, fluffy, soft and white, and a big puffy eiderdown covered with bright satin as the finishing touch for each well-furnished bed. Madeleine pretended to be modern sometimes, and to say it was absurd to have so many, but in her heart, inherited from long generations of passionately homekeeping women, she took immense satisfaction in all the ample furnishings of her pretty little home. What woman would not?

Now, although all this has a great deal to do with what happened to Madeleine, I am afraid you will think that I am making too long an inventory of her house, so I will not tell you about the shining silver in the buffet drawers, nor even about the beautiful old walled garden, full of flowers and vines and fruit trees, which lay at the back of the pharmacy. The back windows of the new bride's home looked down into the treetops of this garden, and along its graveled walks her children were to run and play.

For very soon the new family began to grow: first, a little blue-

eyed girl like Madeleine; then, two years later, a dark-eyed boy like
Jules—all very suitable and as it should be, like everything else that
happened to Madeleine. She herself, happily absorbed in her happy
life and in the care of all her treasures, reverted rapidly to type, forgot most of her modern education, and became a model wife and
mother on the pattern of all the other innumerable model wives
and mothers in the history of her family. She lived well within their
rather small income, and no year passed without their adding to the
modest store of savings which had come down to them because all
their grandmothers had lived well within *their* incomes. They kept
the titles relative to this little fortune, together with what cash they
had, and all their family papers, in a safe in the pharmacy, sunk in the
wall and ingeniously hidden behind a set of false shelves. They never
passed this hiding place without the warm, *sheltered* feeling which a
comfortable little fortune gives—the feeling which poor people go all
their lives without knowing.

You must not think, because I speak so much of the comfortableness
of the life of this typical French provincial family, that there was the
least suspicion of laziness about them. Indeed, such intelligent comfort as theirs is only to be had at the price of diligent and well-directed
effort. Jules worked hard all day in the pharmacy, and made less
money than would have contented an American ten years his junior.
Madeleine planned her busy day the evening before, and was up early
to begin it. The house was always immaculate, the meals always on
time (this was difficult to manage with Madeleine cooking everything
and only a rattle-headed young girl to help) and always delicious
and varied. Jules mounted the stairs from the pharmacy at noon and
in the evening, his mouth literally watering in anticipation. The
children were always as exquisitely fresh and well-cared-for as only
European children of the better classes used to be, when household
help was available at preindustrial pittance payments. Their hair was
always curled in shining ringlets and their hands clean, as those of
our children are only on Sunday mornings. Madeleine's religion was
to keep them spotless and healthful and smiling; to keep Jules' mouth
always watering in anticipation; to help him with his accounts in the
evenings, and to be on hand during the day to take his place during
occasional absences; to know all about the business end of their affairs
and to have their success as much at heart as he; to keep her lovely
old garden flowering and luxuriant; to keep her lovely old home
dainty and well ordered; and, of course, to keep herself invariably
neat with the miraculous neatness of French women, her pretty, soft

chestnut hair carefully dressed, her hands white and all her attractive person as alluring as in her girlhood.

Madeleine saw nothing lacking in this religion. It seemed to her all that life could demand of one woman.

In the spring of 1914, when Raoul was five years old and Sylvie eight, Madeleine was once more joyfully sorting over the tiny clothes left from their babyhood. All that summer her quick fingers were busy with fine white flannel and finer white nainsook, setting tiny stitches in small garments. Every detail of the great event was provided for in advance. As usual in French families, in all good families everywhere, the mother-to-be was lapped around with tenderness and indulgence. Madeleine was a little queen-regnant whose every whim was law. Of course she wanted her mother to be with her, as she had been for the arrival of Sylvie and Raoul, although her mother was not very well, and detested traveling in hot weather; and she wanted the same nurse she had had before, although that one had now moved away to a distant city. But Madeleine did not like the voice of the nurse who was available in Mandriné, and what French daughter could think of going through her great, dreadful hour without her mother by her to comfort and reassure her and to take the responsibility of everything! So of course that special nurse was engaged and her railway fare paid in advance, and of course Madeleine's mother promised to come. She was to arrive considerably in advance of the date, somewhere about the middle of August. All this was not so unreasonable from a money point of view as it sounds, for when they made up the weekly accounts together they found that the business was doing unusually well.

All through the golden July heats Madeleine sewed and waited. Sometimes in the pharmacy near Jules, sometimes in the garden where Raoul and Sylvie, in white dresses, ran and played gently up and down the paths. They played together mostly and had few little friends, because there were not many "nice" families living near them, and a good many that weren't nice. Of course Madeleine kept her children rigorously separated from these children, who were never in white but in the plainest of cheap gingham aprons, changed only once a week, and who never wore shapely, well-cut little shoes, but slumped about heavily in the wooden-soled, leather-topped "galoches" which are the national footgear for poor French children. Like many good mothers in France (are there any like that elsewhere?) Madeleine looked at other people's children chiefly to see if they were or were not "desirable" playmates for her own; and Sylvie and Raoul were not three years old before they had also learned the art of telling at a glance whether another child was a nice child or not, the question being settled of course by the kind of clothes he wore.

July was a beautiful month of glorious sun and ripening weather. For hours at a time in her lovely green nest, Madeleine sat happily, resting or embroidering, the peaches pleached against the high stone walls swelling and reddening visibly from one day to the next, the lilies opening flaming petals day by day, the children growing vigorously. Jules told his pretty wife fondly that she looked not a day older than on the day of their marriage ten years before. This was quite true, but I am not so sure as Jules that it was the highest of compliments to Madeleine.

The last week of July came, the high-tide moment of lush growth. Madeleine was bathed in the golden, dreamy content which comes to happy, much-loved women in her condition. It was the best possible of worlds, she had the best possible of husbands and children, and she was sure that nobody could say that she had not cultivated her garden to be the best possible of its kind. The world seemed to stand still in a sunny haze, centered about their happiness.

Drenched in sunshine and peace, their little barque was carried rapidly along by the Niagara river of history over the last stretch of smooth, shining water which separated them from the abyss.

I dare not tell you a single word about those first four days in August, of the incredulity which swiftly, from one dreadful hour to the next, changed to black horror. Their barque had shot over the edge, and in a wild tumult of ravening waters they were all falling together down into the fathomless gulf. And there are not words to describe to you the day of mobilization, when Jules, in his wrinkled uniform, smelling of moth-balls, said goodby to his young wife and little children and marched away to do his best to defend them.

There are many things in real life too horrible to be spoken of, and that farewell is one.

There was Madeleine in the empty house, heavy with her time of trial close upon her; with two little children depending on her for safety and care and cheer; with only a foolish little young maid to help her; with such a terrible anxiety about her husband that the mere thought of him sent her reeling against the nearest support.

The first hint came when the Mayor in person, venerable and white-bearded, appeared to gather up the weapons in all the houses. To Madeleine, wondering at this, he explained that he did it, so that *if*

the Germans came to Mandriné he could give his word of honor
there were no concealed arms in the town.

It was as though thunder had burst there in the little room. Madeleine stared at him, deathly white. "You don't think . . . you don't
think it possible that the Germans will get as far as *this!*" It had not
once occurred to her that not only Jules in the Army but she and the
children might be in danger. Monsieur le Maire hastened to reassure
her, remembering her condition, and annoyed that he should have
spoken out. "No, no, this is only a measure of precaution, to leave
nothing undone." He went away, after having taken Jules' shotgun
and little revolver, and even a lockless, flintless old musket which had
belonged to some of the kin who had followed Napoleon to Russia.
As he left, he said, "Personally I have not the faintest idea they will
penetrate as far as Mandriné—not the *faintest!*"

Of course when Jules left, *no* one had the faintest idea that his
peaceful home town would see anything of the war. That horror, at
least, was spared the young husband and father. But during the fortnight after his departure, although there were no newspapers, practically no trains, and no information except a brief, brief announcement, written by hand, in ink, posted every day on the door of the
Town Hall, the air began to be unbreathable, because of rumors, sickening rumors, unbelievable ones . . . that Belgium was invaded, although not in the war at all, and that Belgian cities and villages were
being sacked and burned; that the whole north country was one great
bonfire of burning villages and farms; then that the Germans were
near! Were nearer! And then all at once, quite definitely, that they
were within two days' march.

Everyone who could got out of Mandriné, but the only conveyances
left were big jolting farm wagons full of household gear; wagons
which went rumbling off, drawn by sweating horses lashed into a
gallop by panic-stricken boys, wagons which took you, nobody knew
where, away! away! which might break down and leave you anywhere, beside the road, in a barn, in a wood, in the hands of the Germans . . . for nobody knew where they were. The frightened neighbors, clutching their belongings into bundles, offered repeatedly to
take Madeleine and the children with them. Should she go or not?
There was nobody to help her decide. The little fluttering maid was
worse than nothing, the children were only babies to be taken care
of. After her charges were all in bed, that last night, Madeleine
wrung her hands, walking up and down the room, literally sick with
indecision. What ought she to do? It was the first great decision she
had ever been forced to make alone.

The last of the fleeing carts went without her. During the night she had come to know that the first, the most vital of all the needs of the hour was the life of the unborn baby. She was forced to cling to the refuge she had. She did not dare leave it for the unknown until she had her baby safely in her arms.

And perhaps the Germans would not come to Mandriné.

For two days the few people left in town lived in a sultry suspense, with no news, with every fear. M. le Curé had stayed with his church; M. le Maire stayed with the town records, and his white-haired old wife stayed to be with her husband (they had never been separated during the forty years of their marriage); good fresh-faced Sister Ste. Lucie, the old nun in charge of the little Hospice, stayed with some bedridden invalids who could not be moved; and there were poor people who had stayed for the reason which makes poor people do so many other things, because they could not help it, because they did not own a cart, nor a wheelbarrow, nor even a child's perambulator in which to take along the old grandfather or the sick mother who could not walk. Soeur St. Lucie promised to come to be with Madeleine whenever she should send the little maid with the summons.

Madeleine sickened and shivered and paled during these two endless days and sleepless nights of suspense. There were times when she felt she must die of horror at the situation in which she found herself, that it was asking too much of her to make her go on living. At such moments she shook as though in a palsy and her voice trembled so that she could not speak aloud. There were other times when she was in an unnatural calm, because she was absolutely certain that she was dreaming and must soon wake up to find Jules beside her.

The children played in the garden. They discovered a toad there, during that time, and Madeleine often heard them shouting with laughter over its antics. The silly little maid came every few moments to tell her mistress a new rumor . . . she had heard the Germans were cannibals and ate little children, was that true? And was it true that they had a special technique for burning down whole towns at once, with kerosene pumps and dynamite petards? One story seemed as foolish as the other to Madeleine, who hushed her angrily and told her not to listen to such lies. Once the little maid began to tell her in a terrified whisper what she had heard the Germans did to women in Madeleine's condition . . . but the recital was cut short by a terrible attack of nausea which lasted for hours and left Madeleine so weak that she could not raise her head from the pillow. She lay there, tasting the bitterness of necessity. Weak as she was, she was the strongest of their little band. Presently she rose and went back to her work, but she was stooped forward like an old woman.

She told herself that she did not believe a single word the terror-stricken little maid had told her; but the truth was that she was half dead with fear, age-old, terrible, physical fear, which had been as far from her life before as a desire to eat raw meat or to do murder. It was almost like a stroke of paralysis to this modern woman.

For two whole days the town lay silent and helpless, waiting the blow. On the morning of the third day the sound of clumsily clattering hoofs in the deserted street brought Madeleine rushing downstairs to the door of the pharmacy. An old farmer, mounted on a sweating plow horse, drew rein for an instant in the sun and, breathing hard, gave the news to the little cluster of white-faced women and old men who gathered about him. Madeleine pressed in beside her poorer neighbors, closer to them than at any time in her life, straining up to the messenger, like them. What he had to tell them loomed threateningly in their ears. The Germans were in the next town, Larot-en-Multien, only eight miles away. The vanguard had stopped there to drink and eat, but behind them was an antlike gray horde which pressed steadily forward with dreadful haste and would be in Mandriné within two hours.

He gathered up his reins to go on, but paused to add a brief suggestion as to what they might expect. The Germans were too hurried to burn or to destroy houses; they were only taking everything which was easily portable. They had robbed the church, had taken all the flour from the mill, all the contents of all the shops, and when he left (the sight of the shining plate-glass windows of the pharmacy reminded him) they were just in the act of looting systematically the pharmacy of Larot, taking down all the contents of the shelves and packing them carefully into a big camion.

He rode on. The women dispersed, scurrying rapidly each to her dependents, children, or sick women, or old men. The Mayor hurried away to carry a few more of his priceless town records to the hiding place. The priest went back to his church. For an instant Madeleine was left alone in the empty street, echoing to disaster. She looked at the pharmacy, shining, well ordered, well stocked, useful, *as Jules had left it.*

At the call to action her sickness vanished like a passing giddiness. Her knees stiffened in anger. They should not carry off everything from the Mandriné pharmacy! What could the town *do* without remedies for its sick? The first breath from the approaching tornado annihilating all in its path crashed through the wall which had sheltered her small, comfortably arranged life. Through the breach in the wall she had a passing glimpse of what the pharmacy was; not merely a convenient way for Jules to earn enough for her and the children to live agreeably, but one of the vital necessities of the community life, an important trust which Jules held.

And now Jules was gone and could not defend it. But she was there.

She ran back into the shop, calling for her little maid in a loud, clear voice such as had not issued from her throat since Jules had gone away. "Simone! Simone!"

The maid came running down the stairs and at the first sight of her mistress expected to hear that her master had returned or that the French troops were there, so like herself did Madeleine seem, no longer stooping and shivering and paper-white, but upright, with hard, bright eyes. But it was no good news which she brought out in the new ringing voice. She said: "The Germans will be here in two hours. Help me quickly hide the things in the cellar . . . you know, the further room . . . and we can put the hanging shelves over the door so they won't know there is another part to the cellar. Bring down the two big trays from the kitchen. We can carry more that way. Then light three candles up and down the cellar stairs. It won't do for me to fall, these last days."

She was gathering the big jars together as she spoke, and taking out the innumerable drawers.

In a moment the two women, one who had been hardly strong enough to walk, the other scarcely more than a child, were going slowly down the cellar stairs, their arms aching with the weight of the trays, and then running back upstairs. Shelf after shelf was cleared of the precious remedies that meant health, that might mean life, in the days to come. The minutes slipped past. An hour had gone.

From her attic windows where she could see the road leading to Lorat-en-Multien, a neighbor called down shrilly that dust was rising up in thick clouds at the lower end. And even as she called, silently, composedly, there pedaled into the long main street five or six men in gray uniforms on bicycles, calm and sure of themselves, evidently knowing very well that the place had no defenders. Madeleine saw the white hair of M. le Curé and the white beard of M. le Maire advance to meet the invaders.

"We can't do any more here," she said. "Down to the cellar now, to mask the door. No, I'll do it alone. Somebody must be here to warn us. We mustn't be caught down there." She turned to go, and came back. "But I can't move the hanging shelves alone!"

Simone ventured, "Mlle Sylvie? Could she watch and tell us?"

Madeleine hesitated. Sylvie, like her mother at her age, had been asked to do very little with herself except to be a nice little girl.

Then, "Sylvie! Sylvie!" called her mother with decision.

The little girl came running docilely, her eyes wide in wonder.

Madeleine bent on her a white, stern face of command. "The Germans are almost here. Simone and I have been hiding papa's drugs in the cellar and we've not finished. Stay here . . . pretend to be playing . . . and call to us the moment you see the soldiers coming. *Do you understand?*"

Sylvie received her small baptism of fire with courage. Her chin began to tremble and she grew very white. This was not because she was afraid of the Germans. Madeleine had protected her from all the horrid stories which filled the town, and she had only the vaguest baby notions of what the Germans were. It was her mother's aspect, awful to the child, which terrified her. But it also braced her. She pressed her lips together and nodded. Madeleine and the maid went down the cellar stairs for the last time.

When they came back, the troops were still not there, although one could see beyond the river the cloud of white dust raised by their myriad feet. The two women were covered with earth and cobwebs, and were breathing heavily. Their knees shook under them. Taking the child with them, they went up the stairs to the defenseless home. They found five-year-old Raoul just finishing the house-and-farmyard which he and Sylvie had begun. "If only I had three more blocks to do this corner!" he lamented.

Twenty minutes from that time they heard heavy, rapid footsteps enter the shop below and storm up the stairs. There was a loud knocking, and the sound of men's voices in a strange language.

Madeleine went herself to open the door. This was not an act of bravery but of necessity. There was no one else to do it. She had already sent the children to the most remote of the rooms, and at the sound of those trampling feet and hoarse voices Simone had run away, screaming. Madeleine's fingers shook as she pushed back the bolt. A queer pulse began to beat very fast in the back of her dry throat.

The first German soldiers she had ever seen were there before her. Four or five tall, broad, red-faced men, very hot, very dusty, in gray, wrinkled uniforms and big boots, pushed into the room past her. One of them said to her in broken French: "Eat! Eat! Drink! Very thirsty. Quick!" The others had already seized the bottles on the sideboard and were drinking from them.

Madeleine went into the kitchen and brought back on a big tray everything ready-cooked which was there: a dish of stew, cold and unappetizing in its congealed fat, a long loaf of bread, a big piece of cheese, a platter of cooked beans. . . . The men drinking at the sideboard cried aloud hoarsely and fell upon the contents of the tray, clutching, cramming food into their mouths, into their pockets, gulping down the cold stew in huge mouthfuls, shoveling the beans up in their dirty hands and plastering them into their mouths, already full. . . .

Someone called, warningly, from below. The men snatched up what bottles were at hand, thrust them into their pockets, and still tearing off huge mouthfuls from the cheese, the bread, the meat they held, and masticating them with animal noises, turned and clattered down the stairs again, having paid no more attention to Madeleine than if she had been a piece of the furniture.

They had come and gone so rapidly that she had the impression of a vivid, passing nightmare. For an instant she continued to see them. Everywhere she looked, she saw yellow teeth, gnawing and tearing at food; bulging jaw-muscles straining; dirty foreheads streaked with perspiration, wrinkled like those of eating dogs; bloodshot eyes glaring in physical greed.

"Oh, les sales bêtes!" she cried out loud. "The dirty beasts!"

Her fear left her, never to come back, swept away by a bitter contempt. She went, her lip curling, her knees quite strong under her, to reassure Simone and the children.

The house shook, the windows rattled, the glasses danced on the sideboard to the thunder of the innumerable marching feet outside, to the endless rumble of the camions and artillery. The volume of this wild din, and the hurried pulse of haste which was its rhythm, staggered the imagination. Madeleine scorned to look out of the window, although Simone and the children called to her from behind the curtains: "There are millions and millions of them! They are like flies! You couldn't cross the street, not even running fast, they are so close together! And how they hurry!"

Madeleine heard someone come up the stairs and enter the hall without knocking. She found there a well-dressed man with slightly gray hair who informed her in correct French, pronounced with a strong accent, that he would return in one hour bringing with him four other officers and that he would expect to find food and drink ready for them. Having said this in the detached, casual tone of command of a man giving an order to a servant, he went away down the stairs, unfolding a map.

Madeleine had all but cried an angry refusal after him, but, as brutally as on a gag in her mouth, she choked on the sense of her defenselessness in the face of physical force. This is a sensation which moderns have blessedly forgotten, like the old primitive fear of darkness or of thunder. To feel it again is to be bitterly shamed. Madeleine was all one crimson flame of humiliation as she called Simone and went into the kitchen.

They cooked the meal and served it an hour later to five excited, elated officers, spreading out maps as they ate, laughing, drinking prodigiously and eating so rapidly such vast quantities of food that Simone was sure she was serving demons and not human beings and crossed herself repeatedly as she waited on table. In spite of all their haste they had not time to finish. Another officer came up the stairs, thrust his head in through the door, and called a summons to them. They sprang up, in high feather at what he had said, snatching at the fruit which Simone had just set on the table. Madeleine saw one of her guests crowd a whole peach, as big as an apple, into his mouth at once, and depart, choking and chewing, leaning over so that the stream of juice which ran from his mouth should not fall on his uniform.

Simone shrieked from the kitchen, "Oh, madame! The garden! The garden!"

Madeleine ran to a window, looked down, and saw long rows of horses picketed in the garden. Two German soldiers were throwing down hay from the gable end of the Mandriné livery stable which overlooked the wall. The horses ate with hungry zest, stamping vigorously in the flowerbeds to keep off the flies. When they had finished on the hay, they began on the vines, the little, carefully tended fruit trees, the bushes, the flowers. A swarm of locusts could not have done the work more thoroughly.

As she stood there, gazing down on this, there was always in Madeleine's ears the incessant thundering rumble of the passing artillery. . . .

Through the din there reached her ears a summons roared out from below: "Cellar! Cellar! Key!"

She was at white heat. She ran downstairs, forgetting all fear, and, raising her voice to make herself heard above the uproar outside, she shouted with a wrath which knew no prudence: "You low, vile thieves! I will not give you one thing more!"

Her puny defiance to the whirlwind passed unnoticed. The men did not even take the time to strike her, to curse her. With one movement they turned from her to the cellar door, and, all kicking at it together, burst it open, trooped downstairs, returning with their arms full of bottles, and ran out into the street.

And all the time the very air shook, in almost visible waves, to the incessant thundering rumble of the artillery passing.

Madeleine went upstairs, gripping the railing hard, her head whirling. She had scarcely closed the door behind her when it was burst open and five soldiers stormed in, cocked revolvers in their fists. They did not give her a look, but tore through the apartment, searching in every corner, in every closet, pulling out the drawers of the bureaus, tumbling the contents on the floor, sweeping the cupboard shelves clear in one movement of their great hands, with the insane haste which characterized everything done that day. When they had finished they clattered out, chalking up something unintelligible on the door. Raoul and Sylvie began to cry wildly, their nerves undone, and to clutch at their mother's skirts.

Madeleine took them back into their own little room, undressed them and put them to bed, where she gave them each a bowl of bread and milk. All this she did with a quiet air of confidence which comforted the children. They had scarcely finished eating when they fell asleep, worn out. Madeleine heard Simone calling for her and went out in the hall. A German soldier, desperately drunk, held out a note which stated that four Herr-Lieutenants and a Herr-Captain would eat and sleep there that night, dinner to be sharp at seven, and the beds ready.

After delivering this he tried to put his arm around Simone and to drag her into the next room. Simone struggled and screamed, shriek after shriek, horribly. Madeleine screamed too, and snatching up the poker, flung herself on the man. He released his hold, too uncertain on his feet to resist. Both women threw themselves against him, pushing him to the door and shoving him out on the narrow landing, where he lost his balance and fell heavily, rolling over and over, down the stairs.

Madeleine bolted the door, took a long knife from the kitchen table, and waited, her ear at the keyhole, to see if he tried to come back.

This was the woman, you must remember, who less than a month before had been sitting in the garden sewing on fine linen, safe in an unfathomable security.

The man did not attempt to return. Madeleine relaxed her tense crouching attitude and laid the knife down on the table. The perspiration was streaming down her white cheeks. It came over her with horror that their screams had not received the slightest response from the outside world. No one was responsible for their safety. No one cared what became of them. It made no difference to anyone whether they had repelled that man, or whether he had triumphed over their resistance. . . .

And now she must command her shaking knees and hands to prepare food for those who had sent him there. Of all the violent efforts Madeleine had been forced to make, none was more racking than to stoop to the servility of this submission. She had an instant of frenzy when she thought of locking the door and defying them to enter, but the recollection of the assault on the thick oaken planks of the cellar door, and of its splintering collapse before those huge hobnailed boots, sent her to the kitchen, her teeth set in her lower lip. "I never will forgive them this, never, never, never!" she said aloud passionately, more passionately than she had ever said anything in her life, and she knew as she spoke that it was not of the slightest consequence to anyone whether she would or not.

At seven the meal was ready. At half-past seven the four officers entered, laughing, talking loudly, jubilant. One of them spoke in good French to Madeleline, complimenting her on her soup and on the wine. "I told my friends I knew we would find good cheer and good beds with Madame Brismantier," he told her affably.

Astonished to hear her name, Madeleine looked at him hard, and recognized, in spite of his uniform, a well-to-do man, reputed a Swiss, who had rented a house for the season, several summers back, on a hillside not far from Mandriné. He had professed a great interest in the geology of the region and was always taking long walks and collecting fossils. Jules had an amateur interest in fossils also, and this, together with the admirably trained voice of the Swiss, had afforded several occasions of social contact. The foreigner had spent an evening or two with them, singing to Madeleine's accompaniment. And once, having some valuable papers left on his hands, he had asked the use of the Brismantier safe for a night. He had been very fond of children, and had had always a jolly greeting for little Raoul, who was then only a baby of two. Madeleine looked at him now, too stupefied with wonder to open her lips. A phrase from "An die ferne Geliebte," which he had sung very beautifully, rang in her ears, sounding faint and thin but clear, through the infernal din in the street.

She turned and went back into the kitchen. Standing there, before the stove, she said as though she had but just known it, "Why, he was a spy, all the time!" She had not thought there were such people as spies outside of cheap books.

She was just putting the roast on the table when someone called loudly from the street. The men at the table jumped up, went to the window, leaned out, exchanged noisy exultant words, cursed jovially, and turned back in haste to tighten the belts and fasten the buttons and hooks which they had loosened in anticipation of the feast. The spy said laughingly to Madeleine: "Your French army runs away so fast, madame, that we cannot eat or sleep for chasing it! Our advance guard is always sending back word to hurry faster, faster!"

One of the others swept the roast from the table into a brown sack, all crammed their pockets full of bread and took a bottle under each arm. At the door the spy called over his shoulder: "Sorry to be in such a hurry! I will drop you a card from Paris as soon as the mails begin again."

They clattered down the stairs.

Madeleine bolted the door and sank down on a chair, her teeth chattering loudly. After a time during which she vainly strove to master a mounting tide of pain and sickness, she said: "Simone, you must go for Sister Ste. Lucie. My time has come. Go by our back door, through the alley, and knock at the side door of the Hospice . . . you needn't be gone more than three minutes."

Simone went downstairs, terribly afraid to venture out, even more afraid to be left alone with her mistress. Madeleine managed to get into the spare bedroom, away from the children's room, and began to undress, in an anguish of mind and body such as she had not thought she could endure and live. But even now she did not know what was before her. In a short time Simone came back, crying and wringing her hands. A sentry guarded the street and another the alley. They had thrust her back into the house, their bayonets glittering, and one had said in French, "Forbidden; no go out till daylight." She had tried to insist, to explain, but he had struck her back with the butt end of his rifle. Oh, he had hurt her awfully! She cried and cried, looking over her shoulder, tearing at her apron. It was evident that if there had been any possibility for her to run away, she would have done it, anywhere, anywhere . . .

Madeleine's little boy was born that night. She, who of course must needs have her mother to take all the responsibility, and the nurse whose voice was agreeable to her, went through her fiery trial alone, with no help but the foolish little Simone, shivering and gasping in hysteria. She was nothing but a pair of hands and feet to be animated by Madeleine's will power and intelligence. In those dreadful hours Madeleine descended to the black depths of her agony but dared never abandon herself even to suffer. At every moment she needed to shock Simone out of her panic by a stern, well-considered command.

She needed, and found, strange, unguessed stores of strength and resolution. She felt herself alone, pitted against a malign universe which wished to injure her baby, to prevent her baby from having the right birth and care. But she felt herself to be stronger than all the malignity of the universe. Once, in a moment's lull during the fight, she remembered, seeing the words zigzag like lightning on a black sky, a sentence in the first little history-book she had studied as a child—"The ancient Gauls said they feared nothing, not enemies, not tempest, not death. Until the skies fell upon their heads, they would never submit." . . . "They were my ancestors!" said the little Gaulish woman, fighting alone in the darkness. She clenched her teeth to repress a scream of pain and a moment later told Simone, quite clearly, in a quiet tone of authority, just what to do, again.

Outside, all night long, there thundered the rumbling passage of the artillery and camions.

In the morning, when Sylvie and Raoul awoke, they found Simone crouched in a corner of their mother's room, sobbing endlessly from sheer nervous exhaustion. But out from their mother's white, white face on the pillow looked triumphant eyes. She drew the covers down a little and lifted her arm. "See, children, a little new brother."

As she spoke she thrust out of her mind, with a violence like that with which she had expelled the ruffian from the door, the thought that the little brother would probably never see his father. It was no moment to allow herself the weakness of sorrow. She must marshal her little forces. "Come, Sylvie dear. Simone is all tired out; you must get us something to eat, and then you and Simone must bring in all you can of what is left in the kitchen and hide it here under mother's bed." She had thought out her plan in the night.

During the next days Madeleine was wholly unable to stand on her feet. From her bed she gave her orders—desperate, last-resort orders to a defeated garrison. The apartment was constantly invaded by ravenously hungry and thirsty men, but her room was not entered. The first morning the door had been opened brusquely, and a gray-haired under-officer entered. He stopped short when he saw Madeleine's drawn white face on the pillow, with the little red, bald head beside her. He went out as abruptly as he had gone in and chalked something on the door. Thereafter no one came in; although not infrequently, as though to see if the chalked notice were true, the door was opened suddenly and a head thrust in. This inspection of a sick woman's room could and did continually happen without the slightest warning. Madeleine was buffeted by an angry shame which she put aside sternly, lest it make her unfit to nurse her baby.

They lived during this time on what happened to be left in the kitchen, after that first day of pillage, some packages of macaroni, tapioca, and cornstarch, part of a little cheese, some salt fish, two or three boxes of crackers, a little sugar, a little flour. They did unsavory cooking over the open fire till their small supply of wood gave out. The children submitted docilely to this régime, cowed by their mother's fierce command not for an instant to go out of her sight. But the little maid, volatile and childish, could not endure life without bread. She begged to be allowed to go out, to slip along the alley to the Hospice and beg a loaf from Sister Ste. Lucie. There must be bread somewhere in town, she argued, unable to conceive of a world without bread. And in the daytime the sentries would let her pass.

Madeleine forbade her to leave the room, but on the third day when her mistress was occupied with the baby she slipped out and was gone. She did not come back that day or the next. They never saw or heard of her from that moment.

Madeleine and the children continued to live in that one room, shaken by the incessant rumble of the passing artillery wagons and by the hurrying tread of booted feet. And now there was the low growl of distant cannon, to the south. *To the south!* Far in towards the heart of France. Now and again, there were incursions into the other rooms of their home, and as long as there were loud voices and trampling and clattering dishes, the children crept into bed beside Madeleine and the baby, cowering together under the poor protection of their mother's powerless arms. They never dared speak above a whisper during those days. They heard laughing, shouting, cursing, snoring in the rooms all around them. Once they heard pistol shots, followed by a great splintering crash of glass and shouts of wild mirth.

Madeleine lost all count of the days, of everything but the diminishing stock of food. She tried repeatedly to sit up, she tried to put her feet to the floor, but she felt her head swim and fell back in bed. She had little strength left to struggle now. The food was almost gone, and her courage was almost gone. As though the walls of the room were closing in on her, the approach of the spent, beaten desire to die began to close in on her. What was the use of struggling on? If she could only kill the children and herself . . .

One morning Sylvie said in a loud, startled whisper: "Oh, *Maman,* they are going the other way! Back towards Lorat . . . and yet they are still hurrying as fast as ever . . . faster!"

Madeleine felt her hair raise itself on her scalp. She sat up in bed. "Sylvie, *are you sure?*"

The child answered, always in her strained whisper, "Yes, yes, I am sure." Her mother sprang out of bed with a bound and ran to the window.

It was true. The dust-gray tide had turned. They were raging past the house, the horses straining at the heavy artillery wagons, lashed into a clumsy canter by the drivers, leaning far forward, urging; the haggard men, reeling in fatigue, stumbling under their heavy packs, pressing forward in a dogtrot; the officers with red angry faces, barking out incessant commands for more haste . . . and their backs were turned to Paris!

The Frenchwoman, looking down on them, threw her arms up over her head in a wild gesture of exultation. They were going back!

She felt as strong as ever she had in her life. She dressed herself, set the wretched room in some sort of order, and managed to prepare an edible dish out of soaked tapioca and sugar. The children ate it with relish, comforted by their mother's new aspect.

About two o'clock that night Madeleine awoke to an awful sense of impending calamity. Something had happened, some tremendous change had come over the world. She lay still for a long moment. Then she realized that she heard nothing but the beating of her own heart, that the thunder of the trampling feet had stopped. She got out of bed carefully, trying not to waken the children, but Sylvie, her nerves aquiver, called out in a frightened whisper, *"Maman, Maman! What is it?"* She caught her mother's arm, and the two went together to the window. They leaned out, looked to right and left, and fell to weeping in each other's arms. Under the quiet stars, the village street was perfectly empty.

The next morning Madeleine made the children swallow a little food before, all together, the baby in his mother's arms, they ventured out from their prison-room. They found their home gutted and sacked and sullied to the remotest corner. The old brocade on the chairs in the salon had been slit to ribbons by sword-slashes, the big plate-glass windows over the mantels had each been shattered into a million pieces, all the silver was gone from the drawers, every piece of linen had disappeared, the curtains had been torn down and carried away, and every bit of bedding had gone, every sheet, every blanket, every eiderdown quilt. The mattresses had been left, each having been cut open its entire length and sedulously filled with filth.

The kitchen, emptied of all its shining copper and enamel utensils, was one litter of splintered wood, remnants of furniture which had been cut up with the ax for fuel. Madeleine recognized pieces of her mahogany beds there. Through the kitchen window she looked down into the walled space which had been the garden and saw it a bare, trampled stable-yard, with heaps of manure. She looked at all this in perfect silence, the children clinging to her skirts, the baby sleeping on her arm. She looked at it, but days passed before she really believed that what she saw was real.

A woman's voice called quaveringly from the landing: "Madame Brismantier, are you alive? The Germans have gone." Madeleine stepped to the landing and saw old Sister Ste. Lucie. Her face which had always been so rosy and fresh was as gray as ashes under her black-and-white coif. She leaned against the wall. At the sight of the sleeping baby in Madeleine's arms, the gray face smiled, the wonderful smile which women, even those vowed to childlessness, give to a new mother. "Oh, your baby came," she said. "Boy or girl?"

"Yes," said Madeleine, "he came. A boy. A nice little boy." For one instant the two women stood there in that abomination of desolation, death all around them, looking at newborn life—and smiling.

Then Soeur Ste. Lucie said: "There is nothing in the pharmacy, I see. I thought maybe they might have left something, by chance, but I see everything has been taken away or smashed to pieces. You don't happen to have any supplies up here, do you? We need bandages horribly at the Hospice, for the wounded. There are forty there."

Madeleine knew the minute size of the little Hospice and exclaimed: "Forty! Where do you put them?"

"Everywhere. On the floor, up and down the hall, in the kitchen. But we haven't a thing except hot water to use for wounds. All the sheets were torn up two days ago, what hadn't been stolen! If I only had a little iodine, or any sort of antiseptic. The wounds are too awful, all infected, and nothing . . ."

Without knowing it Madeleine took a first step forward into a new life. "There's plenty of everything," she said. "I hid them all in the far room of the cellar."

"God grant 'they' didn't find them!" breathed the nun.

Madeleine lighted a candle, left the sleeping baby in charge of

Sylvie, and went with Soeur Ste. Lucie down into the cellar. They
found it littered and blocked with emptied and broken bottles. A
strange hoarse breathing from a dark corner frightened them. Lifting
her candle, Madeleine brought to view a German soldier, dead-drunk,
snoring, his face swollen and red. The older woman said, "We should
be sure his gun is not available." They looked for the weapon, found
nothing, not even his bayonet in its sheath. They turned from him
then as from an object of no importance and went across the cellar.
With a long sigh of relief they saw that the hanging shelves were still
there, untouched. Madeleine's device was successful.

As they looked for bandages and antiseptics among the heaped-up
supplies from the pharmacy, Soeur Ste. Lucie told Madeleine very
briefly what had been happening. Madeleine listened in a terrible
silence. Neither she nor the nun had strength to spare for exclamations. Nor could any words of theirs have been adequate. M. le Maire
was dead, shot in front of the Town Hall, on the ground that there
had been weapons found in one of the houses. "You know in the
Bouvines' house they had some Malay creeses and a Japanese sword
hanging up in M. Bouvines' study, things his sailor uncle brought
back. The Mayor had never thought to take those down, and they
wouldn't give him time to explain. M. le Curé was dead, nobody knew
or ever would know why—found dead strapped to a bed in an attic
room of a house occupied by some German officers. Perhaps he had
been forgotten by the person who had tied him there. . . ." The
nun's voice died away in sobs. She had been brought up under M. le
Curé's protection all her life and loved him like a father.

Madeleine sorted bandages in silence, her throat very dry and
harsh. Later Soeur Ste. Lucie went on, trying to speak more collect-
edly: "The worst of trying to care for these wounded is not being
able to understand what they say."

"How so?" asked Madeleine, blankly.

"Why, I don't speak German."

Madeleine gave a violent start—and stood motionless, her hands
full of bandages. "Are they *Germans?* Are we getting these things for
German soldiers?"

Soeur Ste. Lucie said gravely, "I felt that way too, at first. But—are
we not taught to do good to our enemies?" Madeleine stared silently
at her. The religious went on, "If it were our army in Germany—if
your husband were terribly wounded like these men—how would you
wish German women to—?"

Of these words Madeleine heard little at the time, although they
were to come back to her, again and again. But one image evoked by

the words burned before her eyes—her Jules, wounded—French soldiers in Germany—would they, if the tide had swept the other way—
would Frenchmen be stamping into strangers' houses, snatching the
food away from the—was it *war* itself not only—.

She cried out as if in a fury of anger, "Oh, of course we'll have to
give them the antiseptics and bandages." She could not have named
the impulse which drove her to say this, nor could she have explained
why she said it, with an intonation so unsuited to the words—with
wrath. It was nothing but self-respect, a bare meager minimum of
the most ordinary self-respect. . . .

But she could not think. Her head ached, her back ached as though
it were being beaten with hammers. She gave up her attempt to think.

"Here," said Soeur Ste. Lucie, staggering with exhaustion. "The
baby is only a few days old. You're not fit to be doing this."

Madeleine, who had lain flat on her back for two weeks after the
birth of the other two children, shook her head. "No, no, I can do it as
well as you. You look fearfully tired."

"I haven't had my clothes off for ten days," said the old nun.

At the street door, with her basket of bandages on her arm, Soeur
Ste. Lucie stood looking around her at the desolate filth-strewn shop,
the million pieces of glass which had been its big windows covering
the floor, its counter hacked and broken with axes. She said: "We
haven't any mayor and the priest is dead, and we haven't any pharmacy and the baker is mobilized, and there isn't one strong, well man
left in town. How are we going to live?"

Madeleine took another step, hesitating, along the new road. She
leaned against the counter to ease her aching body and put back her
hair to look around her at the ruin of her husband's business. She said
in a faint voice: "I wonder if I could keep the pharmacy open. I used
to help Jules with the accounts. I know a little about where he bought
and how he kept his records. I wonder if I could—enough for the
simpler things?"

"You have already," said the nun, as she went away, "and the first
things you have given out are bandages for your enemies. God will
not forget that."

Madeleine received this with an impatient shrug. She was not at
all glad that her first act had been to help the suffering among her
enemies. She had hated doing it. Only some confused sense of decency
had forced her to it. She would have been ashamed not to. That was
all. And yet to help those men who had murdered M. le Maire, so
blameless, and M. le Curé—so defenseless! . . . No, these were not

the same men who lay bleeding to death in the Hospice to whom she
had sent bandages. *They* had not murdered . . . as yet!

Her head throbbed feverishly. She renounced again the effort to
think, and turned to the urgent needs of the moment. It seemed to
her that she could not breathe till she had set the pharmacy as far as
possible in the order Jules had left it. This intense feeling was her
only refuge against her certainty that Jules was killed, that she would
never see him again. Without an attempt to put in order even a
corner of the desolated little home, she began toiling up and down
the cellar stairs carrying back the glass jars, the pots, the boxes, and
bottles and drawers. In her dazed condition it seemed to her that
somehow she was doing something for Jules in saving his pharmacy
which he had so much cared for, that she was almost keeping him from
dying by working with all her might for him there. . . .

In the middle of the morning she went upstairs and found that
Sylvie, with Raoul's help, had cleared the kitchen of the worst of
the rubbish. In a pot-closet under the sink they had found two old
saucepans which had not been stolen. Madeleine made a fire, stoically
using her own broken-up furniture, and, putting a few potatoes (the
last of their provisions) on to boil, sat down to nurse the hungry
baby.

"*Maman* dear," said Sylvie, still in the hoarse whisper of the days
of terror. She could not speak aloud for weeks. "*Maman* dear," she
whispered, "in the salon, in the dining room, I wanted to try to
clean it, but it is all nasty, like where animals have been."

"Hush!" said her mother firmly. "Don't think about that. Don't
look in there. It'll make you sick if you do. Wait here till I finish
feeding the baby. Then don't go away, tend the fire, watch the baby,
and play with Raoul." She outlined this program with decision and
hurried back downstairs. If she could only get the pharmacy to look
a little as it had when Jules had left it, it seemed that Jules would
seem less lost to her.

She shoveled the incredible quantity of broken glass back through
the shop into what had been her garden, hardening herself against
a qualm of horror at the closer view of the wreckage there.

She went back to her work hastily, knowing that if she stopped
for an instant to look, she would be lost.

At noon she climbed the stairs, and with the children lunched on
potatoes and salt.

She was putting the last of the innumerable drawers back in its
place, after having tried it in all the other possible places, when a
poorly dressed, rough-haired, scrawny small boy came into the shop.

Madeleine knew him by sight, the six-year-old grandson of Madame
Duguet, a bedridden, old, poor woman on Poulaine Street. He said
that he had come to get those powders for his grandmother's asthma.
She hadn't slept any for two nights. As he spoke he wound the string
about a top and prepared to spin it, nonchalantly. Looking at his
cheerful, dirty little face, Madeleine felt herself a thousand years old,
separated for always and always from youth which would never know
what she had known.

"It was my husband who took care of your grandmother's asthma
powders. I wouldn't have any idea where to look for them," she said.
The little boy insisted. He was so young he was astonished that a
grown person did not know everything. *"He* always kept them.
Grandmère used to send me twice a week to get them. *Grandmère* will
scold me awfully, if I don't take them back. She's scolding all the time
now, because the Germans took our soup kettle and our frying pan.
We haven't got anything left to cook with."

The memory of her immensely greater losses rose burningly to
Madeleine's mind. "They took *all my sheets!"* she cried impulsively—
"every one!"

"Oh," said the little boy indifferently, "we never had any sheets,
anyhow." This did not seem an important statement to him, apparently; but to Madeleine, emerging from her old world into new
horizons, beaten upon by a thousand new impressions, it rang loudly.
The Germans, then, had only put her in the situation in which a
woman, like herself, had always lived . . . and within a stone's throw
of these well-filled linen-closets of hers! There was something strange
about that, something which she would like to ponder, if only her
head did not ache so terribly. The little boy said, insistently, *"He*
always gave me the powders, right away!"

Through obscure mental processes, of which she had only the dim-
mest perceptions . . . *Jules* had always given the powders . . . how
strange it was that precisely a bedridden woman who had most need
of them should have owned no sheets . . . there came to her a great
desire to send that old woman the medicine she needed. "You go
outside and spin your top for a while," she said to the child; "I'll call
you when I'm ready."

She went upstairs. Holding her skirts high to keep them out of the
filth on the floor, she picked her way to the bookcase. Books were
scattered all about the room, torn, cut, trampled on, defiled; but for
the most part those with handsome bindings had been chosen for
destruction. On the top shelf, sober in their drab, gray-linen binding,
stood Jules' big record-books, intact. She carried down an armful of

them to the pharmacy, and opened the latest one, the one which Jules had put away with his own hand the day he had left her.

The sight of the pages covered with Jules' neat, clear handwriting brought scalding tears to her eyes. Her bosom heaved. She laid down the book, and, taking hold of the counter with all her strength, she forced herself to draw one long, regular breath after another, holding her head high.

When her heart was beating quietly again, quietly and heavily, in her breast, she opened the book and began studying the pages. Jules set everything down in writing, it being his idea that a pharmacist had no other defense against making those occasional mistakes inevitable to human nature, but which must not occur in his profession.

Madeleine read: "March 10, sold 100 quinine pills to M. Augier. Stock low. Made 100 more, using quinine from the Cochard Company's laboratories. Filled prescription. . . ." Madeleine's eyes leaped over the hieroglyphics of the pharmaceutical terms and ran up and down the pages, filled with such items, looking for the name Duguet. She had almost given up when she saw, dated July 30, 1914, the entry: "Made up fresh supply Mme Duguet asthma powders, prescription 457. Dr. Millier. Drawer No. 17."

Madeleine ran behind the counter and pulled out No. 17. She found there a little pasteboard box marked "Duguet."

"Oh, boy, little boy!" she called. She did not know his name. He had lived all of his six years close to her home, and she did not know his name.

When the child came in she asked, "Did your grandmother ever get any other medicine here?"

"No," said the grandson of the bedridden woman, "she hasn't got anything else the matter with her."

"Well," said the pharmacist's wife, "here is her medicine." She put the box in his hand.

"But we never get more than four at a time," he told her. "She never has the money to pay for more. Here it is. Granny hid it in her hair so the Germans wouldn't get it. She hid all we have. She's got more than *five francs*, all safe."

He put a small silver coin in her hand and departed.

The mention of the meager sum of hidden money made Madeleine think of her own dexterously concealed little fortune. She had noticed at once on entering the shop that the arrangement of false shelves which concealed the safe had not been detected, and was intact. She pushed the spring; the shelves swung back and disclosed the door of the safe just as usual. She began to turn the knob of the combination lock. It worked smoothly and in a moment the heavy door swung open. The safe was entirely empty, swept clear of all the papers, titles, deeds, bonds which had covered its shelves.

As actually as though he stood there again, Madeleine saw the polite pseudo-Swiss geological gentleman, thanking Jules for the temporary use of his excellent safe.

She felt the very ground give way under her feet. A cold, cold wind of necessity blew upon her. The walled and sheltered refuge in which she had lived all her life was cast down and in ruins. The realization came to her, like something indecent, that *she*, Madeleine Brismantier, was now as poor as that old bedridden neighbor had been all her life . . . *all her life.* . . .

Somehow, that had something to do with those sheets which she had had and the other woman had not . . . her mind came back with a mortal sickness to the knowledge that she had now nothing, nothing to depend upon except her own strength and labor—just like a *poor* woman. She *was* a poor woman!

Somebody was weeping and tugging at her skirts. She looked down blindly. It was Raoul, her little son. He was sobbing and saying: "Sylvie said not to come, but I couldn't stand it any more. I'm hungry! I'm hungry, and there isn't a thing left upstairs to eat! I'm hungry! I'm hungry!"

Madeleine put her hand to her head and thought. What had happened? Oh, yes, all their money had been stolen, all . . . but Raoul was hungry, the children must have something to eat. "Hush, my darling," she said to the little boy, "go back upstairs and tell Sylvie to come here and look out for the shop while I try to find something to eat."

She went down the silent, empty street, before the silent, empty houses staring at her out of their shattered windows. Not a soul was abroad. At the farm, in the outskirts of town, she saw smoke rising from the chimney and went into the courtyard. The young farmer's wife was there, feeding a little cluster of hens, and weeping like a child. She stared at the newcomer for a moment without recognizing her. Madeleine looked ten years older than she had a fortnight ago.

"Oh, madame, we had three hundred hens, and they left us just these eight that they couldn't catch! And they killed all but two of our thirty cows; we'd raised them ourselves from calves up. They killed them there before the very door and cooked them over a fire in the courtyard, and they broke up everything of wood to burn in the fire, all our hoes and rake handles, and the farm wagon and . . . oh, what will my husband say when he knows!"

Madeleine had a passing glimpse of herself as though in a convex mirror, distorted but recognizable. She said, "They didn't hurt you or your husband's mother, did they?"

"No, they were drunk all the time and they didn't know what they were doing mostly. We could hide from them."

"Then your husband will not care at all about the cows and pigs and farm wagons," said Madeleine very firmly, as though she were speaking to Sylvie. The young farmer's wife responded automatically to the note of authority in Madeleine's voice. "Don't you think he will?" she asked simply, reassured somewhat, wiping away her tears.

"No, and you are very lucky to have so much left," said Madeleine. "I have nothing, nothing at all for my children to eat, and no money to buy anything." She heard herself saying this with astonishment.

The young wife was horrified, sympathetic, a little elated to have one whom she had always considered her superior come asking her for aid; for Madeleine stood there, her empty basket on her arm, asking for aid, silently, helplessly.

"Oh, we have things left to *eat!*" said the farmer's wife. She put some eggs in Madeleine's basket, several pieces of veal left from the last animal killed which the Germans had not had time entirely to consume, and, priceless treasure, a long loaf of bread. "Yes, the wife of the baker got up at two o'clock last night, when she heard the Germans go by, and started to heat her oven. She had hidden some flour in barrels behind her rabbit hutches, and this morning she baked a batch of bread. It's not so good as the baker's of course, but she says she will do better as she learns."

Madeleine turned back down the empty, silent street before the empty silent houses with their wrecked windows. A child came whistling along behind her, the little grandson of the bedridden Madame Duguet. Madeleine did what she had never done before in her life. She stopped him, made him take off his cap, and put into it a part of her loaf of bread and one of the pieces of meat.

"Oh, meat!" cried the child, overjoyed. "We hardly ever had meat!" He set off at a run.

As she passed the butcher shop, she saw an old man hobbling about on crutches, attempting to sweep up the last of the broken glass. It was the father of the butcher. She stepped in, and stooping, held the dustpan for him. He recognized her, after a moment's surprise at the alteration in her expression, and said, "Merci, madame." They worked together silently a moment, and then he said: "I'm going to try to keep Louis' business open for him. I think I can till he gets back. The war *can't* be long. You, madame, will you be going back to your parents?"

Madeleine walked out without speaking. She could not have answered him if she had tried. In front of the Town Hall she saw a tall old woman in black toiling up the broad stone steps with a large package under each arm. She went to help. It was the white-haired wife of the old mayor, who turned a ghastly face on Madeleine to explain: "I am bringing back the papers to put them in place as he always kept them. And then I shall stay here to guard them and to do his work till somebody else can come." She laid the portfolios down on a desk and said in a low, strange voice, looking out of the window: "It was before that wall. I heard the shots."

Madeleine clasped her hands together convulsively, in a gesture of horror, of utter sympathy, and looked wildly at the older woman. The wife of the Mayor said: "I must go back to the house now and get more of the papers. All the records must be in order." She added as she sat down at her husband's desk, "And you? Will you be going back to live with your mother at Amiens?"

Madeleine made no answer.

The Mayor's wife went on, "We will need a pharmacy. There will be no doctor, you know. You could do a great . . ." Her voice failed her.

Again Madeleine said nothing.

In the stillness they heard the banging of a shutter, hanging by one hinge in front of a broken window.

There was another sound. Their eyes met as they held their breath to listen. It was the distant growl of cannon, and it was to the north . . . to the *north!*

A sob of relief broke from Madeleine. "But . . . do you think . . . will they perhaps come back?"

The white lips in the old face were trembling. But the words of the Mayor's widow were—almost—steady. "Perhaps . . . perhaps not." She looked down at the Mayor's desk. It was covered with broken glass and plaster. She lifted a hand to sweep it clear, dropped her hand, and said, "But . . . but it is now that we have our work to do."

Madeleine stooped for her basket. "Yes, I shall keep the pharmacy open," she said. "I used to help my husband. I already know about the simple things. I can study my husband's books on pharmacy at night, after the children are in bed. There will be much I can learn."

She went out at the broken door, and down the broad stone steps. When she was once more on the paving stones of the street, she stood motionless for a moment, gazing into a new, terrifying, and pleasure-less life.

Something stern and mighty rose within her and swept her to meet it. She turned her face toward her ruined home and felt a wind blowing coldly along the deserted street. It was savagely cold. She shuddered. Would she ever be warm again? But she held her head up and walked steadily forward.

In the Eye
of the Storm

"What was in the ground, alive, they could not kill."

&ऽ**T**wo weeks after the German retreat from the
Aisne was rumored, five days after the newspapers were printing
censored descriptions of the ravaged country, and the very moment
the official bulletin confirmed the news, Pierre Nidart presented himself to his lieutenant to ask for a furlough, the long-delayed furlough,
due for more than two years now, which he had never been willing to
take. His lieutenant frowned uneasily, and did not answer. After a
moment's silence he said, gently, "You know, my old fellow, the
Boches have left very little up there."

(Nidart was not an old fellow at all, being but thirty-four, and the
father of two young children. His lieutenant used the phrase as a term
of endearment, because he had a high opinion of his silent sergeant.)
Nidart made no answer to his officer's remark. The lieutenant took
it that he persisted in wanting his furlough. As he had at least three
furloughs due him, it was hard to refuse. There was a long silence.
Finally, fingering the papers on the dry-goods box which served him
as desk, the lieutenant said: "Your wife is young. They say all women
under forty-five were carried off to work . . . forced labor . . . slave
labor . . . in German munition factories."

Nidart swallowed hard, looked sick, and obstinately said nothing.
His lieutenant turned with a sigh and motioned the *fourrier* to start
the red tape for the authorization for the furlough. "All right, I think

I can manage a three weeks' 'permission' for you. They're allowing that, I hear, to men from the invaded regions who haven't taken any furloughs since the beginning of the war."

"Yes, *mon Lieutenant*. Thank you, *mon Lieutenant*." Nidart saluted and went back to his squad.

His lieutenant shook his head, murmuring to the *fourrier:* "Those north-country men! There is no use saying a word to them. They won't believe that *their* homes and families aren't there, till they see with their own eyes . . . and when they do see . . . I've heard that some of the men in these first regiments that followed up the Boche retreat across the devastated regions went crazy when they found their own villages. . . . Nidart has just one idea in his head, poor devil!—to go straight before him, like a homing pigeon, till . . ." He stopped, his face darkening.

"Oh, damn the Boches!" the *fourrier* finished the sentence fervently.

"You see, Nidart is a master mason by trade, and he built their own little house. He carries around a snapshot of it, with his wife and a baby out in front."

"Oh, damn the Boches!" responded the *fourrier* on a deeper note.

"And like all those village workmen, they got half their living out of their garden and a field or two. And you've read what the Boches did to the gardens and fruit trees."

"Isn't there anything else we can talk about?" said the *fourrier*.

Nidart passed through Paris on his way and, extracting some very old bills from the lining of his shoe, he spent the five hours between his trains in hasty purchasing. At the hardware shop, where he bought an ax, a hammer, some nails, and a saw, the saleswoman's curiosity managed to screw from him the information that he was going back to his home in the devastated regions.

At once the group of Parisian working people and bourgeois who happened to be in the shop closed in on him sympathetically, commenting, advising, dissuading, offering their opinions with that city-bred, glib-tongued clatter which Nidart's country soul detested.

"No, no, my friend, it's useless to try to go back. The Germans have made a desert of it. My cousin's wife has a relative who was in the regiment that first followed the Germans after their retreat from Noyon, and he said . . ."

"The Government is going to issue a proclamation stating that land will be given in other parts of France to people from those regions, because it's of no use to try to rebuild from under the ruins."

"No, not the Government, it's a society for the Protection of the

People in the Invaded Regions; and they are Americans, millionaires, every one. And it's in America they are offering land, near New York."

"No, near Buenos Aires."

"The Americans want the regions left as a monument, as a place to see. You'll make much more money as a guide to tourists than trying to . . ."

"Your family won't be there, you know. The Boches took all the able-bodied women back with them; and the children were sent to . . ."

"Give me my change, won't you!" said Nidart with sudden fierceness, to the saleswoman. He turned his back roughly on the chattering group and went out. They shrugged their shoulders. "These country-people. Nothing on earth for them but their little hole of a village!"

Down the street, Nidart, quickening his soldierly gait to an angry stride, hurried along to a seed store.

That evening when he got into the battered, dingy, third-class compartment of the train going north, he could hardly be seen for the innumerable packages slung about his person. He pulled out from one bulging pocket a square piece of bread, from another a slab of cheese, and proceeded to dine, bent forward with the weight of his thoughts, gazing out through the dirty windows at the flat farming country jerking by him in the moonlight. It was so soon after the retreat that the train went no further north than Noyon, and Nidart had lived far beyond Noyon. About midnight, he rolled off the train, readjusted his packages and his knapsack, and, after showing his perfectly regular *sauf-conduit* to five or six sentries along the way, finally got out of town.

He found himself on the long, white road leading northeast. It was the road down which they had driven once a week, on market days. Of all the double line of noble poplar trees, not one was standing. The changed aspect of the familiar road startled him. Ahead of him as he tramped rapidly forward was what had been a crossroads, now a gaping hole. Skirting this, he almost fell as he floundered through the deep mud churned up by artillery caissons. He was panting a little when he regained the hard surface on the other side, but he walked forward steadily and strongly.

The moon shone clear. Something in the lay of the land told him he should have reached the village where his married sister had lived, where he and his wife and the children used to come for Sunday dinners once in a while. Puzzled, he stopped before a low, confused huddle of broken bricks and splintered beams, and looked about him uncomprehending. The silence was intense. In the instant before he could grasp what he was seeing, he heard and felt a rapid vibration, his own heart knocking. Then he understood.

A moment later, mechanically, he began to move about, clambering up and down, aimlessly, over the heaps of rubble. Although he did not know it, he was searching for some trace of his sister's house. Presently his knees gave way under him. He sat down suddenly on a tree stump. The lopped-off trunk beside it showed it to have been an old cherry tree. Yes, his sister's big cherry tree, the pride of her garden. A long strip of paper, one end buried in a heap of broken plaster, fluttered in the night wind. It beat against his leg like someone calling feebly for help. The moon emerged from a cloud and showed it to be a strip of wallpaper; he recognized the pattern; he had helped his brother-in-law put it on the bedroom of the house. His sister's four children had been born within the walls of that bedroom. He tried to fix his mind on those children, not to think of any other children, not to remember his own, not to . . .

The paper beat insistently and rhythmically against his leg like a recurrent thought of madness—he sprang up with the gesture of a man terrified, and stumbling wildly among the formless ruins sought for the road again.

He walked heavily after this, lifting his feet with an effort. Several miles further, at the heap of débris which had been Falquières, where his wife's family had lived, he made a wide detour through the fields to avoid passing closer to the ruins. At the next, Bondry, where he had been born and brought up, he tried to turn aside, but against his will his feet carried him straight to the center of the chaos. When the first livid light of dawn showed him the two stumps of the big apple trees before the door, which his grandfather had planted, he stopped short. Of the house, of the old walled garden, not a trace beyond the shapeless heap of stones and plaster. He stood there a long time, staring silently. The light gradually brightened, until across the level fields a ray of yellow sunshine struck ironically through the prone branches of the murdered trees upon the gray face of the man.

At this he turned and, dragging his feet, his head hanging, his shoulders bent, he followed the road which led like a white tape laid straight across the plain, towards—towards . . . The road had been mined at regular intervals, deep and broad craters stretching across it, enough to stop a convoy of camions, not enough to stop a single soldier, even though he stumbled along so wearily, his cumbersome packages beating against his legs and arms, even though he walked so slowly, more and more slowly as he came in sight of the next heaped and tumbled mound of débris. The sun rose higher. . . .

Presently it shone, with April clarity, on Nidart lying, face down-wards, upon a heap of broken bricks.

For a long hour it showed nothing but that—the ruins, the prostrate trees, the man, like them stricken and laid low.

Then it showed, poor and miserable under that pale-gold light, a wretched antlike procession issuing from holes in the ground and de-filing slowly along the scarred road towards the ruins; women, a few old men, a little band of pale and silent children. They approached the ruins and dispersed. One of the women, leading three children, picked her way wearily among the heaps of stone, the charred and twisted beams . . . stopped short, both hands at her heart.

And then the sun reeled in the sky to a sound which burst strangely on that silent desolation—scream after scream of joy, ringing up to the very heavens, frantic, incredulous, magnificent joy.

There they stood, the man and wife, clasped in each other's arms in the ruins of their home, with red, swollen eyes, smiling with quiver-ing lips, silent. Now that the first wild cries had gone rocketlike to the sky and fallen back in a torrent of tears, they had no words, no words at all. They clasped each other and the children, and wept, constantly wiping the tears from their white cheeks, to see each other. The two older children, a little shy of this father whom they had almost forgotten, drew away constrained, hanging their heads, looking up bashfully under their bent brows. Nidart sat down on a heap of stone and drew the little girl to him, stroking her hair. He tried to speak, but no voice issued from his lips. His wife sat down beside him, laying her head on his shoulder, spent with the excess of her relief. They were all silent a long time, their hearts beginning to beat in the old rhythm, a sweet, pale peace dropping down upon them.

After a time, the youngest child, cowering under the woman's skirts, surprised at the long silence, thrust out a little pale face from his shelter. The man glanced down on him and smiled. "That's a Dupré," he said, in his normal voice, with conviction, all his village lore coming back to him. "He has the Dupré nose . . . exactly . . . he looks just the way my cousin Jacques used to when he was little."

These were the first articulate words spoken. With them, he turned his back on the confused immensity of the world in which he had lived, exiled, for three years, and returned into the close familiar com-munity of neighbors and family where he had lived for thirty-four years—where he had lived for hundreds of years. The material frame-work of this community lay pulverized in ruins about him. But it was

still warmly alive—to him. He looked at the little child whom he had
never seen before and knew him for kin.

His wife nodded. "Yes, it's Louise and Jacques's baby. Louise was
expecting him, you know, when the mobilization . . . he was born
just after Jacques went away, in August. We heard Jacques was killed
. . . we have heard everything . . . that Paris was taken, that London
was burned. . . . I have heard twice that you were killed. Louise believed it all, and never got out of bed after the baby came. She just
turned over and let herself die. I took the baby. Somebody had to.
That's the reason I'm here now. 'They' carried off all the women my
age unless they had children under three. They thought the baby was
mine."

"But Jacques isn't killed," said Nidart; "he's wounded, with one
wooden leg, frantic to see Louise and the baby. . . ." He made a gesture of blame. "Louise always was a fool! Anybody's a fool to give
up!" He held out his hand to the baby and said, "Come here, little
Jeannot."

The child shrank away silently, burrowing deeper into his foster
mother's skirts.

"He's afraid," she explained. "We've had to make the children afraid
so they would keep out of sight, and not break rules. There were so
many rules, so many to salute and to bow to, the children couldn't
remember; and when they forgot, they were so dreadfully cuffed, or
their parents fined such big fines . . ."

"*I* never saluted!" said the boy of ten, wagging his head proudly.
"You have to have something on your head to salute, they won't let
you do it bareheaded. So I threw my cap in the fire."

"Yes, he's gone bareheaded since the first days, summer and winter,
rain and shine," said his mother.

"Here, Jean-Pierre," said his father, wrestling with one of his packages, "I've got a hat for you." He extracted from its brown canvas bag
a horizon-blue fatigue cap, which he held out. "And I've got something for my little Berthe, too." He fumbled in an inner pocket. "I
made it myself, near Verdun. The fellows all thought I was crazy to
work over it so, when the chances were I'd never see my little girl
again; but I was pretty sure *Maman* would know how to take care
of you, all right." He drew out from a nest of soft rags a roughly
carved aluminum ring and slipped it on the child's forefinger.

As the children drew off a little, to compare and examine, their
parents looked into each other's eyes, the deep, united, serious look
of man and wife before a common problem.

"*Eh bien,* Paulette," said the man, "what shall we do? Give up? Move away?"

"Oh, Pierre!" cried his wife. "You *wouldn't?*"

For answer, he shook himself free of his packages and began to undo them, the ax, the hammer, the big package of nails, the saw, the trowel, the paper bags of seeds, the pickax. He spread them out on the clutter of broken bricks, plaster, splintered wood, and looked up at his wife. "That's what I bought on the way here."

His wife nodded. "But have you had your breakfast? You'd better eat something before you begin."

While he ate his bread and munched his cheese, she told him, speaking with a tired dullness, something of what had happened during the years of captivity. It came out just as she thought of it, without sequence, one detail obscuring another. "There wasn't much left inside the house when they finally blew it up. They'd been taking everything little by little. No, they weren't bad to women; they were horrid and rough and they stole everything they could, but they didn't mistreat us, only some of the foolish girls. You know that good-for-nothing family of Boirats, how they'd run after any man. Well, they took to going with the Boches; but any decent woman that kept out of sight as much as she could, no, I wasn't afraid of them much that way, unless they were drunk. Their officers were awfully hard on them about everything—*hard!* They treated them like dogs. *We were sorry for them sometimes.*"

Yes, this ignorant woman, white and thin and ragged, sitting on the wreck of her home, said this.

"Did you hear how they took every single thing in copper or brass —Grandfather's candlesticks, the andirons, the handles of the clothes-press, the doorknobs, and all, *every one* of my saucepans and kettles?" Her voice trembled at this item. "The summer after that, it was everything in linen. I kept just the chemise I had on my back . . . even what was on the clothesline, drying, they took. The American Committee gave us some cotton cloth and I made a couple for me and Berthe, and some drawers for Jean-Pierre and the baby. That was when we could still get thread. The winter after that, it was woolen they took, everything, especially mattresses. Their officers made them get every single mattress in town, except the straw ones. Alice Bernard's mother, they jerked her mattress right out from under her, and left her lying on the bed-ropes. And M. le Curé, he was sick with pneumonia and they took his, that way, and he died. But the Boches didn't dare not to. Their officers would have shot them if they hadn't."

"I can make beds for you," he said. "There must be trenches somewhere, near"—she nodded—"they'll have left some wire-netting in an *abri*. You make a square of wood, and put four legs to it, and stretch the wire netting over it and put straw on that. But we had some wire netting of our own that was around the chicken yard."

"Oh, they took that," she explained—"that, and the doors of the chicken house, and they pried off our window cases and doorjambs and carried those off the last days, too . . . but there was one thing they wouldn't do, no, not even the Boches, and that was *this* dirty work!" She waved her hand over the destruction about her, and pointed to the trees across the road in the field, all felled accurately at the same angle. "We couldn't understand why they were getting ready to leave, but some of them had learned enough French to tell us *they* wouldn't 'do it'—we didn't know what. They told us they would go away and different troops would come. And Georges Duvalet's boy said they told *him* that the troops who were to come to 'do it' were criminals out of the prisons that the officers had let out if they would 'do it'—all this time we didn't know what, and somebody said it was to pour oil on us and burn us, the way they did the people in the barn at Vermadderville. But there wasn't anything we could do to prevent it. We couldn't run away. So we stayed, and took care of the children.

"All the men who could work at all and all the women too, unless they had very little children, were marched away, off up towards the north—to work in German factories, we are told now—with just what few extra things they could put in a big handkerchief. Annette Cagnon, she was eighteen, and had to go, but her mother stayed with the younger children—her mother has been sort of crazy ever since. She had such a long fainting turn when Annette went by, with a German soldier, we thought we never could bring her to life. . . ." The tired voice shook a moment, the woman rested her head again on her husband's arm, holding to him tightly. "Pierre, oh Pierre, *if we had known what was to come*—no, we couldn't have lived through it, not any of us!" He put his great, workingman's hand on her rough hair, gently.

She went on: "And then the troops who had been here did go away and the others came, and they made the few of us who were left go down into the cellar of those old houses down the road. They told us to stay there three days, and if we went out before we'd get shot. We didn't know what they were doing. Just one awful bang, bang, bang after another. When we'd waited two whole days, we didn't hear anything more, and the water they had given us was all used up.

Then old Granny Arnoux said she was all alone in the world, so it wouldn't make any difference if she did get shot. She wanted to make sure that her house was all right. You know what she thought of her house! So she came up and we waited. And in half an hour we heard her crutches coming back on the road, and she was shrieking out. We ran up to see. She had fallen down in a heap. She hasn't known anything since; shakes all the time as if she were in a chill. She was the first one; she was all alone, when she saw what they had done . . . and *you* know . . ."

Nidart turned very white, and stood up. "God! Yes, I know! *I* was alone!"

"Since then, ten days ago, the French soldiers came through. We didn't know them for sure, we were expecting to see the red trousers. I asked everybody about you, but nobody knew. There are so *many* soldiers in an army. Then an American came in a camionette. He brought us bread and blankets and some shoes, but they have leather soles and I make the children keep them for best, they wear out so. Of course I was glad to get them, but I told him that we needed most of all some tools so that we could make a seed bed for our garden. I wasn't sure I made him understand. He seemed to know very little French. But next day he came back with that shovel, a hoe, and the two rakes. He was a kind man. The roads were terrible then. His little car was so plastered with mud that I could hardly see the red cross on it. And now the Government lets the camions going up to the front throw off bread and meat . . . once, a whole bag of potatoes for us. The préfet came around and asked if we wanted to be sent to a refugee home in Paris or stay here, and of course I said stay here. The children and I have come every day to work. We've got the plaster and bricks cleared out from the corner of the fireplace, and I cook there, though there isn't any chimney of course, but I think the tiles of the kitchen floor are mostly all there still. And oh, Pierre, we have one corner of the garden almost cleared, *and the asparagus is coming up!* Come and see! They cut down everything they could see, even the lilac bushes, but what was in the ground, alive, they couldn't kill."

Nidart put the shovel in his wife's hand, and took up the pickax. "Time spent in traveling isn't counted on furloughs," he said, "so we have twenty-one days, counting today. The garden first, so's to get in the seeds."

They clambered over the infernal disorder of the ruins of the house, and picked their way down and back into what had been the garden. A few sections of the wall were still standing, its thick solidity resisting even dynamite petards.

"Oh, see, almost all of the pleached trees are saved!" cried Nidart, astonished. "That part of the wall didn't fall."

"I'm not sure I pruned those right," said his wife doubtfully, glancing at them. "I couldn't remember whether you left two or four buds on the peaches, and I just gave up on the big grapevine. It grew so, it got all ahead of me!"

"Did they bear well?" asked the man, looking across the trash heap at the well-remembered trees and vines. "We'd better leave those till some odd time, they won't need much care. I can do them between other things sometime when I'm too tired to do anything else. Here is where the big job is." He looked the ground over with a calculating eye and announced his plan of campaign.

"We won't try to carry the rubbish out. It's too heavy for you, and my time has got to go as far as it can for the important things. We'll just pile it all up where the walls used to stand. All of us know that line! I'll use the pickax, and *Maman* the shovel. Jean-Pierre will throw the bigger pieces over on the line, and Berthe will go after and pick up the littler ones."

They set to work, silently, intensely. When they reached the currant bushes, all laid low, Pierre gave an angry growl, but none of them slackened their efforts. About eleven the big convoy of camions on the way to the front came through, lurching along the improvised road laid out across the fields. The workers, lifting their eyes for the first time from their labors, saw at a distance on the main road the advance guard of the road menders already there, elderly soldiers, gray-haired territorials, with rakes and shovels, and back of them, shuttlelike, the big trucks with road-metal coming and going.

Reluctantly leaving her work, Paulette went to get the supplies for dinner, and started an open-air fire in the cleared-out corner of the chimney. Over this she hung a big pot, and leaving it to boil she hurried back to her shovel. "The soup kettle and the flatirons," she told her husband, "they were too hard to break and too heavy to carry away, and they are about all that's left of what was in the house."

"No, I found an iron fork," said Berthe, "but it was all twisted. Jean-Pierre said he thought he could . . ."

"Don't talk," said their father firmly—"you don't work so fast when you talk."

At noon they went back to the fire burning under the open sky, in the blackened corner of the fireplace where it had cooked the food during the years past. The man looked at it strangely, and turned his eyes away.

"Now where is your fork, little Berthe?" he said. "I'll straighten it for you. With that and my kit . . ."

"I have my jackknife too," said Jean-Pierre.

They ate thus, dipping up the stew in the soldier's *gamelle*, using his knife and fork and spoon and the straightened iron fork. The baby was fed on bread soaked in the gravy, and on bits of potato given him from the end of a whittled stick. In the twenty minutes' rest which their captain allowed the little force after the meal, he and Jean-Pierre whittled out two wooden forks, two-tined, from willow twigs. "That's one apiece now," said Nidart, "and the asparagus bed is all cleared off. We have made a beginning."

They went back to work, stooping, straining, heaving, blinded with the flying plaster, wounded with the sharp edges of the shattered stones. The sun shone down on them with heavenly friendliness, the light, sparkling air lifted the hair from their hot foreheads. After a time, Nidart, stopping for an instant to wipe away the sweat which ran down into his eyes, said: "The air has a different feel to it here. And the sun looks different. It *looks* like home."

At four they stopped to munch the piece of bread which is the supplementary meal of French working people at that hour. Nidart embellished it with a slice of cheese for each, which made the meal a feast. They talked as they ate; they began to try to bridge over the gap between them. But they lacked words to tell what lay back of them; only the dry facts came out.

"Yes, I've been wounded, there's a place on my thigh, here, put your hand and feel, where there isn't any flesh over the bone, just skin. It doesn't bother me much, except when I try to climb a ladder. Something about that position I can't manage . . . and for a mason . . ."

"I'll climb the ladders," said Jean-Pierre.

"Yes, I was pretty sick. It got gangrene some. They thought I wouldn't live. I was first in a big hospital near the front, and then in a convalescent hospital in Paris. It was awfully dull when I got better. They thought if I had made an application to be *réformé* and retired I could be like Jacques Dupré with his wooden leg. But with you and the children here . . . what could I have done with myself? So I didn't say anything, and when my time was up in the hospital I went back to the trenches. That was a year ago last winter."

"Berthe and Jean-Pierre had the mumps that winter," said their mother. "The baby didn't get it. I kept him away from them. The

Boches shut us up as though we had the smallpox. They were terribly strict about any sickness. The Boche regimental doctor came every day. He took very good care of them."

"He wanted to give me a doll because I didn't cry when he looked in my throat," said Berthe.

"Of course she didn't take it," said Jean-Pierre. "I told her I'd break it all to pieces if she did."

"But she cried afterwards."

"Come," said the father, "we've finished our bread. Back to work."

That night, after the children were asleep on straw in the cellar down the road, their parents came back to wander about in the moonlight over their ravaged little kingdom. The wife was wordless, drawing her breath irregularly, keeping a strained grasp on her husband's arm. For the most part he succeeded in speaking in a steady voice of material plans for the future—how the revetment planks from the nearest trench could be combined with the trunks of the felled trees to make roof and side walls of a one-room cabin; what they could plant in the garden and the field—things which she and the children could cultivate after he had gone back.

At this reminder of the inevitable farewell again before them, the wife broke out in loud wailings, shivering, clutching at him wildly. He drew her down on a pile of rubbish, put his arms around her, and said in a peremptory tone: "Paulette! Listen! *You are letting the Boches beat you!*" He used to her the tone he used for his squad, his new soldier's voice which the war had taught him, the tone which carried the laggards up over the top. At the steel-like ring of it, his wife was silent.

He went on: "There's nothing any of us *can* do but to go on. The only thing to do is to go on without making a fuss. That's the motto in the army, you know. Don't make a fuss." He lifted his head and looked around at his home dismantled, annihilated. *"Not to give up—* that and the flatirons are about all the Boches have left us, don't you see?"

He was silent a moment and went on with his constructive planning. "Perhaps I can find lime enough somewhere to rebuild the chimney. With that, and a roof, and the garden, and the allocation from the Government . . ."

"Yes, Pierre," said his wife in a trembling voice. She did not weep again.

He himself, however, was not always at this pitch of stoicism. There were times when he looked up suddenly and felt, as though for the first time, the downfall and destruction of all that had been his life. At such moments the wind of madness blew near him. The night after they had moved from the cellar into the half-roofed, half-walled hut, to sleep there on the makeshift beds, he lay all night awake, crushed with the immensity of the effort they would need to put forth. There came before him the long catalogue of what they had lost, the little decencies and comforts they had earned and paid for and owned. He sickened at the squalid expedients of their present life. They were living like savages; never again would they attain the self-respecting order which had been ravished from them, which the ravishers still enjoyed. With all his conscious self he longed to give up the struggle, but something deeper than his conscious self was at work. The tree had been cut down, but something was in the ground, alive.

At dawn he found himself getting out of bed, purposefully. To his wife's question he answered: "I'm going to Noyon to buy the seed for the field. We haven't half enough beans. And perhaps they have some young cabbage plants there. I can make it in six hours if I hurry."

He was back by ten o'clock, exhausted, but aroused from his waking nightmare—for that time! But it came again and again.

On the day he began to spade up the field he noticed that two of his murdered fruit trees, attached by a rag of bark to the stumps, were breaking out into leaf. The sight turned him sick with sorrow, as though one of his children had smiled at him from her deathbed. He bent over the tree, his eyes burning, and saw that all the buds were opening trustfully. His heart was suffocating. He said to himself: "They have been killed! They are dead! But they do not know they are dead, and they try to go on living. *Are we like that?*"

In an instant all his efforts to reanimate his assassinated life seemed pitiful, childish, doomed to failure. He looked across the field at the flimsy enclosure he had begun and felt a shamed rage. Was that patchwork hut all he could offer his wife and children as a shelter— a home? He was half-minded to rush over and knock it to pieces.

"Papa, come! The peonies have begun to come up in the night. The whole row of them where we were raking yesterday."

The man found his wife already there, bending over the sturdy, reddish, rounded sprouts pushing strongly through the loosened earth. She looked up at him with shining eyes. When they were betrothed lovers, they had together planted those peonies, pieces of old roots from her mother's garden. "You see," she said again; "I told you what was in the ground alive they couldn't kill!"

Nidart went back to his spading silently, and, as he labored there, a breath of healing came up to him from that soil which was his. The burning in his eyes, the taste of gall in his mouth, he had forgotten when, two hours later, he called across to his wife that the ground for the beans was all spaded and that she and Jean-Pierre could come now with their rakes, while he went back to building the house wall.

He had started to set up one of his heavier planks as a doorpost when a new idea flashed into his mind. He caught up his shovel and hurried off along the road. Inside an hour he was back with a heavy bag on his shoulder.

"Lime!" he called in exultation. "You know the warehouse of Sarazan Brothers . . . just as you are getting into Chauny. All the upper floors have crashed down flat . . . a big shell must have hit it. But I dug until I found the cellar door. I knew where to look. I always bought my materials there. By keeping close to the wall I worked my way around. And there, sure enough, under a section of basement vaulting that hadn't sagged, were what I was looking for . . . bags and bags, stacked up the way they always kept them. A few are still dry enough to use. Now, I'll knock together some sort of a mortar box. I can get sand from the old pit near the river. In a few days my batch will be slacked and tempered enough to hold the chimney bricks together. Then you can have a real draft—no more smoke from your cooking fire."

But such brief periods of enthusiasm made it all the harder to bear the contrasting return of black discouragement. Discouragement! More like total defeat was the hour waiting for him in his garden beside the wall on which the branches of his pleached trees and vines still spread out their carefully symmetrical patterns. He had put off caring for them till some odd moment. He and his wife, glancing at them from time to time, had made estimates of the amount of fruit they would yield, "and for *us* this time—we haven't had a single peach or apple from them. The Boche officers sent their soldiers to get them always."

"Queer they should have left those unharmed," said his wife once, and he had answered: "Perhaps the man they sent to kill them was a gardener like us. I know I couldn't cut down a fruit tree in full bearing, not if it were in hell and belonged to the Kaiser. Anybody who's ever grown things knows what it is!"

One gray day of spring rains and pearly mists, the fire would not burn. Paulette crouched beside it, blowing with all her might, and thinking of the big leathern bellows which had been carried away to

Germany with all the rest. Jean-Pierre shaved off bits from a dry stick and Berthe fed them under the pot, but the flame would not brighten. Pierre, coming down, cold and hungry, from the top of the wall where he had been struggling with a section of roof, felt physically incapable of going on with that work until he had eaten, and decided to use the spare half hour for pruning the pleached trees and vines. Almost at the end of his strength after the long-continued, strained effort to accomplish the utmost in every moment and every hour, he shivered from the cold of his wet garments as he stood for a moment, fumbling to reach the pruning shears. But he did not give himself the time to warm his hands at the fire, setting out directly again into the rain. He had been working at top speed ever since the breakfast, six hours before, of black coffee and dry bread.

Sodden with fatigue and a little light-headed from lack of food, he walked along the wall and picked out the grapevine as the least tiring to begin on. He knew it so well he could have pruned it in the dark. He had planted it the year before his marriage, when he had been building the house and beginning the garden. It had not been an especially fine specimen, but something about the situation and the soil had exactly suited it, and it had thriven miraculously. Every spring, with the first approach of warm weather, he had walked out, in the evening after his day's work, along the wall to catch the first red bud springing amazingly to life out of the brown, woody stems which looked so dead. During the summers as he had sprayed the leaves, manured the soil, watered the roots, and lifted with an appraising hand the great purple clusters, heavier day by day, he had come to know every turn of every branch. In the trenches, during the long periods of silent inaction, when the men stare before them at sights from their past lives, sometimes Nidart had looked back at his wife and children, sometimes at his garden on an early morning in June, sometimes at his family about the dinner table in the evening, and sometimes at his great grapevine, breaking into bud in the spring, or, all luxuriant lines, rich with leafage, green and purple in the splendor of its September maturity.

It was another home-coming to approach it now, and his sunken, bloodshot eyes found rest and comfort in dwelling on its well-remembered curves and turnings. He noticed that the days of sunshine, and now the soft spring rain, had started it into budding. He laid his hand on the tough, knotted, fibrous brown stem.

It stirred oddly, with a disquieting lightness in his hand. The sensation was almost as though one of his own bones turned gratingly on nothing. The sweat broke out on his forehead. He knelt down and took hold of the stem lower down. The weight of his hand displaced it. It swung free. It had been severed from the root by a fine saw. The sap was oozing from the stump.

The man knelt there in the rain, staring at this, as though he were paralyzed. He did not know what he was looking at, for a moment, conscious of nothing but a cold sickness. He got up heavily to his feet, then, and made his way to the next vine. Its stem gave way also, swinging loose with the horrible limpness of a broken limb.

He went to the next, a peach tree, and to the next, a fine pleached pear. Everything, everything, peach trees, apple trees, grapevines, everything had been neatly and dexterously murdered, and their corpses left hanging on the wall as a practical joke.

The man who had been sent to do that had been a gardener indeed, and had known where to strike to reach the very heart of this other gardener who now, his hands over his face, staggered forward and leaned his body against the wall, against the dead vine which had been so harmless, so alive. He felt something like an inward bleeding, as though that neat, fine saw had severed an artery in his own body.

His wife stepped out in the rain and called him. He heard nothing but the fine, thin voice of a small saw, eating its way to the heart of living wood.

His wife seeing him stand so still, his face against the wall, came out towards him with an anxious face. "Pierre, Pierre!" she said. She looked down, saw the severed vine-stem and gave a cry of dismay. "Pierre, they haven't . . . they haven't . . . !"

She ran along the wall, touching them one by one, all the well-known, carefully tended stems. Her anger, her sorrow, her disgust burst from her in a flood of outcries, of storming, furious words.

Her husband did not move. A deathlike cold crept over him. He heard nothing but the venomous, fine voice of the saw, cutting one by one the tissues which had taken so long to grow, which had needed so much sun and rain and heat and cold, and twelve years out of a man's life. He was sick, sick of it all, mourning not for the lost trees but for his lost idea of life. That was what people were like, could be like, what one man could do in cold blood to another—no heat of battle here, no delirium of excitement, cold, calculated intention! He would give up the effort to resist, to go on. The killing had been too thoroughly done.

His wife fell silent, frightened by his stillness. She forgot her own anger, her grief, she forgot the dead trees. They were as nothing. A strong, valiant tenderness came into her haggard face. She went up to him, close, stepping into his silent misery with the secure confidence only a wife can have in a husband. "Come, Pierre," she said gently, putting her red, work-scarred hand in his. She drew him away from the wall, his arms hanging listlessly. She drew him into the sheltered corner of the room he had half finished. She set hot food before him and made him eat and drink.

The rain poured down in a gray wall close before them. The heaped-up ruins were all around them. Inside the shelter the children ate greedily, heartily, talking, laughing, quarreling, playing. The fire, now thoroughly ablaze, flamed brightly beside them. The kettle steamed.

After a time Nidart's body began slowly to warm. He began to hear the children's voices, to see his wife. The horror was an hour behind him. The blessed, blurring passage of the moments dimmed the sound of that neat small saw, the sight of that deft-handed man, coolly and smilingly murdering . . .

He looked at his wife attentively, as she tried to set in order their little corner saved from chaos. She was putting back on the two shelves he had made her the wooden forks and spoons which she had cleaned to a scrupulous whiteness; she was arranging neatly the wretched outfit of tin cans and formless paper packages which replaced the shining completeness of her lost kitchen; she was smoothing out the blankets on their rough camp-beds; she was washing the faces and hands of the children, of their own children and the little foster son, the child of the woman who had given up, who had let herself be beaten, who had let herself be killed, who had abandoned her baby to be cared for by another, braver woman.

A shamed courage began slowly to filter back into his heart. With an immense effort he got up from the tree stump which served for chair and went towards his wife, who was kneeling before the little child she had saved. He would begin again.

"Paulette," he said heavily, "I believe that if we could get some grafting wax at once, we might save those. Why couldn't we cover the stumps with wax to keep the roots from bleeding to death, till the tops make real buds, and then graft them onto the stumps? It's too late to do it properly with dormant scions, but perhaps we might succeed. It would be quicker than starting all over again. The roots are there, still."

He raged as he thought of this poor substitute for his splendid trees, but he set his teeth. "I could go to Noyon again. Someone there must have wax and resin enough for these few stumps."

The little boy presented himself imploringly. "Oh, let me go! I could do it all right. And you could get on faster with the roof. There aren't but ten days left, now."

Nidart considered, "Yes, that would be best. Any camion driver will give you a lift, and no one will bother if a kid like you hasn't the right travel papers. Listen, at Noyon, on the *rue des Merciers,* between the *Hôtel de Ville* and the Cathedral, there used to be a shop, kept by M. Pinchard, an old friend of mine. Hold on, though! That quarter was pretty well shot up in the bombardment. . . . Anyway, if he isn't there, or hasn't what we need, don't give up, keep on . . . as far as Compiègne if you have to . . . but don't come back without that grafting wax."

Jean-Pierre set off in the rain, a small brave spot of energy in the midst of death. His father went back to his house building.

The roads were mended now, the convoys of camions rumbled along day after day, raising clouds of dust; staff-cars flashed by; once in a while a non-militarized automobile came through, sometimes with officials of the Government on inspection tours, who distributed miscellaneous lots of seeds, rolls of tar paper for roof and walls, and once brought Paulette some lengths of cotton stuff for sheets; sometimes with reporters from the Paris newspapers; once with some American reporters who took photographs and gave bars of chocolate to the children. Several times people stopped, foreigners, Americans, English, sometimes women in uniforms who asked a great many questions and noted down the answers. Pierre wondered why those able-bodied young men were not in some army. He had thought all the able-bodied men in the world were in some army.

For the most part he found all these people rather futile and uninteresting, as he had always found city people, and paid little attention to them, never interrupting his work to talk to them, his work, his sacred work, for which there remained, only too well known, a small and smaller number of hours. He took to laboring at night whenever possible.

The roof was all on the one tiny room before the date for his return. The chimney was rebuilt, the garden spaded, raked, and planted. But the field was not finished. It takes a long time to spade up a whole field. Pierre worked on it late at night, the moonlight permitting. When his wife came out to protest, he told her that it was no harder than to march all night, with knapsack and blanket-roll and gun. She took up the rake and began to work beside him. Under their tan they were both very white and drawn, during these last hours.

The day before the last came. They spent every moment they could in the field, never lifting their eyes from the soil. But their task was not finished when night came. Pierre had never been so exacting about the condition of the ground. It must be fine, fine, without a single clod left to impede the growth of a single precious seed. This was not work which, like spading, could be done at night in an uncertain light. When their eyes, straining through the thickening twilight, could no longer distinguish the lumps of earth, he gave it up, with a long breath, and, his rake on his shoulder, little Berthe's hand in his, he crossed the mended road to the uncomely little shelter which was home.

Paulette was bending over the fire. She looked up, and he saw that she had been crying. But she said nothing. Nor did he, going to lean his rake against the reconstructed wall. He relinquished the implement reluctantly, and all through the meal kept the feel of it in his hand.

They were awake when the first glimmer of gray dawn shone through the empty square which was their window. Pierre dressed hurriedly and taking his rake went across the road to the field. Paulette blew alive the coals of last night's fire, and made coffee and carried it to her husband with a lump of bread. He stopped work to drink and eat. It was in the hour before the sunrise. A gray, thin mist clung to the earth. Through it they looked at each other's pale faces, soberly.

"You must get the seed in as soon as you can, after I'm gone," said the husband.

"Yes," she promised, "we won't lose a minute."

"And I think you and Jean-Pierre can manage to nail in the window frame when it comes. I thought I'd be able to do that myself."

"Yes, Jean-Pierre and I can do it."

"You'd better get my kit and everything ready for me to leave," he said, drinking the last of the coffee and setting his hand again to the rake.

They had reckoned that he would need to leave the house at ten o'clock if he were to make the long tramp to Noyon in time for the train. At a quarter of ten he stopped, and, the rake still tightly held in his hand, crossed the road. His knapsack, blanket-roll, all the various brown bags and *musettes* were waiting for him on the bench hewn from a tree-trunk before the door. He passed them, went around the little hut, and stepped into the garden.

Between the heaped-up lines of rubble, the big rectangle of well-tilled earth lay clean and brown and level. And on it, up and down, were four, long, straight lines of pale green. The peas were up. He was to see that before he went back.

He stooped over them. Some of them were still bowed double with the effort of thrusting themselves up against the encumbering earth. He felt their effort in the muscles of his own back. But others, only a few hours older, were already straightening themselves blithely to reach up to the sun and warmth. This also he felt—in his heart. Under the intent gaze of the gardener, the vigorous little plants seemed to be vibrating with life. His eyes were filled with it. He turned away and went back to the open door of the hut. His wife, very pale, stood there, silent. He heaved up his knapsack, adjusted his blanket-roll and *musettes,* and drew a long breath.

"Goodby, Paulette," he said, kissing her on both cheeks, the dreadful long kiss which may be the last.

"I will—I will take care of things here," she said, her voice dying away in her throat.

He kissed his children, he stooped low to kiss the little foster child. He looked once more across at the field, not yet seeded. Then he started back.

He had gone but a few steps when he looked down, saw that the rake was still gripped in his right hand. He stopped short, turned back, left the rake on the bench, and, his right hand empty—the hand that would soon be holding a gun—he went back to war.

The Knot-hole

⚑ In the spring of 1940, a new little son or daughter was on the way, so our dear Emilie-Anne, my goddaughter, wrote me. She made a pretense of knowing as well as I how foolish it was for people living in a country at war to have babies. The pretense was thin. Lianne (as we who had known her from her chubby childhood called her) was obviously as lightheaded with joy and pride as any other young mother-to-be. It was really, she explained, not so crazy as it seemed to us in the United States. True, her husband was at the front, on the Maginot Line, like other French soldiers and officers. But during that quiet winter they had regular furloughs at home. Like vacations. By not taking the next furlough when the time came for it, he would have an extra long one, due in late October, when the baby would arrive.

Yes, yes, even so—can you remember those months of the phony war?—even so did the men of the French Army plan confidently for regular vacations from war. From the military leaders down to the sergeants and privates, even so did the French Army feel that this war would naturally repeat the pattern of the static, trench fighting of the First World War. And even so, in all unfearing ignorant confidence, did the wives go out at intervals, when they could, to spend a week end in some farmhouse, not too far from the front for Army husbands to dash back for an hour or so. Lianne was, when she wrote me, in such a week-end, temporary home. She was, she told me, cheerfully, that very minute looking out of the little rustic window, expecting to see him appear. She said that she and Jean-Jacques felt so strongly about family unity that no effort was too great to be sure their little four-year-old boy did not forget his father. I smiled as I read this. We all knew that the reason for her expensive, uncomfortable trips to the farmhouse near the front was that Jacqui's young father and mother were crazy about each other.

There was no danger that Jacqui would forget his father. Jean-Jacques was the kind of bluff, good-humored, vital young man no boy would resist. In peace times he was a teacher of physics in a small-town high school, a great favorite with his students. In war times he was in an artillery battalion, as great a favorite with his Army comrades. He was one of those who know how to take hold of life by the right end.

In due time another letter came from Lianne. In that first dream-like winter of the war, mail from France was slow but almost regular. The family plans were made for the event, she reported. In July she was to go South to stay with her mother in the old, white-washed, thatched cottage on the farm from which Lianne's grandfather had gone out, eighty years before, to his modest success in the big world. She wrote that they all thought it would be pleasant to have little Paul, or small Thérèse, whichever it was, born in the same room where she had been born, looking out on the hollyhocks at Voillac.

There were medical details in that letter—the last one she wrote from her home near the high school where her husband had taught—the intimate report on this and that detail of her pregnancy which a younger-generation friend makes to an affectionately solicitous older woman. She was, on the whole, she wrote, getting along better than before Jacqui was born. Her doctor said that if she would take things very calmly, relax, go up and down stairs as little as possible, and keep her mind tranquil, she would have no such trouble as with the birth of her first child. Her husband being first in her thoughts, she always passed along his news. He hoped, it appeared, that the new baby would be a girl, exactly like her mother. "But *I* want another boy. There can't be too many like my Jean-Jacques." There had been, her husband had written, some sickness among the horses in his battalion. But that was now past. Jean-Jacques was an intellectual but he was as good with horses as any army vet.

I was surprised. "*Horses?*" I thought. I knew as little about military equipment as most women of my age, but by that date I had seen hundreds of photographs of high-speed tanks, tearing Poland to pieces.

Lianne's cleaning woman had gone to live in another town, she wrote. Since the doctor had forbidden any stooping or lifting for her, she would need to find another helper.

On this trivial homely note, ended that last letter. It was written in April. By the time it came to me, May was drawing to a close. Do you need any reminder of what was happening late in May of 1940?

My desperate feeling is that if you have forgotten—all is lost. We are doomed if we forget. So I assume that you remember the appalling uproar of clanking tanks, screaming dive-bombers, and the sledge-hammer pound-pound-pound of hundreds of thousands of hobnailed boots, which in May of that year shook the earth under us, here, on the other side of the Atlantic from invaded France.

From Lianne nothing. Nothing. Not a word.

Like everybody else of that period, I was naïvely astonished by the failure of the world's postal system to carry letters to their addresses. Of course I did the frantic things which we were all doing then—I wrote and telegraphed to the American Consul in Lianne's home city, "Could any news be had of Madame Jean-Jacques Bergeron? She was last heard from at . . ." I wrote and telegraphed to the Consul in the nearest city to Voillac. And to the Consul in the city where her parents lived. And to other friends in France. And to French-American charitable organizations to which I had long belonged. I beat wildly on what I thought were doors. And then I saw that my knocking fell on unbroken walls. No doors. No windows. No echo from my outcry.

Not a word from Lianne. Not a word.

Then weeks and weeks later—three months after it had been written, a short letter. It must have been mailed on one of the very last days when a French post office was free to accept a letter for the world outside. It had been scrawled in pencil, in a cowshed where Lianne and Jacqui were spending the night. With her little boy, she was trying to reach Voillac. On foot. They had been tramping and hiding and trudging on for eight days before she could get together a piece of paper, a pencil, an envelope, a stamp to let us know that she and Jacqui were alive. She did not know as much of her family. No news of parents, of her husband's parents, of her sister, of her sister's husband—nothing.

And nothing, nothing, nothing of her husband! Her last letter from him, written hastily, was sent just as the horses were being put to the caissons to start the battalion to join the battle of Flanders.

Horses! I laid the letter down, shuddering. The quiet grass of a

Vermont field lay before my eyes. Across it, as I read, there thundered the tornado of motorized war, hurling itself down in steel to meet those horses.

Silence again.

"No. Sorry, no telegram can be accepted for places inside occupied France."

"No, no change in the mail situation. We are informed that no letters are being sent to occupied France. It would be no use to mail them."

Then a letter. A letter! A system had been arranged for excluding letters from France as rapidly as a prison door is slammed shut and locked behind a man brought in by the police. But for a time there were, infrequently, cracks in those prison walls through which a letter in a crumpled soiled envelope could be pushed out—a cautious letter, unsigned, undated, not a name mentioned—short, hurried, a hoarsely whispered message, like what might be caught by the ears of tense watchers at the mouth of a mine, after a cave-in. Hardly loud enough to be heard, for even sound itself was a danger. A spoken word, a mere sob, might be enough to bring down more crashing tons of savagery upon human flesh and blood.

Letters could not reach those in that great prison but they could— by efforts and risks not to be imagined—send out at long, irregular intervals, one of those whispered, anonymous, secret messages. Often those which came to me were not even set down in their own hand-writing, as familiar to me as their dear faces. But every word ringingly, unmistakably personal. Reading one left me trembling and wet with cold sweat.

From the first of these contraband letters, I learned that Lianne had not reached Voillac and her mother. She never did. Three days distant from the cowbarn where she had written me, the fleeing refugees had been stopped. It was their first encounter with the words "By Order" which came to cover the sky, to hang like black curtains before every door, every window, to smother all mouths, to blind all eyes. "By Order" the tragic mass of footsore women, children, old people, were halted in a town none of them had ever seen. Even in this smuggled-out letter, she dared not tell me the name of the town, since she was not sure into whose hands the message might fall.

Because her husband had been a teacher, Lianne and her little boy were directed by the distracted old Mayor of the town to the school. There were seven classrooms and a small office which had been that of the *Directeur*. The building had been meant to provide space for daytime classroom teaching for a hundred and fifty children. In it now, living, sleeping, cooking, being sick, being born, dying, were more than five hundred men, women, children, and babies.

Jacqui was with her. She underlined this. It was a triumph. In the rout, under the scream of the machine-guns in the dive-bombers, many of the fleeing mothers had been separated from their children, she wrote. "Day and night, my son has not once been out of reach of my arm. He and the baby to come are Jean-Jacques' children. I must keep them safe until their father is here to take care of us again. We sleep on the floor. There are so many, we take turns lying down. An old lady beside me died last night. Jacqui is being a good boy."

No news from her husband. No news of what inconceivable horror could be happening to France. All communications cut. To those thousands of French citizens not a word of what was being done to France. People around her told her that Jean-Jacques certainly had been killed in battle. But she would not let him die. *He was alive.* She knew he was alive.

These few secret letters which straggled out after long gaps usually came in the same mail. Probably held for some tramp freighter into which a sailor might smuggle them. In the same mail with this bulletin of news from Lianne was a letter from her mother at Voillac, frantically anxious about her daughter. "We know nothing of Lianne and Jacqui except that her town and home were obliterated by bombs. None of the refugees who have passed this way has heard of her." I, in Vermont, knew that Lianne was alive. Her mother in France, three hours' drive from her, did not. I could not tell her. "No, very sorry, the situation has not changed since you last inquired. No telegrams accepted for occupied France."

Silence. Silence. The calendar turned over one blank leaf after another, day after day, towards the month, the week, when Lianne's baby was to be born. That month, that week passed, another week, more weeks, another month went by.

Then, dated three months before, another scribbled, penciled note came in. It was a muffled scream of joy. "Jean-Jacques is alive. A prisoner. He is alive. The news was on a printed card. *But his name is in his own handwriting.* He is alive."

Then not a whisper, not a breath. For months.

Sometime in 1941, the German conquerors began the system of prisoner-of-war short messages. Do you remember them, the yellow printed slips marked "prisoner-of-war service"? The people of a great nation, prisoners of war! A message of twenty-five words, carefully innocuous and personal, was allowed "By Order." This was sent by the writer to the Paris Red Cross headquarters, then German of course. There the cards were held long enough to make any code-concealed information out of date, and sent to the Swiss Red Cross. In Switzerland, after a prescribed delay, they were sent to our own American Red Cross, and thence on to the persons to whom they were addressed. Mostly they arrived four to five months after they were written.

When one came, you were allowed, "By Order," to write twenty-five words on the back and return it, along the same five- or six-month-long route. Of those twenty-five words every one must count. Every one did count. Pondered on for days as they were, factual, disjointed, so expressed as—first of all—to pass the Censor, those telegraph-short sentences lay like crusted scars on the flimsy yellow paper. It was later they began to bleed again, in the anguished hearts of those who read them.

Through this channel I learned that little Anne-Marie had arrived (she was already six months old by that time), that Lianne was in charge of the two- and three- and four-year-olds of the refugee group crowded into that old school building (she had been a kindergarten teacher before her marriage), that she and Jean-Jacques in his German prison were allowed "By Order" to write each other nine words a week, or thirty-six words a month.

The next message reported that Jean-Jacques now knew that he had a little girl. "He loves her wildly, he writes." So did Lianne. "Anne-Marie sweetest baby. Strong and well. I am nursing her much longer than I did Jacqui. Kindergarten full of children."

The twenty-five words of the message after that ran, "Am passionately excited. Reason to hope J. J.'s release. Jacqui is thinner. I dread weaning baby. Have heard from my parents. Kindergarten full of children."

Then, astonishing, unimaginable—a letter. A real letter though not in Lianne's handwriting. Once in a while this happened. Somebody about to try to escape "over the line" memorized messages given him by those left in the occupied zone. Not the most modern Gestapo sound-detecting machines could locate a memorized message in a man's mind. This was postmarked from near Marseille. It had been transcribed from memory by someone almost illiterate, to judge from the crudely penciled scrawl. Strange to hear echoes of Lianne's young voice, of her own turns of phrase, in this unfamiliar handwriting.

I soon knew it by heart, as well as did the unknown messenger who sent it. It took me straight into the crowded old building, to stand by the emaciated young mother, desperately trying to go on nursing her baby, trying to feed two lives on the only food there was —turnips, chestnuts, apples—and, inestimable privilege, because she was a nursing mother, every day a pint of *whole,* not skimmed, milk.

It was midwinter. She was still wearing the same dress she had on when, in June, she was driven from her home by bombs, wore the same summer-thin underwear and stockings. In her care were forty little boys and girls, all day, every day. Her task was to keep them— so I interpreted the imperfectly comprehended phrases of that letter— from the dismal idleness and barbarian quarreling into which closely confined, undernourished children sink without skilled direction.

There were places where the transcriber—perhaps a sailor? perhaps a cook?—confused the message so that it meant nothing. I suppose none of it meant anything to the near-illiterate who risked his life to pass it on to me. I suppose he (or she) had tried to memorize too many messages. Yet I could make out that Lianne wished to let me know that she was trying to do for the children what her husband was doing for his fellow-prisoners in the German camp. "Jean-Jacques study-classes, chorus, dramatic club, care for the sick, not allowed to say where he is, but climate cold, very damp."

Then for a sentence or two it was quite clearly remembered, clearly enough set down. "We still find each other, *we do meet* as we both try to keep life human, not animal-like. No equipment for kinder-garten, but songs, poetry, games, keep clean, run and play outdoors— but mostly how to live without hurting each other." Then a blurred passage, with names I did not know, names I was sure Lianne had not put in—probably a passage from some other memorized letter—and then, like the clearing of radio reception, Lianne's words came through again, "Jacqui thin. All children thin except those still nursing. They lose weight terribly when weaned. I still nurse Anne-Marie. Loveliest baby. Fair, like Jean-Jacques' family. Beautiful expression in blue eyes. Everyone speaks about this. If only I have milk enough to keep on nursing her."

One item in this message never would have passed the Censor, if she had tried to write it on one of the prisoner-of-war cards. "Man escaped from *Oflag* where J. J. is, hiding in village here. I have talked with him. I touched a man who had seen my husband. He said he would have cut his throat without J. J.'s help and example."

A last paragraph, a long one, alas, so badly written, so blurred on the too-thin paper that I could make out almost nothing of it:—

something about a photograph of the baby having been taken by a relief worker from a neutral country.

No signature. None was needed.

No other letter ever came through. Only the widely spaced-out, telegraph-short messages on official cards. "Hoping every day to see J. J. come in. He is soon to be released. Jacqui is thin. Still nursing Anne-Marie. Kindergarten not so full."

"Many children too weak for kindergarten. Jacqui very thin. Have had official word to expect J. J. soon. Have you received photograph of baby?"

Then one in which not even the twenty-five words were used. "Have weaned Anne-Marie. I had no more milk for her."

That was an open wound from which the blood gushed out as I read. "I had no more milk for her." Misery! Misery! My heart broke with the young mother's, I laid my old-woman's hand in horrified pity on the thin, drying, empty breast, with her I was shamed by the hungry baby.

After that, the short messages were mostly about Jean-Jacques' release and return to France. Over and over this seemed about to happen. "Two weeks ago card from J. J. with news they hear the order for their return has come in. They must be on their way now."

"Intense suspense. Every time the door opens, I think it is J. J. Anne-Marie does not grow. Very few children in kindergarten. Jacqui good."

Then, astounding, incredible—a cablegram delivered at my door. The yellow envelope, just as though there were no war. I cried out, "From France? Did you say a cablegram from *France?* Why, I thought they were not allowed." I tore it open. I was shaken to the heart by the naïve idea that Lianne had been allowed "By Order" to let me know that her husband was released, was with her.

LITTLE ANNE-MARIE DIED LAST NIGHT. NO SUFFERING. FADED AWAY.

Later that day, in answer to my rage of pain, of astonishment, of stupefaction, someone told me, "Oh, yes, hadn't you heard—cablegrams from France which announce a death are allowed by the Germans."

Silence. Silence. Silence.

Months later a battered envelope came in, postmarked from some undecipherable place in Africa. It had been addressed to me in Lianne's own handwriting. No letter in it. Only a small snapshot of

a baby's head, fair, with a great candid rounded forehead, and innocent wide eyes. This came four months after the baby died.

Silence. Silence.

Then I heard at last. Not from Lianne. From Jean-Jacques. At
second hand. No, at third hand. A Swedish war-relief worker (Sweden
was a neutral country) who had been in France passed through the
United States. He had not seen Jean-Jacques, but he had been in close
and continued secret contact with a Frenchman, an escaped prisoner,
hiding in France. This man had promised Jean-Jacques that if he did
make that escape from the boxcar, and ever met an American, he
would try to get word to the godmother of Bergeron's wife.

My Swedish informant told me in such detail that, almost at once,
I broke my tense listening, to ask him wonderingly how the escaped
French prisoner happened to talk at length—how had they had time,
wherever had they found a place safe enough to talk where they were
sure of no enemy ears? He told me, "The man was still frightfully
shaken. I could see that. Everything we saw, or did, reminded him of
those days in the boxcar. He told me about them over and over. They
were just behind him you see. He still could think of nothing else.
And every time he spoke of it, some new detail would come out. He
was no peasant, you see, wordless in pain. He was a skilled scientist, a
professionally trained laboratory worker in chemistry—and, like all
educated French people, highly cultivated too. He had plenty of words
at his command. I think now he would have gone insane if he hadn't
been able to tell it all."

I asked again how they had time. And the place?

The worker from Sweden told me, "We were part of a group helping people marked down by the Gestapo but not yet caught, to escape
over the Pyrenees. We waited, the two of us, night after night, for
months, in a shepherd's abandoned hut, at the end of a mountain
path. When we heard the first sounds of an escaping party, we went
out to guide them over the hidden twisting way through the rocks
of the pass, into Spain.

"They were never there before midnight. Often, if there were old
people or children among them, much later. Some nights no one came
at all. We had time enough, we two, and nothing else to do but talk.
No light, of course, in the hut. We were safe enough. No listeners
there. We could say what we pleased. I could ask all the questions
I wished. I heard his story over and over, till I could tell it myself."

II

He often began his story by saying wonderingly that he probably would never know why he had been put with those in the boxcar. They were not the ones who had been with him the preceding two years of his prison life. He had never seen one of them before.

Perhaps the reason was only that there had been room—if you could call it room—for one more. Perhaps when he was taken from his *Oflag*, the official intention had been to have him shot as a reprisal for something done somewhere else. There were always reprisals of this kind—no connection with the men shot. Then, perhaps—as he puzzled it out—perhaps in the jungle-growth of orders and counterorders in every prison office, someone might have picked up the wrong *dossier* from a desk, got an order for disposing of him, meant for another prisoner.

All he knew was that he and twenty others had been taken away from their prison in a closed truck. When it halted and they were herded out, they were beside a railway track. Not in a station. In the open country. He thought the train was a long one. But it was black night. He could see only the boxcar to which he was pushed. He had no idea what happened to the other prisoners with him in the truck. He never saw or heard of one of them again. His brother was among them.

An armed guard unlocked the sliding door to the car, opened it a crack, and two others shoved him in. The door was slammed shut behind him.

He felt that the blackness was full of men, but he did not, not as strongly as usual in prisons, smell them, for there was a sizable opening in the roof of the car down from which poured a current of fresh spring air which diluted the prison stench of unwashed bodies in dirt-encrusted clothes. He could not see the opening in the roof, but as he strained his eyes to get some idea of where he was, he caught a glint of distant stars immeasurably high above them. Nearer, seen through the roof-opening, a small yellowish glow. He knew what that was. A guard's lighted cigarette.

He flung one arm up to shield his face from blows, and tried to get his back against the wall. Prison technique. But the shove which had pushed him in had sent him stumbling several steps from the door, and when he tried to step back, he felt human bodies there.

Then a voice spoke. It was a French voice. It said neutrally, "We are from *Oflag* (he gave the number of the prison camp), confined there since June, 1940. For the last four months we have been told every day that we would be sent back to France. We have been two days and two nights in this car. Of that time it has rolled for about eleven hours. We do not know where we are."

The voice trembled, whispered in his ear, *"We think we are being repatriated."*

He heard the men about him breathe deeply. There was a silence. The voice went on. "My name is Bergeron. High-school teacher of physics. Of the —— Field Artillery Battalion, Will you tell us who you are?"

The newcomer had been in prison camps for two years, was experienced in prison ways, and knew, he said, before the end of the first sentence that the speaker was the man who set the tone for the group. He knew too that he was safe from violence. He drew a long breath, dropped his arm, gave his name, the number of the prison camp he came from, the regiment to which he had belonged, his occupation in civilian life.

The rules of the place were explained to him. There were too many in the car for them all to lie down to sleep at the same time. So they took turns. The sick and crippled ones had twice the lying-down time given to the others. When it was not your turn to lie down, you had your choice of sitting on the floor or standing. The best sitting places were those around the edge where you could lean back against the side walls of the car. These were also shared turn and turn about. So far, the guards on the roof allowed them to talk—at least most of the time. Silence was enforced when, as nearly as they could judge, the train was in or near a railway station, or a town, where their voices might be heard. But where they were allowed to talk freely, as now, they supposed—

"The train is standing on a siding in the midst of the empty country," the newcomer broke in to tell them.

"Yes, we had guessed that." Bergeron's voice went on explaining the organization of the day. "One of us is a priest. There are morning and evening prayers in one of the corners of the car. No talking by others at that time. One of us was a medical student. He does what he can for our sick and gives a health inspection each morning. Four buckets make up the sanitary arrangements for forty men. With covers," said the voice, ironically. "They are, you know, a very cleanly nation. These buckets are emptied each day. After dark, four of us, each one roped to a guard and carrying a spade, carry them out, dig a hole and empty them. They are never washed out, there is no water for that. Only one cupful for each man, night and morning."

"*Roped?*" the newcomer had asked quickly.

"Roped."

"And did you say '*a spade*'?"

There was a silence. He felt the men move closer to him. Then Bergeron's low voice said—and now it was not quietly firm, it was rough, agitated, anxious, "You understand—didn't you hear me?— *we think we are being repatriated*—on our way home! Our release will be, of course, conditional on absolute obedience to rules. There must be no . . . no . . ."

The newcomer hastily assured the invisible men around him that he understood. There would be no . . .

Towards the last of this talk the train had begun to move again. He had to raise his voice to make his pledge heard above the clatter of the freight car wheels. There was a muffled stirring as of animals at night in a barn. They sat down as best they could. Someone near him coughed rackingly, and from the other end of the car came an echoing series of other dreadful, deep coughs. Tuberculosis, he thought, forebodingly. He was given one of the favored places, where he could lean his head against the wall. As he relaxed against it, he said gratefully to the darkness, "Thanks."

"It is your turn," explained Bergeron's voice.

My Swedish informant had been speaking as tensely as I had been listening. To hear this in Vermont was incredible!

He shifted his position, drew a breath, went on, "The French prisoner did not, of course, tell it to me, up there in the shepherd's hut, as I am now telling it to you, all in one piece. But it ended by coming together in my mind, because I heard it so many times. I came to know just what would remind him of one or another part of it. Dawn for instance. How many dawns did we see together! He never saw the blackness fade to gray without telling me over again about the first dawn in the boxcar."

It was like this, he would say. First I noticed that over our heads the open hatchway was gray. I looked up at it. And when I looked down it was light enough in the car to see the men. There was no surprise for me in what I saw. I had known what they would be. For two years I had been with men like that, gray-faced, thin, their clothes faded, stained, patched, ragged, a stubble of beard on their sunken cheeks. They were sitting or lying down. The bare boards of the floor passed on to their bony frames every jar of the freight car. Yet many, even of those who were sitting up, were asleep, sagging to and fro, their heads fallen on their chests. Those who were awake braced themselves against the incessant shaking by locking their hands around their knees. A rank stench came from the four buckets at the end of the car.

Yet when my eye caught that of Bergeron—I knew at once which one he was, a gaunt, big-boned man, his eyes gray-blue—he saluted me from across the car with a nod, and a brisk wave of the hand. He was standing, wide awake, an alertness in his face very different from the sodden dullness of the usual prisoner's expression. For the moment he said nothing, not to disturb those who slept. But later, when those who had been sitting through the night were on their feet, yawning and stretching their stiff arms and legs, Bergeron came over to me to say, "One more night gone. Every one brings us nearer home—we hope." I noticed that no sour snarl rose from the other men such as, in the prison I had come from, had instantly quenched any attempt to speak cheerfully. All of them, even the sick ones, hoped.

The day began. Those which followed were exactly like it. The only variation was the color of the sky up there above the hatchway, which we saw beyond the rifle butt and the gray-green trousers of the guard seated in a sort of sentry box on the roof. Sometimes that bit of sky was blue and sun-flooded. Sometimes it was covered with lowering gray clouds. Once in a while the slow rattling car jolted for a time under green tree branches. When this happened, every man clutched at his neighbor and pointed to make him look up. Even the sleepers, by rule never to be disturbed during their turn to lie down, wanted to be awakened to see this. Sometimes rain poured in streams down through the hatchway. This, as far as possible, we used hastily as it fell, to clean the skin on our faces and hands and feet. It was, I saw, not only the fresh air from the roof-opening which lessened the fetid prison smell. Sometimes a square patch of sunshine lay on the floor, actual bright sunshine. It was big enough for several men to sit in. This privilege was shared in turn by all, with a double turn for the sick. Some of them, at the suggestion of the medical student, took off their clothes when their turn came for the sun bath. The white bodies they showed then were thin, but not strengthless except for the six or seven sick and crippled men.

This was probably because of the twice-a-day exercises. These were compulsory. As Bergeron had explained, the prisoners were never let out of the crowded car (except for the nightly sortie of the four who emptied the soil-buckets). They would all have been half paralyzed if they had not taken some exercise. These lasted half an hour, twice a day, for each of the three squads into which the men were divided.

There was no room to take more than three or four steps in what space could be cleared. But for their first steps on French ground they were determined to be able at least to walk out of the car steadily on their own feet. The coats were laid down—the thin, threadbare coats—to soften a little the boards of the floor, and the men, by fours, rolled, stretched, kicked, did somersaults (those who could), walked on their hands, or did simple bending exercises, rhythmic, taken in time to an accompaniment of folk-tunes whistled by the spectators. A squad of helpers, directed by the medical student, massaged the sick, carefully flexed and gently moved the arms and legs—what there was left of them—of the crippled.

The food was—well, everyone now knows what prison food is—a little bread, often moldy, floating in what looked and tasted like tepid dishwater. Sometimes a few "eyes" of grease floated on the water. The prisoners, especially the sick ones, mortally dreaded the coming of these rations. But they were so famished that when the sickening food appeared, there was a deadly moment when they became starving animals. The frantic reflex instinct to fight for all they could grab was barely held in check by the rigid self-discipline of the group. At such instants, when the ground-swell of bestiality rose under our feet, Bergeron stopped it, "Now! Now! Turn and turn about is the rule here."

I had not meant to interrupt the narrative of the Swedish relief worker, not even for one question, but at this my wonder broke out. "Is it often that such rigid group discipline . . . ?"

"I asked the French prisoner that question too," said my informant. "It seemed to me a natural one. He scorned me for not knowing the answer. 'That depends, of course,' he said impatiently, 'on who sets the tone. When those who do are like animals, the group is like a pack of wolves—or hogs. When the leaders are human— Why should it be different with prisoners than with other men? It's always like that, everywhere.'

"What they liked best, the Frenchman told me, were the long talks between those who were awake, sitting or crouched near each other."

This talk was personal, casual, wandering, just what came into our heads. Mostly it was of what we would do when we were at home again. As the car jolted slowly on, most of us were surer and surer we were being repatriated. Not all. The coughing, sweating sick did not hope to live till they were free in France. Several older men, of the kind who always believe the worst, insisted that we were being taken to the Russian front, where we would be forced into front-line fighting. They said the trip was taking far too long for a short journey into France from Germany. This point was continuously argued. A younger man, a university undergraduate, had figured out from the stars wheeling over the open hatchway that the general direction of their course was south. But it was impossible to make any real calculations, because the car stood motionless more often and for longer periods than it moved.

Two or three times we could not keep ourselves from talking over, in the lowest of our whispers, what the chances of escape would have been—if we had not been going home anyhow—for at least one or two of us, during the night sorties with the soil-buckets. Those ropes. A spade in each prisoner's hand. A spade has a sharp edge. The darkness. Quick, concerted action. Of course it could have been done only once, would have meant a chance for only one or two men. Reprisals for the others. But it would have been worth it. But this whispered talk was idle speculation. As it was, it would only spoil the chances for all of us.

Mostly we talked as though we were certain that we were being taken back to France. Had we not been told over and over at the *Oflag* that any day we were likely to start home? Had not the *Oflag* been full of widespread rumors of this or that astute way in which *Le Maréchal* would secure the return of the prisoners? Most of us pushed away our doubts and sent our hearts flying forward.

A favorite subject for these rambling talks was the manner of each one's home-coming as it would be if he could have that as he wished. One man said he would send word ahead, and have all the village at the station to meet his train. With the band. He had played the piccolo in the band. Another young fellow would not let even his parents know he was coming. He planned to take the night train to his town, slip away from the station by the back road, turn up the lane to his father's barn, step in, take a milking stool, and be there, milking, his head dug against the cow's flank, when his father opened the door and came in for the morning chores. The farm boy's dream description made us all, even the city gutter-sparrows, even the death-struck sick, feel against our cheeks that warm, living, hairy flank, and smell the barn odors—straw, milk, earth, manure, fresh hay.

Another man said, "All I want is to get drunk—one long, glorious, blind drunk after another. It would be like heaven to be drunk-sick again."

"A hot bath—a hot bath a week long!"

"Girls! Girls! Girls!"

"The heel of a loaf of real white bread, French bread, and a whole Brie cheese . . ."

The young priest saw himself walking up the steps to his country church, and into its incense-fragrant dimness. A mechanic murmured, "To stand in my own garage again, to lift the hood of a car brought in for repairs, to lean over the engine, listening to hear what's the matter with it."

A young research worker from the botanical laboratory of the Jardin des Plantes tried to make us feel the brimming peace it would bring him to lean once more over his high-powered microscope. At this, someone said with the acrid savagery that was like the usual prison-camp talk, "Boy, you won't find any high-powered microscope there. It'll be in Berlin. Four hundred million francs a day drained off from France to pay for the occupation."

But Bergeron had quickly broken in on this bitterness to describe yet once more what his own home-coming would be. Not the little house which had been his home. That house, like all that town, was now nothing but bombed, burned rubble-cinder. But he would be going home, although to a wholly unknown town, because his wife and little son were there. He knew from his wife's nine-word messages through the prisoner-of-war service, just where he would find her—with thirty or forty children in a kindergarten improvised in an old school building, crammed with refugees.

He described over and over just how he would open the door to that crowded room. Quietly. He would not knock. Then he would stand there, looking at his wife and his little boy and those French children she had been taking care of, keeping them decent, saving them from becoming animals. At first she would think the door had been opened by one of the children. She would not turn her head. And then . . .

Bergeron talked a great deal about his wife. He was proud of her.

All the men were unnerved with the incredible prospect of seeing our own again after two years of prison, none more so—in spite of his self-control—than Bergeron. Whenever he spoke of his family his voice roughened and shook, and sometimes it broke.

One of the other men explained to me, one day, in a whisper, that Bergeron had a baby daughter born seven months after the battle of Flanders. He had been taken with an almost dreadful affection for this child of his he had not seen—his wife wrote the baby was like an angel—but of course all women thought that. Night after night the man in prison had waked up wild with a joyful dream that he had held his little daughter in his arms. When his wife had to wean her, he had worried frantically lest she suffer from the coarse, scanty food. Madame Bergeron had nursed her as long as she had any milk. His fellow prisoners had heard all about this again and again, till no one but other family men would listen.

When the rumor began to circulate back in the *Oflag*, that the prisoners were to be sent back to France, Bergeron had almost gone off his head at the thought he would see his baby girl. But three weeks before they had been put on the train, a telegram had been handed him—yes, a telegram!—saying the little girl had died.

He had been broken by this. Could not eat, could not sleep, never spoke, kept his hands clasped over his eyes. His fellow prisoners had thought he would die. He seemed dying before their eyes. But ten days before their departure he had received from his wife one of those brief, officially-allowed messages, "I promise you I will be here with Jacqui when you come back to me."

Then he rose and lived again.

He used to tell us in those long rambling talks in the boxcar, "I always knew my wife was lovely. I never knew she was so strong." He used to say, "My wife does honor to humanity, by her work with those homeless children. It is called a kindergarten. What it really is, is teaching French children they can live together like civilized beings. Not like wild beasts. She upholds human dignity, my wife does." He often said, too, "She would not be allowed 'By Order' to send in the message, in plain words, 'Never give up!' but really in everything she writes me that is what I have heard her say all these two years."

No matter how deep we were in these memories, in these forward-looking hopes, Bergeron never forgot, when the time came, to get stiffly to his feet, motioning those with him to rise, letting the waiting ones move to the better places where they could lean back against the wall.

Then one night the car came to a halt and did not go on. For two days it was stationary. The sky seen through the hatchway was gray-blue, with small clouds. Several men said it looked like a French sky. A graybeard with one arm amputated, answered grimly, "Or Russian."

The guards on the train became bored with nothing to do. We could hear them calling idly back and forth to each other. Sometimes the gray-green trousered legs of the guard at the hatchway disappeared for a few moments. We could hear him clambering down the ladder at the end, and then a sound of several men talking and laughing together, as if he had been joined by others from the other cars. Sometimes there was the measured sound of counting—*ein, zwei, drei*—the numbers pronounced in louder and louder voices, ending in a great burst of laughing and hooting, as though some kind of game were being played, watched from above by those who stayed on guard on the roof, rifles cocked.

During those two days inside the boxcar, we went through the routine planned to keep us alive till we were freed. We ate the dreadful daily slop; we exercised; we played what finger and guessing games we could invent; with no tools but our cups, which were examined and checked every time the food was handed in, we could construct nothing. We took turns at lying down. We said our prayers or were respectfully silent when others prayed. We told the same stories over and over. We imagined again what we would do on the day we reached home. There were occasional brief outbursts of rough, wild, obscene talk when somebody's nerves snapped under the suspense. But we crowded close around the man who had broken, to steady him, to keep the guards from knowing that a Frenchman had given way. A few of the more thoughtful men talked sometimes with Bergeron about plans for serving their country and the country's youth more creatively than ever before—once they were free to do something creative. We ground our teeth in our struggle to remain human.

Over and over someone would say, in a hope that ebbed and rose as we breathed, "It *may* be only a little longer now . . ."

Every hour was exactly like the one which preceded it. In that windowless prison how could anything happen to make one hour, one minute, one day different from another?

And then one of the men darted from the other end of the car with the quick, astonished step of a man to whom something has happened. He put his lips to Bergeron's ear, whispered and turned back to where he had been. With a startled look, Bergeron sprang up and followed him.

In a rush we were all on our feet. There was nothing different to be seen. There could be nothing different. We knew that. But we were like stampeded cattle. The break in the monotony beat on our taut nerves as if a trumpet had shouted, as if—we did not know what, only that one among us had moved swiftly as if—incredibly—something had happened.

Crowding, pushing, shoving to see what it was, the stronger ones using their fists to be ahead of the others, we were a mob. Dehumanized. Bergeron turned, held us back with an upraised arm. "Turn and turn about is the rule here," he said sharply, in a phrase now so thickly encrusted with associations of order that we halted. With a cautious glance up at the guard's legs and the rifle butt at the hatchway's edge, he said, "Before I take another step, I will tell the man nearest me what Carrière said to me. He will tell the next man. And so on. Till we all know. It may be nothing, you understand. Nothing. If it is anything, we will all share it alike. Don't let the guard suspect anything."

He leaned to whisper in the ear of the nearest man, who turned to whisper to the next one. When it came to me, I heard, "Carrière thinks he has found a knot in one of the planks of the wall, loose enough to work out of its hole. He came to ask Bergeron if he thought it safe to do this. We might look through it and see something. But it may be a trap. A guard may be standing just outside. Or the car may be double-planked. In that case the hole would not go through to the outside." I passed this on to the man back of me. We were all on our feet, craning our necks, even those whose turn it was to lie down.

We watched Carrière stooping, the fingers of one hand picking slowly, delicately, at a place on the plank siding. After a time, he looked around at Bergeron, asking a question with upraised eyebrows. Bergeron assumed the responsibility, gave a nod of assent. Carrière brought his fingers together and slowly drew out the knot. The sunlight shone through in a long beam. The hole was as big as a man's thumb. In the light from it Carrière's prison-pale face was chalky. He looked at Bergeron for orders.

Bergeron turned his face to glance up at the hatchway. At the end of the car where we were, we could not be seen by the guard unless he stooped his head down through the hole. There was not a sound inside the car. Bergeron motioned the men to make a screen with their standing bodies around Carrière, said to him, all but soundlessly, "You were the one who found it. The first look belongs to you."

Carrière stooped and put his eye to the hole. The silence in the car was so entire that we could hear the guard on the roof clear his throat raucously, and spit. Our hearts rose at the casual, ugly, unself-conscious sound. It could mean nothing but that there was no guard waiting ouside. We gazed tensely at the back of Carrière's bent head. Would he never look away? What was he seeing?

Then he stood up and turned towards us. Tears were streaming down his cheeks. His mouth worked. He put his bent arm up before his eyes and stumbled away to lean against the wall, his shoulders shaking.

"Your turn next, Fayolle," said Bergeron steadily, motioning to the man who stood nearest.

So all of us looked in turn. I had not liked Carrière crying. It made me sick to see one of us, who had endured so much, in tears. But every man was half-blinded by tears when he turned away to let the next one see. I was resolved to be calm.

But when my turn came, what I saw—oh! it was France I saw there under the gentle French sunshine—a narrow green meadow; next to it, on one side, a rolling, half-plowed brown field, two great work horses, nodding their heads as they stepped strongly forward throwing their shoulders against the tall collars; on the other side, a long, straight, white road bordered with slim poplar trees leading to a gray village in the distance, with red roofs and a white church tower; on the road a farm cart with two high wheels slowly approaching, the metal trimming on the harness winking in the sun; between the railroad tracks and the meadow, a slow-moving, dark-green little brook bordered with silvery pollarded willows—the earth, the grass, the water, the very sky of home. . . .

Bergeron was the last one to take his turn to look at France. We watched his tall form stoop, we gazed at the back of his head, seeing through it what he saw. We stood in a long orderly file beside him, eager for our second look at France.

When Bergeron stood up and turned towards us, his face was white. His lips moved. In a rhythm we all knew as we knew our own pulses, his hand began to beat time. He began to sing in a low clear voice—we knew the words—we sang with him in the same hushed voice: *"Amour sacré de la patrie"*—and *"Liberté, Liberté chérie—"*

"Nicht singen!" shouted the astounded guard, shoving the barrel of his gun down the hatchway.

We gave a convulsive start. We had not known we were singing. We were like men wakened roughly from a dream, who for an instant do not know where they are. Bergeron motioned for silence. He looked as startled as we. He, too, had not known what he was doing. For an instant, even he had forgotten the tense self-control which had focused all our faculties on one thing—to do nothing which might risk losing our release. . . .

Carrière, who had been stooping at the knot-hole to look, stood up now, and again whispered into Bergeron's ear. Bergeron whirled, stooped, looked out through our tiny window, and continued looking. Carrière tiptoed around our circle, telling us in a whisper, "I was looking out while you were singing. An old man sitting in that cart beside the driver stood up and looked this way, as if he had caught the sound."

We were terribly affected by this. To have made ourselves known to a fellow countryman, not a prisoner, still living on the sacred soil! But Bergeron turned back to us, shaking his head. "It couldn't have been," he said. "We were singing too low. Nobody could have heard. They were still a long way off. I watched closely as the cart jogged by. Neither of them so much as turned his head this way."

For the next day there was not one hour of the twenty-four when one of us was not feasting his eyes on the look of France. Even at night, someone was watching the golden lamps in the village, or the French stars in the French sky. The car had now stood still for three days.

Small as the hole was, it was possible, by shifting one's position a little lower, higher, to one side or the other, to take in perhaps a quarter of what we could have seen through a window. The far end of the car where the hole was, and where one man after another was perpetually stooping to look out, was not visible to the guard up at the edge of the open hatchway. We always kept a cluster of sitting or lounging men directly under him. Of course, twice a day when the slop food was brought in, the gnarled wood-brown knot, preciously preserved, was carefully inserted into the hole. Since only one could look at a time, we shared with the others whatever we had seen. "An old woman pushing a wheelbarrow was going along the road when I was looking out. The way her black headkerchief was tied made me think we are in the *Ile de France.*" Yes, the others who had seen that stooped old figure agreed that the kerchief's twist did look like the center of France. "My grandmother tied her kerchief on with that knot at the back."

The first morning the watcher at the hole whispered, "School children," and stood back to let the fathers among us take quick looks at five little boys and girls in black aprons, clattering along in their wooden-soled *galoches,* their leather school bags swinging. There was something special about the way those children stepped, set their feet down on the ground—we felt it in our own feet. They were our children; we were again children clattering to school along a white, straight, poplar-shaded road. Thus to possess with our eyes the longed-for home scenes swept us beyond what we knew was real. We were not prisoners; we were out there, walking freely on the French road as the early sun sent long rays down through the thin mist.

An hour or so after they had passed, something exciting began. An old workingman, very shabby, his shoulders stooped under a faded blue blouse, carrying a long-handled spade, plodded his way slowly out from the village along the road. When he reached the sagging, weather-beaten gate to the meadow just across the little stream from the tracks, he stopped and pushed it open. How many times had each of us in imagination laid his hands on that gate to push it open! We touched, handled, smelled, felt everything we looked at, as we pored over that piece of our home country, framed in the knot-hole. Each one of us, as we took our turn to look, told what he did. "He is going into the meadow. He has shut the gate behind him. He has stopped, as if to get his breath. He has his lunch with him in a package. He has put his package down on a stone. He is going to stay all day. He has begun to spade. To turn under the sod."

At first, we wondered at anyone, let alone an old man, spading away in the open country, in a meadow. That was land for plowing, not spading. The guards evidently wondered, too. Presently, one of our watchers at the knot-hole reported that a green-gray uniform went out from the train towards the meadow, stood on the side of the little stream, and shouted something across to the old workman. The words were French, but the heavy voice sounded as writing looks which is done with a coarse pen in thick ink. But as we listened tensely, holding our breaths, we heard another voice—purely French, the clearly spoken vowels, the resonant consonants, the rise and fall of the familiar speech tune as accurate to our ears as, to our eyes, the tracing of fine lines made with a drawing pen. The sound of it was music, poetry. It took an instant for us to hear the prosaic words it uttered. "Potatoes," it explained. He was preparing a patch of ground to plant potatoes.

The watcher of the moment whispered back to us, "The guard isn't satisfied. He keeps standing there. He is going to order the old man off."

But he did not. He stood uncertainly for a while, calling something back to—we supposed—another guard on the train. There was an exchange of hoarse German. A moment of suspense. Finally, so our watcher reported, the guard came back, leaving the old man there. A long breath of relief went around the car. "What is he doing now?" we asked the watcher.

"He has gone back to spading. He is shaking out the earth from a sod." We felt, sifting through our own hands, the soil of our motherland. We smelled the fresh healing fragrance of earth newly turned over.

All day we shared what that free man did out there under the gray-blue home sky. Through that hole, which any one of us could have closed by putting a thumb into it, we flung our hearts, our senses, our souls. We stooped stiffly with the old man, we slowly spaded with him. With him we turned under what was alive, so that that something of more value could take root and grow. We stopped with him to rest, sitting down on a stone sucking a cold pipe meditatively. He evidently had no more tobacco than we. The stone happened to be so placed that when he dropped down on it to rest, he faced the railway track. Several times that day we saw his lifted glance run along the roofs of the cars indifferently, and drop from there to the ground, to his work, to his shoes, to the grass. He leaned to knot a loose shoe-lace, to finger a clod, he sat up again, looking off towards the horizon. He yawned, took his dead pipe out of his mouth, lifted his faded blouse to stuff it into his pocket, took up his spade again.

He did not get on very fast with his job, it seemed to some of us who knew about farm work. The farmer's son, every time it was his turn to look, whispered to us, "Listen, fellows, I don't believe he *is* a workingman. I never saw anybody try to spade with that kind of a push from the shoulders. You do it with your back and legs."

At the end of the first day, he had spaded only one strip across that narrow field. But he was old. How old? We all made a guess. Sixty, perhaps? Probably had served as Territorial in the last war. "I've got an uncle sixty-one, looks about like that."

The next morning began the fourth day since the car had stirred. Bergeron had insisted it would do no good to question the guards, since they probably knew no more than we. But on this fourth day he was overborne, and a man who spoke a little German was delegated to ask the guards who brought in the morning pail of food, "Why? Why so long waiting?"

The guards looked at each other, hesitated, said nothing, turned back to the door. The older one went out. The younger one went after him, stopped, said in broken French, "Not know. Hear that—"

The older guard shouted at him angrily. He stepped out and began to slide the door shut. Through the crack he called a word or two more, hurriedly. But strain our ears as we might, we could make nothing out of them. His accent was too heavy. They sounded like nothing we had ever heard.

All that they told us was that some reason for the delay existed.

We did not even try to guess what it might be. We sat motionless, sickened by frustration, by the intimate humiliation of total helplessness. Silently we looked down fixedly at the pale brown liquid in our tin cups, the drops of grease congealing as it cooled.

Bergeron lifted his cup and began resolutely to eat. But he was breathing very fast as though he had been running with all his might. He swallowed down what was in his cup and got up. "If no one else wants a turn at our lookout, I'll take mine now," he said.

He stooped to look. Over his shoulder he whispered, "The old man is certainly looking at our car. He *keeps* looking. He darts his eyes up and down the train. Perhaps the guards are all down on the ground on the other side playing that gambling game." We looked up at the hatchway. Our guard was not there. A whisper ran about from mouth to mouth, "Make him a signal! Let the old man know—" One of us went close to Bergeron and whispered this in his ear. He looked up at the hatchway, saw that it was still empty, nodded to us, put his thumb through the knot-hole, and slowly turned it up. Everyone's heart began to pound. Bergeron withdrew his thumb, stooped again to look and gave a great start. "The old man is running this way," he reported on a sharply indrawn whisper.

There was an instant in which we did not breathe. Then Bergeron let his breath out in a gasp and murmured, "He has turned back. He evidently saw a guard. He has picked up his spade. He has gone on working."

We pulled Bergeron back to whisper urgently, utterly at a loss, "What does it mean—what do you think—?" His gaze was darkly inturned in thought. "Perhaps he *did* hear us singing. And he must have seen my signal," he said. And then, shaking his head, "But there is nothing he—nothing anyone can do. He will be shot if he tries."

"Tries what?"

He lifted his shoulders. "There is nothing he could even try."

After that, we never took our eyes from the old man in the blouse. Late that day the watcher at the hole reported, "He has taken out a white handkerchief. He is unfolding it to wipe his forehead."

"A *white* handkerchief?" went rapidly around among us. "That's no workingman."

But what—what—? We could not think what.

We only never took our eyes from him. . . .

Late that afternoon, our guard was again not at the hatchway. We had for some time heard the thick voices talking and laughing together down on the side of the train away from the road. Then, as sometimes happened, the brawling sound of a quarrel broke out. One of the players had perhaps cheated. We had heard them before this, shouting angrily at each other. Now the noise was louder than usual, more voices joining in, as if the guards still up on the cars were leaning over the side and taking part in the row.

"Bergeron! Quick! Here!" the man at the knot-hole called in a loud whisper. Bergeron sprang to the hole. He saw the old man in the field racing towards us. He had something white in his hand. He sprang across the little brook. Looking fearfully up and down the train, he darted to our car. A paper, rolled up, was pushed through the knot-hole. We rushed to see.

Bergeron unrolled it, and held it up to the ten or eleven men near enough to read it. A question in one word, "French?" Bergeron scribbled on it *"French"* and thrust it back. The man outside darted a look up and down the train, took the paper and wrote feverishly. The tiny white roll came back through the hole. Bergeron held it up. On it was written, "Courage, Faith, Hope."

The thronging men leaning over Captain Bergeron's shoulder read the words at a glance, and motioned him fiercely to send an answer. "Tell him—" "Say that we—" Their pulses pounded with the answer that must go back, to say what must be said. "Tell him that we—" There were no words.

Bergeron was stretched on the rack with them, brains and hands paralyzed by the longing to speak, by the need for haste. The pencil in his hand hung suspended over the paper while his eyes plunged into those around him.

From somewhere in the car, a voice—we never knew whose—perhaps several at once—called hoarsely, *"Never give up."*

Bergeron's hand set the three words down all in one rushing line and pushed the paper through the hole.

He saw the old man read it at a glance, look up, his face convulsively working. He nodded over and over—his lips said soundlessly, "Yes, yes, yes, yes." He thrust the paper in under his blouse, and clasped one hand closely on it over his heart. With his other arm he made a long gesture towards the town. He was gone, racing back to the field.

The brawling voices were dying down. We heard our own guard climb up to the roof of our car. We saw his legs and the rifle butt. He hawked and spat. We sank back limply. The man at the knot-hole reported in a whisper, "The old man is sitting on the stone. He keeps his left hand pressed closely over his heart. He is looking straight at us." We took hasty turns to meet that long gaze.

When twilight began to fall he went away towards the village, taking his spade with him.

The next morning before dawn the man who was at the lookout said, *"Pst! Pst!"* Several of us went at once. "It seems to me I make out people walking by on the road," he said.

We all looked in turn. Yes, people were certainly passing there, dim shapes at first, which might be anything. As the light grew stronger, the shapes became men—old men—and women, boys, more women— children, big girls, little boys, small girls. They did not come together or abreast. Sometimes singly, sometimes by family groups, sometimes two or three. At times, the road would be quite empty all the long way to the gray houses with the red roofs. Then, from the end of the village street we would see a group, or a couple of people coming out towards us. They did not look—not more than once—at the train. They only walked by on the long white road bordered with poplars. As they approached the train, each one looked at it once, turning his full face towards us. Then as they passed on, everyone pressed his hand over his heart and held it there. Even the little children.

Not one of us needed to be told what it meant. The old man had answered "Yes!" to our message. He had understood it. He had pointed to the town. He had meant he would tell them. They were telling us that they understood, that they would not forget.

We saw that our guard stood up several times as if to look. We heard the others shouting questions back and forth. But there was nothing for them to see except groups of quiet people—men, women, children, blacksmith, priest, shopkeeper, fine lady, old farmers— quietly walking along a dusty white country road, their eyes straight before them. They were still passing when twilight thickened so that our eyes could no longer see them.

None of us slept much that night. It would have been a waste of the first moments of happiness we had known for two years. We talked in low tones, each one adding to the common store what he had seen of the procession. "There was a little girl with curly fair hair exactly like my Claire. The old blacksmith with the leather apron—my grand-father looked like that." "The tall dark-haired good-looking girl in the blue dress—one of my girls at home walks just as she did."

Would we see them again, we wondered, the next day when dawn came?

About midnight the door to the car slid open a little—yet it was long before the time for food. And hours before, the soil-buckets had been emptied. A flashlight played on us, sitting there, silent, our hands clasped around our knees. We were counted. The alien voices mechanically pronounced the numbers, *ein, zwei, drei*— The alien hand turned the flashlight on the paper and made a check mark.

The flashlight was held to another paper. The voice began to read aloud rapidly, rattling off the words drily. But they were not of the alien tongue. They were our men. We heard the words, "Sabotage.

Reprisals." The door slid shut with a bang. In the smothering black stillness, the lock rattled loudly.

We were being sent back.

We were being sent back to prison.

We were being sent back to Germany.

One of us began to shriek out curses as if he had been stabbed. His screams stopped with a strangling choke. Bergeron had sprung upon him. Bergeron's voice sounded out in a cry as sharp as if he also had been stabbed—"Order! No screaming. We are men!"

We heard the other man struggling frantically to breathe through the hand pressed over his mouth. We heard Bergeron, too, fighting to breathe, when, after an instant, his voice came—breaking, dying, as he tried with long gasps to draw air into his lungs. "We have pledged ourselves to—" he said, "all those people. We gave them our promise. They promised us—" He gave up trying to speak. We heard his panting—loud, rough, strangling, as if he had been struck a terrible blow in the chest. Or was it our own struggle to breathe that we heard?

When he spoke again, his voice was under control. "We have been home," he said. "We have been home to France. We have made a promise to France."

The car jolted to and fro and began to roll slowly. On each side of me in the dark, I could hear groaning. But not loud. . . .

After a long time, Bergeron's voice said in my ear, in a faint whisper, "Now about those ropes—"

Memorial Day

May 30, −1913

&§Anyone watching from the cemetery could have seen the distant little cloud of dust in the valley which announced the approach of the first car. But no one was watching from the cemetery. A thrush was absorbed in his liquid song. The dead lay quiet. The grass and trees and all things living thrust their roots deeper into the warm moist earth and lifted their heads towards the spring sun. There was no one among the living or the dead who cared in the least that the first Model T Ford was approaching from the village.

Presently it appeared, and ground slowly in low speed up the steep sandy road, a small American flag standing stiffly at attention beside its radiator cap. Similar flags lay flat on the wreaths of flowers held by the little country boys who filled the car to the brim. When it stopped at the gate of the cemetery, the little boys spilled themselves out. Like the grass and trees and other growing things, they were quivering and glistening with vitality. Their small bodies were clad in their Sunday clothes, their hair was smoothly brushed back from their round, well-soaped faces. Everyone wore a necktie. Everyone carried on his arm a wreath to decorate a soldier's grave.

"Now, don't go and get everything mixed up, the way the boys did last year," cautioned the middle-aged citizen who was driving their car. He was chairman of the committee for the annual ceremony of remembering the dead soldiers, and responsible for the careful spending of the small sum voted at Town Meeting for this purpose. He slammed the car into reverse to turn it around, calling out, "Keep your minds on what you're doing." The car was now pointed down-hill ready to return to the valley. He turned off the switch and continued, "Now, boys, *listen* while I tell you what to do. Be sure not to bother with any graves except those that have the G.A.R. standard on them. They're kind of rusty now, but you can make them out if you look sharp. If last year's flag is still left in the socket, take that out, but don't leave it lying around. Put it in your pocket. And then stick in your this-year's flag. But be sure about it. We haven't any flags to waste."

The little boys listened seriously. "Lay your wreath down near the head of each grave," the chairman told them. He had a second thought, "No, lean it against the tombstone. It shows up better there." The little boys nodded. They walked on. It made them feel important to be walking. They were at the age when boys usually skip or trot.

More cars came slowly up the hill. From them more clean-faced little boys with wreaths clambered out. From others, mothers and fathers emerged, extra wreaths over their arms. Like the cleaned-up little boys, they were carefully dressed in holiday clothes, suitable for the beautiful spring weather. Their faces were good-humored and comfortable. In one of the cars sat the elderly minister in black broadcloth, who had come to "say a few words and pronounce the benediction." His hair was white, his pale, broad face had a genial, pleasant expression.

Inside the cemetery there was no dust. It was not thought decorous for cars to roll in over the weedy gravel of those driveways—except for funerals, which were of course serious occasions. Now there were ten or twelve little boys. They walked forward. The smaller ones once in a while gave a skipping hop to keep up with the bigger ones. Their mothers and fathers sauntered beside them, the wreaths over their arms, their eyes dreamily fixed on the quiet valley below, its small white homes peaceful in the sunshine.

When they reached the older part of the cemetery where the grayer, weather-beaten tombstones stood, they separated into groups and began to look for those graves where a limp last-year's flag drooped from the small metal standard.

JOHN HEMINWAY ANDREWS

Died in Camp Fairfax, Virginia

In the Twenty-second Year

of his Life.

A round-cheeked little boy stopped with a wreath at this first grave he saw. He did not read the inscription, although, in spite of many summers' and winters' weathering, it was still legible. He had not been told to read the inscription. He did what he had been told to do, took out of its socket the limp and grizzled flag, leaned over the grave and set his wreath against the tombstone.

Instantly a silent scream burst up from the grave. The first of the soldiers had awakened.

All the year around, they rested quietly in their graves. They had been country men, at home under the open sky. Neither the furious rages of winter nor the heat of the summer suns could disturb their sleep. Year by year, the shroud of their oblivion was thicker and softer. . . . If only little boys could be kept away from their grassy beds . . . little boys with clear eyes and small harmless hands. At the touch of those small hands, the dead men who had been small and harmless little boys themselves awoke in the old agony to what they were trying to forget.

It had been in an army hospital in Camp Fairfax that John Andrews had died in 1863, screaming his heart out while surgeons were amputating his leg without anesthetics. When he awoke, it was always in the midst of that shriek. But now it was at the little boy he screamed to tell him—to let him know—to warn him. He was horrified by the child's rosy calmness, by his awful unawareness. Yet he could never think of words to warn him. He could only shriek silently from his grave, till the trees quivered to it, till the clouds echoed it back, till the thrush was silenced. But none of the little boys ever heard him. Nor did this one.

He looked carefully at the standard to make sure that it had on it the letters the man had told them about—G.A.R. He had no idea what the letters meant. Older people always take for granted that children know. But, unless children are told—in words, or in what they live through—they do not know. And if they have lived through it—it is too late.

Yes, the rusty letters were the right ones, he could see them plainly. He stuffed the dingy old flag into his pocket. It was the first time he had been old enough to be included among the boys who placed wreaths on Decoration Day. He wanted to make no mistake with the flag. Sure that he had it right, he turned away to his father with a gesture which said, "Well, that's *one* disposed of." His father smiled indulgently at his small son's brisk competence.

A little distance away from him was a bigger, older boy, who was already placing his second wreath and flag. He had been quicker about it because this was not his first trip to the cemetery on Decoration Day. He knew what to do. He took the old flag from the standard, set in the new one, and leaned up against the tombstone his wreath of already-drooping lilacs. His mother had told him not to take longer than he need because they were going on a picnic afterwards. Fishing, too. It had turned out lovely weather. As she sorted out the fishing tackle, her little son had heard her say to his father that it certainly was handy, having Decoration Day come after the opening of fishing season.

Under the matted shaggy old grass of the grave he had just decorated lay a dead man who had been very poor and who had gone away to war because he had been offered five hundred dollars to take a rich man's place. With the money he and his young wife had planned to buy a small farm. It would provide a home for his children and his wife, where he could take good care of them all as they grew up. Very dear to him were his three sons, so like this little boy who now bent his round child-face over the old grave. The dead man had not been able to think of any other way to earn so large a sum as five hundred dollars.

He had killed other men because he had been told to, killed and maimed men whom he had never seen before, who had never done anything to him: and then one of them had maimed and killed him. He had died in battle, an expression of astonishment on his face. He had never been very bright and had not at all understood what was happening to him. The last thing he remembered was the unknown face of the unknown man who was killing him, although they had never seen each other before. Death had sealed that stranger's face upon his eyes, so that when, with a start, once a year, he awoke from his sleep, he saw two faces . . . the set, strange features of the man who was driving a bayonet into his side, and a little boy's face, clear and harmless, like the face of one of his own little boys. He had died without a sound, but now as the child leaned upon his breast to set the wreath in place, he broke into a groan.

But no one ever heard him. This little boy brushed his hands together lightly to dust them off, and was about to turn away when he saw a tiny fly buzzing in terror in a spider's web. That was a groan he could hear. He stooped over the helpless, trapped little living victim, broke the threads and freed the small flying creature. It spun up into new life with a joyful, whirring beat of gauzy wings.

At this act of pity, the soldier in his grave groaned "Misery!

Misery!" straining to be heard, till the blades of grass growing over him shook.

The little boy, having correctly placed his wreath and flag, ran down the weedy gravel path to slip his hand into his mother's. Now they could go fishing.

A thin little boy had halted beside another grave. His clothes were threadbare and faded. And not very clean. This was the first year he had been included in the Decoration Day celebration at the Old Burying Ground. He had never been in any cemetery before, and looked around him admiringly at the tombstones; some were plain weather-beaten slabs, some were sort of little elegant playhouses, stone ornaments all around. It was like the village in the valley, he thought, with its many houses—only here so small.

He had seen little—of anything—except his own run-down home. His father was very poor and could not do much for his children. Yet this was not the father's fault. All that he had done was, when he was a very young man, to marry because he pitied and loved her, a pretty young girl with a gentle smile. She was hired girl on the next farm. After they were married, she remained pretty and gentle and he still loved her, but she had turned out to be, as country people say, "not quite all there," and there must have been something amiss with the health of her family. So she never could really take care of the house or the children. Her husband did what in most families the wife did, as well as what in most families the husband and father does. She "forgot things." In the middle of plowing or haymaking, he often left his work and went back to the house to make sure she had not forgotten something important. Of course neither the farming nor the housework was done well and the children were sickly.

But the farmer never told anybody why, because he didn't want to complain of his smiling, gentle wife who was like his oldest child. He didn't want other people to criticize her. So they criticized him.

The little boy knew very well, although no word had ever been spoken to him about this, that his father was looked down on by the neighbors because "things weren't kept up as they should be." The shutters were unpainted, hung first by a hinge and then fell off and lay on the grass to rot. The porch steps had broken boards, which had been broken ever since the little boy could remember. The neighbors said, "Wouldn't you think he'd have gimp enough to—" Their cows got sick, more often than other people's, and sometimes one died. People said, "Wouldn't you think that he'd realize—" Their kitchen was always in a clutter and sometimes when you stepped in from outside, it didn't smell as it should. People said, "Wouldn't you think—?"

The little boy saw his silent father at Town Meeting, or where men gathered, looking humble and defeated among the others whose wives were "all there." He could see without being told that his father had nothing to be proud of and never would have. His heart almost burst with his longing to get for his father something to be proud of. There was in the village street a great old house, well-painted, with green shutters, lilac bushes, peonies and green grass smooth around it—much grander than any other. One of the little boy's earliest memories was looking wistfully up at it, and feverishly trying to hope that someday when he grew up, he could earn money and buy it and take his father and mother to live in it. He imagined his father standing in its front door, proud and looked-up to.

But how could he even hope? He was so small for his age that although he was ten, he was often taken for seven or eight. He tried to help his father on the farm, but he was not only little and strength-less—he had a sore on his knee that did not heal. He told no one about it because he feared if he did someone would tell his father he ought to be taken to the doctor. There would be no money to pay the doctor and his father would never have left a debt unpaid. It would be dreadful to owe money and not to be able to pay. The sore on his knee was not so very big. Maybe it would heal of itself. His gentle, smiling mother never noticed it. If the teacher at school asked him why he limped, he told her he had just stubbed his toe.

He limped a little now as he walked about among the graves, but in his sober little face his eyes shone with happiness. It was the first time in all his life that he had held a proud position of trust. He had ridden in an automobile, with flags on it, with other boys, well and strong, whose fathers kept up their farms and whose mothers were clean and knew how to keep house neatly. And just like anyone, he was now laying wreaths on the graves—trusted—nobody watching him to see that he did it right. He walked carefully and glanced down at his knee once in a while to be sure that the oozing matter from his sore had not soaked through the cheap material of his trousers.

He chose a grave—one with a fine great monument, marked with the name of Captain Elijah Hatwell on it. He was not going to take a plain, little slab when he could just as well have a fine one.

The dead man under the fine marble monument had been a country boy too. Not sickly—strong, broad-chested and always tall for his age. He had left the life in the valley and on the mountain which he had loved, and gone to war because he had thought it his duty to defend his country's unity and to free black men held as slaves. He had not been taken unawares. He knew why he had enlisted. Year after year, on this day when his dead comrades lost their courage, he had kept a righteous silence. He had winced at the touch of little boys' hands, but had been sternly mute. Yet year after year, his silence had worn thinner. He had stirred in a growing restlessness. Those few moments when the people from the valley strolled in over the graveled paths of the cemetery—with easy, quiet pulses, talking together of the day as a holiday!

Yet their little boys were beside them!

It must be that they did not *know!* But he still kept his silence. If they did not know there was no way to tell them.

If he could only think of a word so short that even as it was cried out, one out of all those sauntering people might understand.

But what was it—that one word? What one word—?

The little boy with the unhealing sore on his knee replaced the faded flag in the rusted standard with a new one, leaned his wreath against the fine marble monument and stood to admire the tall urn on top. The monument towered among the small slabs like the great old house in the village street that was so much better than any other.

The sickly little boy knew now that he would never own that fine house, would never take his father and mother there to live. But looking up at that richly ornamented tombstone, his heart leaped. Why, yes—*this* he could do!

He put his clawlike little hands together in front of his chest. Once in a while a kind neighbor family stopped to take him to Sunday school. So he knew how to pray. He bowed his head over his folded hands. His face shining with joyful hope, he prayed, "Jesus, please—make me grow up to be a soldier. Dear Lord Jesus, let me be a fine soldier and after I die have a grand tombstone. And then my father will have something to be proud of."

The desperately silent, dead soldier under the fine tomb had begun to hope that this year he would be passed by, had felt himself already sinking back into blessed blackness. The murmured prayer of the little boy startled him from his gaze into oblivion. He had no time to prepare himself, to stiffen, to resist. The child's helpless, empty ignorance of all that the soldier knew drove to his vitals like the bullet that had killed him, and as instinctively as he had screamed then, he screamed now . . . the thing the little boy did not know, and that he knew. "Blood! Blood! Blood!" he shrieked noiselessly.

It was the word he slept to forget. All eternity would be too short a sleep to forget that word. Awake now, with a living little boy standing beside him, his scream of "Blood! Blood! Blood!" rose from his grave like a scarlet spray and fell back in dripping red drops upon the child's bowed, praying head.

The little boy heard voices and a shuffling of feet on the gravel. Near the entrance of the cemetery the exercises were going on. The light breeze brought some of the phrases to his ears: ". . . over our fair land . . . the last meed of true devotion . . . with unflinching heroism to defend the right . . ."

Turning their backs on the scattered graves where they had left their wreaths, the little boys straggled towards the entrance. In front of them a group of people stood about the minister who was finishing his few remarks with a solemn dip of his voice intended as the transition to the benediction: ". . . unfailing grateful remembrance of our fallen heroes," he said and stopped to draw breath.

Back of the little boys, the dead soldiers had all taken up the cry of the last awakened, the strongest, the best, the one who had always till now been silent. Now they knew what it was that must be said and heard. "Blood! Blood! Blood!" they screamed after the harmless little boys, trotting lightheartedly through the flickering tree-shadows.

The minister slid into the benediction: "And now . . ." He raised his hand and lifted his face. The little boys knew what to do when a minister prayed. They stood still and looked down at their shoes.

". . . the peace of God which passeth all understanding . . ."

"Blood! Blood! Blood!" screamed the dead soldiers soundlessly.

The exercises were over. The little boys swarmed up over the sides of the automobiles and perched three deep on the seats. Some of them took off their neckties and put them in their pockets. The little sick boy's face shone. Someone had carelessly given him a flag to keep (they were bought by the dozen anyhow, and one more or less . . .). He had never had a flag of his own before. He waved it with all his might as the Ford turned and started back down the hill. It had been the happiest day of his life. For once he had been an accepted part of things. He thought with pride of the great stone monument where he had laid a wreath. Perhaps his monument after he had been killed would be like that. He imagined his father standing proudly by it, admired by other men. A throb of pain from his knee made him look down with apprehension. No, it had not soaked through his trouser, yet.

The dust cloud settling in the distance marked the departure of the last car. The dead soldiers lay silent, fumbling with their dead hands to draw up over them once more the blessed black of oblivion. Nothing else in all the world could reach them to rend asunder that sheltering pall . . . if only no little boys came near them, little boys with clear eyes and honest faces and kind, harmless hands. Raw and shaken, the dead soldiers huddled down under the shreds of their forgetfulness.

The thrush rolled his rounded liquid note into the silence. The trees and grass and all the rooted living things quivered and glistened with vitality. In the hot sun the flowers of the wreaths, their life oozing from their amputated stems, began to hang their heads and die. The little new paper-crisp American flags, bought at wholesale, stood stiffly at attention. The last cloud of dust blew away in the distance. The cemetery lay quiet.

The soldiers, having been remembered, were now once more forgotten.

The Old Soldier

◆§ **N**o matter how I set this story down, you will take it, I fear, as a fable. But it is not. Although it happened in a dead-end, over-the-mountain, up-state valley, more than a century ago, the chain of supporting evidence proves it no less literally true than any local news item in this morning's newspaper.

For a long time after the Revolution, the little settlement of Sunmore had made a great day out of the Fourth of July. People there had not forgotten what it meant. More clearly than city or big-town dwellers, they seemed to hear the very sound of the old Liberty Bell in Philadelphia as it rang out in joy over the signing of the Declaration of Independence.

As the years went by, a set form grew up for the day's celebration. At dawn, the big boys fired again and again the old cannon which stood on the village common. There was a meeting about eleven in the morning at the Town Hall, where people made speeches and sang patriotic songs. After that, a picnic lunch was eaten out on the green. If it rained, the lunch was eaten inside the Town Hall. Then, rain or shine, the procession formed to escort the old soldiers out to the Burying Ground, a mile from town, where they put flags on the graves of their comrades among Sunmore men, who, like them, had been soldiers in the Revolution.

Nearly everybody in town marched in this procession, carrying flags and flowers, and keeping step with the music of the town drum and fife corps. "Whee-dee-deedle-dee" went the high thin voices of the fifes. "Boom-boom-boom" went the deep voices of the drums. "Tramp! tramp! tramp!" went the feet of the Sunmore men and women and children.

The boys especially looked forward to this celebrating from one year to the next, chiefly, of course, because it was like passing a milestone on the road to growing up when you were given a chance to join in the cannon-firing. Ordinary people never doubted that this cannon had been used in the Battle of Bennington. But more cautious folk would only go as far as "Well, it *might* have been. Where else would it have been likely to come from?" The truth was that no one could be sure because, as thirty, forty, fifty years and more went by after the battle, fewer and fewer people could remember much about it.

Naturally also with the passing years, the Sunmore men who had been in the Revolutionary Army grew older and older, fewer and fewer. Up to their eightieth birthday these veterans marched in the procession like everybody else. But beyond that date, Dr. White, who took care of all the sick and ailing in town, put his foot down, ruled that their joints were too stiff for much walking. He carried them in his own chaise behind his ancient roan horse. Dick was rather stiff in his joints too, and was glad to walk with ceremonial slowness.

Dr. White knew more about medicine than anybody else in town. This was to be expected because nobody else knew anything at all about it. But on the subject—local history—of which many people knew a great deal, he was also the local specialist. On the shelves of his library, mixed up with his medical books, stood more histories of Vermont than the rest of Sunmore people had all put together. When anyone wanted to find out something about what happened in the past, Dr. White was asked. He always knew the answer.

When May ended and June began in 1848, seventy-one years after the Battle of Bennington, people began to plan as usual for the Fourth of July celebration. But now there were no old soldiers to be found. For the past five years there had been only two, both of them very old. A year ago, one had reached ninety, the other eighty-six. Now both were gone. The elder had died in the winter; the family of the other had moved " 'way out west into York State," and taken the old man with them.

It was too bad. It was terrible. Without even a solitary veteran how could people remember what the Fourth of July was really about? The ancients had always sat on the platform of the Town Hall while the singing and speech-making went on, their long-barreled fire-arms across their knees, and some of them had their leather soldier's belts strapped on over the Sunday coats. Of course their uniforms had all gone to pieces years ago . . . that is if they ever had any, which was most unlikely . . . buckskin being the wear in those early days. They had ridden in Dr. White's chaise, just behind the little girls in white dresses carrying the bouquets, ahead of the marching men and women four abreast in the road. When the procession reached the cemetery, the little girls handed the flowers to the big boys, and they passed them out to the hobbling old soldiers, who laid them on the graves of their comrades in the Revolution. The smaller boys had the honor of planting on the graves fresh American flags to wave, red, white and blue, above the flowers.

Clem Bostwick's son Andrew heard his family lamenting that the celebration wouldn't be much without the old soldiers in it to connect the town with the Revolution. He was a bright boy of ten, had finished the fourth reader in the district school, and long before he had learned the alphabet, he had listened to plenty of stories about the Battle of Bennington and the Revolutionary War. He was just beginning to be old enough to help fire off the cannon and to hand flowers to the old soldiers in the cemetery. And now there weren't any old soldiers!

One day in June he was sent out to look for a lost cow which, the night before, hadn't come back to the barn from the mountain pasture. Up there he met a schoolmate, Will Hunter. Will was picking wild strawberries for his mother on that sloping clearing. The two boys sat down on a ledge to have a talk. Before long Andrew brought out what was weighing on his mind . . . the Fourth of July celebration without any old soldiers, not a single one.

The other boy told him, "There's an old fellow lives in Hawley Hollow . . . 'way up beyond our house. Maybe he fought in the Revolution. He's old enough anyhow. They say he's ninety . . . more."

Andrew's ten-year-old mind was already lodged behind the Chinese Wall of Town lines. "That's not in Sunmore," he objected. "We have to have a sure-'nough Sunmore soldier for our Fourth."

"Yes, it is, too, in Sunmore." Will was positive. "His folks don't trade in Sunmore stores much, because from where their farm is, it's easier to go out the far end of the Hollow to Canbury. But they vote in our Town Meeting, all right." The two boys looked at each other.

Thinking no more of the cow and the strawberries they set out for Hawley Hollow.

So there was to be a genuine Revolutionary soldier after all for the Fourth of July celebration. Everybody was talking about the old man eighty-nine years old, or maybe ninety, maybe more, back on the far side of Westward Mountain, who had been remembered just in time. After the boys had told their fathers about him, two of the Town Selectmen had gone over the mountain to see him. On their return they reported that his back was bent with rheumatism, he was almost stone deaf, and he hobbled along with two canes to steady him. But he still had his old rifle, and even his cracked leather soldier's belt. *And* when, shouting loudly in his ear, they had asked him if he had fought in the Revolutionary War, he had nodded his head. Still louder questioning whether it had been in the Battle of Bennington brought the answer, when he finally made out what they were asking, "Yes, yes, *sir*, it certainly was."

Furthermore the young couple he lived with guaranteed his acceptance of the Selectman's invitation. Weak and failing though he might be, they said he never was a bit crotchety, and was always cheerfully willing to do what was expected of him. They had felt some misgivings over the arrangement at first, but when, a couple of years back, his last surviving grandson had been killed by a falling tree while lumbering, they felt duty-bound to leave their little cottage in Canbury and come to look after him. "I'm his great-great-granddaughter," explained the young woman, "the only blood kin he had in the world, so far as we know. We're to take care of him so long as . . ." she dropped her voice—"and see to his funeral. And he's made a will leaving the house and farm to us. We've never regretted the bargain a minute. Such a good sweet old man!"

Naturally neither husband nor wife had any idea what he had been doing seventy-odd years ago . . . neither of them was over twenty-five. But they remembered always seeing the old long gun laid on pegs over the fireplace, and the old belt hanging near it.

Wasn't it remarkable, Sunmore people said, that just that very year when the last of the old heroes had passed on, this other Revolutionary soldier had been found? And who had found him? Why, Andrew Bostwick and William Hunter, two little boys. Pretty smart they were to have known enough history to understand about the Fourth of July. Patriotic too! The Program Committee arranged that during the meeting they were to stand on the platform on each side of the old soldier, and to march in the procession just in front of Dr. White's chaise, each one carrying an American flag. They were to be called the "Young Guard of Honor." You don't need anyone to tell you that those boys could hardly wait for the Fourth of July to come.

On the morning of the Fourth, Andrew's father got up early, took the boys and drove his farm wagon all the way around the mountain and up into the Hollow to fetch the old man down. It was ten o'clock when they got back into Sunmore Street. A crowd was waiting in front of the Town Hall. They began to clap their hands and cheer when Mr. Bostwick helped lift the bent old man out of the wagon and led him into the Hall. Andrew and Will, the Young Guard of Honor, carried his ancient gun in and put it across his knees. Strapped over his coat he wore his leather soldier's belt, fresh-blacked and polished for the occasion.

When they took his gun to carry it, he gave them such a pleasant smile of thanks that they understood why his great-grandchildren thought so much of him. He was a very nice-looking old man, everybody thought, clean and neat . . . with quiet gentle eyes . . . and although he hadn't a tooth left in his head, his mouth still looked as though he liked jokes.

The crowd came into the Town Hall, took their seats and began fanning themselves. It was a hot day, as the Fourth is apt to be. The speaker was there, a lawyer from Canbury. The chorus of local singers stood below the platform facing the audience. Their leader rapped his stick. They stood at attention. But they did not begin to sing. For at this point Dr. White, who always sat on the platform with the Selectmen and the speaker, called out to Andrew, "Here, let me look at that gun! Pass it over to me."

Andrew was surprised. He put his hand on the gun, and leaning down to the old man's ear said to him as loudly as he could, "Dr. White wants to see your gun."

He shouted with all his might but could not make himself heard. The old soldier was almost stone deaf. He understood Andrew's gesture, though. His cheerful old face remained bright. He felt the friendliness all around him. He smiled, nodded, and passed the gun to Andrew.

The doctor took a sharp look at it and motioned to the singers in the chorus. "Wait a minute," he told them.

Then he put on his glasses (he was the first person in Sunmore to have spectacles) and looked very carefully at a certain place near the trigger. Everybody wondered what was on his mind.

When he looked up, his face was all astonishment. He spoke so loudly that everybody in the whole Town Hall could hear him. "This is a German gun! The old man must have been one of those Hessians who fought against the Americans!"

There was such a silence in the Town Hall you could hear a wasp buzzing at one of the windows.

He was a Hessian. He had fought on the other side. People's mouths dropped open, they were so taken aback.

The old man hadn't heard any of this because he was so deaf. He sat quietly there, between the two little boys, his gentle old eyes looking around at the people in the hall.

For a minute nobody said a word. Nobody could think what to say. Or what to do.

Then Andrew ran out to the front of the platform and began to talk very fast. "Listen," he said, "that was a hundred years ago. Well, more than seventy years anyhow. No matter how mad you are at somebody, you don't keep it up forever. The Bible says not to. He's lived close to us all that time, and farmed it like anybody, and had his family, and paid his taxes. He's old, so old . . . it would be *mean* of us to . . ."

Andrew had never even spoken a piece in school. He had forgotten where he was. When he realized what he was doing, he stopped talking and hung down his head. He went back and put one hand on the old man's shoulder. The wrinkled face lifted to smile at him. Andrew smiled back. But his lips were trembling.

People began to rustle and move their feet. But when Dr. White stood up to say something, they were still again. "It comes back to me now," he said. "When I was first starting to practice medicine in Sunmore and began to be interested in Vermont history I remember reading in one of those old books in my collection that some of the Hessians, too badly wounded to be moved, were cared for in near-by farmhouses, and a few of these are supposed to have stayed in Vermont . . . never went back to the British Army. That's all the history book said. But I was interested and questioned all the old folks about it. Finally I heard some more from old Mr. Hale." The doctor looked down into the audience at a middle-aged man in the second row. "It was your grandfather Jim Hale who told me the rest. He couldn't say about more than one. But one, he was sure of. He, Mr. Hale I mean, was sort of connected . . . in-laws somehow . . . with a family down Bennington-way, and he heard it straight from them . . . the day after the battle a young Hessian, pretty badly wounded, was found unconscious in the woods . . . carried into their farmhouse. By the time he was well enough to get around, many months afterward, there weren't any soldiers or armies left in those parts. So they let him stay on with them. They'd grown to like him. In time he learned enough English to tell them his story. He had always had it hard in the Old Country, he said. He was an orphan, very poor, seventeen years old when a recruiting gang picked him up on the street, marched him off to the barracks in Brunswick. He never liked soldiering, he said. He never had any notion what the fighting was about. While Mr. Hale didn't know any more for sure, he thought the young Hessian moved away after a while into the back country . . . he'd never heard just where." The doctor took a long breath before he went on. "I believe I know now where he went . . . and where he is. He's right on this platform." The doctor still had the old rifle in his hands. He turned around now and laid it back on the old man's knees. Then he faced the audience. "I also believe young Andrew Bostwick had the right idea. Seventy years *is* too long to keep on bearing a grudge. I think we'd better go ahead with our celebration. Maybe the Reverend Hardwick might have something to say about this."

The old man from Hawley Hollow had evidently supposed that it was all part of the program . . . that the doctor had been making one of the planned speeches. Now, seeing the minister step forward in his black clergyman's clothes, he thought the prayer was to be said. He composed his face, leaned forward in his chair in the respectful position you take when somebody is praying in public, and dropped his eyes to the ground.

As a matter of fact, the Reverend Hardwick did pray. He was silent a long time. Then he said, "May war pass and peace be with us. Amen."

He sat down. The Moderator of the Town took his place. He was a burly, powerful-looking man with a serious, responsible face. He said soberly, "I think this is something we ought to take a vote on. Don't you agree, Mr. Hardwick?"

The minister nodded. "Yes. It is something for each one of us to decide. But before we vote, let us sit quiet for a moment. And think."

The Moderator reached for the clergyman's cane, and with it struck a gavel-like blow on the table. In his big official voice he announced, "The question before this house, as I see it, is: has the Revolutionary War ended? Or is it still going on?"

They all sat still.

The deaf ears of the old soldier had, of course, not heard any of this. It looked all right to him. Without anxiety he had settled his old bent rheumatic body into a more comfortable position. His hands lay thin and knotted on the arms of his chair. His clean old face was calm. During the silence his eyes shifted from one person to another in the audience. He smiled a little. After a moment, he turned his white head to look around at his little-boy guard of honor. There they were, one on each side of his chair. He nodded, and leaned back as if to say, "It's all right if you are there."

The water came into Andrew's eyes.

The people in the rows of chairs on the floor were all looking up at the old soldier and the little boys. A man stood up and said, "Mr. Moderator, I move you that the celebration proceed as planned."

Several voices said, "I second the motion."

Then the vote was taken. Everybody voted "Aye."

So, that afternoon, when the usual speaking and singing had been done, and the picnic lunch eaten out on the Common, the procession formed as usual, to march out to the cemetery.

The old soldier looked very tired by this time, but still cheerful. He came out of the Town Hall on Dr. White's arm, and was helped up into the chaise. The Young Guard of Honor held their flags high, so that they stirred in the breeze. The little girls in white dresses were pushed by their mothers into line, two by two. They carried the flowers, lilies, roses, carnation-pinks.

The men and women formed, four by four. The doctor slapped the reins over the old horse's back. The band-leader lifted his hand and said commandingly, "A-a-all ready!"

The marchers held their flags straight.

"Forward, *march!*" cried the bandmaster.

The fifes sang out "Whee-dee-deedle-dee," in thin high voices.

In a deep roar, the drums said "Boom! Boom! Boom!"

And away they all went.